GALE HARBOUR

This is a work of fiction. All of the characters, organizations and events portrayed within are either products of the author's whimsical imagination or are used in a fictitious manner. Any resemblance to actual persons, living or dead, is purely coincidental.

Gale Harbour Book 3:
Dirtbag Satan Worshippers From Down by the Bay

ISBN: 978-0-9947704-5-5

Published by Stories I Found in the Closet www.cdgallantking.ca

First Edition
Copyright © 2025 C.D. Gallant-King

Edited by Maddy D.

"Stories I Found in the Closet" Logo by
Ann McDougall Design & Creative Services
www.facebook.com/AnnMcDougallDesign

For Ben and Evie.
Hopefully you'll both grow up to be better writers
than me.

GALE HARBOUR BOOK 3:
DIRTBAG SATAN WORSHIPPERS FROM DOWN BY THE BAY

C.D. Gallant-King

PROLOGUE

Space Cadet
October 26, 1978
Outside Clarenville, Province of Newfoundland
5:25 pm

Barbara Whillet stood on the side of the road next to the broken-down Pacer, waiting for cannibal hillbillies to come and murder her.

Now to be fair, she didn't actually *know* if there were homicidal rednecks on this stretch of the highway, but she *had* watched *The Hills Have Eyes* at the Avalon Mall cinema a few months ago, and the film was indelibly burned into her brain. Nor did she know Clarenville very well, so there could have been cannibal rapists out there. Somewhere.

Barb had come in from St. John's for her friend Diane's wedding. The service was lovely, and she was very happy for Diane and Stanley (if only a little jealous). Still, now she was convinced that coming to Clarenville was a tremendous series of mistakes, and not just because she was going to end up in a filthy bayman's belly.

Coming alone was her first gaffe. She was supposed to go to the wedding with another friend, Ivy, but Ivy had fallen ill at the last minute and couldn't make it. Barb, Diane, and Ivy worked together in the president's office at Memorial University. Barb was feeling under the weather, too, and probably should have stayed in St. John's with Ivy.

Taking Ivy's green Pacer with the shoddy transmission was the next mistake. Getting lost on her way back to the hotel was yet another bonehead move. When the Pacer finally gave out on a deserted section of Route 230, she had no idea where she was.

She'd passed a gas station a couple kilometres back. Was it still open? The sun was nearly down; even if she started now, she might not make it back there on foot before it was pitch black. She weighed the prospect of being alone in the car in the middle of nowhere against being at least close to a phone when the darkness descended and the cannibals found her.

Barbara got out of the car and, still wearing her pretty yellow dress and high heels from the wedding, started to walk. She tightened her brown suede jacket around herself and tried to ignore the deep shadows in the scraggly trees on the left-hand side of the road.

She thought briefly of Johnny O'Neil. Johnny would have known what to do. She had broken up with him three years ago when she moved to St. John's to attend secretarial school, but that didn't mean she didn't think of him sometimes. More than she should have, in fact. Especially when she was lonely or scared.

Johnny was tall and handsome, but he could be monstrously frustrating sometimes, like refusing to shave a ridiculous moustache that made him look like a hippie. But he still made her feel safe. Since moving to St. John's, Barbara dated several other guys, but they all had that god-awful East-coast Townie accent. She couldn't imagine spending her life with any of them. If she had to listen to them for the rest of her life, she'd throw herself in front of a bus.

Johnny was also educated. He got a bookkeeping degree from the adult centre in Gale Harbour. He travelled, too, having toured around Canada and the States on the bowling circuit. Barbara's mother always told her that he was probably screwing around on her while he was away, but Barbara didn't believe that. She trusted Johnny... but she did miss him while he was away. And he was away a lot. It was part of the reason they broke up. She gave him an ultimatum: her or the bowling, and he chose bowling.

Well, maybe she hadn't *explicitly* said those words exactly. But she mentioned that Johnny spent too much time on the road. He said he would cut back after the regional championships, but then there were the nationals, and then he went to the States for that tournament in Ohio. She dropped hints about getting married for months before he left that last time, too, on a pilgrimage to the grave of Tommy Ryan, the so-called Patron Saint of Canadian Bowling. And it *was* the last time for her. When he returned, she was gone, without so much as a letter explaining why or where she'd gone.

The sun had set on the lonely stretch of road, and the moon was rising. Of course, there were no streetlamps, so the only light shone down from the silver half-circle above. Barbara could still make out the edge of the road, at least, and wouldn't walk into the ditch.

Think about other things, she told herself. Anything but the murderous, flesh-eating rapists hiding in the bushes.

So, she continued to think about Johnny and the day he tracked her down somehow and begged to know what he'd done wrong. He brought flowers and followed her for three days while Barbara refused to speak to him. Her friends told her that if he really cared, he would keep trying and never give up. Barbara agreed to give him one more day, and then she would hear what he had to say.

On the fourth day, he didn't come back. He returned to Gale Harbour, and she never heard from him again.

She finally reached the gas station, and her heart sank. A few security lights revealed the parking lot, and the attendant's booth was empty. No late-night service in a small town on a desolate highway—what kind of hick town was this? The rapid beating of panic began to rise in her chest once again, and she choked it down. Losing her cool and being unable to concentrate would not help her situation.

From the corner of her eye, Barbara caught a glimpse of green light out over the bay, but a copse of trees prevented her from getting a good look at it. *Strange*. Was it a low-flying aircraft? She was two hours away from any airport.

As she skirted around the parking lot to follow the light, her eyes fell on a brightly lit phone booth just outside the station, and she felt weak with relief. At least she could call for help.

But who was she going to call?

She didn't know any local numbers and couldn't very well call anyone in St. John's. She was two hours out of the city. What help would any of her friends be out here? Hopefully, there was a phone book in the booth. She could call a garage or the hotel where she was staying. They would know what to do. *Please, please, let there be a phone book in the booth.*

There was no phone book.

The dangling, bare cable that was supposed to prevent the theft of the phone book mocked her. Who cuts off a steel cable to steal a phone book from a gas station in the middle of nowhere? Who needed the Yellow Pages so badly that they carried bolt cutters out to the boonies?

She slammed her fist against the plexiglass wall of the booth in frustration. Her hand stung from the impact. *Think, Barbara, think. Who could you call?* Maybe she *should* call someone in St. John's. Someone could look up a garage or towing company number for her.

Who did she know that might be home? She pumped a few coins into the slot. Diane was nearby in Clarenville, but she didn't know how to reach her. Ivy was sick, so she had to be home. Barb dialled Ivy's number and let it ring nearly two dozen times before she hung up. The coins rattled into the return. Dammit, where was she? Maybe she was too sick to come to the phone? Or maybe, thought Barbara heatedly, Ivy was faking being ill to get out of the trip, and now she was out tearing up the town while Barbara waited to be murdered or worse? Barbara's anger deflated as swiftly as it came. No, more likely, Ivy was staying at her mother's place. She often went there on weekends when she didn't go out with the girls from work.

Barb fished the coins from the return slot and pumped them back into the phone. She wished she could call her mother. She would know what to do. She wished she could call anyone from Gale Harbour. She knew a hundred people she could call back home to help her. Her parents, her brother Archie, one of her dozens of cousins, and even Uncle Herbert would help her out in a pinch. She could call Johnny. Johnny would come to help her in a heartbeat. She still remembered his number, of course.

The phone line started to ring in her ear, and Barbara nearly dropped the receiver in shock. She had dialled Johnny's number. What the hell was she doing? She should have hung up, she knew, but her hand didn't want to move. It probably wasn't his number anymore, and she didn't know if he still lived in the same place. She should have hung up before she wasted her coins...

Why was the sky getting lighter?

"Hello?" came Johnny's voice on the phone.

Barbara froze. The coins dropped inside the payphone, and Barb didn't know if she had enough money for another call. She would have to ask Johnny to call someone for her.

The lights in the sky were nearly blinding. Barb felt like she was staring into the high beams of a truck, so she shielded her eyes.

"Hello?" Johnny's voice again. "Who is this?"

Barbara opened her mouth, and the world became a featureless blaze of white light. She heard nothing, felt nothing, and soon saw nothing.

After a moment of emptiness that may have lasted thirty seconds or thirty years, Barb felt herself falling, and she forced her eyes open.

When her eyes focussed, Barbara was swaying next to the payphone. The receiver was hanging at the end of the cord by her knees. She picked it up and put it back to her ear. The line was dead.

As she replaced the receiver on the cradle, Barb heard an approaching car. She leapt out of the telephone booth to wave it down, beyond caring now whether it was cannibal rednecks or not. Amazingly, it turned out to be an RCMP officer. Maybe her luck was finally changing.

A burly officer not much older than herself stepped out of the driver's seat. "Is there a problem here, Miss?"

Barbara was never so relieved to see another soul. She didn't understand why she felt nauseous, and her head was swimming. "Oh, thank God. My car broke down a ways back there, I'm trying to find the way back to my hotel."

"I saw the car," said the constable, stepping away from his vehicle. "I was worried. It's not safe to be out here alone at night."

Barbara's heart leapt. She had been right all along. "Are there murderers on the loose?"

"What? Oh, no, go on with you. I just mean it's unsafe to walk along the highway in the dark. Kids out here drive like fools. Just a minute."

The radio crackled inside the car. The officer reached in and grabbed the microphone. "This is Constable Blackwood. Go ahead."

Barbara couldn't quite make out the garbled, static response from the radio inside the car, but Blackwood seemed to understand it. His brow furrowed with concern. "Lights over the bay? You sure it's not just the boys getting into the moonshine again? No, no, I'll go check it out. Near the Lethbridge place on Marine Road. On my way."

Blackwood replaced the receiver. "Sorry, my dear, I've got to go to a call. But I can drop you off on my way."

"Thank you." Barbara moved to get in the car. The RCMP constable watched her in confusion.

"Aren't you going to take your kid?" he asked.

Barbara turned back toward the phone booth. A young boy, no more than three years old, was standing there, staring at her with wide, imploring eyes. His fair hair was long, hanging down in his face, and he was dressed in plain, rough wool clothes. She hadn't noticed him before. She was sure he hadn't been there before she tried to call Johnny, before the weird light. How long had he been standing there?

"My kid?" she asked. "I don't know... He's not..."
"Mommy?" said the boy.

CHAPTER ONE

Burn
Wednesday, October 19, 1994
Gale Harbour, Province of Newfoundland
8:15 pm

There is a scene in the 1994 film *The Crow* where Brandon Lee, his character struggling with returning to life, full of broken memories of his and his wife's brutal murders, smashes a mirror and then paints his face like a sad Pierrot clown. Moody music by The Cure plays throughout. It's supposed to be a stirring scene to show the character's disorientation, barely controlled rage, and propensity for completely unnecessary theatrics. Since seeing the movie, fourteen-year-old Niall O'Neil had tried to recreate the drama of that scene many times but only succeeded in making a fool of himself.

First, his older brother, Nelson, had walked in on him, and once he stopped laughing, he demanded to know why Niall was painting himself up like a depressed Krusty the Clown. His brother also suggested, sniggering at his own wit, that Niall ask their mom for makeup tips.

Next, there was the time that Niall couldn't find his CD, *The Crow (Official Movie Soundtrack)*, which was essential to setting the mood, so he put on a Cure CD instead. Midway through applying his makeup, Lovecats came on. Niall recalled his friend Skidmark dressing up like Mr. Mistoffelees for drama club, and laughing, he poked the Revlon #7 eye pencil he was using in his eye, spoiling the gothic mood he was going for and necessitating the use of an eye patch for several days.

Most recently, he'd punched his bedroom mirror a little too hard and accidentally broke it for real. *That* resulted in a trip to the emergency room, four stitches on his hand and no end of weird looks and rude comments from other ER patients. Niall had gone into the hospital with his makeup half-finished and streaked from his tears. He looked like someone had beat up a mime. The doctor, who had provided Niall's eye patch several weeks earlier, was mercifully silent.

The truth was Niall was trying to find a way to express his misery, but he was screwing it up.

Sixteen months ago, Niall killed someone using preternatural powers he inherited from his grandmother while she was possessed by the soul of a dead witch. No longer possessed, Nana's magic didn't work anymore. Niall's powers, which he barely understood, only worked when he was in physical contact with the blood of his ex-girlfriend, Harper Jeddore. Apparently, she was the "blood of the Blood", the last surviving descendant of Kluskap, an ancient mystical warrior, and Niall could use her hemoglobin to do things like create fire, protect himself and his friends from injury, and banish otherworldly entities. It all sounded ridiculous, so he tried not to think about it.

To ensure that he never hurt anyone with his magic again, he broke up with Harper and hadn't spoken to her in over a year. He had regretted it every day since.

Heartbroken but unburdened by a healthy level of self-consciousness, Niall contemplated joining the drama club so they could show him how to do his makeup correctly. The lady at the cosmetics counter at the drugstore where Nelson worked was another possible alternative. Of course, if he did that and Nelson found out, he would make his life hell, and not in a cool cinematic way. He couldn't talk to his mom about it. He found he had a lot of trouble talking to his parents. His dad blamed it on him becoming a "surly teenager." Niall felt it was more likely due to all the secrets he was hiding and being unsure of what he could talk about. Killing monsters and burning down half the town really ruined the ability to have regular dinner table conversations.

So, with no other options, Niall was left to figure out how to apply eyeliner alone. At least tonight, it would be quiet, with no interruptions. His brother was at work, his mom and Nana Josephine were playing cards at the seniors' lounge, and his dad was gone to do whatever his dad did on Wednesdays. Poker? Hockey? Niall didn't care as long as it left him some time by himself. Usually, he used his alone time to watch vaguely inappropriate anime like *Dirty Pair* and *Ranma*

½. Tonight, he would listen to Nine Inch Nails and decide which shade of eyeshadow suited him best: Obsidian Beauty or Midnight Enigma?

Another drawback of killing Keenan was that he was the only guy Niall had ever met who wore makeup. He would have been the perfect person to ask for tips.

With his meagre supply of Halloween makeup laid out atop his dresser beside his Oxy wipes and an old bottle of his dad's Ralph Lauren Polo cologne, Niall stared at himself in the mirror. He was wearing his favourite plain black t-shirt, his blond hair was wet and spikey from gobs of Dippity-Doo gel, and he could clearly see in his mind's eye what he wanted his face to look like. He picked up an eyeliner pencil and set to work turning his vision into reality while the dulcet tones of Trent Reznor wailed in the background.

About fifteen minutes into his routine, Niall heard screams outside the house.

With reflexes honed by years of paranoia from fighting creatures from another world, Niall leapt into action. He raced out of his room and down the hall, snatching up the baseball bat he kept in the porch closet for such situations. The bat had been a gift from Keith Doucette last Christmas. Keith gave them all aluminum baseball bats— both as a memento of surviving an alien invasion and a handy weapon in case of the next one. Niall kept quietly placing it back by the front door every time his mom found it and yelled about the kids leaving their crap everywhere. She always blamed Nelson. No one imagined Niall doing anything sports related.

The bat served its purpose tonight as Niall raced outside to find a blond girl being savaged by a large black dog. He didn't recognize the girl or the animal. Aggressive strays weren't uncommon in Gale Harbour, but he never heard of anyone being attacked by one.

Two years ago, Niall would have frozen in panic at the sight of a werewolf-sized canine mauling a human being. Hell, he probably wouldn't have come out of his room. But after everything he'd been through, all the sacrifices they'd made to protect this town from freaking aliens, there was no goddamn way he was going to let a poor girl get taken out by a stupid dog on his watch.

Without hesitation, Niall rushed into the fracas and swung the bat at the dog's rib cage with all his might. He felt a sickening crunch, and the animal howled a horrible, guttural screech of pain. It leapt away, then backed up, limping.

In the light of a streetlamp with some distance between them, Niall got a good look at the animal. Though it was large, at least as tall as Niall's waist, it was thin and bony. Its matted black fur was falling out in clumps, and its eyes appeared to be bleeding. He realized with an unpleasant shock to his guts that the beast was probably rabid, and he started to second-guess his eagerness to jump into this particular situation.

Fortunately, the dog must have been badly hurt because it turned and limped away into the darkness. Niall watched it go and almost pitied it. He should probably call the dog catcher. That animal was definitely not right.

Something heavy slammed into Niall, and he nearly swung the bat again before realizing it was the girl he'd just saved. She threw her arms around him like a drowning swimmer grabbing onto a rope.

"Oh my God," she breathed, her face buried into his shoulder. Her shampoo smelled like oranges and berries. "Thank you so much. The dog came out of nowhere, and I panicked."

"You're okay now." Niall awkwardly patted her on the back. He wasn't used to close physical contact with any female that wasn't his mom or Harper. "I think I scared it off. What about you? Are you okay?"

The girl pulled away, and Niall looked at her for the first time. She was cute and couldn't be more different from Harper in every possible way. Where Harper was dark of complexion, she was pale and freckled with strawberry-blond hair. Harper was tall and wiry, while this girl was short and curvy. Where Harper was always dressed in baggy jeans and army surplus jackets, this girl wore a tight pink top and a colourful puffer vest.

Niall suspected that whoever she was, she probably wouldn't appreciate being compared in such detail to his ex-girlfriend, but honestly, Niall had no other frame of reference.

"I think so," she said. She looked down at her arm. Her pink sweater was torn, and blood was soaking through the material. "Ah crap, maybe I'm not okay. Am I going to need a tetanus shot?"

She was surprisingly level-headed for someone who had just been mauled by a wild dog. "No, that's for stepping on a rusty nail. You will probably need a rabies shot, though." Niall was well acquainted with different types of shots and vaccines after being kidnapped and held in a filthy underground bunker two summers ago. He didn't bother telling her that she would need *several* rabies shots. No sense in upsetting her further.

"Oh, that's just great. I hate needles."

"It's no worse than getting bitten by a dog, and you seem to be taking that pretty well."

"The dog came at me so fast. I still don't know what happened."

"You're probably in shock." Again, he had first-hand experience. "We should get you home. Do you live around here?"

"Just down on St. Anne Street. And I think you may be right. I'm starting to feel light-headed."

"It's okay, I'll walk you home. Do you need to lean on me?"

"Thank you. I'm Stacey, by the way."

"Niall."

They started to walk, with Niall holding her forearm to keep it elevated. That was good; he would focus on her physical injuries, so he didn't have to think about the fact that he was *holding a girl's hand*.

"I haven't seen you around," said Stacey. "Have you lived here long?"

"Just my whole life." He didn't add that he had spent most of that life in the house playing video games and watching movies, which explained why she'd probably never seen him. "I don't think I've seen you around either. You must go to the Amalgamated. I would remember meeting you."

The Amalgamated High School was for everyone who wasn't Catholic and was the bitter rival of St. Paul's, which Niall and his friends attended. It was only Christian to teach Catholics and Protestants to hate each other from a young age. "And why would you remember me, huh?" she asked him.

Niall almost said, "Because you're cute," but stopped himself. Was that appropriate? Were they flirting now? Unsure of the social rules in this situation, he said instead, "I would have remembered the dog bite on your arm."

Stacey laughed. It was an easy, girly laugh. Harper didn't laugh so easily; when she did, it was more of a chortle. Like she was laughing at you. Which she often was. "I don't usually go around with dog bites on my arm, silly."

"Oh, well, that's good then. Probably for the best." It was good to keep her talking and distracted. Niall noticed that blood was still soaking through her sleeve, so he squeezed her arm a little harder.

"I usually wear them on my face, like right about here. It goes better with my earrings that way."

Niall was embarrassed that it took him a moment to realize she was kidding. "Oh, right. Yeah, the blood would go well with them, wouldn't it? Would look nice with your eyes, too."

Stacey laughed again, and Niall joined in with her, uncomfortably. He was so far beyond everyday conversations with the opposite sex that there was no way to know if it was going well or not. Maybe he should ask her.

Instead, she asked him an awkward question first.

"Niall, not to judge or anything, but are you wearing black lipstick and eyeliner?"

Niall almost threw her on the asphalt and ran back home. He completely forgot about the makeup. What the hell was he supposed to do now? How did he explain that he was testing out being goth because he was depressed about accidentally killing somebody and dumping his girlfriend?

"Oh... I... I just..." Niall said eloquently.

"Hey, you just saved me from a rabid dog. You could be wearing a clown nose and fishnet stockings for all I care."

"I was just... experimenting..."

"I told you, don't worry about it. I think it actually looks kinda good on you. But if you want some pointers, I can show you how to keep your eyeliner from getting so smudgy. And your lipstick must be the cheap Halloween kind. It's all chunky and flaking. I can hook you up with some good stuff."

As they walked along Woodward Avenue toward St. Anne Street, Niall noticed his heart felt the lightest it had in a long time. Somehow, this cute, funny girl dropped out of the sky right into his front yard, and she came with makeup tips? How was it possible that she could be so perfect? They continued to laugh and talk the rest of the way to her house, and Niall registered that for the first time in a year, he had gone twenty minutes without thinking about Harper or about Keenan's dead face being zipped into a body bag.

It wasn't until hours later, when he was lying in bed replaying that evening's events in his mind, that he realized why the dog looked so strange while it was walking away. It had a freakish, hairless tail, like a rat's, over a metre long. It dragged on the ground behind the creature as it slunk off and disappeared into the darkness.

CHAPTER TWO

All I Wanna Do
Thursday, October 20, 1994
6:35 am

Jake Cutler was a fisherman. His father before him was a fisherman, and his father before that was a fisherman. Jake didn't know any farther back than that because his grandfather was an orphan, found in the woods by men cutting firewood in December of 1904. According to family legend, great-grandmother Cutler had called it a Christmas miracle. According to that same legend, great-grandfather Cutler just called it another damn mouth to feed.

Jake had seen it all while out on the water. He'd seen orcas and dolphins swim alongside his boat. He'd caught a great white shark on a line and dragged it for hours, trying to tire it out before it eventually broke free. He'd been there when his father and a couple of other men found a giant squid washed up on the rocks near Musgrave Harbour. The beast was over ten meters long, and they couldn't get close enough to bring it onto the boat to haul it back home. That was back before they'd moved to Gale Harbour, a few years before Dad died and he'd taken over the boat and fishing licenses.

This cold day in October wasn't the first time he'd found a corpse while fishing. Two years ago, he'd come across the bodies of Mike and Will O'Quinn, drowned on their boat. That never sat right with Jake, and he still had nightmares about it. It wasn't right for two men to drown *on* their boat. The mounties were never able to explain it. It was a sign of something wrong, some unholy deal with the devil, Cutler was sure. It was no coincidence that a dozen more people ended up dead that same weekend. Gale Harbour was a cursed place, make no mistake about it.

Jerome called him over, saying something was caught in their net. Not yet thinking much about it, Jake tossed the butt of his cigarette overboard and crossed the rolling deck to the other side of the boat with the effortless swagger of a veteran mariner. Jerome Wheeler, Jake's fishing partner for the last twelve years, struggled to pull the net out of the water. "What're you gettin' on with, Jerome? Since when can't you pull in a load of mackerel?"

"The line's tangled, and I don't want to blow the motor on the winch again," Jerome grumbled, grunting and gasping for breath as he yanked on the ropes. Jerome was a big man, close to 140 kilograms, and heavy lifting was not his strength. He preferred to drink, watch hockey, smack his wife around, and drink some more, in that order. "Just stop yer yappin' and give me a hand."

Jake was half the size of his partner but much stronger, and between the two of them, they were able to pull the large knot of net and fish onboard. Jake could tell there was something wrong. He'd never seen a net tangled like that before, and there was no way that fish alone would have caused it.

"There's something caught in the net," said Jerome as he leaned in to cut loose whatever was tying up their line. It would hurt to cut it and cause a lot of work for later, but it was better than losing half their catch if they couldn't get the rest of the net onboard. Jake got a sick feeling in the bottom of his stomach. Jake was never a jumpy man before the events of two years ago, but now his nerves were dancing on a knife's edge, and his guts were twisted in knots.

Something flopped onto the deck, and Jerome nearly leapt out of his boots. "Jesus, Mary and Joseph!" He backed so far against the rail that he almost fell over into the bay.

A pale white human hand and forearm hung out of the tangled net, surrounded by wiggling mackerel. *Not again*, Jake thought silently.

Jake Cutler crossed himself and picked up Jerome's dropped knife. He approached the mound of snarled netting.

"What the hell are you doing?" Jerome's voice cracked as he spoke. Jake didn't answer, nor did he look back at his partner. He could still hear the man mumbling under his breath.

They would call the Coast Guard in a moment—well, Jake would do it; Jerome was turning into a blubbering mess—but first, Jake wanted to know if it was someone he knew. With shaking hands, he continued to cut at the lines around the arm so he could pull the body out.

"Don't touch it!" Jerome screeched.

Jake continued to ignore him. He yanked the arm, ignoring the off-putting feel of cold, clammy flesh. A head and torso came free of the lines, revealing a man with a mangled, bloodless face.

Jerome threw up over the side into the water.

With the bloating of the body and the damage to the skull, Jake couldn't identify the corpse. He was average-sized, probably Jake's age, but that was all he could tell. The flesh was pallid and lumpy; the chest was bare to the waist and covered with scars, and it looked like someone had tried to rip the man's jaw off with a crowbar. It was possible the twisting of the net could have done the damage, but Jake couldn't be sure.

"Oh my God, oh my God, oh my God," Jerome was hyperventilating and sobbing, but he couldn't look away. His voice continued to increase in pitch. "What in the Jesus—Jake, look, he's breathing!"

Jake saw it, too. The corpse's chest was definitely moving. But there was no way he could be alive, could he?

He knew he should leave well enough alone and call the Coast Guard, but what if, by some miracle, the man was alive? He needed to at least check, didn't he? Jake knelt back down on the deck and slowly approached the body. For the first time in thirty years, he was aware of the swaying boat beneath him. Or was it his head that was swirling?

Jake leaned in close to listen for breathing. With his face just centimetres from the scarred, purple chest, he could tell that it was not air in the dead lungs. Something was moving inside the corpse's chest. He could hear scratching and crunching inside. Could it be a fish or an eel? It sounded almost like... *chewing*...

The dead man's chest burst open, and something leapt at Jake Cutler's face. It tore out his eyes first, so Jake never saw what it was that killed him. The last thing he heard was Jerome screaming.

CHAPTER THREE

No Excuses
Thursday, October 20
8:25 am

"I'm trying to get four Sol Rings for the new deck that I'm building. Do you have any Sol Rings? I tried to trade for some with Mitchell Kenny, but he wanted two Serra Angels for each of them, which is totally not worth it."

Pius Jeddore was very good at tuning out his friend, Brian Hawco, also known as Skidmark. They were standing at their lockers, grabbing their books for the first period, and Pius was nodding along as if in rapt attention, even though he was only registering about ten percent of the words. Since ninety percent of what came out of Skidmark's mouth was incomprehensible, it worked out rather well.

The two fourteen-year-old boys closed their lockers and headed for homeroom, Skidmark having barely stopped to catch a breath. "The part in Time Cop was so cool when Jean-Claude Van Dam punches that guy, and he goes flying." Pius missed where Skidmark transitioned from Magic cards to Time Cop, but since Magic had been a non-sequitur from last night's episode of Lois & Clark, Pius didn't bother trying to make sense of it.

As they walked down the hall, Pius noticed he was now slightly taller than Skidmark. He'd experienced a growth spurt over the last year, though his weight hadn't changed. He now possessed the build of what could generously be described as an uncooked noodle. Skidmark hadn't gained any height but had put on a few kilos since his family got a new computer, and he somehow became even more sedentary. Despite being shorter, he was about four times the overall mass of Pius, and now bullies described the pair of them as—cruelly, though not incorrectly—Spaghetti and the Meatball.

One of Pius' cruellest former bullies popped up and slapped the Meatball on the back. "What's up, boys?" asked Keith Doucette. His freshly braces-free teeth shone white and perfectly straight. Before waiting for an answer, he pointed to his ear. "Check it out!"

"You got an earring!?" Skidmark gasped. Pius was equally shocked. Keith lost his other earlobe two years ago in one of their adventures and always seemed self-conscious about it. For him to purposely stick a hole in the good one was... surprising.

Skidmark was looking at the cheap fake diamond stud and poking at it with his pudgy, filthy finger. Keith winced. "Watch it, dipshit."

"Is it infected?" Pius asked.

Keith shrugged. "Probably. Jessica Skinner did it with her mom's sewing needle. I told her to disinfect it, but I don't think she did a very good job. So, what do you think? Pretty cool, right?"

Pius tried not to think about the toxins probably flowing through Keith's bloodstream. "Yeah, it's... pretty cool."

"Right on. Hey, we're meeting up after school to go to Arlene's to buy Magic cards, right?"

"You ask that knowing full well that there is literally nothing else I would rather be doing in my life," replied Skidmark.

Keith winked and gave them finger guns. "Cool. I'll see you boys then."

"He's in a good mood," said Skidmark.

"Yeah, weirdly so."

"Maybe he's drunk. He has a drinking problem, you know."

"Yes, we all know, Brian."

"He's been drinking so long, he's probably building up a tolerance for it. Like, he's probably always at least slightly drunk, buzzing on one or two beers that would knock us on our asses, but for him, it takes way more to get really drunk. Maybe he downed a forty-ouncer this morning before school. Or maybe he started to take drugs, like hash or whippets. I heard a guy in Toronto did so many whippets he fried the inside of his nose, and they had to surgically remove his sinuses and nose, so now he just has a big gaping hole in the middle of his face..."

Skidmark's tirade was mercifully interrupted by Pius' best friend, Niall O'Neil, who was beaming even brighter than Keith. "Pius! I have amazing news! Oh, hey, Brian."

Skidmark snorted and rolled his eyes. "We know, we saw last night's Superman. We already talked about it. Hey, did you know someone saw the Satan worshippers up behind the dump road again? Scott Legge said Dave Rideout's cousin found a skinned cat in a circle of candles the other night."

Niall completely ignored Skidmark. Pius was jealous of his ability to tune out the short, round boy.

Niall wasn't in Pius' homeroom this year, so they had little time to talk. They didn't walk to school together anymore, either. Niall didn't want to run into Harper, who still lived with Pius' family. Having his best friend and his cousin as exes was incredibly awkward for Pius and caused him no end of anxiety. He constantly struggled to remember who he wasn't or wasn't supposed to say things to because he didn't want to upset anyone or make anyone jealous. He started to keep track of all the notes in a specially-made binder that he organized and colour-coded himself. He wrote "Break-Up Rules" in large black letters on the cover and made a point of carrying it so both Niall and Harper could see it, and they could see what kind of trouble they were causing him.

It was nearly a year and a half since they broke up. The fact that they still hadn't gotten over themselves was ridiculous. Pius wished they would either get back together or stop being weirdos and start acting like normal people again.

Pius had no experience in romantic relationships himself. His only point of reference was his parents' marriage, which was also pretty complicated.

"I met this awesome girl last night," Niall said, smiling. Pius was so stunned he nearly dropped his books. He couldn't remember the last time Niall looked so happy. "Her name is Stacey. She's smart, funny and super cute. She goes to the Amalgamated."

Brian snorted again. "Ew, I stay away from girls from the Amalgamated. They have asbestos in their ceilings and lead in their pipes over there. There's no telling what kind of brain damage she might have from heavy-metal poisoning."

Niall shot Skidmark a dirty look but said nothing. They all knew that Skidmark had somehow less experience with girls than Pius.

"How did you meet her last night?" Pius asked.

"She got mauled by a dog outside my house."

Pius and his friends were used to weird occurrences, but Pius was not expecting that. "Seriously? Is she okay?"

"She just got a little bite on her arm. She's fine. I knocked the dog off of her with that bat Keith gave me, and I walked her home afterward. We talked for a while before her mother came out screaming 'cause her arm was covered in blood, then she rushed her off to the hospital. But Stacey gave me her number to call her after school!"

"If she's not dead or still in the hospital," Brian said, always optimistic.

"So do you, like, like her?" Pius asked.

"Yeah, I mean, I think so. She's really great."

It was nice to see Niall smiling. At least he wasn't using his mom's make-up to make himself look like a sad clown again, but Pius was torn. If Niall found another girlfriend, maybe it would finally clear up whatever weird, uncomfortable aura surrounded him and Harper. On the other hand, there was a possibility that Niall seeing someone else could just make it all worse...

Why did Pius have to be in the middle of this?

Harper must have sensed Pius thinking about her because she chose that exact moment to walk past them in the hall. Niall's neck spun around so fast he looked like he had performed a Mortal Kombat-style Fatality on himself. Nearly every head in the hall turned in shocked disbelief.

Niall gasped. "Is she wearing... a dress?"

She was, indeed. Before school that morning, Harper combed out her long, silky black hair and put on a yellow babydoll dress over black tights. It was the most feminine she had ever looked, though she still wore her Doc Martens. Pius' parents were so surprised they nearly spit out their tea at the breakfast table. After Kurt Cobain died, she'd worn the same jeans and sweatshirt for months, so the current look was particularly shocking.

"Why... is she dressed... like that?" Niall seemed to be having palpitations.

Pius knew why, but he wasn't supposed to say. It was on Page One of the Harper section in his Break-Up Rules binder.

Harper stopped and turned around. She hesitated momentarily, then seemed to decide and approached the boys outside Mr. Noseworthy's homeroom.

"Harper... Your hair looks... really nice." Niall turned suddenly into a tongue-tied prepubescent twerp. He had gotten much better after he and Harper started dating, but now he sounded like he was twelve years old again, trying to ask Sally Alexander out on a date.

She smirked but made no comment on it. He'd probably never seen her hair outside of its regular messy braid. "Look, Niall, can I meet you after school? I wanted to talk to you about something."

"Of–of course." Niall stammered. "I'm not in trouble or anything, am I?"

She smirked again. "I'll see you after school. Out back by the soccer field?"

Harper walked away, and Niall whirled on his best friend.

"What does she want to talk to me about?"

Pius gulped and took a step back. Niall was closer to his face than his dentist. "I can't tell you."

"Pius, you're my best friend. You have to tell me."

"It's best if she tells you herself."

Niall was beside himself. He threw up his hands in exasperation. "Come on, man, you can't make me wait all day to find out what she wants! That's cruel and unusual punishment. I bet that's against the Geneva Conventions."

Pius felt bad. He would be a nervous wreck if he knew he had a potentially uncomfortable conversation coming and was expected to wait six hours to find out what it was. Hell, he got so scared of dentist appointments that his mom couldn't tell him he was having one until she showed up at the school to pick him up. Otherwise, he would worry himself to the point of vomiting.

"Pius, you have to tell me!" Niall insisted, and the bell rang.

Niall turned, frustrated, and hurried down the hall toward his class. He called back, threateningly: "I'm going to find you at recess!"

Pius, wondering if he could hide in the music stand closet at the back of the auditorium during recess, headed into class and sat down. Skidmark was already there, eating a Fruit by the Foot and discussing his favourite flavours with the unlucky kid beside him. Pius hadn't noticed he'd walked away while he and Niall were talking.

Pius reviewed his notes for Math class while the morning announcements played over the school PA system. There was something about an intramural basketball game at lunch, a reminder that sweatpants were not permitted to be worn in class, and...

"Pius Jeddore, please proceed to the principal's office."

All eyes fell on Pius. There were a few *"Oohs"* from his classmates, the typical sound kids made when someone was in trouble, but Pius didn't hear them. The blood was pounding too hard in his ears. Pius was an honour roll student and often helped with school clubs and activities, so being called to the office was not unusual, but something about this summons felt different. He gulped and looked up at Mr. Noseworthy, who nodded toward the door but said nothing. How could he be so nonchalant? Didn't he know his star student might never come back again?

Pius picked up his books and headed out of the room. He hoped no one had figured out that he was the one who burned down the school at the end of grade seven.

The homeroom period was not quite over, and the school hallways were empty. Pius' long walk to the office was terrifying. He was fourteen years old. This shouldn't scare him so much, especially after the literal other-worldly monsters he faced down the prior two years. But his heart was racing, his cheeks felt hot, and the rest of him felt icy shivers from the cold snap shooting up and down his spine. Why was he so terrified? Surely, they just wanted to talk to him about re-starting the junior chess club, junior math club, or any of the dozens of other clubs he dropped out of this year, all of which folded without him. There was no way anyone could have found out about the incident with the exploding filing cabinet in the Principal's office. It had been fifteen months; if someone was going to figure it out, it would have happened by now. And yet, he was sure he was about to show up at the Bourgeois' office, and there were going to be a dozen RCMP constables there, and Pius was going to spend a long time in prison.

The administrative offices, as well as most of the front end of the school, were completely rebuilt after the fire. Everything was still white and new-looking, and it seemed very off to Pius. There were far fewer pictures and awards on the wall, along with graduation photos of old classes. Many of those items were irreplaceable. Pius was destroyed by the thought that, because of him, no one would ever again see that guy with the metre-wide afro in the Class of 1977 or that girl from 1984 who was holding her cat.

The secretary led him into the principal's office, and Mr. William Bourgeois was seated behind his desk, scribbling away intently at something. Probably a writ of execution.

Pius stood waiting for what felt like hours, but it was probably only half a minute. It took Mr. Bourgeois that long to acknowledge his presence. The tall man was very absorbed by whatever he was writing, and all Pius could see was the top of his shiny bald head.

Finally, Mr. Bourgeois put down his pen, closed the folder before him, and sat up to address Pius. Pius stifled a yelp and withered under Bourgeois' gaze. The principal was disconcertingly tall and anemically pale, with a gaunt, angular face and eyes that seemed to be carved from broken beer bottles. He was smiling, which should have been a relief, but Pius once saw the man smile while a kid with a broken leg was carried out of the school and into a waiting ambulance. And there were rumours that Bourgeois once laughed when he slammed Chris Tobin's fingers in a locker door. Whether or not it had been on purpose was up for debate.

"Mr. Jeddore," said the Principal, gesturing to one of the two chairs in front of his broad, neat desk. "Please have a seat."

Pius sat down heavily, his books sliding out of his hands and landing on the floor with a thud. Pius gurgled and bent down quickly to pick them up. Mr. Bourgeois didn't acknowledge it.

"I noticed, Mr. Jeddore, that you are not very active in extracurricular activities this year. You did not sign up for any school clubs. I also noticed that your marks have slipped."

He got an A-minus on *one* math test and was getting called into the office? What would they have done if they found out about the fire? Executed Pius' entire family by firing squad?

"Ah, yeah, sorry sir, I've just been busier this year at home."

The Principal raised a hairless eyebrow. "At home? I certainly hope you haven't been required to take up a part-time job to support your family."

"No, nothing like that." His dad's bid to go back to school kind of fell apart after he screwed his tutor, but he still had a decent job. "We have a new baby, and my mom isn't doing so well, so I've been helping out around the house."

"Of course. How could I forget? A new child can certainly throw a family into chaos."

Especially when Pius' mom found out she was pregnant when they were on the verge of breaking up over the tutor. That was a hard few weeks, with Pius' parents fighting more than he ever remembered. Then, abruptly, it stopped, and there was an uneasy truce in the house ever since. His mom and dad didn't seem particularly *happy*, but they never fought anymore, and Pius wasn't brave enough to ask exactly what their resolution was.

"Yeah, Rebecca just turned six months old. She's cute but a lot of work, so Harper and I have to help out. Cooking meals, cleaning, that kind of thing."

"I see. So I imagine you have to head straight home after school every day?"

That was weirdly pointed. "Um. Yes?"

"Which means you don't have time to play at Satanic rituals like this?"

Mr. Bourgeois pulled a handful of playing cards out of a drawer and tossed them on his desk. Magic the Gathering cards.

Pius' mouth dropped open. This wasn't what he was expecting at all.

"I don't... I mean, I haven't...." Pius thought quickly and decided this was one of those situations in which lying was the best course of action. "No. No, I do not."

Bourgeois stared at Pius for a long time. Pius wasn't sure if he believed him or not. Finally, he said, "I confiscated those cards from a student last week. Can you imagine bringing such filth into our halls of learning? Goblins, magic rituals, demons. It's blasphemous and obscene."

"Um. Yeah. No, I don't play."

"Are you sure?"

What was he getting at? Obviously, Pius was lying about playing Magic, but after years of covering up monsters and alien invasions, being less-than-truthful was becoming easier. But why did Mr. Bourgeois call him in here to ask about Magic? Was the cards really that big of a problem at school? Did he think Pius was some kind of ring leader, seducing other kids into the Cult of Cardboard?

Or was the Principal actually asking for some other reason?

"So, no dallying at the homes of your evil friends? No late-night excursions to do the devil's work? You stay home and mind your sister like a good Christian youth?"

How the hell was Pius supposed to answer that? He wasn't sure if Mr. Bourgeois experienced some sort of brain injury over the summer, but he was acting stranger than usual. He had just returned from some kind of vacation for a few weeks. The rumour was he'd been attending some sort of extreme born-again Christian Bible camp. Maybe something happened at the camp that got his dander up about Magic cards. Perhaps it was some kind of baptismal accident that cut off oxygen to his brain for too long.

"Um. Okay?"

Bourgeois stared at Pius for a moment without saying a word. A very long moment that seemed to stretch into hours. The Principal's black eyes made Pius' skin crawl, and he fought with all his might not to squirm in the seat. Finally, he asked, "Is there anything else you need to tell me, Pius?"

The man's eyes flickered, ever so slightly, toward the corner of the office. Pius may not have noticed if he hadn't been staring at him so intently. Unconsciously, Pius glanced toward the corner as well...

There, sitting atop a filing cabinet that looked exactly like the Principal's old cabinet where he kept contraband he confiscated from students, was a black, scorched bookbag. Pius couldn't stop the gasp that escaped his lips, but he stifled it quickly.

It was his bookbag. The bookbag he'd lost and assumed was destroyed the night of the school fire.

Pius' gaze snapped back toward Bourgeois' grotesque eyes. His chest was tightening, and he couldn't breathe. How did the principal get it? Did he know who it belonged to? Did he mean to draw Pius' gaze toward it? Did he know Pius saw it?

"Pius?" asked Bourgeois. "Is there anything—"

"—No sir," Pius choked. "Nothing."

There was another long pause, and Pius feared he would pass out. His lungs couldn't draw in any air, and he was sure the principal could tell he was turning blue. Instead, Bourgeois smiled another one of his bilious grins. "That's good to hear, Mr. Jeddore. There are a lot of godless heathens in this school, and you would do your best to stay away from them. Now hurry back to your class."

"Thanks, Mr. Bourgeois." Pius hurriedly got up. He staggered and dropped his books twice before composing himself enough to get through the door.

CHAPTER FOUR

You Don't Know How it Feels
Thursday, October 20
8:50 am

She sat in the car for a long time. The detachment's entrance was only a few meters away, but she was having trouble walking to it.

Marie-Ann Tanguay was scared.

She knew now how Pius Jeddore must feel, going through life terrified of everything. It was not the same, of course—she wasn't afraid of lawnmowers and greenhouse gases like the scrawny kid with the ugly rat tail—but she felt more fear in the last sixteen months than she had in her entire life.

First, she was afraid she was going to die. Lying on the asphalt of the old airstrip, looking up at that bastard Mason, she was more fearful than in pain. It wasn't the dying that scared her, though. If she died, she might get to see her daughter Lynne again. But if she died, she wouldn't be able to protect her other kids—Pius and Harper and Niall—and she couldn't bear to leave them alone.

Then she was afraid she was never going to walk again. Mason's bullet had shattered her pelvis, and it took numerous surgeries to put her back together. Physiotherapy was many long months of gruelling torture, re-training her legs like a toddler learning to walk.

Next came the fear of whether she would ever be able to work again. It seemed unlikely. Before, she was the fastest, fittest and toughest officer at most detachments where she'd been deployed. She could outrun and outfight men twice her size and never backed down from a challenge. Now, she couldn't get out of bed without excruciating pain, a long hot bath, and a Percocet or two.

She overcame all of it. She was alive, she could walk, and she was about to return to work for the first time in nearly a year and a half. It was an incredible feat and one she should be proud of. Yet, she was still petrified.

It was going to hurt to walk across the parking lot, stand on the concrete floor of the detachment, and sit at a desk. She was on a modified workload to ease her back into the job and see if she could do it, but she already knew the next few hours were going to be agony, and she feared every minute of it.

Marie-Ann fingered the bottle of pills in the pocket of her uniform pants. Perfectly pressed and creased pants, same as always. Of course, before the injury, it didn't take her an hour to iron them because she had to sit down to rest after a few minutes standing at the ironing board. It was the memory of ironing her pants that convinced her to pull out the bottle and pop another Percocet into her mouth. She hated taking more of these than necessary, but she needed to make it through the door.

Tanguay took a deep breath, grabbed her cane from the passenger seat, and stopped herself. The cane was automatic the last few months, but she couldn't take it in there. It would be an obvious sign that she wasn't the same person she was and should not be back at work. She sighed, dropped the cane, and climbed out of her car.

The detachment cheered for her when she walked in. Bruce Bennett, the rotund Constable with a heart three times the size of his brain, and not just because of the clogged arteries. Burt Brake, the rat-faced Constable with a pornstar 'stache that was more crooked than his teeth. Cheryl Murphy, the dispatcher, already had a cup of tea waiting for her. Constable Forrest had been new when she left but was made permanent while she was away. His most distinguishing feature was that he wasn't one of the other three.

And then there was Sergeant Peters, the man who had taken her job.

Andrew Peters was a tall, handsome man with a broad chest, sandy hair and a mailbox-shaped chin. He looked like that He-Man toy the kids played with (did they still play with that?) He sported an impeccable track record and numerous commendations. He smiled at Tanguay warmly.

"Welcome back, Sergeant Tanguay," he said.

Marie-Ann hated him immediately.

It wasn't his fault he was assigned here while she was out injured. Bennett and Brake were so grossly incompetent and corrupt, respectively, that there was no way either of them would be made acting Sergeant. It was inevitable that her replacement was going to come from outside. It wasn't his fault that he did the job well and kept everyone in line while Tanguay was away.

It wasn't Peters' fault that Inspector Williams from St. John's sent her a letter last week. In no uncertain terms, it stated that if Marie-Ann could not return to work as outlined in her modified work agreement, she would be transferred to Montreal, some 1200 kilometres away.

Sergeant Peters shook her hand. Marie-Ann pretended to smile. "So," she said, "what did I miss?"

Cheryl fell upon her like a doddering mother, taking her by the hand like she was leading an old woman across the street. "Now, now, let's not rush into anything, Sergeant. Let's go to your desk and sit for a spell. I've got a tea waiting for you, just the way you like."

Tanguay shrugged her off, more aggressively than she intended, and felt bad instantly. Cheryl had probably been taking care of her whole family like this since the horrific accident that burned down their house last year. It was her nature. Marie-Ann tried to soften her tone. "I'm fine, Cheryl. I don't need to sit down. How is your family, by the way?"

"Oh, they're good, well, good as can be expected, I suppose. Todd and Sheila are mostly back to normal, though Sheila wakes up screaming in the middle of the night sometimes, and Todd has some nasty scars on his face. Course, he was always a homely boy, but still, it's a sin. He looks like the Phantom of the Opera now."

Marie-Ann remembered Todd. He was a very smart boy but incredibly weird, and he always stared at her chest.

"My husband, Harold, is the worst off. Well, I think he's actually fine, but he complains worse than Todd did when he was lying in the hospital with half his face burned off."

"I'm sure you'll kick his arse back into shape." Marie-Ann grinned and took Cheryl's hand. She squeezed it. A few years ago, she would never have shown that kind of familiarity with her subordinates, but they had been through a lot together. They were her odd little family. She had no idea how she was supposed to leave them.

"There's a stack of paperwork and files piled up you may want to look at," said Bennett. "Sergeant Peters came up with a new filing system you may want to familiarize yourself with too. It's very efficient."

Brake snorted, and Bennett glared at him. "I said it's efficient. I didn't say I'm actually going to use it."

So, Peters was already making his mark, though some things didn't change. "I assume the paperwork is all your reports you didn't finish, Bennett?"

Bennett's face and thick moustache fell. He looked hurt. "Well, I didn't feel right finishing all those files without you here, Sergeant."

"I don't know how you can read that man's handwriting," commented Peters. He smiled. His teeth were annoyingly perfect, too.

"I'd rather not sit around doing paperwork all day." She knew she should sit; she was exhausted from standing and talking for five minutes. She just didn't want to. "Are there any cases or calls? I've been cooped up too long."

Peters gave her a long, inquisitive stare, but he said nothing. Finally, he grabbed a file from his desk. "Just two. Simon Delaney called to say his neighbour poisoned his dog."

"Again?" Marie-Ann groaned. "He's claimed that at least twice before."

"Three more times while you were away as well," Peters said. "How many dogs does that man have?"

Delaney and his neighbour were awful people, and their feud had been going on for years. The neighbour, Claude Martin, kept poisoning Delaney's dogs. Delaney kept "accidentally" knocking down trees onto Martin's car, shed, or wife. "Sounds like a Brake case," said Tanguay. Bennett was related to both of them.

Brake grumbled, and his thin, creepy moustache twitched like a rat's whiskers. "Peters already assigned it to me."

So, Peters knew the team. That was good, she supposed, though she didn't like it. Christ, she wanted to sit down but tried her best not to show her discomfort. She leaned on the back of an office chair. Her lower back was on fire. "What's the other case?"

"A couple of teenagers didn't come home last night," said Peters. "They were probably out fooling around and got lost, maybe ran away. Their parents said they've done similar things in the past, but some of the kids' friends called this morning and sounded concerned, so the parents reported it."

Tanguay's heart sank. There were two missing teens out there, and they were just standing around *jasser*? Her heart was racing, and her blood pounded in her ears, but she tried to keep her voice steady.

"Who are the kids?"

Peters glanced at the file. "Robert Brown and Shelly Parsons. Both aged seventeen."

Merci Dieu. They weren't her kids, at least. Still, the kids in this town got into weird sorts of trouble, so you could never be too careful. "Who did you assign to that one?"

"I'm going to talk to the parents, take a statement and get a full report." Bennett nodded and patted his broad stomach. He didn't say, "And hopefully, he would wrangle a bowl of soup or a slice of molasses bread," but Tanguay knew he was thinking about it.

It was another good choice. Despite his appetite for free food, or maybe because of it, Bennett was good at talking to people in distress. He was calm, caring, and non-intimidating, like a teddy bear in a uniform.

"I'm coming with you," Marie-Ann said. All eyes turned to her. "I can do the paperwork later. And you know me, I've got a soft spot for dumb kids."

Bennett smiled. "You got it, chief. You wanna drive?"

"Nah, you take this one. I'll grill you on the way and take notes on the new filing system."

"Oh, you're going to like it," Bennett said as he grabbed his hat off the coat rack. "It's got colour-coded tabs."

Usually, Tanguay might have been interested in a new filing system—she was a sucker for classification and organization—but right now, she didn't give a shit. She didn't want to drive because she needed to take another Percocet. There was no way she would make it through the morning without it.

She discreetly popped a pill into her mouth on the way to Bennett's cruiser.

CHAPTER FIVE

Doll Parts
Thursday, October 20
2:50 pm

Niall was anxious the rest of the day. He barely spoke to Harper for over a year, and now, out of the blue, she wanted to talk to him about something after school. Something important enough that she couldn't just do it then and there. Something that she needed to do in private.

And she was wearing *a dress*.

He was so freaked out that he couldn't eat his lunch. He completely zoned out during Biology class and missed the entire review for tomorrow's test. He would have to ask Pius for his notes later. Pius would complain about it, but he would eventually give in.

What could it be? Another girl was interested in him now, so of course, this would be the time she wanted to get back together. Girls always made things complicated. Then again, he was the one who broke up with her. It was unlikely she wanted him back.

Maybe she was pregnant. He hadn't spoken to her in sixteen months and they hadn't had sex anyway, so the chances of her being pregnant was pretty slim. Unless it was someone else's baby. The thought made his stomach churn and twist. This was stupid. He broke up with her. He wasn't allowed to be jealous. Still, he really hoped she wasn't pregnant. That would really mess with the life of a fourteen-year-old. Her mother hadn't been much older when she'd gotten pregnant, and it left Harper with a serious parental complex.

Niall was a wreck all day. He told himself he shouldn't be freaked out. They were still friends, after all. They only broke up so they didn't risk disintegrating anyone with their weird magical powers.

Niall found Harper, as promised, out by the ball field after the final bell. He raced outside so quickly when it rang that he forgot his books in class and nearly bowled over Alexander Bartlett, a grade 12 hockey player who was one of the biggest school bullies since Chris Tobin graduated. The only reason Niall survived was because he was moving so fast Alex couldn't identify him.

Harper looked glorious, leaning on the chain link fence, her hands folded in front of her. Her onyx hair shone in the sunlight. She glanced around nervously, which gave Niall the slightest moment of pause. Harper wasn't afraid of anything and rarely looked anxious. There must be something pretty significant going on to rile her up. Niall really hoped she wasn't pregnant.

She looked at him and smirked. Niall nearly threw up from excitement. Harper hadn't smiled at him in 16 months. "Hey, Niall."

"Hey, Harper." Niall tried to sound cool, he really did, but he was pretty sure he sounded like he'd just sucked back an entire balloon full of helium and drank a half-dozen cans of Crystal Pepsi. "How's it going?"

"It's fine."

Unsure of what else to say, Niall asked, "Is that creepy weirdo from across the street still watching you with his binoculars?"

Harper's eyes widened, and her head snapped back as if she had been slapped. "What?"

"Pius told me." It made Niall angry when he heard about it, and he almost stormed over there to give the guy a piece of his mind. He chickened out, of course.

"Right. Yeah, no, I took care of it."

Of course, she did. More than anyone Niall knew, Harper could take care of herself. "Your dress is pretty."

"Thanks."

"What's the occasion?"

She bit her lip and glanced around awkwardly. "That's kinda what I wanted to talk to you about."

"Oh my God, you're pregnant," Niall blurted out. His cheeks started to burn with embarrassment.

Harper recoiled in disgust. "What?! Ew, no, Niall. Gross."

Thank God.

"Why would you think that?"

"I don't know, I just... I don't know... what you do in your private life these days..." Thanks to his regular reports from Pius, Niall was pretty confident she didn't have a boyfriend, but he couldn't let Harper know that he knew that. "I just... I mean... It's possible..."

"Shut up, ass wipe. I'm fourteen!" She shuddered. "Why did you have to make this more awkward?"

Niall was good at that. It was his specialty.

They stood in uncomfortable silence for a moment. Some kids ran across the field behind them, kicking a soccer ball. A rumble of conversation drifted, along with a choking cloud of cigarette fumes, from the smokers' corner a few dozen paces away.

Finally, her annoyance passing or at least suitably diminished, Harper spoke, "I wanted to talk to you because my mom is coming to see me."

Niall was taken aback. The mom that, for years, he assumed was dead but recently found out that was actually alive. She was a drug addict living away who seemed to want nothing to do with her daughter. Harper had been raised by her father, who died at the hands of the Psycho Hose Beast. "I thought you hadn't spoken to her in ages."

"I've spoken to her a few times over the last year," Harper explained, and Niall cringed. Of course, he wouldn't know that. He hadn't spoken to her since they broke up. "She went to rehab. She's been clean for a year. She has a job and an apartment in Toronto, and she's getting her life back together."

"That's... great," Niall said, hoping he used the proper adjective.

"No, it is. Her life has been a mess for years, so it's good that she's getting back on the right track. She even remembered my birthday."

Niall was still conflicted. Harper was saying positive things but didn't sound positive or particularly happy about them. "You're not sure if you want to meet her," Niall guessed.

She nodded, and he thought he saw a glimmer of a tear in her big brown eyes. She brushed it away quickly. It was so rare for Harper to show vulnerability.

"You've been mad at her for a long time."

Harper nodded again. "I know I should be happy for her, but I don't know if I can. There's so much I want to say to her, so much I need to get off my chest."

"Then tell her."

"But she's so fragile right now, and she's trying to be nice, it doesn't feel right..."

Niall cut her off. "The Harper I know wouldn't pussy-foot around like that. She would tell her mother what she felt. If your mom is serious about making things right, she needs to know how she's hurt you. She needs to hear the anger and the disappointment that I heard when she called you drunk and high and barely remembered your name. Just because she wants to heal doesn't mean you have to. If you need to get these things off your chest, then you do it. If she still wants to make peace afterward, then at least you're coming from an honest place."

Niall looked down and realized he was holding Harper's hand. He wasn't sure who grabbed whose fingers first. And there were definitely tears in her eyes now.

They pulled their hands away simultaneously, both embarrassed and confused by the moment. The last time they touched, they disintegrated a giant insect monster powered by interstellar glowing bugs. The time before that, Niall accidentally killed somebody.

"Thank you," Harper said. "I needed to hear that."

"Of course. I know you. You don't kowtow to anybody, certainly not a mom who hasn't been in your life for fourteen years. Is that why you asked to talk to me?"

"Yeah. Uncle Raymond and Aunt Samantha are careful about what they say around each other and with me. Their advice about my mom is so wishy-washy. They're the ones who set up the meeting today."

"Today? You're meeting her today?"

"Of course. That's why I dressed up." She pulled on the skirt of her dress for emphasis. "I'm going to meet her at the coffee shop. Actually, I wanted to ask if you would—"

"—Niall?"

Niall whipped around to find Stacey standing a few metres behind him, down the hill that led up to the soccer field. She was dressed in a pink tank top and a blue skort (he thought that's what it was called?), and her curly red-blond hair was blowing in the wind.

A million odd emotions ran through Niall's mind in a heartbeat. At first, he felt guilty, but then he realized he only *thought* he should feel guilty. He wasn't actually doing anything wrong. He and Harper broke up, and nothing happened between him and Stacey. They were all neutral single parties who happened to bump into each other. Yet... his stomach was twisting into knots, like that time he ate bad lobster. Guilty was the best way he could describe it. But who should he feel guilty about? Stacey or Harper? Why were they both here at the same time?

"Stacey?" Niall asked, his tongue dry and swollen in his mouth. Maybe he was having an anaphylactic reaction to something and was about to die. That would be good. "What are you doing here?"

She approached with a smile. "I came to meet you after school. My parents let me take the day off, and I wanted to thank you again for saving me last night."

Harper's brow furrowed. "Save you? From what?"

Stacey put her hands—one of which was heavily bandaged—possessively on Niall's arm. "Niall rescued me from a wild dog last night. It was the craziest thing. It probably would have torn my arm off if Niall hadn't scared it away."

"It was no big deal," Niall said, blushing. He saw Harper looking at Stacey's hands on his arm, and he felt mortified. He felt like he should pull away, but a part of him really liked her touching him. He enjoyed it last night, too, holding her hand while he walked Stacey home. Why did the situation have to be so uncomfortable now?

"I'm Stacey Peters." She extended her good hand to Harper. "And you are...?"

Niall realized he should have introduced them instead of just standing there like an idiot. "Sorry, Stacey, this is Harper, she's my..." Niall didn't know what to call her. It didn't feel right to say "ex-girlfriend."

Harper smirked. "Me and Niall go way back. We've rescued each other from monsters a bunch of times."

Niall nearly choked, and Stacey looked confused. "I'd love to hear that story sometime. Anyway, Niall, I wanted to take you out to thank you. Do you want to go for ice cream?"

She was asking him out. Stacey was asking him out right in front of Harper. Niall felt the sweat pouring down his face and the back of his neck. He hoped the girls didn't notice. He felt like he had just jumped into a boiling swimming pool.

He forgot how to speak. He opened his mouth and released a dry wheeze. Some grunts that vaguely resembled words tumbled out. "Well, actually, I... Harper was just..."

Now, it was Stacey's turn to be embarrassed. "Oh, I'm so sorry! Were you guys planning to do something? Don't let me interrupt!"

"No, it's fine." Harper's tone was perfectly level. Niall was relieved she said it but unnerved because he couldn't tell what she was thinking. "You guys go do your thing. I've got an appointment anyway."

Niall breathed a sigh of relief. He could almost kiss Harper. He was so happy at how she diffused that situation. And yet, something felt wrong. "Harper, were you just about to ask me something?"

"Don't worry about it," she said, walking away. "You guys have fun."

"Good luck," Niall called out to her, a heavy weight settling back into his chest. He hoped she would be okay.

"Thanks," Harper said and disappeared around the corner of the school.

"So, what kind of ice cream do you like?" Stacey asked and slipped her hand into Niall's. He was shocked for a moment but then realized he liked the feeling of her fingers in his—a lot. Her hand was warm, and her smile was infectious. Some of the pain in his chest subsided, and he grinned slightly.

"Pralines... and dick," Niall said, and Stacey's jaw dropped. He felt embarrassed again. "Crap. That was supposed to be funny."

"It's from Wayne's World, right?"

"Yeah."

"I love that movie! The second one kinda sucked, though. So I Married An Axe Murderer was much better."

Niall relaxed again. Stacey was so good at making him feel good. He just felt so oddly comfortable around her. "Yeah, that was really good."

"You should come over and watch it sometime. We've got a big TV in our family room."

They weren't on their first date, and she was already asking him on a second one? What was this madness?

By the time they left school property, walking hand in hand and laughing about Mike Myers movies, Saturday Night Live, and Kids in the Hall, Niall completely forgot about the question Harper was about to ask him.

CHAPTER SIX

Scream of the Butterfly
Thursday (?), October 20 (?)
???

Robbie Brown was known as a hard case. He talked back to teachers, bullied junior high kids, and stole his parents' booze from time to time. He was flunking most of his classes and would only graduate because the teachers didn't want to deal with him anymore. He knew he was an asshole, and he wasn't always proud of it, but that didn't mean he should be kidnapped and murdered by Satan worshippers.

Robbie didn't know who snatched him and Shelly from the rusted-out van off the old dump road. They snuck out there to make out like hundreds of kids did before, and were just getting into it when the strangers in white robes burst into the van and grabbed them. Local kids had joked for years that there were Satan worshippers "up in those woods," so at first, Robbie thought it was a prank. But the freaks threw bags over their heads, bound their hands behind them and hauled them through the woods before shoving them into another vehicle. They drove for a long time, over rough roads, until Shelly finally stopped screaming and passed out. Robbie dozed for a bit, and when he woke up, his arms were in agony from lying on them awkwardly.

Finally, they were dragged out of the vehicle at their destination. Robbie knew Shelly was with him because he heard her cursing and swearing at their captors; the girl had a mouth on her like a sailor. It was one of the reasons he liked her. He wasn't planning on marrying her or anything, but she was fun to fool around with. Robbie was eventually dumped onto a hard floor and heard a door slam and lock nearby. It didn't take him long to determine he was in a small, empty room, not much bigger than a closet. He heard muffled voices through the walls but couldn't make out any words. He had no idea where Shelly was.

Robbie was left alone for a long time. He couldn't take the hood off, couldn't free his arms. He could do nothing but lie on the floor and wonder how they were going to kill him.

He didn't know who took him or why. His dad was a fisherman, and his mom worked at Woolco. It wasn't like they could afford a ransom. Robbie hadn't pissed off any criminals or anyone who might do this for revenge. Could his parents have been involved in something? Unlikely. His parents were the most boring people on the planet. His dad drank hard, but he wasn't involved in drugs or anything.

Robbie didn't want to die. There was so much he hadn't done yet. He hadn't finished high school, bought his first car, or gone to see the Toronto Maple Leafs in person. He was supposed to lose his virginity tonight, but obviously, that didn't happen.

He was shaken from his delirium when a girl yanked the bag off his head. As his eyes came into focus, he tried to make out her features in the dim light. She was wearing a white robe like the people who grabbed them.

Robbie could not tell how much time had passed—hours, days?—all he knew was that he was starving, sore, and had pissed himself more times than he cared to admit.

"Wake up, sleepyhead!" The girl smiled. Her face was round and disconcertingly friendly. She wore smudged black lipstick and eyeliner, and her messy, long black hair was growing out to show lighter roots. Her white robe-thingie was pulled tight across her huge boobs.

"Get the hell away from me, you crazy bitch!"

The girl pouted. "That's not very nice. I'm here to make your day a little brighter, and that's how you talk to me?"

Robbie looked around to find himself in a small room with chipboard walls about the size of a small shed. Daylight streamed in from the open door behind the psycho woman.

Robbie screamed for help.

"No one here can hear you," said the girl. "No one that matters, anyway."

He smelled the faintest scent of seawater and heard gulls, but that could be anywhere on the island. "Where's Shelly?" Robbie demanded.

"She's close by. She's safe."

"As safe as me?"

The girl laughed. "You're perfectly safe, for now. But bad things are coming. We need you to help protect the rest of the world. You can be a hero, Robbie."

"How do you know my name?"

"We've been watching you and Shelly. We don't take just anyone, you know. We told you we need you to help us save the world. Not just anyone will do."

This was insane. This Townie bitch was telling him he was going to see the world. "Why couldn't you just tell me that instead of hauling us off into the night like goddamn Candy Man?"

She smiled. "Would you have believed me?"

Screw this. The door was open. Though his hands were bound behind him, Robbie wasn't going to sit here and listen to this nutjob. He pushed himself off the floor and to his feet. Robbie wasn't a small guy and had seen his share of fights. One stupid skank wasn't going to slow him down. He put his shoulder down and charged toward the door, ramming the girl out of the way. She collided hard with the wall.

And then Robbie was outside. His eyes, so accustomed to the hood's darkness, were blinded by the sunlight. He staggered, disoriented, catching a glimpse of a circle of small wooden buildings surrounded by trees. The ground beneath his feet was bare and full of twisted roots, like the area had recently been cleared. Where the Hell was he?

Just as Robbie started to get his bearings, something hit him in the face with crushing force. Judging by the smell of dirt and the clang it made when the weapon collided with his skull, he was pretty sure it was a shovel.

Robbie didn't remember falling, but when he came to his senses, he was on the ground and being dragged back into his shed. His face throbbed in agony; he couldn't see out of one eye, and he felt blood running over his mouth from his nose. He tasted it in the back of his throat.

"Are you hurt, Sister Pearl?" asked a voice he didn't recognize. Sounded like a bayman from out by Cape-de-Cape, with the strong, vaguely French-sounding dialect that was nearly incomprehensible to people who weren't from around here.

"I'm fine, Brother Limeville," said the girl's voice from nearby.

"You should be more careful." Brother Limeville dropped Robbie unceremoniously back on the floor of his cell. He was too loopy to think about protesting. "Want me to break his knees so he don't try to run again?"

"I don't think that will be necessary, will it, Robbie? You know there's no way to get away, nowhere to go. Besides, if you leave, you won't be able to help us with the Reckoning. When he returns, you want to be on the right side, don't you? Those out there will suffer unspeakable horrors as punishment for their sins. But those of us in the Order will be safe. We will prevail, and we will be rewarded for our faith."

Robbie couldn't have answered if he wanted to. His throbbing head couldn't remember how to form words. His jaw ached, and the only sound he could make was a choked moan. There was no point talking to this woman. She was obviously unhinged. She was going to hurt him and Shelly, and Robbie was now absolutely certain that he was going to die.

A child whimpered softly, kneeling on scattered uncooked rice on a hard wooden floor. She didn't know how long she'd been here. An hour? Two? It was impossible to tell. Her father was still preaching, but it was difficult to hear his words. She blocked everything out to disassociate from the pain.

Mother and Father had always been hyper-religious. Anna knew she was going to Hell before she learned to walk. There was a strict series of rules she was to follow in everyday life— prayer, penance, and piety were the big three, but deference to her parents and their fellow church members was also important. As a child, she had no rights except to honour her mother, father and God. She was pretty sure that was how it went. Her parents followed new leaders so often that it was hard to keep track.

When kids at school asked her what religion she was, Anna couldn't answer. She wasn't Catholic, Anglican, Lutheran, or Pentecostal. Mother and Father always said that the so-called "real" churches were all heretics, and they didn't know the True Story. Long ago, Anna stopped asking her parents what the "true story" was. It always resulted in too many beatings.

However, since they came back from Switzerland, Mother and Father were worse than ever. They said they had finally found the Right Path and other True Believers like themselves. They were so excited and convinced that they had found the right thing that they sold their house in Mount Pearl and moved to a new community of like-minded individuals in Quebec. Her father abandoned his import business, as far as she could tell. Or maybe he'd given it to the new church leaders? All Anna knew was that they used to be pretty well off, with a nice house and lots of toys and new clothes all the time, and now they were living in a tiny shack with another family, dressed in faded hand-me-downs and eating pitiful meals in a communal cafeteria with the other members of the congregation.

"Christ is coming," her father was saying now, holding his mysterious new bible-like book above her in his thick hands. "He will come from the sun in a blazing ship of fire and unite all the religions in one true church! We must be ready. He will reward His truest followers, and we will be among them. You must understand this."

"Yes, Father," Anna muttered. She felt something warm and sticky under her knees. They were bleeding again.

"If you understand this, why do you slut yourself out like a common trollop? You are to be pure! To give your body to another member of the Temple!"

"We must ensure the line remains pure." Mother's head bobbed up and down like a hen pecking for seed in a barnyard. "You must save your virtue for a husband chosen for you by the Synarchy!"

Anna had worn shorts to school. It was hot. When she came home, her mother yanked her to the floor by her hair, and her father slapped her bare thighs with a belt. Then they made her kneel on rice while they preached from their new book and berated her for hours. The sun was gone down now.

Anna was ten years old.

She didn't know what a slut was. She'd heard the word on a re-run of Taxi at her friend's house but was too embarrassed to ask what it meant. She didn't want old men she'd never met to pick her husband, either. She didn't even like boys! They were all so dirty and smelly. They picked their noses and talked about hockey and He-Man all the time.

She had always assumed her parents would tell her how to grow up and who to marry, but they had grown more adamant about it since they found their new calling. They talked about her getting married all the time now. They said there was a great calamity coming, and they needed to expand the members of their faith before the end of the world.

None of it made any sense to Anna, but she dared not question her parents.

CHAPTER SEVEN

Black Hole Sun
Thursday, October 20
4:05 pm

"I'm telling you, you can use it to take infinite turns!" Skidmark insisted.

"I'm calling bullshit," Keith said again. "I don't believe it."

Pius was only half paying attention. He was still thinking about his encounter with Mr. Bourgeois earlier.

The late October sky was threatening rain as the trio emerged from Arlene's discount department store on Main Street, a brown, ugly building with large front windows. Arlene's sold a bit of everything—sewing supplies, kids' winter coats, souvenirs and cheap toys—and it was also the only place in town where you could buy Magic: The Gathering cards. Skidmark, Keith and Pius came out with fistfuls of packs, eager to start ripping into them to discover what kind of cardboard goodness was waiting inside.

Pius wondered if he could still play Magic in prison.

Skidmark had by far the largest stack of shiny cellophane-wrapped card packs. "It's really simple! You put Animate Artifact and Instill Energy on Time Vault. Then you can keep untapping Time Vault so you can take infinite turns!"

Skidmark looked smugly proud of himself for having figured this out. He stuffed another handful of colourful Nerds candy into his face, though more of it spilled down his Beavis and Butthead sweatshirt than into his mouth. Noticing his little red and blue cardboard box was empty, he chucked it on the ground and fished another box out of the pocket of his sweatpants. He awkwardly balanced his packs of cards in one hand while tearing open the fresh candy box with the other.

Still picturing that scorched bookbag in the principal's office, Pius absently picked up the empty candy box while Keith grumbled, "I don't think that's how that works. That's stupid! Pius, is that how that works?"

Pius didn't really want to get into an argument with his friends. He was too distracted by the panic rising in his chest and the fear that cops were going to show up any moment and drag him off to prison for burning down the school.

He chose his words carefully. "I don't think that's what the designers necessarily intended, but by how the cards are worded, yes, that's exactly how it would work."

"That's nuts!" Keith started ripping open his first pack of cards as they walked back down the street. They had planned to stop at Jerry's Video Shack to see if NHL95 was available to rent. Pius wasn't a big hockey fan, but Keith and Skidmark loved it, and Pius could also go through their decks while the other two played. "I've never even seen this 'Time Vault' card. I'm not sure it's real."

"Todd has one," Pius confirmed, referring to Todd Murphy, another kid their age who went to a different school. Todd was unwillingly and inadvertently pulled into their adventures last year when they blew up his house and nearly killed him. "I've never seen him use that combo, though."

Skidmark tried to open a pack and dropped half of his cards and most of his freshly opened box of Nerds. He cursed, picked everything up, and promptly dropped them again. "I'm all thumbs today. The Satan worshippers must have cursed me."

"Will you shut up about the Satan worshippers?" Keith scoffed.

"I told you, Scott Legge said Dave Rideout…"

"Scott and Dave are idiots! They're just making up stories to screw with you."

Skidmark tried to stand up, juggling his cards and candy and failing miserably. "Well, don't say I didn't warn you when they steal your dog for their weird rituals. Crap, where did Serra Angel go…?"

"Why don't we sit down?" Pius suggested, gesturing to a bench on the sidewalk just a little way down, next to White's Hardware store. Jerry's Video was across the street, but he knew they were all eager to tear into their packs, so they might as well get it over with. His legs were weak and shaky, so sitting was a welcome relief.

"I don't know how you can afford so many cards," said Keith, adjusting his Blue Jays baseball cap and lopsided haircut underneath. Keith grew his hair long to conceal the missing earlobe on his left side. The earring on his one good ear looked redder and angrier than it had earlier in the day.

Skidmark shrugged. "I get a good allowance. My parents are quick to reward my exceptional behaviour and helpfulness around the house."

"I've met your parents," Keith reminded him. "They hate you."

"I've never seen you do a chore unless there was a threat of physical violence," Pius added.

"Well, I'll have you know that my repeated near-death experiences have caused my parents to appreciate me more and realize they were taking me for granted, so they started showing that they love and care about me and buying me stuff. And spend time with me and junk, too, but it's the buying stuff that's important."

Keith shook his head. "I saw your mother take a swing at your head with her shoe just last week."

"Oh, look, I got a Sol Ring!" Skidmark exclaimed, completely ignoring Keith's comment.

Pius started to look through his own cards, but he was distracted. Not only was he being crushed by the paralyzing fear of his impending arrest and incarceration, he also just realized that they were sitting at nearly the exact spot where he and Keith had sat in the aftermath of the butt monkey invasion last year. Pius and Keith had shared a quiet moment, where Keith disclosed some of his own troubles. He showed Pius more empathy than he had ever thought possible. After that moment, Keith really did become his friend and never went back to his asshole, bullying ways, at least not with Pius and their other buddies.

Keith's parents were broken up, and his mother lived on the other side of Newfoundland. Pius came to learn that Keith somehow blamed himself for his mother's leaving, but he never really understood why. Pius was worried that Keith might resent him since Pius' own parents got back together after their problems a while back, yet Keith never seemed anything but supportive. Keith shocked everyone, including himself, with his friendlier, more positive behaviour over the last year or so.

Pius traced the beginning of that change to the moment he and Keith had sat at this very spot while half of downtown burned around them. He wondered if their conversation had changed Keith's outlook on life. It was equally possible that the change started from watching another of their friends, Keenan, being loaded into a body bag across the street from where they now sat.

Pius was so lost in his thoughts, and the others were so engrossed in their cards that no one noticed a man approaching them. Dozens of people walked past them on the sidewalk while they passed around their cardboard treasures, so it was a shock when one of them stopped and screamed in Keith's face.

"What the Jesus hell are you doing?"

Pius felt every organ inside his body contract, and he was amazed he didn't wet himself. Having an adult stranger yell at him was very high on his exhaustive list of fears. He felt like he was three years old again and had done something horribly, unforgivably wrong, like eating a Lego or drawing on the wall with crayons.

But it wasn't a stranger yelling at them. It was Keith's dad. Pius had seen him only once or twice, but he would recognize him anywhere. Mr. Doucette looked much like his son—tall, solidly built, with a square jaw and sandy-coloured hair. He wore a few days' worth of stubble on his chin, his Arctic Cat jacket was scuffed and dirty, and he carried a general air of disheveledness. He was also red in the face, probably from screaming at Keith at the top of his lungs.

"Christ, Dad, you scared the crap out of me." Keith fumbled with his cards and tried to stand, but his father stood so close to him that he couldn't get up. Pius and Skidmark instinctively slipped away and off the bench.

"What do you think you're doing?" Mr. Doucette demanded again.

"I don't know... the cards? They're just trading cards, Dad. Like hockey cards."

Mr. Doucette slapped the Magic cards out of Keith's hands, sending them fluttering all over the sidewalk. Pius heard Skidmark whimper, but Keith's dad was laser-focused on his son. "I don't care about the frigging cards. What the Hell is this?"

He grabbed Keith's ear, and Keith winced in pain. Pius wanted to help, say or do something, but every synapse in his body told him to run away. A small crowd of people was gathering, but none seemed to want to help either. It took every quantum of willpower just to stand his ground.

"Ow, dammit, Dad, it's just an earring! Ow!"

"An earring?" Mr. Doucette was seething, spitting with rage. "Just an earring? What are you, a faggot? No son of mine is going to wear a goddamn earring!" He shoved Keith's head away. "Take it out. Now!"

Keith gingerly touched his ear. "I can't take it out; it's infected and swollen. If I take it out now, they said the pus could heal over, and it would get worse."

"Jesus Christ, you take that goddamn thing out of your ear right now!"

A half-dozen adults were standing around watching now. Why wasn't anyone doing anything? Was it because Mr. Doucette was one of the wealthiest people in town? Were they afraid of him? Or did they just not want to get involved?

"Dad, no, I'm not taking it..."

Without warning, Mr. Doucette's hand shot out, grabbed the small silver stud in his son's right earlobe, and yanked it out. Keith screamed. So did a couple of young girls who had been watching.

Keith held his hand to the side of his head, blood trickling through his fingers. His father stepped back, seemingly stunned by his actions, and some of the colour drained from his face. He finally went silent.

Pius watched Keith intently. The shock and pain in his eyes faded, to be replaced with a red-hot anger to rival his father's. Mr. Doucette must have also seen this because he started to get his voice back, "Go. Get in the truck."

"Go to hell," Keith growled through gritted teeth.

"What did you say to me?" Doucette shot back.

Keith stood up to his full height and looked his father in the eye. "I said go to hell, you son of a bitch."

"Ungrateful piece of shit. You get in the truck right now."

Pius thought for sure one of them was going to start swinging. Keith had hit plenty of people for less, and his dad seemed like the type to not take backtalk. But instead of fighting, Keith stepped back and walked away. Mr. Doucette called after him a few times, but as more people continued to gather, his anger seemed to falter. Keith kept walking. Eventually, Mr. Doucette ran across the street and jumped into a blue pickup truck. He took off, squealing his tires and nearly taking out two pedestrians at the crosswalk.

A few dozen meters away, Keith disappeared around a corner. Pius knew he should follow him, but he found himself frozen. Why didn't anyone do anything? Why didn't *he* do anything? Why didn't he at least say something? He had just been thinking about how he and Keith had become good friends, and then, in Keith's moment of need, Pius did nothing. He was no better than all those other faceless strangers who wouldn't raise a finger to help a kid who was being beaten by his own father.

What the Hell was wrong with people? What was wrong with him? Pius felt sick to his stomach. Time and time again, when faced with danger and things that scared him, he screwed up, just like when he set fire to the school and destroyed Theolina's journal. He failed himself, and once again, he failed his friends.

Beside him, Skidmark crawled around on the sidewalk, collecting Keith's dropped cards. At least he was doing something to help. Pius still hadn't moved.

CHAPTER EIGHT

Big Empty
Thursday, October 20
4:40 pm

Robbie Brown lived with his family in a trailer court on the South side of Gale Harbour, near the road to Port Hanson. Despite the area's reputation, many of the trailers were done up with pride and care by their residents, with neat yards and gardens, painted porches and maybe a pink flamingo or two on the lawn. The Browns' trailer possessed none of these. The grass was overgrown with weeds, one of the windows was boarded up, and the front step was made of cracked, pitted concrete that had nearly crumbled away to rubble.

Tanguay could feel the disappointment settling into Bennett as they exited the car. He wasn't likely to get a decent lunch here.

They knocked on the screen door, and a large, middle-aged woman in a shapeless blue dress appeared. "Teddy, the cops are here," she called back to someone in the house before she opened the screen.

An impatient male voice called from somewhere inside. "Well, talk to them. You're the one who called them!"

"I ain't talking to no Jesus Mounties. You get off your arse and come to the kitchen. I'll put the kettle on."

The woman walked away, still having not opened the screen door. Tanguay and Bennett exchanged glances. "Um, Mrs. Brown?" Bennett called to her.

"What're you doing just standing there on the step like warts on a horse's backside? Come on in, you're letting the heat out."

They looked at each other again. Bennett shrugged, his thick moustache bristling. "At least we're getting a cup of tea."

The inside of the trailer was dimly lit, with faux wood panelling and orange shag carpet. A cloud of bluish cigarette smoke hung in the air, but at least the nicotine masked most of the cat piss smell.

"You've got a kitty?" Bennett asked, trying to be friendly.

"Cat died last year," grumbled the woman's voice.

"Did you find it?" asked Bennett, and Tanguay shot him a withering glare.

The officers found themselves in a small kitchen/dining room, where the woman was noisily banging around preparing a kettle and mugs. A balding, bent man in a wrinkled shirt and pants entered from the other end of the room, leaning heavily on a cane. Tanguay looked at him and cringed, wondering if that would be her fate too.

"Friggin' wife calls the cops and then can't be bothered to talk to them," grumbled the man. "I told her Robbie's fine, but she goes on with her 'mother's intuition' crap and gets all teary and squeamish. Go on, sit down, sit down."

Marie-Ann gratefully took a seat, though the hard wooden chair only made her hips hurt in a different way. She would have to find an excuse to stand up again in a few minutes.

"Now, now," Bennett said, "a mother knows best. It's understandable if she's worried about her little boy."

While that may be true, the woman in the kitchen looked like a rhino in a mumu; Marie-Ann couldn't picture her ever being "teary" or "squeamish."

"Are you Mr. Brown, Robert's father?" Tanguay asked. She pulled out her notebook and pen.

"That's me, Theodore Brown." He sat down heavily at the table beside them. "My wife's name is Bridget. Robbie goes off all the time, sometimes days at a time. There's nothing to be worried about."

Mrs. Brown put down something on the counter with a clattering bang, apparently out of passive-aggressive denial of her husband's claims.

"If he's fine, why did he leave his car up the back of the dump?" Bridget grumbled.

Tanguay looked back to Teddy, who tsked and shook his head. "Go on with you, woman. You sound like your mother. They left Robbie's car because they went off in that Parsons girl's car. We spoke to her parents."

"That's Shelly Parsons?" Tanguay asked.

Teddy nodded, his bald round head bouncing like a fishing bobbin on the water. "Nice-looking girl, but she's got a mouth on her. She had words with Bridget the last time she was over."

"That one is no good for our Robbie!" Mrs. Brown spat.

"Quiet with you. You think Mother-bloody-Theresa isn't good enough for our Robbie."

Bennett raised his hands as if to somehow ease the tension and quiet the situation with his beefy palms. It never worked, but he tried it every time. "Sounds to me like a couple of kids running off being foolish. If they try to go to Vegas to get married, they'll be sorely surprised how far it is."

Teddy slapped his hand on the table in a victorious gesture. "See? I told you! Isn't that the same thing I said?"

Bridget glared daggers at him. Bennett looked infinitely pleased with himself.

"Actually, we would like to do more investigation before we write off any possibilities." Tanguay tapped her notebook with her pen. Bridget returned to the table with a tray of steaming tea mugs, and Tanguay deliberately looked her in the eyes. They were puffy and red, as if from crying. "Do you believe something happened to your son?"

Teddy moaned, but Marie-Ann ignored him. Bridget nodded slowly. "Something ain't right. It's not like him to go missing. Not like this."

"I believe you." Tanguay stood up to show she didn't have time to wait for tea. She also needed to take the pressure off her lower back and hips. "We will do everything possible to find your son, Mrs. Brown."

She didn't add that Gale Harbour had a strange history of kids disappearing under unusual circumstances. Mrs. Brown likely already knew all about it.

"Was you the one what found those kids in that bunker a couple years ago?"

"It was," Marie-Ann acknowledged.

Mrs. Brown's lip quivered. "You find my Robbie, then."

They were heading back to the car when the call came that two men had been found dead on a boat near Port Hansen. Tanguay's head swam with déjà vu to the Quinn brothers, the drowned men who started it all two years ago.

Sainte Mère de Dieu, thought Tanguay. *Please, let it be a coincidence.*

CHAPTER NINE

Fell on Black Days
Thursday, October 20
5:30 pm

Stacey thought the face paint was cool. She told him over ice cream at Silver Scoops while they chatted about nonsense, getting to know each other. Stacey told him she did figure skating in winter and played soccer in the summer, and her favourite bands were Ace of Base and Boyz II Men. Niall wasn't too keen on her choice of music, but he held his tongue. Her favourite movie was *Robin Hood: Men in Tights*, which earned her back some points.

Talking to Stacey was easy; it was almost like talking to one of the guys. Talking with Harper was different—it's not that it was hard, but Niall just felt nervous all the time. Was that because he wasn't as confident around her? Had he since learned to be more comfortable around girls?

Niall mentioned that his favourite movie was The Crow, which is what brought them to the topic of face paint. He was initially embarrassed, but she assured him there was nothing to be embarrassed about. Brandon Lee and The Crow were the coolest things going right now, and she was sure there would be tons of guys dressing like him for Halloween.

"But it would take a powerful, confident guy to be able to wear that any other day," she'd said, leaning in close to Niall in the booth at the ice cream shop. "I mean, maybe not the whole getup, but I think a little eyeliner or black nail polish or something would be cool. Goth is in, right?"

"You wouldn't be embarrassed to be seen with me like that?" Niall asked.

"I wouldn't be embarrassed to be seen with you anywhere." Stacey took his hand, smiled, and then looked away meekly, the first time either of them had been the least bit shy all day. They talked a long time, so long that Niall had to run off to be home in time for supper. Nana Josephine was making fish and brewis—a meal of boiled salt cod and hardtack that was considered a delicacy by older generations of Newfoundland—and she hated when anyone was late.

"You didn't eat very much," Nana asked Niall over supper, scooping another helping onto his dad's plate. Johnny O'Neil was engrossed in his newspaper, his small dark eyes scanning pages from behind his glasses. Nana and Niall's mom were staring right at him, however. Nana's round face turned into a scowl. "You didn't spoil your supper, did you?"

Niall had eaten what he could and fed Joey Smallwood more fish under the table, but his and the cat's combined efforts weren't enough for the motherly figures in his life. "Sorry, I went out for ice cream after school," he said without thinking and immediately regretted it.

"Ice cream?" his mother asked. She cocked her head inquisitively. Her dusty-coloured hair, the same colour as his, didn't move from all the hairspray she'd put in this morning before work. "That's not like you and your friends."

Niall considered his options. Niall was used to lying to his parents about alien invasions and murderous monsters and had become pretty good at it, so he hated telling more lies than he strictly needed to. "It wasn't my friends. It was Stacey."

Nana and his mom's eyes lit up. His dad's gaze briefly came up from the paper. "Stacey?" asked his mom. "Who's Stacey?"

"You don't know her. She goes to the Amalgamated," Niall said quickly, trying not to make a big deal about it. "I met her a few days ago. She's nice."

"Does that mean you're finally over that Jeddore girl?" Nana asked, and Niall felt his cheeks grow hot.

"That's too bad," said his father, returning to the newspaper. "I liked Harper."

Barbara O'Neil slapped her husband on the arm and told him to hush. "We all liked Harper, but Niall can go out with whoever he wants. As long as she's not a Mercer, she's not a Mercer, is she?"

Unable to speak, Niall just stared at his plate and shrugged.

"We're related to Mercers on both sides. It would probably be best if you steer clear of them, you know. So your babies don't grow two heads or anything."

"Mom!" Niall snapped, louder than he'd intended. "We just went out for ice cream!"

"I know, I'm just thinking long-term. Something to keep in mind."

"There's a lot of prostate cancer on the Mercer side too," added Nana.

"That's true," his mom agreed. "You just have to think about your hypothetical children, is all."

Niall wanted to die.

After dinner, Pius stopped by unannounced to hang out. This was unusual, as Pius nearly always called first, but Niall was happy to have the chance to play video games or Magic, avoid his mother and Nana, and chat about his date with Stacey.

Oddly, Pius came straight in and sat on the Chesterfield in the living room instead of going to Niall's room. Nelson was still at work, and his dad was preparing to leave for his night shift at the matchstick factory. His mom and Nana were in the kitchen playing cards. Niall tried talking to Pius, but the gangly boy was distracted. He absently flipped through some photo albums and scrapbooks Niall's mom had left on the coffee table.

"So yeah, I was hanging out with Stacey at Silver Scoops after school," Niall said.

"Uh-huh." Pius' head bobbed up and down, but he didn't look up.

"I like hanging out with her. She's funny and cute. She has terrible taste in music, but she likes Wayne's World and The Crow, so that's cool."

"Uh-huh." Pius turned the page in a scrapbook.

In the kitchen, Nana cheered, and Niall's mom groaned so that Niall could guess who was winning.

Niall rolled his eyes at Pius. "Her sister is a harpy. No, like literally, she has wings and talons."

"Yeah."

"She flies around and eats stray cats. Sometimes, she picks up small dogs and flings them to their gruesome demise onto the rocks at Little Port Hanson."

"Yup."

Niall sighed. "Pius, what's going on? You've got something on your mind. Is the series finale of Star Trek getting you down again?" Pius had been nearly as broken up about the end of The Next Generation as Harper had been about Kurt Cobain's death.

Pius glanced up for the first time, but only briefly before looking back at the books. "I saw something today. It was really upsetting."

"Was your dad walking around with no pants on again?" Niall asked. He'd slept over at Pius' house plenty of times and had seen Mr. Jeddore's wang more than he cared to admit. That was before he'd broken up with Harper, of course. Niall hadn't stayed at their house in over a year.

"Niall, it's not a joke. It was Keith's dad. We were on Main Street, we'd just bought some Magic cards at Arlene's, and Keith's dad just showed up out of nowhere. He started screaming about Keith's earring and called him horrible names. He was so angry. I've never seen anyone so angry at their kid before."

Keith's earring was pretty awful and he looked like a douche with it, but since Niall was considering eyeliner and nail polish, he was hardly one to talk. Pius was shaking; he was so upset his long rat tail trembled over his shoulder. Niall knew now was not the time to make further quips.

"And then... then he just yanked Keith's earring out of his ear, right in the middle of the street! Keith was screaming, and all these people were staring, and Keith's dad was still yelling at him to come home."

"Jesus Christ," Niall breathed. "Then what happened?"

"Keith just walked away. He wouldn't go with him. He just stormed off."

"That's probably a good thing. What did you do?"

"Nothing!" Pius said so loudly that it surprised both of them. The voices in the kitchen quieted momentarily before they resumed their conversation. Pius lowered his head and his voice again. "I froze! I didn't say anything or call for help. I just stood there."

"Pius, come on," Niall said. "What were you supposed to do? You going to hit Keith's dad?"

"I don't know. Maybe."

"Nobody expects you to stand up to anyone."

"That's what I mean! I don't ever stand up to anyone!"

"Pius, that's not what I meant..."

"But it's true!" Pius was getting agitated, but conscious of the adults in the next room, he kept his voice to a hissing whisper. "With everything we've been through, I've been too scared to do anything every time. You, Harper, Keith, even Skidmark, you've all stood up to all kinds of crazy stuff, but I froze every time! The one time I tried to do something useful, I burned down the school!"

"That was an accident."

"It doesn't matter. I still screwed up."

"So what are you going to do?"

"I have to do something about Keith's dad. I just don't think it's right for him to get away with that."

"I mean, Skidmark's parents have been pretty abusive to him for years..."

"This was different. We joke about Skidmark because his parents threaten him, which is not good either, but Niall, you didn't see this. I've never seen someone so angry, so violent. He tore the earring out of his ear! His own son! What if he does something worse next time?"

Niall admitted it was pretty horrific. He wasn't sure if he would have been any more helpful in that situation, but Pius always took these things to heart. He was a good guy who always wanted to help people... but he wasn't good at it. He always froze in any kind of crisis situation.

Pius took a deep breath. "We've got to make sure he never hurts Keith like that again."

"Are you suggesting we... kill him?"

"No! I think I should go to the police."

They were on a friendly basis with the local RCMP Sergeant. They heard she had just come back to work, too. Still, going to an authority figure with big news like that, especially since Pius was still hiding the whole burning down the school thing, would be a big deal for his best friend. "Are you sure? Keith's dad is a big shot in town. He owns the hotel, a couple of bars and other property. My dad says he will probably run for mayor one of these days."

"All the more reason I need to tell the cops! The guy's an asshole. He shouldn't be in charge of anything."

"You sound like you made up your mind."

"Yeah. I'm going to talk to Sergeant Tanguay after school tomorrow."

"Do you want me to come with you?"

Pius' shoulders fell with visible relief. "Will you?"

"I figured that's why you came over. Of course, I'll go with you. For moral support."

"Thanks, man." Pius flopped back onto the couch. "I'll do the talking. I would just really appreciate having a friend with me."

Niall felt like he'd been punched in the stomach. Realization dawned on him so clearly that he couldn't believe he'd missed it the first time.

"I didn't know your dad bowled professionally," Pius said out of the blue. He was looking intently at an old newspaper clipping in the scrapbook. He kept flipping back and forth between the scrapbooks and the photo albums, but it hardly registered to Niall. It was now Niall's turn to nod without really paying attention.

Harper. After school. When she wanted to talk to Niall. She had been about to ask him to go with her to meet her mom. And he went off with Stacey instead.

How could he be so stupid?

"Niall," asked Pius, oblivious to the turmoil inside his best friend. "When was Nelson born again?"

CHAPTER TEN

Nelson O'Neil had that dream again.

In it, he was trapped at the bottom of the ocean. He always panicked because he couldn't breathe, and inevitably, he found he didn't need to. The panic changed to anxiety, then to dread, and finally to boredom.

Being at the bottom of the ocean was neat the first time. He watched some weird fish swim by and saw a couple of jellyfish. One time, an octopus crawled right past him. In the dream, Nelson couldn't touch anything or move his arms. He wasn't sure he even had arms. The first time, this was just an odd observation. After a while, it just became annoying. He wanted to swim around and see whatever interesting stuff he could find at the bottom of the sea. Maybe some sunken ships or pirate treasure or something. Maybe even a topless mermaid. He used to dream about girls a lot (and once about his buddy Dale, which was super weird) before he started having this stupid ocean dream.

It wouldn't have been so bad, except for the next part.

The ground beneath Nelson opened up, and there was nothing beneath. Just blackness and the endless expanse of space. And then he was falling, falling into the infinite abyss, and he knew he would fall forever until he starved or died of fear, except it never ended that way. It always ended the same way, with an unearthly monster appearing out of nowhere beneath him, so large it covered his entire field of vision. It was covered in red eyes the size of dump trucks, and every one of those unblinking crimson orbs was staring right at him. And the endless blackness wasn't outer space; it was the monster's open mouth, and Nelson knew he wouldn't fall forever after all. He screamed and screamed...

...and then he woke up.

Nelson found himself covered in sweat, dressed only in his boxer shorts, sitting on a bare mattress in his dark bedroom. He'd kicked off all his blankets and sheets sometime through the night, but he wasn't cold. His skin felt like it was on fire.

He rolled onto the floor, cracking his knee against a rollerblade he'd discarded carelessly there days ago. He tossed it aside with a muttered curse, where it crashed into hockey sticks stacked in the corner, and they all clattered to the floor. He really should clean his room. He regretted that he'd banned his mom from coming in and cleaning years ago.

There was a knock on the door, and Niall's voice came through. "You okay in there?"

Nelson got up, unlocked the bolts he'd installed himself, and threw open the door.

"Screw off, dillwad," Nelson muttered as he shoved his younger brother aside and headed for the bathroom.

Niall had recently experienced a growth spurt, but Nelson was still taller. He was also far more muscular and stronger than his brother, so Niall crashed into the wall. Their parents would give him a hard time about that later. Niall was their precious little baby, and Nelson was the big dumb moocher who barely finished high school and would probably still live at home when he was forty. They always took Niall's side.

Nelson locked the bathroom door and forced himself to look in the mirror. He looked like shit. His skin was pale, he had deep purple bags under his eyes, and he was covered in sweat. His shoulder-length hair, slightly darker than his brother's, was drenched. He looked like this most mornings, to the point his parents were worried he was on drugs. He wasn't. He hadn't touched any drugs besides drinking with his buddies on the weekends, so they took him to a doctor. He was physically in perfect health but prescribed some anti-anxiety medications for his bad dreams. Nelson tried them a few times but didn't like how they made him feel light-headed and dizzy, so he flushed the rest down the toilet.

He crawled into the shower and turned it on to icy cold. He didn't know why he felt so hot. He hadn't been like this when he saw the doctor. Maybe he should tell his parents about it.

The cold water washed away the heat, the dreams faded, and Nelson became less worried. He started thinking about work, his new girlfriend, and the car he was saving up to buy.

He wanted the car for freedom, of course, but more importantly was the prestige. Having a cool car was a sign he was doing something right. He didn't need a college degree or a fancy job. So what if he stacked boxes of panty liners for a living? It would all be worth it once he had a sweet ride and a cute girl sitting in the passenger seat.

He was eying a '68 Firebird advertised on Tele-Shop a few weeks ago. Tele-Shop was a call-in radio show for people around the Gale Harbour area to buy and sell everything from used cars to hockey equipment to cords of wood to babysitting services. When Nelson heard that someone out in Gale Harbour Crossing was selling a Firebird for ten thousand bucks, he knew it was out of his price range, but he went to see it anyway and immediately fell in love with it.

Blood red with a 5.7L V8 engine and original leather seats. It was gorgeous and perfect and Nelson was confident he could talk the owner down a little on the price, but he would need to get the money soon. That meant taking every shift he could get at the drugstore, and he was considering taking a second job to make more on the side. The Christmas season was coming; surely, he could find extra work somewhere. Maybe that would make his parents respect him more if they saw him working toward something.

Thinking about the car and making plans helped Nelson get his head back on straight, and the dream faded into the back of his mind. The car needed work, but he was sure he could get Nana to help him. His grandmother was great with cars; her husband ran a garage years ago. Nelson would ask her to teach him how to change the oil and stuff before she kicked the bucket. She was a spry old bird, but weird shit happened in this town. She was dragged out of the senior's home and held at gunpoint in a bunker by a psycho woman a couple of years ago; that's why she ended up coming to live with Nelson's family. God knows when another fuel tank would explode, lightning would strike a power transformer, or the next murderer would break out of prison. Or, you know, she could die of cancer or a heart attack like a regular old person.

Nelson walked down to the mall. His parents had gone to work with both their vehicles, not that they would have offered him a ride anyway. It was only a fifteen-minute walk, and he listened to Faith No More on his Walkman to pass the time. He was still jamming to "Midlife Crisis" when he entered the Gale Harbour Plaza and the busy drug store across from Sobey's supermarket. He was so caught up in his music that he didn't realize he was humming and pretending to drum along, and a dozen customers were watching him. As was Irene, standing behind the register, cashing out a little, old, blue-haired woman.

Irene was a pretty girl with dark straight hair, cat-eye glasses, and dimples. Nelson had tried several times to get up the nerve to ask her out but never succeeded. Now, here she was, watching him rock out like an idiot. He realized, vaguely, that he should be embarrassed. Niall would have run back home, hid in his room, and cried for days. Fortunately, Nelson was not his brother.

Instead of shying away from his foolishness, Nelson leaned into it. He drummed harder, threw in a few wails that would have made Mike Patton proud, and finished off with windmilling his arm on an air guitar, Pete Townsend-style. Several customers near the shampoo aisle backed away, and the old lady at the cash register nearly had a heart attack, but Irene laughed and smiled. Nelson winked at her, and she blushed.

It was funny. The best way to feel confident enough to flirt with girls was to get a girlfriend. Nelson never would have acted that way a few weeks ago.

Nelson went to the staffroom, dropped off his Walkman and windbreaker, then returned to the floor to check shelf stock on the more popular items and note what he would have to fill up first. Usually diapers, toilet paper and cases of Pepsi. No one bought Coke in Newfoundland anymore after they closed their bottling plant and pissed off a lot of very loyal Newfies. He would also have to check the seasonal aisle to make sure there were still plenty of those ugly Power Rangers costumes on the rack.

Irene flagged him down from the cash register on his way to the paper aisle.

"Nelson, this customer would like to speak to you."

The girl at the counter, standing with her back to him, was tall, with jet-black hair growing out at the roots, and was dressed in a weird bodice-kind-of-thing and a long black dress. Nelson recognized her, and his heart skipped a beat.

She turned, and Nelson felt a smile spread on his face. She was deathly pale, with black around her eyes and lips. She looked like a frigging ghost, but Nelson thought she was the sexiest woman in the world.

"Hi!" Anna chirped. "I'm looking for bleach. And do you have any duct tape? The hardware store was all out."

CHAPTER ELEVEN

Longview
Friday, October 21, 1994
9:05 am

Seagulls cawed their obnoxious song overhead as Tanguay and Bennett stepped out of the cruiser at Port Hansen. The smell of saltwater and rotting fish nearly made her throw up her lunch. She hadn't eaten much, just bread and a cup of tea, but that didn't mean she was any more excited to see it again.

They were not coming down to Port Hansen to investigate the two dead men found yesterday. Sergeant Peters had taken that case himself. He said it looked like some kind of horrific freak accident like the two men somehow got entangled in their net's winch and were torn to pieces by the motor. In Tanguay's experience, there was no such thing as freak accidents, but she did not have the energy to push her way into Peters' case. It took everything she had to focus on finding Robbie and Shelly.

"That's Squires' boat." Bennett pointed at a long blue fishing boat tied up to the wharf. "Billy works with his father."

Tanguay nodded but said nothing. Her head was spinning, her equilibrium taking its sweet time returning after sitting in the cruiser for a while. It was a side effect of the Percocet, and it was getting worse. Probably because she was popping them like Bennett (should be) popping breath mints.

The pair headed across the gravel road toward the boat, and Tanguay was struck with the memory of another boat on this wharf when they were investigating some of the first victims of the Psycho Hose Beast. Dick Jeddore had hinted that there was something strange going on then. At first, she didn't see it and couldn't believe him, but she didn't take long to figure it out.

She hoped this current case wasn't about something equally supernatural, but anything was possible in this town.

Jake Cutler's green boat was tied up and cordoned off farther down the wharf, and forensics investigators from St. John's were going over it with a fine-toothed comb. Cutler was one of the dead men from yesterday. Tanguay had questioned him about the Quinn Brothers' deaths. Another coincidence. Something about it made Tanguay's stomach turn. Or maybe it was the pills.

"Billy Squires?" Bennett called as they approached the blue boat, and a tall young fisherman in oil slickers appeared to meet them.

"That's me," Billy called back, cigarette dangling from his mouth. He was scrawny, with a long face and puffy, bloodshot eyes. "You the ones looking for Shelly and Robbie? Or is this about Cutler?"

Bennett nodded. "We called about Shelly and Robbie. Permission to come aboard and ask a few questions?"

"I ain't the captain." He scratched his shaved scalp and looked around. "Dad already unloaded all the poached lobster, so sure, come on aboard."

Tanguay hoped he was joking because she didn't have the fortitude to deal with another crime. It was awfully strange that he would be cracking jokes when his friend was missing. Billy was young, though, barely out of high school, and young men his age didn't often have the best judgment when it came to humour.

Getting onto the boat was a struggle. Stepping over the gap between the wharf and the boat and leaning down to step onto the deck was a direction her surgically repaired body did not want to move. Bennett offered her a hand, but she refused. She nearly fell into the bay when her foot hit the deck boards. The pain shooting up through her hip was excruciating. It took a moment to steady herself.

"We already spoke to Robbie and Shelly's parents," said Bennett, watching Tanguay carefully. "We wanted to talk to you because you might be one of the last people who spoke to them before they went missing."

"You think I got something to do with that?"

Bennett smiled. "No, just standard questions."

"Look, Robbie and I goes drinking sometimes, but we're not that good of friends. And I knows Shelly runs off on her own all the time."

Tanguay forced herself to speak to keep from zoning out. "Shelly's parents said she left home a few weeks ago."

"'Left home,' is that what they told you?" Squires chuckled, took a drag of his cigarette, then tossed the butt into the water. His fingers and teeth were already starting to take on the stained yellow of nicotine addiction. "Shelly didn't leave by her own choice, that's for bloody well sure."

"What do you mean by that?"

Billy sighed and scratched his head. "Look, I didn't know she was back with Robbie. Last time I saw Rob, he told me she left him for another girl. Shelly's parents heard about her sucking face with a girl and threw her out of the house."

"So you haven't heard anything from Rob or Shelly?" Bennett scribbled some notes in his pad. "When did you last see Rob?"

"About two weeks, maybe three." Billy spit overboard. "Haven't heard from him since we went on a bender for our buddy Chris Tobin's birthday."

Tanguay nonchalantly leaned against the rail to relieve pressure on her hip and because the vertigo was worsening. She didn't want to fall. "Is there any place Rob and Shelly may have gone to? Any friends out of town?"

"Nah, I don't think so. Neither of them got many friends. Well, I suppose they may have shacked up at the make-out van."

"Excuse me?" Tanguay shivered. Something about it made her skin crawl.

"There's a rusted-out Ford van parked out behind the old dump road. Kids use it to hook up all the time. Robbie said he and Shelly've been out there a few times."

The thought was so gross it made Tanguay's teeth feel greasy. Still, it might be worth checking out.

Bennett cleared his throat. "What about the girl she was... *ahem*... kissing? Do you know who she was?"

Tanguay cringed. She wasn't sure whether to be embarrassed for Bennett or of him.

Billy shook his head. "Think she was from out of town. Rob didn't know her. He said the girl had her face painted up all weird, like pedrolino."

Bennett's pencil went still. "Like what?"

"You know, the clown from the 17th century Italian *Commedia dell'Arte*. The sad comic servant that's always put down by the other characters."

Tanguay's jaw dropped, but Bennett was unfazed.

"Like Geoffrey from Fresh Prince?"

Billy sighed. "Something like that. But with black and white clown makeup. Can I get back to work now? I gotta finish unloading these boxes, or my dad's gonna tan my hide."

So did Robbie call her that, or did Billy make that... never mind. Tanguay didn't want to know. She decided to assume that young men in Gale Harbour were really into old Italian theatre for some reason. What she wanted to know was the identity of that girl. A painted-up sad clown from out of town? There wasn't much to go on, but she knew one person who fit that description. She met her briefly in the aftermath of the explosion on Main Street last year. What was her name?

They asked Billy a few more questions, but nothing much came of it. It sounded like Shelly and Robbie were much the same—not many friends, from unstable homes, and a history of running away. Kids that could go missing without anyone noticing right away.

As they walked back to the car, Tanguay struggled with every step; she tried to think of the girl's name but kept coming up blank. Was it brain fog messing with her memories again? Did she ever know her name? To be fair, that night ended with Tanguay bleeding out on the tarmac of the old airfield. She never did get a proper debriefing of the situation.

"Burt, there was a girl last year who sounded a bit like what Billy described. All done up in makeup—"

"Anna Chaffey, born 1974, from Mount Pearl," Bennett rattled off without hesitation.

Tanguay raised an eyebrow. "She really left an impression on you, eh?"

Bennett blushed a little. "Well, she did cry on my shoulder for a bit after her boyfriend died. And not to mention she has knockers on her like this."

Bennett held up his hands in front of his chest like he was carrying a pair of watermelons.

Tanguay, disgusted, turned her head away quickly—too quickly, as the snapping motion led to a sudden surge of vertigo. It hit her so hard that she stumbled and fell to her knees in the gravel.

"Christ, boss, you okay?" Bennett knelt beside her.

"Yeah, just a bit light-headed," she lied. "Haven't eaten anything today, skipped breakfast."

"Well, why didn't you say so?" Bennett asked cheerfully. "Let's head over to Nanny's Kitchen for lunch, eh? My treat?"

Tanguay groaned, cursing her frailty and Bennett's terrible taste in food. The only reason he ate at that crappy diner in the mall was to flirt with the waitress. When did Bennett become such a horndog?

Tanguay really did not feel like eating, but she had lied now and would have to follow through. "Sure, sounds good."

Bennett offered her a hand. Usually, she wouldn't have taken it, but today, it felt like she had no choice. He helped her up, and she staggered to the cruiser, trying to be as steady as possible.

Tanguay was reeling. Between the pain and the nausea, she knew she should go home and rest.

Instead, she said, "After we get food, I want to go check out that van Billy Squires was talking about. And we should probably look into Anna Chaffey too."

Bennett looked at her with sadness and uncertainty, but he said nothing. Tanguay hated that look. It made her feel weak and ashamed. At least he didn't say anything. Finally, after a moment, the grim visage disappeared from Bennett's face, and his usual jovial smile returned.

"Sure thing," he said and turned the ignition. "You're the boss."

Probably for not much longer, thought Tanguay miserably.

<u>CHAPTER TWELVE</u>

Fall Down
Friday, October 21
3:55 pm

Pius sat, squirming uncomfortably in a grey waiting room chair at the police station. Niall was beside him and also seemed distracted. Pius assumed it was because of a girl since Niall didn't have to worry about being arrested for arson.

It was the same chairs they had sat in two years prior when they came to tell Sergeant Tanguay about the monster in the tunnels under the town. At that time, Pius was so terrified that he ended up in a catatonic stupor. He was well on his way again this time, and only the breathing exercises his therapist had shown him were keeping him from a complete meltdown.

Breathing was the one useful thing Dr. Isaac had taught him. Since Pius couldn't tell the psychologist about the monsters or burning down the school, they mostly talked about his parents' messy situation. Sure, that brought on some stress, but his parents' separation was not what caused him to wake up screaming in his urine-soaked sheets.

Constable Murphy waddled by and asked them if they wanted anything. "Cup of tea? Some lemon cookies?"

Pius wouldn't be able to keep anything down, so he shook his head. Constable Murphy turned to Niall. "You haven't been by in a while, Niall. What have you been up to?"

"Uh, girl stuff," Niall muttered, keeping his blond head down. Niall blamed himself for nearly getting Mrs. Murphy's son Todd killed and always felt terrible when he saw the scars on his face. He avoided hanging out with them when he could.

Constable Murphy's rosy, round cheeks rose with a smile. "I understand. I wish Todd would spend some more time with girls and less with those computers of his. He gets so obsessed with them sometimes that he starts to act a little weird."

A little weird? Todd was the oddest person Pius knew by a long shot, and he knew some pretty messed up people.

"Anyway, Sergeant Tanguay still isn't back, but you can speak to Sergeant Peters."

Pius' butt clenched at the thought of speaking to a different authority figure he didn't know. "No, that's okay, we can wait for Sergeant Tanguay..."

Constable Murphy put on her best motherly look. "You know, if you need to report a crime, you should tell someone right away..."

Pius' intestines were about to turn inside out and wrapped around his throat. A mixture of a cop and mother guilt? Pius could feel the icy fingers of paralysis starting to squeeze his heart.

Niall saved him. Pius didn't think he could form words anymore. "It's fine, Mrs. Murphy. We don't need to wait for Sergeant Tanguay. We can talk to you or—"

"—Boys, come over here," said a new voice. They glanced across the office and saw a tall, good-looking officer standing at a desk near the back door. He had a perfectly square chin, like Batman. They hadn't noticed him come in, and Pius wasn't sure how much he had heard.

The boys must have looked terrified because Constable Murphy nudged them to their feet and toward the other officer. "Go on, Sergeant Peters is an old softie. He'll take your statement. And he loves kids too."

Pius and Niall shuffled across the office, Niall having to practically drag Pius the whole way. They flopped down into two seats across from the new Sergeant's desk. The man grinned at them. "I'm not going to bite. No need to be scared. You wanted to report a crime?" He pulled out a pencil and a notepad. "What are your names?"

Pius was quiet for so long that Niall answered for him again. "I'm Niall O'Neil, and this is Pius Jeddore. Pius actually has something he wants to report; I'm just here for moral support."

Sergeant Peters looked sideways at Niall. "Niall O'Neil? You're the boy who saved my daughter from the wild dog the other day."

Niall nearly choked. He turned deathly pale. "You're Stacey's dad?"

Peters smiled. "Don't worry, son, I just wanted to thank you for saving Stacey. That was very brave of you. And she goes on and on about how wonderful you are. To tell the truth, I think she's a little sweet on you."

Niall slid down in his chair, trying to make himself look smaller. Pius had seen this many times and knew that whatever help his best friend might have provided was now gone out the window.

When it became clear that Niall wouldn't say another word, Sergeant Peters returned to Pius. "So, what was it you wanted to tell me, Pius?"

Pius took several deep breaths like Dr. Isaac had taught him. It barely worked, but at least he had enough oxygen to form a few words. "I saw one of my friends get hurt by his father."

The Sergeant's face suddenly became dark and serious. "It's very good that you came to tell us, Pius, that was the right thing to do. Is your friend okay?"

"I don't know. I haven't seen him since it happened."

"It's okay, Pius, we'll check on him. Tell me everything that happened."

And so, Pius told him everything. About how Mr. Doucette showed up from nowhere, started berating Keith, and then tore out his earring. Sergeant Peters asked for more details here and there but didn't otherwise question Pius' account. He seemed to treat the report very seriously and took copious notes.

"Do you know the names of any of the other people who witnessed this?" Peters asked when Pius was finished.

"Just our friend Skidmark—I mean, Brian Hawco. There were a half dozen more people there, but I don't know any of them." Pius started to get nervous again. Would they believe him without any witnesses? Worse, what if they talked to *Skidmark*?

Peters obviously sensed his discomfort. "That's okay, son. You did the right thing telling us. I'll contact child services, and we'll send someone to talk to Mr. Doucette."

Pius was both relieved and terrified. "Is he going to jail?"

"That's a complicated question and not up to me. We'll do an investigation, and if there are charges, then it will be up to the court to decide. But most importantly, we need to make sure your friend Keith is safe. Now, if you and Niall just wait here for a few more minutes, I need to grab a couple of forms, okay?"

The Sergeant stood and walked away to the far side of the office, where he conferred a few moments with Constable Murphy. Pius guessed he was getting her opinion on the two boys, but he didn't care.

He did what he came to do. The Sergeant must not know about Pius' part in the fire, which was what he suspected since no one had arrested him yet.

Pius slumped back into his seat, relieved that this hadn't blown up in his face. He noticed Niall was flailing his hand weirdly by the side of his chair, below the sight line of the table. He seemed to be gesturing at the Sergeant's desk.

The desk was neatly organized and only held a few notepads, in/out filing baskets, and a caddy for pens and pencils. Niall was pointing at some papers sticking out from under the notebook. It looked like a photocopy of a newspaper clipping. Pius craned his neck and tried to read the headline nonchalantly, though, to be fair, Pius couldn't be nonchalant to save his life. He was the most chalant guy on the planet.

"UFO Sighted over Clarenville - October 26, 1978."

This was weird. Clarenville, a small town on the other side of Newfoundland, rivalled Gale Harbour on the spectrum of boredom. They had alien encounters, too? It seemed like one of those newspapers you read in the grocery store checkout line, but Pius knew that UFOs and aliens were all too real. It might have just been a coincidence that there were more sighted on the island not too long ago.

It was an odd coincidence that October 26 was Niall's brother Nelson's birthday, as Pius had just discovered yesterday.

But why was Sergeant Peters looking up UFOs? Did he know what had happened in Gale Harbour over the last two years? Was he trying to piece something together?

The Sergeant returned to the desk, and Niall and Pius snapped upright in their seats. They tried not to look guilty, but Pius felt like he had just robbed a bank and pushed an old lady into traffic, trying to make his getaway.

"Since Constable Murphy knows you both, and we have your phone numbers on file, you boys can go. But don't leave town or anything. We might have more questions for you.

The boys jumped up and headed for the door. Pius wished he had read more of that newspaper article, but he hoped he could find more about it at the library. He told Niall as much.

"You're going to the library now?" Niall asked as the two boys grabbed their bikes outside the RCMP detachment.

"It's on the way anyway. Do you have something better to do?"

"Actually, yes. I need to go check on Harper. I did something really dumb after school yesterday and need to apologize for it." They hopped onto their bikes and began to pedal down the sidewalk.

"Yesterday? You mean when Harper went to talk to her mom?"

Niall looked a little green. "Yeah... Do you know how their meeting went?"

Pius' chest clenched. He had been so worried about Keith and the meeting with the police that he'd forgotten entirely about the family secret he wasn't supposed to tell Niall about.

"Oh, crap. You haven't heard..."

"Heard what, Pius?"

Pius slammed on the brakes of his bike, and Niall skidded to a stop beside him.

"Heard what, Pius?" Niall asked again.

There was no way he would get out of not telling him now. "Niall, I have something to tell you. And you might want to sit down..."

CHAPTER THIRTEEN

Heresy
Friday, October 21
Somewhere on St. Stephen's Bay
11:58 pm

Sister Mary hated boats. It's not that she got seasick; it was just being out on open water with unimaginable fathoms between her feet and the bottom of the ocean. It just kind of freaked her out. It didn't help that she was a crappy swimmer either.

Being out at night didn't help. Everything was just so black; it all seemed endless, like the infinite void of space. It made her dizzy. The stench of rotting fish made it worse. *Why the hell did they have to use a fishing boat?*

A dozen Church of Christ the Sun Redeemer members were on the boat, all dressed in white robes. Many wore jackets and hats over their vestments. It got cold on the water at night. Sister Mary didn't know the real names of anyone in the group. They called each other by their hometown: Brother Fogo, Sister Burgeo, and so on. She was Sister Mary, short for Marystown. It was impossible to address Brother Dildo with a straight face. Some congregation members tried calling him Brother Dill, but that was worse. Everyone knew what it was short for.

Sister Mary knew the actual name of only one of their group—Brother Vee, their leader. She knew his name from her childhood days before the church became what it was now, but Mary never dared say the name aloud in his presence. Her family were among his oldest converts, but Sister Mary had seen him kill people for less. She wasn't taking any chances.

Sister Mary's family joined the congregation with Brother Vee for the same reasons as many others—to show their love for Jesus and worship him with like-minded individuals. The teachings of the Catholic Church and most Protestants never sounded honest in her ears, but the Church of Christ the Sun Redeemer spoke the truth. Christ was returning far sooner than anyone imagined, and his retribution would be righteous and calamitous.

The rumbling beneath Sister Mary's feet cut out, signalling they had arrived at their destination a moment before Brother Limeville called out, "We're here!"

How could he possibly tell? Sister Mary had no clue. They were surrounded by the blackness of the ocean on all sides and the dark sky above. They could have been on the arse-end of Pluto, for all she knew.

Brother Vee stepped out on the deck from his tiny cabin. A white hood obscured his face, but Sister Mary knew his height and shape well and recognized him before he began to speak.

"Thank you, everyone, for being here. You are fortunate to have front-row seats to the dawning of the new world."

His voice boomed loudly and confidently out over the water. Brother Vee was a strong speaker and a ruthless leader. He was the kind of man soldiers would follow into battle. "The Saviour is returning. It is not the messiah, prophet, or charlatan but a true God, an old God who has existed beyond the stars since the dawn of the universe. They are coming to remake the world in their image. Those who oppose the Primordial One will suffer merciless death and eternal misery. Those who prepare the way will be The Chosen, will be granted respite and clemency and a place at the Primordial One's side in the new world."

Sister Mary had heard this speech many times, but it still gave her goosebumps. It sounded mad, but she knew every word of it was true. Christ was not the gentle man that the heathen Bible wrote about. The true Saviour was not merciful or forgiving and would show only righteous discrimination against the unbelievers once he returned. The events in Gale Harbour these last two years only proved their teachings true.

"And it is to our Lord that we make this offer, of flesh and life, to appease their great hunger, to ease its passage into this world. May the Primordial One remember our sacrifice and look upon us fondly with love and mercy."

Every worshipper in every faith was at least a little brainwashed. The difference between Catholics and those who followed the Sun

Redeemer was that Sister Mary had experienced God's power firsthand. The whole town had. They didn't need to have faith when your deity walked down Main Street, and your divine servants dropped out of the sky like manna from heaven.

Brother Vee gestured to the large metal door at his feet, and two of the larger men in the congregation stepped forward and opened it. Inside the hold were eight bound, gagged and slightly drugged sacrificial victims.

"Victims" was a bit of a misnomer. Sure, these people were about to be sacrificed to an ancient god from another galaxy, but at least they would die quickly. If this little offering didn't work, every other human on the planet was in for a much less pleasant death.

"Sister Pearl, if you would, please."

One of the faithful stepped forward, a woman who had recently become Brother Vee's favourite pet. It was a great honour to stand by the First Brother's side and share his bed, and the other women in the congregation were jealous of Sister Pearl—jealous and more than a little afraid.

Sister Mary had seen Sister Pearl without her hood. She was young, barely out of her teens, curvy and brazen. She dyed her hair black and wore dark makeup. She would seem a feckless child, a plaything for First Brother and nothing else except for the aura of darkness that enveloped her. Her grey eyes were haunted, and her gaze felt like it could stare into the secrets of your soul.

Sister Pearl stood opposite Brother Vee on the other side of the open hold. Someone placed the box at her feet. Just the sight of the thing sent shivers through Sister Mary's boots, up the backs of her legs and through her spine. It was thrilling and terrifying at the same time.

The box was about a metre square and half as tall, made of riveted metal and held closed with a heavy padlock. One of the other sisters unlocked the box and quickly scampered away. Most of the congregation stepped back, but Sister Pearl did not flinch. She was either courageously stupid or completely lacked any fear of death.

Sister Pearl opened the box, revealing a writhing mass of giant insects, like June bugs nearly as large as a fist. They were less active than when Sister Mary had last seen them. Some of them weren't moving at all, probably starved to death from being locked in the box for so long. Good riddance. Sister Mary knew the scarabs were servants of the Redeemer and were instrumental in bringing about his return, but they still gave her the willies.

Sister Pearl picked up one of the creatures and held it in her hand. Its long legs twitched as it crawled across her hand and up her arm. She watched it in fascination. Sister Mary forced herself to keep watching, though others around her turned away. The undulation of the plates that made up its exoskeleton made Sister Mary shiver. She thought she could feel its hooked pincers crawling up her own arm.

The prisoners in the hold whimpered in horror. Sister Pearl nodded, and the hulking Brother Limeville pulled the first sacrifice out of the hold. It was an older man, naked and covered with scars and bruises, his long grey hair and beard matted with blood and dirt. He was a homeless drunk they'd collected from St. John's, someone who would not be missed. Still bound and gagged, Brother Limeville forced the old man to his knees in front of Anna. She held the scarab over his face.

The old man's grey, bloodshot eyes grew wide, and he began to scream through his gag. He shook his head violently, but Brother Limeville snatched off the gag and grabbed him by the face. His powerful hands reached into the old man's mouth and forced it open. From across the deck, Sister Mary heard his jaw crack, and the old man howled a muffled scream that made her blood run cold.

Sister Mary continued to stare despite the roiling in her stomach. She needed to watch this. She needed to prepare herself. Far worse was coming. Sister Pearl seemed unfazed. She withdrew a red-covered notebook from her robes and began to read as the scarab continued to crawl on her arm and the bound man howled in agony.

She was a witch. Although she drew her power from the Redeemer and was his divine chosen, she was still a witch, which frightened Sister Mary. The young woman could cast actual magic spells.

Sister Pearl held the scarab over the man's gaping, bleeding mouth and closed her eyes. The bound man moaned horribly, but the witch didn't notice. She said strange words from some old foreign language Sister Mary didn't understand. The very sound of the vowels and consonants was like nails scraping across the inside of her eyelids. She felt the nerves of her spine tighten.

The scarab skittered down the witch's arm and, without warning, jumped from the tips of her fingers. It leaped into the victim's broken, gaping jaw, and Sister Mary finally had to look away. The old man's cries became more pitched before turning into choked bleats as the insect burrowed its way down his throat. The other prisoners were screaming and thrashing now too. Sister Mary kept telling herself that this was necessary. This was necessary to appease the Redeemer before he returned to Earth. She felt bile creeping up her throat, and she forced it back down.

She needed to be strong. She had to follow the teachings of the Sun Redeemer. Otherwise, it could be her in the ship's hold next time.

It took all of Sister Mary's will to open her eyes and return her gaze to the scene. The old man was twitching on the deck, blood pooling around his head. Eventually, the man went still, except for the pulsing and stretching flesh of his throat as the scarab clawed its way down his esophagus. Ligaments and muscles popped and snapped in his neck.

Sister Pearl looked at Brother Vee and shook her head. Whatever miracle they had hoped for wasn't going to happen tonight. He ordered the prisoners tossed over, and Sister Mary could hear the anger and frustration in his voice. These sacrifices were to appease the Primordial One and make it stronger, but what they really wanted was to awaken a mortal host to its glorious power.

As the men pulled the struggling people out of the hold, Sister Mary couldn't help but feel bad for them, as she did when her brother used to feed crickets to his pet spider. Though they were stupid and useless creatures, they had done nothing wrong to deserve their fate. It was just part of the circle of life. In the case of the humans on the boat, their circle consisted of being fed to a hungry god at the bottom of the sea, the god being satiated enough that it would lay dormant a little longer until the Church of the Sun Redeemer could ready themselves to receive it.

It wasn't a large circle, but it made sense to her. And the man with the scarab in his stomach was the lucky one. He had died quickly, if painfully. From what Sister Mary understood, drowning *sucked.*

The dead homeless man was the first over the side, and he sank quickly beneath the waves. Sister Mary wondered how the scarab would react to the waters beneath. Then there was the fisherman lost at sea a few weeks ago. He was missing and presumed dead already, so tossing him in only completed what their families believed had actually happened to him. It was only a stroke of good fortune that the Temple found his boat before he really did die in that storm.

Then there was the old woman, who lived alone and whose disappearance would take even longer to notice than the drunk. She sank without a whimper, and Sister Mary wondered briefly if the Primordial One would care if they gave it an already-dead offering.

Finally came Robbie and Shelly. These were the only two that Sister Mary felt a little uncomfortable about. Despite their shitty family lives, the disappearance of these two would be missed. Brother Vee insisted that it couldn't be helped, that at least some of the offerings must have traces of the blood of Kluskap. The witch Sister Pearl had translated the book of the Redeemer's teachings and claimed that Robbie and Shelly were their best bets of anyone outside the Jeddore family. Or close enough, anyway.

Sister Pearl tried shoving a scarab down Robbie's throat as well. He struggled harder than the old man and nearly bit off one of Brother Limeville's fingers. Brother Fogo stunned him with a blow from the butt of his gun so the witch could complete the ritual.

Robbie Brown died choking on the scarab, like the old man. It was impossible to say whether Sister Pearl did something wrong or his blood wasn't strong enough.

She shook her head again, and Robbie Brown was thrown thrashing into the icy waters of the North Atlantic.

Shelly struggled the longest in the water. She must have been a pretty good swimmer and managed to tread water for a few moments, though her hands and feet were bound. Her gag also came free, which was unfortunate as she began to scream and beg for help. They were several kilometres out to sea, and it was the middle of the night, but they still couldn't take any chances with her voice.

Brother Vee caught Sister Pearl's gaze and nodded. She nodded back. He always gave her the most important missions. She was more than just his plaything and pet witch.

Sister Pearl crossed the deck to Brother Limeville, who produced a rifle from the cabin. He handed it to her with bloody hands. She took it and checked to ensure it was loaded and that the safety was off.

"You go take care of that finger," she told Brother Limeville and took aim out at the water.

Despite the darkness and the rising and falling of the boat on the waves, it only took one shot, and Shelly screamed no more. That's why Brother Vee asked her to do these things—she did them quickly and efficiently without question.

The boat's engines roared back to life before the echo of the gunshot died away. On the off chance anyone had heard the screams or the gunshot, they wanted to put as much distance as possible between themselves and the location of the sacrifice.

Like Brother Vee and Sister Pearl, Sister Mary was disappointed as the ship pulled away. The spell's failure was bad enough, but she had hoped to at least catch a glimpse of whatever was going to come up to accept their offerings.

At the bottom of the Atlantic, something stirred...

Food?

Where was the food coming from?

It had been gathering strength, feeding off the dim life essence of fish and other simple, stupid creatures. It needed power to seek out the vessel, but it was taking too long. True, time was essentially meaningless to the Primordial One, but it desired revenge against particular mortals, mortals who would be long dead with the rate it was gathering strength.

And then, someone was so accommodating as to provide fresh fuel to accelerate its return. Tonight was not the first time someone dumped fresh food into the sea. But why? Why were those mortals so eager to bring about their own destruction?

Human beings were unfathomably stupid, hardly more intelligent than their backward, brutish ape forebears. They were rushing toward extinction, thinking they were saving themselves, when all they were accomplishing was the hastening of their annihilation.

It wasn't the dead humans it was feeding on. Their lives extinguished long before they reached the seabed, the mortals provided no sustenance. Fortunately, each corpse came with a special little treat...

The harbingers. The energy beings from the meteor shower, imprisoned and doomed to travel the galaxy for eternity. It knew the beings sometimes crossed the orbit of this forsaken rock, but it had been eons since it was active at the same time as their arrival.

Why were the humans forcing them into the corpses of their deceased?

It mattered not. The denizens of Earth would be little more than a forgotten memory in the grand history of the universe. Their frantic insistence to hasten their demise would only bring about the Primordial One's revenge faster. It drained the energy from the harbinger, the power equal to a hundred pitiful mortals flooding through the formless, eternal entity.

It left a little power, just as it did every time the humans gave it an offering such as this. Just enough energy to complete the trick the idiots had been trying to accomplish.

The corpse of Robbie Brown opened its glowing eyes.

CHAPTER FOURTEEN

Mary Jane's Last Dance
Friday, October 20
8:10 pm

Niall knocked on the Jeddores' door again, but no answer came. He knew it was locked; he'd just checked it. The sky grew dark over Townsview Street, and the day's last warmth faded quickly. A cold wind picked up. He should have called first.

"Niall."

He had started to leave when he heard Harper's voice. He walked around the yellow house to find her sitting on the back patio. He could only see a shadowed silhouette against the street lamp a few houses away, but Niall would have recognized her anywhere.

"Pius isn't here. Uncle Ray and Aunt Samantha took the baby for a drive to get her to go to sleep."

Niall stepped up onto the brown, wooden back porch. "I was looking for you."

"Why?"

Harper was back to her regular baggy jeans and wore a grey hoodie against the cold. The hood was pulled over her head, so Niall couldn't see her eyes and tell what she was thinking.

"I'm so sorry about yesterday. About meeting your mom. You wanted me to come with you, didn't you?"

She turned her head away. "Whatever."

"How did it go?"

Harper was quiet for a long time, as if she wasn't sure if she would answer. "Fine."

"Just fine? I know this is the first time you've seen her in years. You must have been freaking out."

"I was fine."

"I would be freaking out. Like, pants-wetting, seizure-inducing terror. Like Pius when we made him watch Child's Play."

"She asked me to come live with her."

Niall felt sharp, thorny fingers squeeze his heart. He knew it, Pius had told him earlier, but it hurt like hell coming from her. "Pius told me." It was a struggle to get the words out. He was finding it hard to breathe.

"She wants me to come stay with her in Toronto. She's doing really well. She's clean, in therapy, and has a job. She says she wants to get to know me."

Niall put a hand on the railing of the patio. He might have fallen over otherwise. Harper? Leaving? "You're not going to go, are you?"

She shrugged. "I'm considering it. There's nothing for me here. Dad's gone, Aunt Sam and Uncle Ray have their hands full with Rebecca. No one wants me around—"

"I want you—" Niall said abruptly and cut himself off just as quickly. What the hell was he doing?

"What about Stacey?"

Niall's throat went dry and clenched so hard he could barely get any air. What about Stacey? He had just met her a few days ago. She was great, but he didn't know what to call whatever was happening between them. "Stacey is just a... I mean, she's only..."

Harper snorted dismissively. "Don't worry about it. She seems nice. And you already said you don't want to be with me anymore, so..."

"That is not what I *meant!*"

"That's what you *said!*"

Both of them had raised their voices, and now they fell silent. Niall's intestines were threatening to crawl up his esophagus and pull out his eyeballs. His hatred of conflict, combined with his awkwardness around girls and his feelings for Harper, was creating a perfect storm of gastrointestinal anxiety.

"Look," she said, finally. "We broke up a long time ago. We were barely dating to begin with. We both need to move on."

Every word pierced Niall's heart.

"I think I will go live with my mom, at least for a while. See how it goes."

Niall sat down on the bench. His swimming head couldn't take anymore and threatened to make him vomit or fall over. Probably both. Gale Harbour without Harper? He couldn't imagine it. "If that's what you think is best," said Niall, which was absolutely the farthest thing away from what he thought was best.

He couldn't look at her. If he did, he might cry. He had never wanted to break up with her. He was scared. He pushed her away, kept her away for a year, and now… He never dreamed she would leave his life altogether. He assumed that they would still be friends even if they never got back together. Right? He assumed they would always be… something.

Niall couldn't help himself. He reached over and hugged her. He squeezed her as hard as the talons crushing his heart. To his shock, she didn't fight him. She hugged him back.

He wanted to ask her to stay, but he couldn't. He was the one who broke up with her. She had every right to try and build a relationship with her mother; Niall had no say in the matter. He wished she would say that she wanted him back. He would come back in an instant, fear of their powers be damned.

Tears ran down his cheeks. He was pretty sure that Harper was crying, too.

Niall wasn't sure who the first to break the embrace was, but it lasted a long time. Both of them wiped their eyes.

"I guess I should go," said Niall.

Harper nodded. "Yeah. I guess so."

He stood up and started to walk away.

"Goodbye, Dork-pie," she said.

Niall walked home in a daze, locked himself into his room, and blasted The Cure as he set about doing his make-up again. He didn't care who heard or saw him this time.

CHAPTER FIFTEEN

Until I Fall Away
Saturday, October 22
10:15 am

"God, it smells like a used gym sock in here."

Bennett peered through the backdoor of the rusted-out old van, panning his flashlight beam over rumpled sleeping bags, empty beer bottles and condom wrappers. His moustache twitched. "What's wrong with kids today? Can't they find anywhere more romantic than this to fool around?"

She might have laughed if Tanguay hadn't felt so much like *merde*. "You think they should have gotten a room up at Doucette's Motel?"

"At least do it in the backseat of your parents' car like normal kids." Bennett sighed. "Or on the floor of your grandmother's shed like I did. Okay, maybe that's not romantic either, but she had these nice floral aprons hanging on the back of the door that were downright whimsical."

Tanguay worked a full shift yesterday instead of the half one her return-to-work plan called for. She was in excruciating pain when she got home, pain that no amount of heat or rest could fix, and though she tried to hold off on taking more pills, eventually, she had no choice. She woke up this morning in a hazy cloud of disorientation and more agony. She ended up being late for work for the first time since she could remember because it took her so long to get herself together and out the door. Her hair was falling out from under her hat in every direction, and she was sure she was visibly swaying on her feet.

"You feeling okay, Sarge?" Bennett asked, and Tanguay realized she had no idea how long she'd zoned out. "Here I am, spilling my guts about my first roll into the arms of the fairer sex and not so much of a smile from you."

Actually, every Mountie on the West Coast of Newfoundland had heard how Burt Bennett lost his virginity to Cathy Bungay in his grandmother's shed when he was seventeen. It was Bennett's favourite story to tell whenever he was drunk. But no matter how often she'd heard it, it usually made Tanguay laugh. Something about the combination of Bennett's brazen descriptions and his goofy reminiscence about the girl was endearing in a gross way. Obviously, he had been in love with her, and the burly man still blushed whenever he spoke of her.

"I'm just worried about these kids," Tanguay lied, and Bennett nodded.

"We sure have a problem with kids disappearing around here, don't we? You think the Satan worshippers got them?"

Tanguay froze. Her head would have snapped in his direction, but she was too dizzy. "*Excusez-moi*?"

Bennett patted his belly and laughed. "I'm joking. The kids tell stories trying to scare each other, saying there are Satan worshippers up in these woods. Every now and then, someone finds a dead cat, but it's just other kids messing with their friends."

The last thing Tanguay needed on top of everything was wannabe Satan worshippers getting people riled up. She didn't think Bennett had ever pieced together what was going on in Gale Harbour— he was way too naive and lacking in imagination. Of course, at least Satanic idiots were human and not aliens or monsters like she usually dealt with. It would be a lovely change of pace.

There were signs that many kids had used this van over the last few weeks, but any chance they could find any specific clues about Robbie and Shelly was slim. They could dust for prints but didn't have the kids on file, so it wouldn't confirm if they'd been here. Still, if they found the prints of a known criminal, at least that was someone they could question... She wondered if she could order one of those new DNA tests, but again, there were so many potential samples in this thing. God knows what they would find.

"Speaking of Doucette's Motel," said Bennett as they pawed through the sleeping bags wearing rubber gloves. "Did you hear Pius

Jeddore came in yesterday evening and accused Cecil Doucette of child abuse?"

This time, Tanguay actually did a doubletake. She turned on Bennett so fast she twinged her hip and nearly screamed in pain. She let out her discomfort as anger instead. "Cecil Doucette assaulted Pius Jeddore? Why didn't anyone tell me?"

Bennett was so shocked he was stuttering. "No, no, the Jeddore kid said he saw Cecil attack his own kid in broad daylight on Main Street. Allegedly ripped the earring right out his ear."

Tabrrnak, Keith. The poor kid. Tanguay had not handled him well. She knew he was dealing with problems at home but never followed up. Between tracking a missing atom bomb and then dealing with her own injuries, Tanguay dropped the ball on her other responsibilities.

"Is Keith okay?" she asked.

"We haven't found him yet. He ran away from home."

Hosti. "And why didn't anyone tell me?"

"Sergeant Peters took his statement and said he would deal with it himself."

Of course, he did. He was acting like he was already the new permanent Commanding Officer. The others were probably trying to keep her load easy by not telling her about additional, stressful cases. Of course, that only pushed her farther away and jeopardized her career and position.

What was she supposed to do? She didn't want to admit it, but her constables were right. She couldn't handle any more than one case in her current state. The one she had was almost proving to be too much as it was.

Shelly's parents were equally unhelpful as Robbie's. Their friends weren't much better, except for leading them to this van, which was proving to be fruitless. A hundred kids had probably fooled around in here. What was she hoping to find?

Bennett seemed to have come to the same conclusion. "So, Sarge, I guess we have two options here. Give up for the day, head back to town and grab some Timmies, or you and I can make use of these sleeping bags and fool around ourselves."

Tanguay nearly threw up in her mouth. She couldn't think of anything less appealing than sleeping with Burt Bennett. Except maybe sleeping with Bruce Brake. "Ew, *c'est dégoutant.* And you're married."

"The wife and I have an arrangement," said Bennet. "She lets me fool around as long as I don't tell her about it."

"That's not true."

"No, you're right, I'm lying. But you smiled and considered it for a moment." He winked at her, and Tanguay smacked him on the back of the head. She finally did smile a little when Bennett wasn't looking. She never would have let a subordinate get away with jokes like that when she started here, but Tanguay had grown to love her weird little Gale Harbour family. Not just the other Mounties, but the townspeople, too. And the kids. She felt as protective of those dumb kids as she would have her own. Josephine Whillett, Niall O'Niall's tough grandmother. She hadn't known him long, but Tanguay still missed Harper's dad, Dick Jeddore. He would have been a great cop, and she wished he was here now to work on this case. He was so good at noticing things. She was, too, usually, but between the pain and the meds, she was not operating at anything near full capacity.

She needed another set of eyes, better eyes than Bennett's. Dick Jeddore knew the woods here, knew the people, was an expert tracker...

Tracks. The path through the woods off the Dump Road to the van was well-travelled and beaten down, but what about around it? Tanguay took a few steps back and walked around the vehicle. The ground was hard and rocky. She expanded her circle a little and found numerous footprints of various shapes and sizes. Many people had been through here recently, but that still didn't tell her anything definite.

But then she found it. Five metres from the van, in the opposite direction of the road, she found marks on the ground where something had been dragged and broken alder branches at the edge of the clearing. She followed the tracks and saw that they intersected with the other sets of prints until they all converged, heading deeper into the brush.

"Where you going?" Bennett called out. "Need to take a piss?"

"What's in this direction?" Tanguay called back.

There was a short pause as Bennett thought about it. "An old logging road, I think. About a kilometre. Not sure how accessible it is."

A kilometre? A year ago, she wouldn't have hesitated, but today... She didn't trust Bennett to follow the trail, though; she had to do it herself. "Go get the car and meet me on the road."

"It's all grown over. I just got the car waxed!"

Tanguay glared at him, and Bennett ambled off. She turned her attention to the brush.

Newfoundland, a barely habitable rock with harsh soil and constantly pelted with seawater, did not have thick forests. But it was overgrown with bogs and scrubby brush that were miserable to crawl through. Tanguay tripped twice, sending stabs of shooting pain through her hip and spine, but she pressed on. She needed to do this and prove to herself and everyone that she could still be normal.

She focused on the trail to distract herself from the pain. Someone was definitely dragged through here, probably more than one, and by numerous assailants. It was like a gang of people swooped out of the trees and carried off whoever was in that van. Maybe it wasn't Robbie and Shelly, but *someone* was attacked here. With the thrill of clues and the prospect of making progress, the burst of adrenaline left her the most energized and clear-headed she had been in days. Months, probably.

Sadly, the elation passed quickly, replaced once again by the throbbing pain and sharp stabs of agony that had become her way of life for the last year. She kept on the trail, but every step became a struggle. She pushed through branches and dragged herself through the underbrush until she wasn't sure if she could go further.

Tanguay had no idea how long it was—minutes, hours—until she staggered back out of the woods on the narrow access road. Bennett was standing a few dozen paces away alongside the cruiser. "There you are! I was starting to get worried."

"I found something." Tanguay started to walk toward Bennett, but he never got to hear what she was going to say. Her legs finally gave out, and Tanguay collapsed on the dirt road.

CHAPTER SIXTEEN

I Like to Move It
Saturday, October 22
7:50 pm

"Keith is dead, man!"

That's what Skidmark said when he called. Pius was so freaked out he took off out the door without thinking. The last time he'd done that was when he'd heard Jerry's Video Shack had gotten VHS copies of Robotech.

"Keith is dead, man!"

Skidmark was known for hyperbole and flat-out lies, but he seemed sincere at the moment. He'd been on the verge of tears on the other end of the phone, so something must have upset him. Skidmark wasn't that good of an actor. Pius had seen him in the school play last year.

Pius' parents were gone with the baby, and Harper was pulling her usual disappearing act she'd been working on lately, so there was no one to ask for help. Pius told Skidmark to hang up and call the police while he called Niall. He wasn't home, either. With no choice but to do this alone, Pius ran out the door and pulled his bicycle out of the shed.

He regretted telling Skidmark to call the police. Skidmark was barely coherent at the best of times. In his current state, he sounded like Kurt Cobain gargling marbles.

"Keith is dead, man!"

Skidmark said he'd found him behind the Black Bowler, the dirty bar down on Main Street, not far from the Video Shack. He was calling from the payphone at Tim Hortons. It took Pius less than five minutes to ride down there, which was just enough time for him to think about what a terrible idea this was.

Did he really want to see Keith's dead body? Was there anything he could actually do for him? Would his already-battered psyche survive another horrific experience like this?

The answer to all those questions was no, but Pius kept riding anyway. He did it because there was a part of him, deep in his gut, who was afraid it was somehow his fault that Keith was dead. Because he had gone to the police.

What if his father had killed him?

Pius found Keith sitting propped up against a dumpster behind the Bowler, with Skidmark sobbing over him. The whole area smelled like rancid booze.

"It's okay!" Skidmark gasped. "He's not dead! Just drunk!"

Pius wanted to scream. "You... I nearly had a heart attack, you jerk! You said he was dead!"

"I thought he was dead! Look at him! He looks like shit!"

Skidmark had a point. Keith looked like he'd passed through the digestive tract of a very large and ill manatee.

Keith was covered in vomit, presumably his own. His hair was a mess, revealing his missing ear on one side and the scabbed mess that his father had left on the other. Why did people always go after his ears?

"Keith, are you okay?" Pius asked. "Should we call somebody for you?"

"Who you gonna call?"

"Did you know I heard Dan Akroyd is working on a script for another Ghostbusters movie?" Skidmark asked. "I hope it comes out soon. The first one was awesome, but the second one was just okay. It ended with them being big heroes and stuff, so I kinda want to see them as—"

"Shut up, Skidmark!" Pius snapped, then turned back to Keith. "What happened? Did your dad kick you out?"

"Dunno. I haven't been home since yesterday."

"Where did you sleep last night?"

Keith gestured vaguely at the dumpster.

Skidmark gagged. "That's gross, man. There's like fifty different types of hepatitis in there."

Pius wasn't sure what to do. Did Keith need to go to the hospital? He understandably didn't want to go back to his father's house. Pius wasn't sure where his mother lived, but he knew he wasn't around here.

Might as well start with something simple. "Pius, help me get him up. Let's take him into the Tim Horton's bathroom and clean him up."

"Do I have to touch him?"

As the boys struggled to get Keith to his feet, Pius noticed someone standing by the corner of the Bowler, watching them from the sidewalk. Numerous people went back and forth down Main Street, but this was the first to stop. Pius was about to call out for them to help, but when he glanced up again, the figure was gone. Did they take off when they saw Keith was hurt? *Jerk.*

They made it to Tim Hortons and shuffled Keith into the men's washroom, much to the chagrin of the employees, who were probably envisioning all the mess they would have to clean up later. Pius figured that being nestled between two bars and with several more down the street in either direction, they should be used to it.

There wasn't much they could do with water and paper hand towels besides scoop off the worst of the puke, but they did their best. Keith's ear was nasty, and Pius didn't want to touch it—it was probably getting infected. Maybe Pius could bring him home and get his mom to look at it. She was a nurse, after all.

They dragged Keith back into the restaurant and shoved him into a booth. The walls and counters were decorated with cheap plastic ghosts and witches. Pius ordered some coffee and donuts, and while they tried to get food into Keith, Pius thought more and more that their best bet would be to bring Keith to his house. His parents would know what to do with him.

"What are you looking at, asshole?"

Keith yelled at a short man in a red trucker's cap and a hunting vest seated a few tables away. Pius was aghast.

"What are you doing?"

"That weirdo's following me. I saw him last night, too."

It was a small town, so you often saw the same people around, not to mention that Keith was drunk and not thinking straight. But was that the same guy Pius had seen behind the Bowler? He couldn't be sure, and now the man turned his face away, sipping from his brown cardboard cup.

"Keith, you're paranoid," said Pius, possibly the most hypocritical words ever spoken. Pius was rapidly thinking up a list of insane possibilities of who that guy was, including a vampire, possessed alien spawn, or Elvis Presley. In this town, you could never be sure.

Still, he didn't want Keith to freak out. They were trying to sober him up, not feed into his hysterical delusions.

Except maybe it wasn't a delusion. The man in the cap was definitely staring at them again. His small, dark eyes were burrowing right into Pius' chest.

Pius stood up. "We need to leave."

Keith looked at him in a daze. "I'm only halfway through my coffee."

"And I'm only on my third donut," added Skidmark. "I bought a half dozen. I also got my Magic cards in my bag. I thought we could play a few games since we were just sitting around. Hey, Keith, did I tell you I opened the rest of your packs from yesterday? You got a Ball Lightning in your Dark pack. It's frigging awesome! I mean, I got a Ball Lightning, you got a, uh, a Scavenger Folk. Yeah. It's pretty cool."

Another man sat down with the guy in the red hat. This one was barrel-chested and had a thick salt-and-pepper beard. They exchanged a few quiet words, and both glanced at Pius.

They really needed to leave. He was getting a weird vibe from those two men, and he didn't want Keith to get into an argument with them. Pius might be a little paranoid, but he had survived this long, so he must be doing something right.

"Hey, let's go back to my place. My mom made cookies today, and we can play Magic there."

"I thought your mom didn't want us coming over after supper anymore?" Skidmark stuffed his fourth (fifth?) honey cruller into his mouth. He continued to talk, spitting crumbs all over the table. "Something about us disturbing the baby?"

Keith snorted. "Yeah, you get really loud and whiny when you lose."

"I didn't know the baby was asleep. Plus was cheating! I saw you drawing extra cards!"

"Look, I will give each of you guys one of my Lords of Atlantis if we leave right now." Pius started physically nudging them out of their seats, but Skidmark was already heading for the door.

"For real?" asked Keith, stumbling to his feet.

"Either that or my Angry Mob, your pick."

A moment later, they were outside in the cool October air, crossing Main Street and heading toward Pius' house. It was true that his mom would be mad that he brought the guys home without asking, but Pius was counting on his mother being so concerned over Keith's condition that she might go easy on him.

They hadn't finished crossing the Foodland parking lot when Pius noticed the two men were following them.

Pius tried to remain calm. "Keith, I know you're still drunk and angry, but I need you to listen to me and not freak out when I tell you something."

"I know Skidmark stole my Ball Lightning."

"No, it's about the guy in the red hat. He's still following you. And now there's another guy with him."

Keith turned around, nearly falling over. "Son of a bitch, I'm going to kill 'em..."

Pius grabbed his arm and pulled him down the road. "They're very large, grown men, and you're in no condition to fight. We just need to get to my house as quickly as possible."

Skidmark was already gone, hustling down the street with his trademark waddling gait, his heavy green bookbag full of cards swinging from one hand and a box of donuts in the other.

"Skidmark, you jerk!" Pius tried to run after him, dragging Keith. "Get back here!"

Skidmark darted to the right, disappearing into the yard of a blue house with several large trees out front. Pius cursed under his breath—they needed to get home, not hide. He was ready to ditch Skidmark and keep running, but when they got to where Skidmark disappeared, they saw him crouched in the darkness behind a garden of lupins. He waved them over.

Glancing back to ensure the men hadn't turned the corner of the Foodland, Pius and Keith took off across the yard after Skidmark. "What are you doing?" Pius hissed.

"We can cut through this yard. There's a gap in the fence out back. Then, we can squeeze behind the shed by the house on the other side, go through the playground by the Lion's Club, and cut through that lot across from the old library. Then we're almost at your place."

Pius was mildly impressed. "How do you know that?"

"When you get chased by bullies as much as I do, you get to know all the shortcuts."

They followed Skidmark's directions, and their route led them most of the way without a hitch. Until they got to the empty lot across from the old library. They were cutting through the waist-high grass when Skidmark abruptly ducked out of sight. It took Pius a half-second to realize what was happening, and then he dove into Keith, pulling him down into the grass with him.

Keith shoved Pius aside. "What the hell, man?"

"Shh!" Pius gestured to Keith to keep his voice down. "It's the guy in the red hat."

Pius caught a glimpse of him standing in the streetlight on the far end of the field. He was looking up and down the street, presumably watching for them.

Keith struggled to get up. "Let me at him..."

Pius held onto his sleeve. "Seriously, keep quiet! We don't know who this guy is or what he wants!"

"He might just be looking for his lost dog or something," Skidmark suggested.

Realization crept into Keith's face. "I think he works for my dad. He does maintenance at the hotel and a couple of the clubs."

That might explain why he was looking for Keith. "And that's a good reason to avoid him, right?"

"I should tell him to tell my dad to piss off..."

Skidmark yelped. "He's coming this way."

As the man approached them quietly, the boys shuffled on their hands and knees through the grass, farther away from the path. He scanned the street at the far end of the field, looking for something. Or someone.

His right hand rested on something tucked into the back of his belt. He approached the boys' hiding space, and Pius tried to make himself as small as possible. If only Keith remained quiet for a few moments, they should be fine...

He stopped just a few metres from where they lay in the grass, and Pius could see what was tucked into the back of his belt. A handgun.

Why the hell would he need a gun?

There was, of course, one very obvious reason he might have that gun, though Pius didn't want to admit it.

The other boys must have seen it, too, because they all froze, holding their breath. The man's gaze swept across the field. There were no streetlamps here; it was dark, and they were well concealed. There was no way he'd be able to see them, right?

Who was Pius kidding? If the guy took two steps off the path and looked down to his left, they were all dead.

"Jim, you see them?"

The voice came from the street. It must have been the other man, the big one with the beard.

"Nah," replied the man with the red cap. He seemed to relax and took his hand off his gun. "I lost them."

"Shit. Better go tell the boss."

The man in the red hat walked away. Pius took his first breath in several minutes. After a few more moments, the boys risked looking over the grass to confirm that the two men were gone.

"So, Keith," said Skidmark. He fished his last donut out of the crushed box beside him. "Want to share why your dad sent a couple of rednecks to kill you?"

Keith looked more bewildered than he had all night. "He didn't... I don't... I got nothing."

After a few minutes with no sign of the men's return, the boys crept out of the grassy field and the rest of the way to Pius' house. They went back and forth, arguing about whether they should tell Pius' parents about the guy with the gun. It was a moot point because they were still out when the boys got home.

They did find Harper sitting alone in the dark living room. She straightened up and wiped her face when they came in, but Pius could tell by the redness of her eyes that she'd been crying.

Pius started to ask what was wrong, but Harper spoke first.

"What the hell, Keith? You look like crap."

Keith puffed up his chest. "Hey, someone just tried to kill me. I'd like to see what you would look like after that."

"People have tried to kill all of us," Skidmark reminded him. "We know what we all look like after cheating death. You look worse right now, but that's only because your dad ripped your ear off, and you've been on a bender for twenty-four hours."

Harper's smugness switched to concern. She looked closer at Keith and cringed. "Holy shitcrackers. What happened to your ear? The other one, I mean."

Skidmark was heading to the fridge. "I told you, his dad ripped it off. It's probably still lying on the sidewalk outside Arlene's. Do you guys have any Pizza Pockets?"

"Your dad tried to kill you?"

Keith shrugged. "Nah, he just yanked my earring out. He sent one of his dirtbag employees to pull a gun on me."

Harper recoiled. "He pulled a gun on you?"

"Hey, you pulled a gun on me last year."

"I wasn't going to shoot you!"

"He didn't actually pull out the gun," Pius clarified. "But we all saw it. He was following us, and just before we lost him out on the field by the old library, he had his hand on a gun."

"You guys need to call the cops."

Keith shook his head. "I'm not calling the cops on my dad. That's a pussy thing to do."

Pius shrunk back. He hadn't told Keith yet that he had spoken to the police.

Harper folded her arms, annoyed. "If he hired somebody to kill you, asshat, that's a perfectly reasonable course of action."

"He didn't hire him to kill me. I don't think so, anyway. I'm pretty sure he's a bayman from Cape-de-Cape who dad hires to do plumbing."

The microwave dinged, and Skidmark withdrew a steaming plate of Pizza Pockets. "So killing his son is just a job perk? Like dental?"

CHAPTER SEVENTEEN

Always
Sunday, October 23
12:00 pm

Nelson came out of the Holiday Inn meeting room with Anna, where her Church had been holding its service. "If you like it, you should come out to our retreat sometime. It's a lot of fun."

This was Nelson's third service of the Church of Christ the Sun Redeemer, and oddly, he had to admit that he enjoyed it.

"Everyone is so nice," he said as they walked through the hotel lobby into the shopping mall attached to the hotel. "At the Catholic Church, everyone just kinda sits there quietly, waiting for it to be over or for someone else to do something they can gossip about later. But here, everyone is smiling, singing, shaking hands and hugging. It's kinda contagious." Nelson would have sat through black-and-white French movies to spend time with Anna, but the positivity of the Church was rubbing off on him too.

Anna was unlike any other girl he'd ever met. Most of the girls he knew were shallow and interested only in their hair and nails and whether they were going drinking on the weekend. Anna was different. She was smart, funny, and unpredictable, and though she put a lot of effort into how she looked, she did it to look like Morticia Addams, not to impress anybody. Today, she wore a variation of her usual outfit: a long black skirt, a tight red bodice that could barely contain her womanliness and long fingerless gloves.

She reminded Nelson of Niall's old girlfriend, Harper, not in her dress but in her personality. He used to think Harper was a pain in the ass, but now he could kinda see what his brother saw in her. He was loathed to admit he shared a taste in women with that spoiled little shit.

"It's the one good thing my parents did, introducing me to the Sun Redeemer. So many other religions are concerned about death and being afraid of the punishment for things you do in life. But the Sun Redeemer says that God is coming soon, and it's a good thing. We should celebrate."

Anna alternated between saying crazy things that would make a sailor blush and sounding like a Jehovah's Witness trying to get him to take a brochure. The good news was that her religion didn't seem to frown on premarital relations. Anna flirted with him shamelessly. For all his bluster, Nelson never had much success with girls, and no one ever flirted with him. Usually, he just turned girls off with his bad pickup lines. He had been on a few dates, but they usually ended up with him being too desperate, and they never called him back. Anna acted like she wanted to be around him and talk to him, and like she wanted *to do* things to him.

"So, did you celebrate by burying any bodies?" Nelson asked with a smirk.

Anna turned a whiter shade of pale. "What?"

He laughed. He felt underdressed in his jeans and faded Adidas sweatshirt, but all eyes were on Anna as they left the mall and crossed the parking lot. No one spared him half a glance. "Remember? When you came into the store the other day, and I said it sounded like you were trying to dispose of a body?"

Anna's expression turned to one of relief, and her black-painted lips widened in a smile. "Oh, no, I was just kidnapping somebody. They're still alive, just locked in a shed."

She said the wildest shit.

"So what do you want to do?" Nelson asked. "I'm starving."

"Me too. Let's get some food, and then we'll makeout in your car."

Nelson's stomach sank. "I don't have a car."

Anna winked. "Oh well, then I guess you lost out." She grabbed his hand and pulled him across the parking lot. "Come on, I still want food."

"I mean, I could go borrow my parents' car..."

"Too late. You missed that boat, at least for today. Didn't you say you were getting your own car, anyway?"

Out of the parking lot, they turned toward West Street. In her towering, heeled boots, Anna was half a head taller than Nelson, but he didn't care. He liked the way she swayed when she walked. "I have my eye on one, yeah. I've been saving money. I should have enough for it soon."

"Your parents going to help you out?"

Nelson grimaced. "Yeah, right. My parents say I should save up myself, build character and that crap. But I know they're still pissed off that I didn't go to university."

"So they're punishing you for not going to school?"

"Something like that," he said. If Niall wanted a car, they'd buy him a Lamborghini and wrap it up with a bow. They always bought him new video games and whatever else he wanted.

Anna snuggled up against him. She tousled his dirty blond hair. "And I never went to university either. Do you think less of me?"

"Hell, no." He wasn't even mad that she was messing up his hair, and he had spent thirty minutes and half a bottle of gel on that.

"Anyway, don't put too much stock in a car. Sometimes, you need to get around, but you don't need a car to make you a better person or to prove anything. You're perfect the way you are. My parents never let me drive, and I turned out okay, right?"

"Were your parents very strict?"

"Let's just say they wished medieval torture never went out of style."

"Shit, I'm sorry." Nelson's parents may have been hard on him sometimes, and he was pretty confident they genuinely loved Niall more than him, but they never raised a hand against him.

She shrugged. "Don't worry about it. It's made me into a strong, confident woman."

Anna smiled, but Nelson couldn't tell if she was being truthful.

They were heading up West Street now, with the road to Port Hansen and the Atlantic Ocean on their left. Nelson realized that, despite hanging out with this girl for the last few weeks, he knew little about her. "So what is your story, Anna Chaffey? I know you're from St. John's, and your parents were assholes, but not much else."

"I'm an only child. I ran away from home before I finished high school. That's about it."

"You ran away from home? Where did you live?"

"With friends. I just kinda bummed around from couch to couch for a while until I met a guy, and I moved in with him."

Nelson cleared his throat. "You lived with a guy?" That was intimidating. Nelson still hadn't slept with anyone, let alone lived with them.

She must have sensed he was uncomfortable because she put a black-gloved hand on his arm. "He's not around anymore, don't worry. After that, I ended up back with my parents."

"How did that work out?"

"Have you ever tried to give a cat a bath? Me fitting in at home was like a stray cat in a bathtub, except I probably bit and clawed more."

"That's awful."

Anna playfully pretended to claw him, then leaned her head onto Nelson's shoulder. It was awkward in her high heels, so she readjusted and put her arm around him instead. She was so touchy-feely, he didn't know what to do with it. Cautiously, he put his arm around her too. She didn't pull away. "It worked out. It got me back to the Church, which helped me get my head on straight. We've worked out our shit, and I'm in a better place than I've been in for years. What about you, Nelson O'Neil? You said you have a brother?"

Nelson said that he did and proceeded to tell her all about Niall and his idiot friends. Most younger siblings were pains in the ass, but Niall's shenanigans were on another level—getting kidnapped by a loony old woman, surviving a house fire, and nearly being blown up when an old military fuel tank exploded under the town last year. Niall and his friends seemed to be a magnet for the most messed-up stuff in Gale Harbour.

Anna looked concerned. "Yeah, I heard about some of those things on the news. Is he okay?"

"He still has all his fingers, but he's probably going to need a ton of therapy when he's older."

"Don't we all?"

"I guess."

"Is it hard on the family, with your brother getting into so much trouble? Is it hard on you?"

No one had ever asked Nelson that before. Everyone—his parents, Nana, his teachers, the cops—was always so worried about Niall that no one ever asked how he was doing.

"It must be so hard." Anna touched his hair. "I bet he gets a lot of attention."

"You have no idea."

Anna cocked her head to the side, like a puppy in mime make-up.

Nelson sighed. "Even before he started getting into trouble, he was always my parents' favourite. I remember when Niall was born, all of a sudden, it was like he could do no wrong, and I could never get anything right. Learned to walk faster, talk faster, and he does better in school. And they always take his side. He quit playing baseball, and they said, 'Oh well, you'll find something that suits you better.' I gave up hockey, and I was a quitter and had wasted their money on all that equipment. I'm always a disappointment to them."

Nelson felt a surge of terror and relief at the same time. He had never told anyone this before; now, he was spilling his guts to a girl he'd only known a few days. It was scary, and he couldn't believe he was doing it, but it felt good.

Anna smiled and touched his face. "I'm so sorry, Nelson. That must be awful. Do you feel angry?"

"Yeah, I guess I do."

"You have every right to be angry. You deserve better than that."

Nelson nodded. He did deserve better.

"When my parents treated me like shit, I was always so anxious. I could barely sleep. Are you anxious? Do you have bad dreams?"

Nelson felt a shiver run through his spine, like someone dropped an ice cube down the collar of his shirt. Anna must have sensed it.

"Do you have bad dreams?" she asked again.

Nelson had never told anyone about his dreams, either. He thought they made him sound crazy, but something about Anna made him want to talk to her. Talking to her was so easy. He wanted to get everything off his chest.

So Nelson told her about the bottom of the sea, about the monster, about falling into space. She just listened and nodded and made no judgement or comment. When he was finished, he felt embarrassed and ashamed. "You probably think I'm nuts."

"That is pretty screwed up, for sure. And I do think that maybe you need therapy. But you're not scaring me away if that's what you're worried about."

"You're not freaked out?" Nelson breathed a sigh of relief.

"Nah, I know some pretty damaged people. It's not like I'm in mint condition myself."

They walked so long they had looped around and now were at the other end of Main Street, in front of the ZigZag Pizza parlour. Paper jack-o'-lantern decorations hung in the window. Anna took Nelson's hand and pulled him away from the door.

She looked him in the eyes. "You know what? I'm not that hungry anymore. I think I might have something that can help you."

"What's that?"

Anna leaned in and kissed him.

Keenan arrived at the party fashionably late as always. He carried a six-pack in his left hand as he knocked on Melissa's door with his right. He'd washed his perpetually greasy black hair and dressed in his best black silk shirt and tight black jeans. His thin moustache was a bit embarrassing, but it was the best he could do. Maybe he should have shaved it off altogether.

Keenan Quick had crushed on Melissa Power since Junior High. Of course, she'd barely noticed him; this was how these things always worked, but he'd always been polite to her and friendly and there to help out. The previous summer, he'd spent a week searching every dumpster and backyard in Mount Pearl looking for her lost cat. He helped her study for her exams last year. Now after everything, his hard work was paying off: Despite the vast gulf in their social standings, Melissa had invited him to the big Christmas party at her house. With no parents!

Melissa was on several of the girls' sports teams and was a cheerleader for the boys' team. She was part of all the cool cliques. Keenan was the smelly, weird kid who wore Iron Maiden t-shirts, had a dragon painted on his Trapper Keeper and suffered from frequent nose bleeds (his parents said it was from him picking it, but he vehemently denied that preposterous accusation). They may have travelled in different stratospheres, but if romantic Eighties movies taught Keenan anything, they were *precisely* the type of people who would get together.

The front door opened, and Melissa's older brother, George, appeared. He was roughly the size and shape of a gorilla and only slightly hairier. He worked at the gas station, which explained the smell of gasoline wafting off the brute, and he had a reputation for selling cigarettes to underage kids.

"Who the hell are you?" George demanded.

Taken off guard, it took Keenan a moment to remember his name. "Uh, Keenan... Keenan Quick. Melissa's friend... uh, I'm in her class. She invited me to the party?"

"Frig off, loser." The door started to close, and Keenan was too shocked to protest. Thankfully, the voice of an angel called out from somewhere in the house.

"Georgie! Are you messing with my friends?"

The brute didn't take his beady eyes off Keenan, whose testicles retracted a little. "This little nerd says you invited him. I told him to piss off."

Melissa appeared beside George, and the world became a little brighter. Her blond hair caught the glow of the warm lights inside the house like the sun coming over the horizon. Her smile gleamed whiter than the fresh layer of snow outside. "Georgie, stop being a dick to my friend. I'm sorry, Keenan, come on in."

She reached out and took Keenan's hand, and he followed without question. She could have led him into the fiery bowels of hell and he wouldn't have questioned it, so passing by her growling brother was easy. Keenan did keep his gaze down, though, and wouldn't look the gorilla in the eye.

The room was a sea of faces and blinking Christmas lights. "Ice, Ice Baby" was blaring on the stereo so loud it was impossible to hear any conversation. Keenan just focussed on the back of Melissa's head, trying to stay close to her in the writhing mass of obnoxious music, neon-coloured sweatshirts and cheap perfume that definitely wasn't Calvin Klein. And the choking stench of beer, so much beer. Her hand was still in his; she was leading him somewhere, and his teenage brain was racing with thoughts of where that might be.

Keenan stopped, and Melissa slipped away from him, momentarily forgotten. There, sitting alone by the tinsel-suffocated Christmas tree, sat the most fascinating girl he had ever seen.

She wasn't, strictly speaking, beautiful or gorgeous, though she was certainly pretty. She had bushy auburn-red hair that hadn't been washed or brushed and pale, pasty skin with numerous blemishes. She was *very* pleasantly plump—the baggy Memorial University sweatshirt she wore couldn't completely hide her assets. But it was her eyes that struck Keenan dead in his tracks. From across the room, her eyes caught him like a wild animal's claws, seizing and dragging him into her aura. The lights and sounds of the party seemed to bend to this girl, to her steel grey eyes, and for a moment, there was nothing in the entire world except for this girl's gaze, locked with his.

Melissa grabbed him by the hand again, momentarily dragging Keenan out of the spell. "Hey, Keenan. What's wrong? There are some people I want you to meet."

"Who is she?"

Melissa glanced toward the tree and made a weird sound in her throat. "Oh, that's just Anna. She goes to Bishop's College. Well, went to. Looks like she dropped out. You probably want to stay away from her."

Keenan turned away from the red-haired girl for the first time in seemingly hours and looked in shocked disbelief at Melissa. "Stay away from her? Why?"

Melissa sighed and rolled her eyes. "Look, she's just kinda odd, okay? My parents call her a hard case. They only let her stay here over Christmas because she has nowhere else to go, but they plan to kick her out after New Year's."

Years of pining after Melissa thoroughly wiped from his mind, Keenan ignored the party's hostess and headed straight for this mysterious Anna. He never approached girls this brazenly but didn't question his sudden injection of confidence. It just seemed *right.*

"Hey," he said.

"Hey," said Anna. She glanced behind him. "Melissa told you to stay away from me?"

"Yeah, kinda."

Her gaze locked back on his. "You didn't listen."

From up close, he could see the dark circles under her eyes. A burn mark on her temple, where some of the hair had been scorched away. He saw fresh scars on her forearm before she pulled down her sleeve to cover them.

Keenan sat on an old leather ottoman next to her. "I kinda do my own thing."

"You should probably listen to her."

"Maybe. Melissa said you were staying with her. What brings you to Mount Pearl?"

"I was born here. My parents dragged me away when I was a kid and joined a cult. A few months ago, I stabbed my mother and escaped."

Keenan nodded. She may have been kidding. She was probably joking. It may have been a test to see if he was really interested in her. Either way, it was obvious she had some demons, and he should take

Melissa's warning seriously. He should walk away and forget about this 'Anna' person.

Instead, Keenan handed her a can of beer and opened one of his own. "Really? Tell me all about it."

<u>CHAPTER EIGHTEEN</u>

Having An Average Weekend
Sunday, October 23
8:10 pm

It was raining in Gale Harbour. Niall was sitting on a bench, alone in the park overlooking Rose River, and his black "raincoat" was doing nothing to keep the rain out. His black T-shirt, black jeans, and even his white underpants and white socks were soaked, which reminded him that he needed to ask his mom to buy him black socks and underwear.

His makeup was running. He had done a pretty good job applying it today, but now the rain was completely ruining it. Niall was surprisingly okay with this. He had caught his reflection in a store window and looked morbid and creepy with the eyeliner running down his cheeks.

Niall recognized he was being overdramatic and self-indulgent and was also okay with that. Maybe it was new teenage hormones, perhaps it was getting in touch with a dramatic side he never realized he had, or perhaps he was just genuinely heartbroken. Whatever it was, sitting alone in the rain, looking like a depressed mime, somehow made him feel better.

Harper was leaving. She was moving to Toronto with her mother, of all people. He knew he screwed up last year, but a part of him always believed they would get back together. It was probably adolescent naivety, but he honestly thought he and Harper were meant to be together.

This was all his fault. He had pushed Harper away because he was scared, but he still cared about her. When she came to him, looking for help, he completely ignored her. He was a massive dickweed, and he deserved to be alone and miserable.

Damn, he was good at wallowing. Maybe he should write some poetry...

Niall didn't notice the two girls approaching him at first. They were quiet, whispering among themselves, and Niall was too occupied with staring at his sodden Reeboks and indulging in the shame and agony of shattered teenage love.

"Niall?" one of the girls asked from beneath her pink umbrella. It was Stacey Peters. "Are you okay?"

"Is he wearing mascara?" asked the other girl. Niall didn't recognize her. She wore a ponytail and wore huge, round-framed glasses.

Niall turned his face away, ashamed of a million things. "Yeah, yeah, I'm fine."

Stacey moved closer to cover Niall with her umbrella. He could smell her strawberry shampoo. "Why are you out here in the rain?"

"Sometimes you just need to walk in the rain." Niall's words sounded astoundingly stupid in his own head, but Stacey smiled at him.

"See, Erin? I told you he was poetic."

Did Stacey hit her head?

The girl in the glasses nodded. "Yeah, but he's also going to catch pneumonia in the rain."

Stacey took Niall's arm. "You're coming with us."

Niall had no intention of fighting, but he was somewhat confused. "Where are we going?"

"To Jennifer's house. To get you dried off. I like you, and I don't want you to die of consumption or something."

Niall allowed himself to be dragged along. His feet felt light, as if he was floating above the wet grass. Stacey was touching him. She said she liked him, in front of her friend. And she didn't want him to die! That was one of the nicest things a girl had ever said to him.

Jennifer lived close by, just across the bridge on the base. It was the part of town that used to belong to the American military, and the lines of drab, institutional-looking row houses hadn't changed much in over thirty years. Of course, Niall didn't pay them any notice whatsoever. He was too focused on the two girls doting on either side of him.

"I kinda like the makeup, actually." Erin's glasses were fogged up from the cold and damp. Pius always had the same problem. "You look kinda goth. Like that Skinny Puppy guy. Or Uncle Fester."

Niall wasn't sure who the Skinny Puppy guy was, but he certainly knew who Uncle Fester was, and it wasn't a compliment.

Stacey was hugging his arm tightly, sharing her umbrella with him, so he certainly wasn't going anywhere, Uncle Fester analogies or not. "So who is Jennifer?"

"A friend of ours from school. We were just going to hang out. It was supposed to be a girls' thing, but we can't leave you alone in the rain like that. If you get any more tortured, you might slit your wrists on me."

"I'm not tortured..." Sure, he was *acting* like he was tortured, but when she said it, he just sounded lame.

"I like my guys a little tortured." She put her head on his shoulder. "You're way more interesting than the skeets in our class."

Erin groaned. "Kyle Bartlett asked me out again. Did I tell you?"

"Kyle's cute," replied Stacey.

"As if I would ever go out with Kyle. Shirley Brown went out with him once, and he cut off some of her hair when she wasn't looking. He still keeps it in his locker!"

"No way!"

"Way!"

"What a freak!" Stacey looked up at Niall. "You wouldn't do something like that, right?"

"No, of course not." Niall was undoubtedly not going to mention that he may have considered something exactly like that.

Jennifer was a tall, gangly girl with a chipped tooth and frizzy hair. She instantly became one of Niall's favourite people when she greeted them at the door and said, "Holy shit, you look like the Crow. That's wicked!"

Stacey waltzed into the house, pulling Niall after her. "Hi Jenn, this is Niall. I told you about him, right? I hope it's okay he comes in."

"Yeah, sure, no problem. My parents aren't home anyway. Why do you look like you fell in Rose River?"

Erin took off her wet boots and headed for the living room. "We found him acting all sad and goth, sitting in the rain."

Niall wasn't sure if they were making fun of him. "Hey now—"

"—It's okay," Stacey explained. "He just broke up with his girlfriend."

What?

Stacey must have sensed his consternation because she elaborated. "I assume? I know you met her the other day, and something weird was going on between you two. And then here you are, looking all dopey and sitting in the rain."

The girl was perceptive. "Actually, we broke up a while ago. We were really good friends. I just found out she's moving away."

Stacey took him by the hand. "That sucks. I'm sorry. Come on, we'll help you forget all about her."

What was happening? This was like the start of one of those movies his brother kept hidden under his bed.

Jennifer took his other hand. "But first, we have to get you out of those wet clothes."

Holy crap, did they read the script to Naughty Neighbours 4*?!*

What the girls had planned turned out to be far less racy than Niall expected, which made him relieved, to be honest. They led him to the bathroom, closed the door, and a few minutes later, it opened a crack to toss him a towel and some of Jennifer's brother's clothes.

Niall dried off, handed the girls his wet things, then examined what they'd given him. "Are you serious?"

"They should fit!" Stacey called through the door. "I think they'll look good on you!"

Niall sighed. He would either have to put them on or hide in the bathroom until his clothes were dry. Or he could ask for the wet clothes back and then run away, but there was no way in hell he was doing that. He was alone in a house with three girls! He would mop the floors and clean the toilet if they wanted, if only for an excuse to hang out here a bit longer.

A few minutes later, Niall came out of the bathroom wearing an old Motley Crue T-shirt and black leather pants.

Jennifer *tsked,* and Stacey shook her head. "Ah, you wiped your makeup off," said Stacey. "We wanted to see it with the pants."

"My brother went through a phase." Jennifer rolled her eyes. "He could never pull those off, but they look good on you."

Niall doubted that was true and still wasn't convinced they weren't making fun of him. In fact, he knew all of this might be some elaborate plot to humiliate him. Then Stacey ran her hand down Niall's leg, and he didn't care whether they were mocking him or not.

"These are so cool." Stacey gave him an appraising look. "But they would look much better if we fixed your makeup."

"I'll get my caboodle!" Jennifer ran for the stairs. "Erin, we need your makeup expertise."

Erin groaned from the couch. "But *My So-Called Life* is coming on!"

"Multitask!"

Erin groaned again. "Fine! But if I miss Jordan Catalano with his shirt off, I'm going to murder somebody!"

Jennifer tied back her dark, wild hair. Erin sharpened an eyeliner pencil. Niall gulped, sat back in a chair at the kitchen table and let the girls have their way with him... but not in any way he ever would have expected. They took turns fiddling with his hair, brushing powders onto his cheeks, outlining his eyes and lips with god-knows-what. Their hands were far more deft at this than his, and they poked him in the eye significantly less than he ever did.

Part of him was terrified. There was no mirror, and he couldn't see what they were doing. The bigger part of him was ecstatic—not one, not two, but *three* girls were touching him. And they were so friendly and gentle, so how could he be afraid? They were talking about people from their high school he didn't know, about boys they thought were cute (Niall noticed he wasn't mentioned this time), and their church group.

"I thought you girls went to the Amalgamated?" Niall asked, feeling left out.

Stacey chuckled. "We're protestant, not atheist. Sorry, we're monopolizing the conversation."

Erin made a flourish of something around his left eye. "Yeah, tell us about yourself, goth boy."

"Nothing too exciting. I live with my parents, my older brother and my grandmother. I play video games, read, listen to music..."

...fight hideous monsters from beyond space and time, cast magic spells, save the world...

"He was in the fire that burned Todd Murphy last year," said Stacey, bringing up something he'd told her at the Silver Scoops.

Jennifer nearly dropped her eye pencil. "No way! How come you didn't get burned up like Todd?"

"Just lucky, I guess."

"Todd's actually doing really good," said Erin. "Did you see him at school last week since he got the bandages off after his latest surgery? His face almost looks... normal."

Jennifer nodded. "Yeah, I mean, he's not winning any beauty contests or anything, but at least everything's in the right place now. His eyes aren't crossed anymore."

"Seriously?" Niall was shocked. Before the accident, Todd's eyes looked like two marbles floating in a glass of oily sweat, spinning freely in every direction. He must have a good surgeon, or maybe getting a house dropped on his head fixed it somehow. Niall hadn't seen the poor guy in a while, though Pius and Skidmark met with him often to play Magic. He would think they'd have mentioned something.

"Okay, finished!" Erin stepped back to admire her handiwork.

Stacey seemed to approve. "Not bad."

Jennifer fished a hand mirror out from somewhere and handed it to Niall. He took it apprehensively. "You didn't make me look like Krusty the Clown, did you?"

Niall looked into the mirror and found a stranger looking back at him. This wasn't his crude smudges, vainly trying to ape Brandon Lee's look from The Crow. His eyes and lips were perfectly black. His skin tone was lighter but not clownishly white. The black lines trailed down from his eyes and mouth exquisitely as if drawn by an artist, which Erin was, in Niall's opinion. His dirty blond hair was artfully mussed. He wouldn't look out of place on stage with Robert Smith or Alice Cooper, except he looked better than either.

"Holy shit," Niall breathed.

All three girls pouted. "You don't like it?"

"No, it's great. It's amazing. You'll have to teach me how to do this."

Erin held up a bottle of black nail polish. "We still have to do your nails. And you should probably dye your hair if you really want to complete the picture."

"But first, we should celebrate!" Jennifer ran into the kitchen as the girls giggled in agreement. Niall paid them little mind. He was too caught up in the mirror. With the makeup, hair, and leather pants... *Did he look... cool?* He wasn't sure if most people in Gale Harbour would appreciate it, but he liked it. Stacey and her friends seemed to, too.

He was so caught up in his own reflection that he was shocked when someone shoved a cold glass bottle into his hand. He looked down in horror to see a brown bottle of Labatt's Blue beer.

"What the hell?"

"I told you, we're celebrating." Jennifer clicked her bottle to Erin's and took a long swig.

"You girls drink?" Niall asked, horrified.

Erin finished her gulp and covered a burp with the back of her hand. The girls laughed. "Just on special occasions."

Stacey nuzzled up next to Niall. Her strawberry-scented blond curls tickled his nose. "What, you don't drink?"

Niall wanted to say "no." A voice in his head that sounded suspiciously like his mother was yelling at him to say "no," but he shut that voice down faster than he closed the lingerie section of the Sears catalogue when someone came into the room.

It's not that his parents were particularly forceful about him avoiding alcohol. Sure, they always said, "Not until you're older," but they knew that Nelson drank sometimes, despite being underage, and never said much about it. They were known to indulge from time to time. No, it was just that Niall was never interested in it. To him, alcohol smelled gross, it tasted gross, and it made people sick and do stupid things when they drank too much of it. He just never saw the appeal. Pius was loudly against alcohol and would have berated Niall for holding an open bottle, but Pius wasn't there. The only people here were three cute girls chugging back Labatt's Blue like it was Kool-Aid and offering it to him like it was nothing. Like it was perfectly natural, as natural as eating Hostess chips or talking about Jared Leto's dreamy eyes.

These girls accepted him into their group, not only as he was but helping him be the person he wanted to be. This wasn't the weirdos he hung out with in his basement, playing D&D and Super Nintendo, who didn't know what they wanted to be and wouldn't know what to do with a girl if one fell out of the sky like a meteor and smacked them in the face (which, in Gale Harbour, was not outside the realm of possibility). This certainly wasn't Harper, who had cut him out of her life as thoughtlessly and painfully as popping a pimple. These were real girls who genuinely seemed to like him, and Stacey, who *really* seemed to like him.

Wouldn't it be worth a few sips of beer to hang out with them, even if it tasted like dog pee? And yes, he knew what dog pee tasted like, thanks to his lovely brother.

Smiling weakly, Niall raised the bottle to his lips.

<u>**CHAPTER NINETEEN**</u>

Where Did You Sleep Last Night?
Sunday, October 23
10:25 pm

Marie-Ann Tanguay awoke in agony. She had no idea where she was.

Instinct kicking in, she reached for her sidearm, but her gun belt was gone. She was still in her uniform but lying in a bed. Her bed? How did she get into her bed?

The curtains were closed, and no light leaked through the edges. It must be night. In the shadows, she saw the boxes that contained her life, and she'd moved three times now back and forth across the country and never bothered to unpack.

She tried to sit up and screamed. Everything in her body hurt. She lay still a moment, waiting for the throbbing spears of pain to pass. Her breath was ragged. Tears welled up in her eyes.

Her bedroom door creaked open, and a tall, broad-shouldered figure stepped in. Quickly, she wiped her eyes and tried again to rise to a sitting position. She could barely get her head off the pillow.

"Easy," said a male voice Tanguay barely recognized. *Peters?* He flicked on the bedside lamp, revealing his features, and sure enough, the man trying to steal her job was standing in her room.

Tanguay closed her eyes and struggled to piece her memories together. "How did I get here?"

"Bennett helped me drag you out of the bush," he explained. "He thought we should bring you to the hospital, but I doubted you would appreciate that."

"What the hell are you talking about?"

Peters produced a bottle of pills and gave them a rattle. Was that her Percocet? "I have a prescription for that."

He produced two more bottles. "Yes, and so do Patricia Gilmour and Rhonda Flynn, but for some reason, their pills were in your pocket, too."

Tabarnak. "Going back to work has been harder than I expected. The script they gave me wasn't enough."

Peters cocked his handsome, square-jawed face at her. "You don't see a problem with that?"

She said nothing. Just closed her eyes and put her head on the pillow. She did not have the strength for this. She had fought monsters and arms dealers, but in the end, it was her own frail body that was going to do her in.

When she opened her eyes again, Peters held out two small white pills and a glass of water to her.

She was in too much goddamn pain now to be noble. She took the pills and swallowed them dry.

"I want to help you, Marie-Ann. You can't keep doing this."

"I will keep doing this as long as I have to."

Peters shook his head. "If you keep doing this, you're going to kill yourself. Or worse, you'll end up fired or in prison."

"I'll be fine."

"We both know that's a lie. This is going to kill you. Take the job in Montreal. You'll save your career and your reputation."

Montreal. Sitting on her ass at a desk. Sure, it was easier, but who would take care of this town? Of these kids? "That's not who I am."

Peters shook his head. The corners of his blue eyes wrinkled with concern. "Maybe it's not who you were, but maybe it's who you have to be for now. You can still do some good there. You can still help people. You can't help anybody if you're dead."

Tanguay took several deep breaths. Peters' words were hitting too close to home. How did he know her so well? When she was mostly confident her voice wasn't going to crack, she continued. "I'm the only one who can deal with the *merde* that goes on in this place."

Peters smiled. "You've protected this place for the last two years. Maybe it's time you let someone else help."

"You wouldn't understand..."

"I understand that there's weird stuff happening in Gale Harbour. Aliens-type stuff. Stuff that the government covered up."

She was taken aback. He knew? Did the RCMP brass tell him? Did he figure it out on his own? "What are you talking about?"

"Look, no one told me anything, but I'm not stupid. I can put the pieces together. Unnatural things have been happening in this town." He paused, letting the words sink in. "Is that what you think happened to Shelly and Robbie?"

Tanguay sighed. "There were tracks near the van. Like someone dragged them through the woods."

Peters was quiet for a moment. Finally, he sighed and said, "Bennett and I searched that area for hours. We couldn't find any tracks or trail."

How stupid were they? "I saw it. I followed it. There was a trail there..."

"I know you think you did, but are you sure you're thinking clearly? You're in a lot of pain, Marie-Ann. Are you sure it's not affecting your judgement?"

Tanguay felt bile rising in her throat. Who the hell did he think he was? "My judgement is clear."

"Are you sure? You're a good cop, but you are still recovering from a massive trauma. You can't keep pushing yourself like this."

"Please leave."

Peters nodded and stood up. He crossed to the door, pausing before he left the room. "Please think about what I said. I don't want you or anyone else to get hurt." He glanced down at the small, framed picture on the dresser before he left, the only photo in the house.

"Is this your daughter?" he asked.

Tanguay merely nodded.

"What happened to her?"

"She died," replied Tanguay, without emotion.

"I'm sorry for your loss." Peters slipped out of the room. A moment later, Tanguay heard the front door open and close.

Her heart climbed up into her throat, and Tanguay began to sob.

CHAPTER TWENTY

No Excuses
Monday, October 24
2:35 pm

"You did *what*?" Pius asked incredulously. He nearly dropped the books he was putting into his locker.

Niall smirked and slid his own books into the locker beside Pius. "I just hung out for a few hours."

"With girls?" Pius asked. "Three girls? And why are you wearing black nail polish?"

"I think it's awesome." Skidmark was in a locker a few doors down, chewing on a Fruit Roll-Up while he stacked a teetering tower of white card boxes. "Samantha in the drama club has black nails and lipstick. I think it's hot."

Pius threw up his hands. "It's not hot. It's Niall! And since when do we hang out with girls? We are at the bottom of the social strata! We are the plankton of the social food chain!"

Skidmark scrunched up his face in consideration. "Eh, Amalgamated girls probably have lower standards."

"And maybe *we* don't hang out with girls," Niall corrected, "but *I* do."

Niall's words slapped Pius in the face harder than any bully had in a long time. Pius didn't particularly want to hang out with girls, but his best friend wasn't supposed to treat him like that.

"Ouch." Skidmark smiled, little bits of red candy goo stuck in his teeth. "Sick burn. Good thing I don't need a girlfriend."

"Oh, and you have a girlfriend?" asked Niall.

Skidmark winked. "A gentleman never kisses and tells."

Pius groaned. "He thinks Mrs. Walsh is his girlfriend."

"The drama teacher?"

Skidmark batted his eyelashes. Or maybe he got some dirt in his eyes; he looked foolish either way. "I can neither confirm nor deny anything of the sort. It would be improper and untoward for me to talk about my conquests, especially when it's an affair with a married woman."

Pius hated it when Skidmark tried to sound smart. "How about when it's gross and illegal? And also completely untrue?"

"Then why did she give me, a lowly grade nine, the lead in the school play this year?"

"Because you saved her life last year from alien bugs, and she feels like she owes you something!"

Skidmark stopped to consider this. "Nah, it's more likely my good looks and natural talent. I took acting classes last summer, you know."

They all knew. He'd told them about it constantly from July through September. He once called Pius at midnight on a Sunday to tell him about Uta Hagen, whoever the heck that was.

"Fine, whatever, you're hot stuff." Pius tried to roll his eyes to show he was being sarcastic, but he didn't think Skidmark noticed. "Do you guys want to come over after school? We could play some D&D or Magic..."

"I would love to kick your ass with my new blue control deck," said Skidmark, "but I've got drama club. Mrs. Walsh would be lonely without me."

"I'm hanging out with Stacey and her friends," said Niall.

"Again?" Pius knew he sounded angry, but it was better than letting out his hurt and sadness. He tried to change the topic. "We need to do something to help Keith."

"We did something to help Keith," said Niall. "We told the cops what happened, and they're looking into it. What else are we supposed to do?"

"I don't know, we could workshop some ideas. I hardly see you anymore..."

"I'm allowed to have other friends, Pius."

At least when Niall was dating Harper, they were all friends and could do stuff together. When he was avoiding Harper, they still did stuff without her. But now, Niall seemed to be creating a new life without his old friends, and Pius didn't like it.

"Yeah, whatever." He slammed his locker closed. "That's fine. I'll see you guys later."

Pius turned and walked away before his emotions got the better of him. He didn't want to fight with Niall in front of half the school. He didn't want to fight with him at all. Pius missed the old days when he and Niall and Harper hung out together, and it wasn't complicated. Skidmark and Keith would tag along sometimes, and they would all have fun together. But now Harper was moving away, and Niall was looking for a new girlfriend. Keith was being hunted by his father's hitmen, and Skidmark... Well, Skidmark was still Skidmark. He had only replaced his obsessions with comic books and Star Trek with Magic: The Gathering and drama club.

Pius was afraid. Afraid of what these changes meant for him. He liked the way life used to be. But nothing was the same anymore, and he couldn't blame most of it on aliens and other monsters. People were changing, his friends were changing, and Pius was getting left behind.

As was rapidly becoming the norm, Pius walked home alone. He was so embroiled with anger at his friends, guilt and fear over burning down the school, and anxiety over whatever household tasks would fall on him tonight that he couldn't think straight. Had he been clearer-headed, he might have noticed the short man in the trucker's cap and orange hunting vest following him.

CHAPTER TWENTY-ONE

Closer
Monday, October 24
11:03 pm

Nelson was lying alone in his bed when there was a knock at his window.

He'd been lying on his bed, staring at a poster on his wall he'd pulled from the Sports Illustrated swimsuit edition and wondering what Anna would look like in a bathing suit. He'd been thinking about going to the beach with her next summer and had been thinking about doing a lot of stuff with her, actually. He hardly thought about the Firebird anymore and certainly didn't think about his family, who didn't care much for him anyway. He just thought about the wonderful woman and all the wonderful things she could show him.

The knock came again, thoroughly shaking him out of his daydreams. Unable to ignore it any longer, he jumped out of bed and stormed across his room. Assuming it was one of Niall's idiot friends looking for him and knocking at the wrong bedroom, Nelson slid open the window and was about to bawl out the intruder when he found himself face-to-face with the deathly-pale face and black-painted lips of the woman he loved.

"Anna?" he whispered.

She flashed him a coquettish smile. "Sorry, I didn't want to knock on the door and wake anyone. Plus, I wasn't sure your family would approve of me."

Nelson found himself seething at the thought of his family not liking her. "I don't care what they think about you."

"That's very sweet of you. Do you wanna come with me? There's something I want to show you. Call it an early birthday present."

Nelson would have followed Anna to the pits of hell or Gale Harbour Crossing.

Anna wore a black leather jacket over her usual dress and corset getup. Nelson was grabbing his pants and sweater when his bedroom door opened. Nana Josephine poked her head in, and Nelson froze, half-dressed.

"I knew I heard voices," said Nana, smiling. "Sneaking in or out?"

Nelson's mouth was so dry he could barely speak. "Out?"

"Oh, well, that's fine then." She stepped in, wearing one of her trademark tracksuits despite it being nearly midnight. You never know when you might need to go for a brisk walk. "You're a grown man, Nelson. You don't need to go sneaking out like a child. Think your girl's dressed up early for Halloween, though."

Nelson breathed a sigh of relief and finished pulling up his jeans. Of all his family members, Nana was the most reasonable. If one of them had caught him, his mom or dad would have bawled him out despite his age. Niall would have run off to tell Mom or Dad. "Thanks, Nana. I don't know if Mom and Dad would agree with you."

"They don't need to agree if they don't know." Nana disappeared out of the room again.

"She seems nice," said Anna, still standing outside on her tiptoes.

"She can surprise you," Nelson agreed. "Though she has lightened up considerably since she went crazy and broke out of the retirement home a while back."

Nelson was just pulling his sweatshirt over his head when Nana reappeared. "Here, take your coat with you, it's chilly."

He took the battered brown jacket and chuckled. "Thanks, Nana."

"Aren't you going to introduce me to your friend?"

Nelson froze again. He appreciated Nana's understanding, but her ease in the situation unnerved him.

Anna saved him. She waved from the window. "Hi, I'm Anna. Nice to meet you."

"Where you from, Anna?"

"Mount Pearl, originally."

Nana tsked. "A townie? Oh well, nobody's perfect. You two kids have fun. But Nelson, if you gets that girl pregnant, I swear to God I'll be standing at the altar with the shotgun at your back myself."

Nana left, closing the door this time, leaving Nelson standing red-faced in the middle of the room and Anna laughing in the window.

"Your grandmother is quite the character," Anna said a few minutes later as they drove away in a beat-up old green station wagon. "Did she really break out of the old age home?"

"Kinda? It was never really clear if she escaped or if her neighbour kidnapped her. But she seems chill about it, so I always assumed she went willingly."

Anna nodded. Nelson watched her hands on the steering wheel, and his gaze kept slipping to her legs. He caught glimpses of her fishnet-stockinged leg as she worked the gas and the brake.

"Aren't you wondering where we're going?" she asked.

Nelson cleared his throat and flicked his eyes forward. "I was just enjoying the ride."

"We're going to a church function."

"In the middle of the night?"

"Trust me, you'll like this one."

She drove West, down through Keeping and towards Cape-de-Cape. The car choked and rumbled, and Nelson commented that it might need service. Anna joked that she wouldn't need it much longer. "Once you get your Firebird, you'll drive me everywhere, right?"

Nelson just smiled. He had nearly forgotten about the car. Anna was the only thing in his thoughts lately. He loved spending time with her, and when he wasn't with her, he counted down the minutes until they were together again.

The drive through the twisty, rocky road along the coast seemed to fly by as the pair talked about music and movies. Not surprisingly, but to Nelson's dismay, Anna was into bands like Depeche Mode and The Cure, which were far closer to Niall's wheelhouse. At least they could agree on Faith No More and Queensryche being cool.

They pulled off on a deserted stretch, heading down a narrow gravel sideroad. They pulled up behind a line of other parked vehicles. Nelson was filled with a mixture of excitement and fear. Fortunately, he trusted Anna; otherwise, he was worried she was bringing him out somewhere to sacrifice him to Satan.

Anna led him through some trees and down to a secluded beach, where about two dozen adults were gathered around a bonfire, singing songs and laughing heartily.

Nelson began to relax. "This is a church function?"

Anna nuzzled against him as they approached the group. "I told you, the Church of the Redeemer is about celebrating life, about enjoying the time we have on Earth now." She leaned in and whispered. "Some people might be extra enthusiastic, but don't get freaked out, okay?"

Now Nelson was freaked out but didn't have time to think about it. Anna was already introducing him. "Hi everyone, this is Nelson, the guy I told you about? You probably saw him at service a few days ago."

Several voices called out greetings, and a short-haired woman in a green jacket walked straight up to him, said, "Hi, Nelson!" and began kissing him passionately.

Nelson panicked, unsure of what to do. The woman forced her tongue into his mouth, and he responded weakly. He put up his hands in a gesture of surrender, but her hands were all over him, her grip pulling him tighter. He finally pulled away, gasping for breath, and saw Anna smiling.

"He's cute," said the short-haired woman.

"I think you freaked him out," Anna replied.

Nelson felt hot all over. He could still taste the woman's mouth, which tasted like beer and cherry lipgloss. "I didn't mean, she just jumped on me, I don't..."

"Relax, Nelson," Anna replied. She squeezed his hand. "I told you people here are enthusiastic, and everyone worships in their own way."

Nelson was shocked that Anna wasn't angry. "So this is okay?"

"It's more than okay," she replied, and then she was kissing him, and Nelson's mind was completely blown. Anna was okay with this? With him kissing another woman right in front of her?

He felt another set of hands on his chest and hot breath upon his neck, and he guessed that was his answer. He let himself go, enjoying the moment, his mouth moving back and forth between the two women. He was dimly aware of guitar music strumming somewhere nearby, and someone passed him a bottle. He drank deeply, then went right back to the women.

Nelson had no idea how long he was touching and kissing the two women, but he was broken from his revelry a few minutes later when a man's voice interrupted them.

"Sorry, folks, it's time to start the service." It was a tall, gruff man wearing rubber boots. Nelson couldn't make out his features with the bonfire illuminating him from behind.

Anna looked put out. "Already?" she said breathlessly. Her cheeks were flushed with more colour than Nelson had ever seen. "Sorry, Nelson, this is for senior members only. I have to do this, but I'm sure Brother Vee wouldn't mind if Gladys and Sandra keep you company."

Nelson didn't get a chance to ask who Gladys and Sandra were before Anna slipped away and another woman took her place on the log beside him. She started kissing him as well, more hungrily, if that was possible. She tasted like peppermint schnapps. Nelson pulled away and looked up at Anna, who was straightening her dress.

"This is okay?" he asked, unable to believe it was.

"It's more than okay." She leaned over and kissed him on the forehead. "It's what we do. You girls take care of him, okay? But save some for me."

Anna winked, and then she was gone, off to deal with a group of people gathering down the beach. Nelson found himself being led away by two women he didn't know, didn't know which one was Gladys and which one was Sandra, and he didn't have any ability to resist. He wasn't sure if the fuzziness in his head was from the booze or the craziness of the situation. One of the women had her shirt unbuttoned, the other one was fiddling with the button of his pants, and they were leading him toward a pickup truck with a white cap over the flatbed.

Nelson was so bewildered that he didn't notice Anna and the other congregation members on the beach pulling out white robes. He was already in the truck by the time they started dragging victims out of the woods with hoods over their heads. He thought he heard a garbled scream a few minutes later, but then Gladys or Sandra was on top of him, and all his awareness of the outside world completely faded away.

Anna joined them a little while later. As she grabbed his face and kissed him, Nelson noticed some blood on her hand, but by then, he was too far gone to care.

CHAPTER TWENTY-TWO

Self-Esteem
Tuesday, October 25
8:50 pm

Niall was sitting on the same bench overlooking Rose River. It was dark, the sky was clear, and he wasn't alone this time.

"He was such a loser!" Erin giggled and nearly fell from where she was perched on the garbage can beside the bench. Her ponytail flapped around wildly, and she stopped to adjust her glasses. She noticed she'd spilled nearly half her bottle of beer. "Ah, dammit."

"He was nice," Jennifer said, pouting. "And sweet. He used to bring me candy and flowers."

"That his mom bought for him. Did she help him kiss you, too?"

Jennifer recoiled, her lips curling to reveal her chipped tooth. She paled, her freckles fading as if trying to hide from embarrassment. "Ew, gross. It might have been better if his mom had taught him how to kiss. He was terrible. His lips were all dry, and he tasted like cabbage."

"Maybe he did learn from his mom?" Niall suggested. "Maybe she ate cabbage for dinner, and he got the taste from her mouth."

The girls cackled with laughter. Jennifer gagged a bit, and Niall took a gulp of his own beer. He certainly wasn't getting used to the taste, but he was strangely enjoying the weird light-headedness he was feeling. It helped him relax. And he wasn't sure, but he thought it made his jokes funnier to the girls.

It was only his second time drinking. The first time, at Jennifer's house, he had just sipped it a bit because it tasted so gross. Erin had laughed at him, but Stacey told him it would get better.

This time, Niall was determined to be more successful at this drinking thing.

He finished his second bottle and started a third. He was developing quite a fuzzy head. It wasn't altogether bad. He often felt weak and dizzy when he used his magic powers, but this was different. In addition to needing to puke, he felt braver and more eloquent.

"I can teach you how to kiss if you're wondering how it's supposed to be done."

The girls' mouths dropped open in unison. Not as an invitation for Frenching, but with bewilderment. Niall felt his ears get hot, but he didn't care. He knew he should be embarrassed, but it was as if he forgot how.

Erin guffawed. "I think Stacey would get jealous."

"Hey, he hasn't even kissed me!" Stacey shot back.

Now, Niall felt his face flush, but he seemed to have forgotten what an inhibition was. "I didn't know you wanted me to."

"She was waiting for you to make the first move, duh." Jennifer gave him a friendly shove that probably left a bruise. Those gangly arms were strong.

"I didn't... I just..." Harper always made the first move. Niall had never been forward or really knew what to do around girls. But this seemed like an invitation if there ever was one.

Niall stood up and sat on the back of the bench next to Stacey. He leaned in, eyes closed, to kiss her.

Suddenly, he was falling. Not in a pleasant, lovestruck way. He and Stacey literally fell off the bench and hit the ground, hard.

Niall cracked his head on the hard-packed Earth, but it didn't hurt nearly as bad as he would have expected. He and the girls kept laughing.

Stacey's blonde hair was in his face, and he breathed deeply of her strawberry shampoo. "Oh my god, are you okay?" He struggled to get up, pulling her with him. They continued to giggle, and she held him tight. She reached up to kiss him, the fingers of her bandaged hand brushing through his hair. Her fingers touched the side of his head, and he winced.

Stacey pulled away. "You're bleeding!"

"It's okay, I'm fine. Just keep doing what you're doing."

"Poking you in the side of your bloody, concussed head?"

"No, before that."

"Oh, you mean this?"

She leaned in again, keeping her hands well away from his head. Niall closed his eyes and braced himself, hoping that she wouldn't mind his smelly alcohol breath since she probably smelled the same way.

"Niall?" called a voice. His stomach dropped into his shoes.

Niall pulled away. "Harper?"

Harper was approaching from across the field, dressed in her regular baggy jeans and flannel shirt. She was walking with an older woman dressed in a leather jacket, her red brown hair pulled up, revealing numerous earrings and tattoos on her neck.

Harper stopped a few metres away and looked away, obviously uncomfortable. "Niall, sorry, I didn't mean to interrupt anything..."

Niall wanted to climb into a hole and die. If he'd had a shovel, he would have already started digging. "No, Harper, it's fine, I just..." He felt cold, and he needed to vomit.

"So you decided to go full goth, huh?"

The make-up. "I can explain."

She rolled her big brown eyes and pointedly tried not to look at him, and especially at Stacey. "You don't need to explain anything. Not why you're drinking or why your head is bleeding. We're not dating anymore."

She was right, of course. Niall had broken up with her. A long time ago. So then, why did he feel so guilty?

"So this is the famous Niall, huh?" asked the woman beside Harper. The gaze of her cold, dark eyes felt like it was burning a hole through Niall's soul. Why was she looking at him like that? Why did he feel so naked and exposed in front of her, somehow more ashamed than he felt in front of Harper? Who was she anyway? She was scrawny, with sunken eyes and gaunt cheeks, hardly intimidating. Why were his intestines trying to strangle his liver?

Harper sighed. "Yeah, Mom, that's him."

Oh, shit...

Niall threw up. His supper and two-and-a-half beers all came back up right at Harper and her mom's feet. They both leapt out of the way. He wasn't sure if he splattered them or not.

Harper's mom looked at the puddle, at her shoes, and then at Niall. He couldn't tell which one disgusted her more. "Really dodged a bullet there, didn't you?"

"Come on, Mom, let's just go."

Niall couldn't look at them. He fell to his knees, staring at the puddle of his own puke as they walked away. Why did he feel like this?

Why did it feel like there was a monster in his stomach trying to climb out of his throat? Was it the beer? Was it the shame? His guts hurt so bad. Who the hell was she to talk to him like that? Harper's mom was a junkie who had practically forgotten she had a daughter for thirteen years. Where did she get off judging him?

Someone put a hand on his shoulder, probably Stacey, but Niall shoved her away.

"Who the hell was that?" asked Jennifer.

Erin grunted in disgust. "His ex-girlfriend."

"Her mom's a bitch. And she's not that good-looking. Is she a jackytar or something?"

"Jennifer, shut up!" Stacey hissed.

Niall stood up and pushed away from them. He was feeling woozy and staggered, but he refused to fall this time. Once again, Stacey tried to put a hand on him, but he pushed away.

"Niall..."

He turned and started walking away, stumbling, his face burning hot. His head began to ache nearly as badly as his stomach.

Stinging tears burst out of his eyes. What was he doing? Why wasn't he over Harper? Why did he let her mom talk to him like that? Why wouldn't he let Stacey confront him? At least she was nice to him. And she was cute and funny and way less complicated than Harper.

He was screwing everything up. Was this his punishment for killing Keenan? He hadn't thought about it in a long time, but the guilt remained. Murdering Keenan was the reason he had broken up with Harper, which had started this whole misery he was living in now. Was this some kind of karmic retribution? Did he deserve this?

A crack of thunder split the night and nearly knocked Niall off his feet. It was accompanied by a flash of brilliant lightning that, for a split second, the cold October night was as bright as a sunny afternoon.

Niall froze. His mind flashed back to two summers ago and the lightning he saw with Harper and Pius over the bay, the lightning that started all of... this.

It was probably a coincidence. A weird twist of fate at a dramatically opportune moment. Sometimes, lightning was just lightning. It didn't always herald the arrival of some other-worldly, unkillable monster.

The sky opened up, and it started to rain. Niall continued to walk, the rain mingling with his tears.

CHAPTER TWENTY-THREE

Here Comes the Hotstepper
Wednesday, October 26
2:10 pm

Tricia looked up when Keith walked into the office. She was Cecil Doucette's secretary, a bull of a woman from Marystown, and one of the more likable adult figures in Keith's life. Despite her broad, stern face and large hands, she always softened when Keith came around.

She nearly leapt up from behind her desk. "Keith, my God, are you okay?"

Keith was confused, mostly that anyone in his dad's circle gave a crap about him. "Yeah, why?"

"The police were here. They questioned your dad, and then they started asking where you were." She noticed the bandages on his face and rushed up to hover over him in a motherly fashion. "What happened to your ear?"

"Cut myself shaving."

"Keith... Wait, have you been drinking?"

Keith had to admit that he'd had a few beers to get up the courage to confront his dad in his office above the shoe store. Courage probably wasn't the right word. It would be more like reckless abandon if Keith understood what those words meant properly.

"Is he here?" Keith pointed to the inner office door with his aluminum baseball bat.

"Yes, he is, but Keith don't—"

He didn't hear the rest. She might have said, "Don't take any guff from a clown," for all Keith cared. He kicked open his dad's office door, surprising his old man so much that he dropped the phone receiver out of his hand.

"You son of a bitch," Cecil Doucette growled. "Did you call the cops on me?"

Cecil had once been a tough, ruggedly handsome man, but now his hair was receding, and the buttons of his shirt strained against his gut. His desk was messy, his walls covered with local business awards and pictures of famous athletes. Keith didn't need to look to know there wasn't a picture of him in the place.

Keith laughed. "You ripped my ear off, and you're pissed because I called the cops? I should have called the cops about the assholes you hired to kill me."

"What the hell are you talking about?"

"That plumber from out the Cape that works for you. Joe McDonald, or McCain or whatever his name is. You hired him to kill me. Or at least beat me up."

"The hell is wrong with you? I haven't seen Joe McFatridge in over a year. And I sure as shit didn't hire him to kill you."

"Like I should believe you. Sounds like the kind of stuff you would do. Don't want to get your own hands dirty, so you pay some skeevy bayman to do it for you."

"You piece of shit, I don't need anyone's help to tan your hide." Cecil stepped from behind the desk and raised his hand to strike, but Keith pointed the bat at his father's face.

"Go ahead and try it."

Cecil laughed bitterly. "Coward. Sure, take a swing at me with the bat that I bought you, you ungrateful little shit."

Keith didn't hesitate. He swung the bat with enough oomph to put a ball over the centre-field fence. His father ducked backward, but Keith wasn't aiming for his head. The bat flew from his hands and crashed into the wall of awards and recognitions. A plaque for "Local Entrepreneur of the Year" shattered and smashed to the floor in pieces.

Keith grinned. "Made you flinch."

Cecil came at him, but Keith was younger and quicker, hardened from years of playing sports, and walloped his father with a vicious punch to the jaw. He collapsed to the floor.

Keith stood over his father, momentarily stunned at what had just happened. One punch? He had spent his life in terror of this man, cowed and cringing, flinching away every time he said "boo." He had let this man drive his mother away. Had made him ashamed to be himself. And he had dropped him with one punch?

"You're a frigging pussy!" Keith howled. His father moaned, rubbing his face, and tried to grab his son's leg. Keith kicked him away and retrieved his bat.

"Please," Cecil begged. "Please don't hurt me."

Keith stepped away, disgusted. He could've beaten his father to a pulp for all the misery he had put him through over the years. Could have killed him right there on the floor of his own office. There was so much anger clawing at his chest, struggling to get out. Anger that he used to direct at other kids he bullied at school. The poor kids whose lives he made miserable. It was all because of him. And now that Keith had him at his mercy and could have let out the rage that he'd built up for so long... He couldn't do it. He didn't want to be that person anymore. He didn't want to hurt anyone else, not even a piece of shit like his dad.

Instead, Keith turned and swung his bat at the computer on his dad's desk, sending the heavy monitor crashing to the floor. When he bought it, his old man had bragged that it was the most expensive computer in town. Keith wondered if he'd ever been half as proud of his son as he was of that stupid computer.

Keith stormed out of the office, unable to look at his dad anymore. Standing in the door and watching the whole thing, Tricia moved to reach out to Keith. She stopped and withdrew her hand at the last moment. Her lip was trembling, and her eyes were full of tears.

Keith ran down the stairs and burst out into the bright afternoon sun. The air was cool and felt fresher than it had in a long time. He ran across Main Street, dodging a blue Chevy, and ducked between two buildings on the opposite side. He found himself in a small parking lot beside a rusted dumpster, behind an accountant's office. He didn't know where to go. Beyond the parking lot was an overgrown vacant lot, and beyond that was the trailer court. He contemplated heading to the Bowler, just a little down the road, to bum some half-full bottles of beer, but he stopped himself. The thought of it disgusted him.

He looked down at the prized Easton bat in his hand. He had hit so many home runs with that bat. It had saved his life against alien June bugs last year. It was battered and scratched, and most of the paint was worn off, and he loved it more than any of the other expensive crap his father had given him. But his father had given him the bat, too. His father had given him everything, and he didn't want it anymore. The bat felt heavy in his hand.

Without thinking, Keith ran to the vacant lot and tossed the bat as hard as possible. It crashed with a clang against some rocks and disappeared into the tall grass.

Keith turned and walked away, back up Main Street, following his feet wherever they would lead him.

CHAPTER TWENTY-FOUR

Spoonman
Wednesday, October 26
3:30 PM

After school, Pius walked home alone. He'd been doing that a lot lately. After Harper and Niall broke up, she started taking a different route. Now Niall was doing his own thing more and more after school, and Pius was all alone. A few years ago, he would have been terrified to walk this far on his own, especially with the higher speed limit on the Harmon Highway. But walking home was now a small terror compared to facing horrible monsters, alien invasions, or a future without two of his best friends.

At first, he didn't think anything of the car parked across the street from his house. It was just an old, rusted-out Monte Carlo, and it looked like it was parked in front of Mister Parsons' house. Someone is probably visiting or trying to sell him a set of encyclopedias. Pius wished his parents would get a new set of encyclopedias. Theirs was over ten years out of date and didn't have anything about 15760 Albion, carbon nanotubes, or other important discoveries. If they didn't get an encyclopedia, he wished they could at least get a new computer with Internet access.

But then he noticed someone in the car, wearing a dirty baseball cap and a hunter's vest. The man did his best to avoid Pius' gaze, becoming obsessively interested in something in his glove box as Pius passed.

Pius could not be sure it was the same guy who had followed them home the other night, but he had a gut feeling that it was. This was not good. He wondered where Keith was and what these people actually wanted with him.

He dashed the last twenty metres home, cutting across the front yard and burst into the door, slamming it behind him. The plastic skeleton door hanging in the window fell to the floor. "Mom!"

"Shush!" his mother hissed, diving across the kitchen to meet him. It took me over an hour to get your sister down. If you wake her up, I swear to God I will stuff your pockets with rocks and throw you off the wharf at Port Hansen!"

Samantha Jeddore's last year had been hard on her. Between nearly breaking up with her husband and having an unplanned child in her late thirties, she was no longer the "hot mom" that Niall once pined for. Her cheeks and eyes were puffy, her once fiery hair was greying, and she had perpetual bags under her eyes from lack of sleep. Rebecca refused to stay down, and Pius felt guilty for nearly waking her. Still, that didn't ease the seriousness of the situation.

"I'm sorry," Pius whispered, his voice still urgent. "Where's Keith?"

"He left this afternoon. I hope he went home to his family."

"What?" Pius couldn't believe his mother was being so dense. "You let him go? After I told you people were looking for him?"

"Pius, I think you're overreacting—"

"No! We were followed home Friday night, and someone is watching the house right now!"

A look of concern flashed across his mother's face, and she got up to look out the dining room window. "Pius, there's no one out there."

Pius had to look for himself, and sure enough, the car was gone. "He was just there... but Keith can't go home anyway. His dad assaulted him!"

"Pius, I don't have time for this. I was waiting for you to get home because I need to run to the store. If Rebecca wakes up, there's a bottle in the fridge, okay? You know how to heat it up." She grabbed her car keys off the counter and headed for the door.

Pius' indignation was replaced by panic. "You're leaving me here? Alone?"

"Pius, you're fourteen years old. You'll be fine. And I'll be back in twenty minutes."

"What if Becca and I come with you?"

She shook her head. "I told you, Rebecca needs her nap. I'm not waking her up. Now go on with you, be quiet and wait until I get back."

And then she was gone, leaving Pius alone in the quiet kitchen. He went to the door and locked it.

What was he supposed to do? What if that guy came back? He was looking for Keith, but what if they didn't realize he'd left? Pius didn't know who they were or what they wanted, but he had to assume the men were dangerous. They had guns. And if there was anything Pius had learned over the last couple of years, everything in life was indeed out to kill you.

Pius entered the living room and sat on the edge of the worn brown leather couch, wondering what to do. At least he could watch the driveway and the road from here so he would see anyone coming. But what would he do if they came? Harper had her dad's old gun in her room in the basement, but his mom made Harper keep it locked up, and Pius didn't know where the key was. Not that Pius knew how to use a gun. He would most definitely shoot his eye out and probably his brains, too.

Someone knocked on the door, and Pius' heart nearly slingshotted itself off his diaphragm out of his throat. He froze, like that deer in the headlights a couple of years ago, right before his father plowed into it with his pick-up truck.

He couldn't get the gun. Maybe the knives in the kitchen drawer. Where was the bat Keith gave him last Christmas?

The knock came again, and a voice came with it this time. "Pius?"

A woman's voice. He recognized it but couldn't place it, muffled through the door. It wasn't his mom. Was it Harper? Did she forget her key? Maybe Harper's mom? She was in town...

Pius stood and slowly crept across the kitchen to the front door. He could see a figure through the window but could not make out its features through the gauzy curtain. He took two cautious steps toward the knife drawer.

"Pius, I know you're in there. It's me, Anna Chaffey."

Anna? What in the heck was she doing here?

Since the last time she'd been in town had been to warn them about an alien invasion, Pius' fear only switched targets instead of easing altogether. He quickly rushed to the door, unlocked it, and swung it open.

It was indeed Anna. As usual, she was dressed all in black with a push-up bustier and corset. She looked more dishevelled than usual. Her dark hair was sticking out in all directions, and lighter, undyed roots were showing close to her scalp. Her long, fishnet gloves were full of more holes than usual, and her mascara was running as if she'd been crying.

"Anna, what's wrong?"

She sniffled a little. "Pius, I'm sorry."

"For what?"

"For this," she said as she drew a knife and stepped into the house.

Melissa was awakened from a dead sleep by the sounds of screaming.

She knew it was Anna. That girl had caused her so much trouble since she moved in.

Melissa Power lived in a one-bedroom apartment on Elizabeth Avenue in St. John's. She worked at Zellers and took part-time esthetician classes at the community college. She had a boyfriend who treated her well, and she was saving up to go on a trip to Bermuda with him that winter. Life was going great until Anna Chaffey showed up a few weeks ago.

Melissa and Anna had been friends—briefly—in high school. Anna was homeschooled until grade nine, when she crashed into Bishops College High School like an angel cast out of heaven. She was a girl out of place and time, ethereal and awkward, innocent and obscene, filled with a relentless, chaotic energy. At first, Melissa thought she was a blast, throwing parties and getting them into all kinds of trouble. But soon, Anna's erratic behaviour got harder to take, and she got into drugs and started hanging around with a bad crowd. Melissa barely saw her in grade eleven, and she dropped out in grade twelve.

Melissa hadn't seen or heard from Anna in several years until she showed up on her doorstep, sopping wet from the rain, her clothes filthy and torn. She looked like she hadn't eaten or bathed in days. Out of pity, Melissa took her in and regretted it almost immediately.

Anna often woke up screaming, so on this particular night, Melissa didn't think much of it. She had terrible nightmares and traumatic flashbacks. Melissa learned bits and pieces of it over the ensuing weeks, about how Anna had been abused as a child, about her struggles with drugs and alcohol, and about how her boyfriend had died just a few months before.

On this particular night, Melissa thought Anna's screams of "get away from me" were just another of her nightmares until she heard other voices outside her bedroom door.

"You're coming home," said a female voice Melissa didn't recognize.

"I don't want to!" Anna screamed.

"You don't have a choice!"

A male voice. And then an unmistakable smacking sound, and Anna cried out in pain.

Melissa shot bolt upright in her bed, clutching her blankets around her. *Shit, shit, shit,* she hissed through gritted teeth. Her stomach turned to ice.

There were other people in the apartment. And they were hurting Anna.

She should call the police, but the phone was on the end table next to the couch where Anna slept. Had Anna tried to call the police? Did she have any warning before these people attacked her? How did they get into the apartment?

"We've let this nonsense go on long enough," said the unknown female voice. "You had your dalliance with that effeminate twat. It's time to come back to the church."

"The hell I am!" There was another crash, probably the lamp in the living room, and then a scream and the sound of someone crying. *Anna?*

Melissa's eyes darted around the room. What could she use as a weapon? Her curling iron? A high-heeled shoe? Maybe she could go out the window. It wasn't very big though, and they were on the third floor...

What kind of church were they talking about?

"Now is not the time for childish defiance." The woman's voice again. "Peronnik's prophecies are coming true. The way of the Sun King is open."

"I know!" Anna wailed. "I know! But it's not what you think!"

"Blasphemy!"

"I saw it, Mother! I saw the signs! I saw the Harbinger with my own eyes. But there will be no justice. There will be no rapture. It's going to kill *everyone!*"

"Stupid bitch." The man's voice. "Hold your tongue."

Mother? Were those Anna's parents out there? Melissa had only met them once, years ago. They were painfully polite and proper people. Her father always wore a tie, and her mother wore a skirt and jacket as if she were going to church. Anna always said they were weird church freaks. But this didn't sound like Pentecostal or, God forbid, Jehovah's Witness stuff.

Melissa pulled the blanket over her head and tried to be quiet. She would just hide until they left.

"You won't need to wait for the coming of the Sun King, Anna. If you don't come with us, we will kill you right here and now."

A heavy, thick silence hung over the apartment. Melissa held her breath, hoping they wouldn't hear her whimpering under the covers. It took her a moment to realize it was Anna who was whimpering.

"Get your things," said the woman. "We're leaving now."

Melissa heard the rustle of bags and a few cupboards slamming open and closed (were they taking her food?). Then the front door opened. Now, it was completely quiet. Were they gone?

Melissa counted to one hundred, then slowly lowered the covers and crawled out of the bed. She tiptoed across her bedroom floor and put her ear to the door. She held her breath and listened. Nothing. No sobs, no footsteps, no voices. Slowly, she turned the knob and opened the door.

Melissa's bedroom opened into the main living area, and she saw the apartment was wrecked. Cushions were ripped off the couch, glasses were shattered on the floor, and the phone had been ripped out of the wall. Melissa wondered if it still worked. She needed to call the police.

Her gaze drifted across the room, from Anna's clothes scattered across the floor to the ceramic angel that her mother had given her, which was now in pieces, to the overturned chairs at the small table in the kitchen area. Her gaze followed to the front door, which was wide open. A man was standing there, dressed in a brown suit. Melissa barely had time to register what she was seeing before he turned and looked directly at her with dark eyes.

His clean-shaven face turned into a snarl. "Anna! I thought you said your roommate wasn't home?"

He stepped into the apartment and closed the door behind him.

Melissa ducked back into her bedroom and locked the door. She searched frantically around the room but knew there were no weapons or escape. She fell back and slumped against the door. Her throat felt like it was closing up, and she couldn't breathe.

The door behind her jumped as something heavy slammed against it. She heard the wooden door frame crack under the weight. Despite her leaning with all her weight against the door, it wouldn't take him long to break through.

Melissa began to cry.

CHAPTER TWENTY-FIVE

What's the Frequency, Kenneth?
Thursday, October 27
12:15 pm

Brian Hawco was walking home from Arlene's, his backpack stuffed with new packs of Magic cards and daydreaming of Mrs. Walsh, when he bumped into Craig Muise. Craig and his bike went careening off the sidewalk and hit a parked car. Skidmark barely noticed.

"Hey, Skidmark!" Craig howled after him, wincing as he picked himself up off the asphalt. "Watch where you're going!"

Brian finally turned around and saw the carnage he'd caused. "I was watching where I was going. You ran into me. Most people just intentionally run into me and keep going, so I ignored you. I didn't want to give your bullying the satisfaction of getting me riled up."

Craig looked exasperated. He was a tall, thin kid with crooked teeth and short, dark, curly hair. He threw up his hands in frustration, which quite a few people did when talking to Skidmark. "I'm not bullying you! It was an accident. You just kinda take up an inordinate amount of the sidewalk. I couldn't get around you."

Brian looked down at himself and nodded in agreement. "I find no fault in that statement." He watched Craig drag his bike back up into a vertical position, making no offer to help. He wasn't purposefully rude; he was just annoyed that Craig had interrupted what was turning out to be a very interesting daydream about Mrs. Walsh.

Craig was in Brian's grade at St. Paul's and was in a couple of his classes. They didn't interact much; Craig was on the honour roll and wrote for the school newspaper. He wasn't involved in the drama club or played D&D or Magic, so he was outside Brian's circle of interests. "Hey, I heard about Pius," said Craig.

"Heard what?" Brian was vaguely aware that Pius hadn't been to school that day but didn't think much of it. He didn't think about much of anything these days if it wasn't drama club, Magic, or Mrs. Walsh. He'd been trying to teach her to play Magic so that all three of his interests could collide in blissful harmony, but she'd spurned his advances so far.

Craig looked at Brian oddly. "I figured that's why you were off school early."

"No, I just skipped off to buy Magic cards. What's up with Pius?"

"He and his sister disappeared last night. The cops are looking for them."

Skidmark nodded. "Oh, that happens all the time. I'm sure they'll be fine."

Craig scoffed. "Holy crap, man, I thought he was your friend. I thought you'd be more concerned."

Taking a half-melted Cookies & Creme bar out of the pocket of his sweatpants, Brian thought about this for a moment. "No, I don't think more concern is necessary. I mean, it could be aliens or vampires or something, but either way, they'll be fine. Hey, do you play Magic? I'm looking for a couple of Dark Rituals if you have some to trade."

"You are unreal, you know that? Would you care that there are also cop cars in front of Keith Doucette's house?"

"Really? I hope they're arresting his dad. He's an abusive dirtbag and probably a child molester. I keep asking Keith if it's true, but he just says I'm an idiot. Since he didn't say I was wrong, I have to assume it's true."

"Keith is my cousin, and his dad is my uncle. That's why I skipped off school. I'm going to go check it out."

Skidmark didn't care why Craig skipped school, but as he got ready to peddle away, Brian surprised himself by blurting out, "I'll come, too. Wait for me."

Craig's face sank. "What?"

"Keith's my friend. I should go check on him. Did I tell you some redneck assassins tried to kill him the other night? Me, Pius, and Keith had to run from them and hide in the field across from the old library. I hope the rednecks didn't kill him. Or molest him. Did I tell you about last year when I got locked into a hotel room with child molesters? Well, they weren't really child molesters, and they weren't really in the room;

I thought they were in the room, but it was just the Secret Service coming to arrest them..."

Craig started peddling down the street toward the Doucettes, and Brian followed him. He kept calling for Craig to slow down so he could keep up, but the lanky kid on the bike kept pulling farther and farther away. If Brian hadn't known better, he would have thought Craig was trying to get away from him. Brian just talked louder so Craig could hear him.

"...it was totally like something out of X-Files. I love the X-Files. Probably my favourite show now that Star Trek is over. Did you see the new one where Scully gets abducted? I mean, it sure looks like she got abducted. Do you think she'll come back? I heard they wrote her out of the show because the actress is having a baby, but I hope she's not gone for too long. Maybe she'll come back with an alien baby, like that movie Abraxas: Guardian of Time and Space, where the girl gets impregnated by that alien body-builder dude and Jesse Ventura has to save her..."

By this point, Craig was so far ahead that Brian was practically yelling to still be heard, but he was getting tired of talking and half-jogging at the same time, so he gave up and started eating his Cookies & Creme instead, which was now mostly a melted puddle in his hand. Still, it was a damn good chocolate, so he could hardly let it go to waste.

Brian saw the flashing red sirens well before he reached Keith's large, white, and black house. Two cop cars and an ambulance were parked out front, and a small crowd was gathered to see what was going on. A skinny officer with an ugly moustache that Brian recognized was trying to keep the crowd back. Craig was harassing the cop, asking him questions.

"C'mon Officer, that's my uncle's house." Craig was aggressively trying to get in the cop's face. Probably those newspaper reporter instincts. "Can you please tell me what's going on?"

"Kid, I already told you, please back off," said the cop, his nose and thin moustache twitching like some kind of rodent.

Brian approached, wiping his sticky fingers on his grey sweatpants. The cop nodded to him and said, "Hey, Skidmark."

Craig turned at Brian and glared at him.

"What's up Constable... Bennett?"

"Brake, actually. Bennett is my partner."

"Really? That's super dumb. Why would they put two guys with such similar names together? I bet that confuses everybody. Anyway, is everything okay? Did something happen to Keith?"

Constable Brake shook his head. "It's not Keith."

At that moment, a pair of medics carried a long black bag on a stretcher out of the house. Some of the women in the crowd gasped. Brake tried to back them away, but the onlookers just pressed closer. Brian wondered if it was a body in the bag or just like some hockey equipment or something.

Craig was hopping up and down trying to get a look, and Bryan had never seen anyone that worked up about smelly ice skates or corpses. "Is that Cecil Doucette? How did he die?"

"Was it Satan worshippers?" Brian asked.

Craig's neck whipped around so hard he nearly gave himself whiplash. "*What?!*"

"I heard it from kids at school. Did you know they sacrifice people up behind the dump?"

"Back off, kids. I'm sorry, I can't say anything." Brake bodily pushed the skinny kid away while ignoring the other onlookers, trying to get a closer look more subtly.

A pair of cops came out of the house, one of whom looked like the bad guy from Abraxas, except clean-shaven. He was tall, buff, and blond, like He-Man in an RCMP uniform. He appeared to be in charge.

Brian, who was pretty confident he could read lips thanks to all the episodes of Star Trek he watched with the sound off in the middle of the night while his family was asleep, carefully studied the blond sergeant as he talked to the other cop. He was sure the boss told him to, "Grope Hiccup Key the Deuce Set." Or maybe it was, "Go Pick Huh Pack East Douche Hat." He wondered if it was some kind of code. Those Mounties were sneaky, using codes designed to stump skilled lip-readers from eavesdropping on their conversation.

Of course, Brian could also be completely wrong. What they said might have been, "Go Pick Up Keith Doucette," but Brian quickly brushed that off. That one couldn't possibly be right.

CHAPTER TWENTY-SIX

I'll Remember
Thursday, October 27
3:55 pm

Niall dreamed about people he didn't know.

He saw their faces, frozen in horror and death. Were they... underwater? It was dark and murky. Sometimes, he had dreams like this, being at the bottom of the sea. Usually, the dreams didn't bother him. Sure, it was weird and disconcerting, but he usually didn't see drowned corpses.

These dead souls had come a long way, dragged across the bottom of the sea. He could see the trail on the mud and the murk, like the path worn into the field across from the library that the kids cut across on their way to school. How many bodies had been dragged out here? And why?

He felt the weight of unfathomable tonnes of water pressing down on him. It was mildly uncomfortable but not debilitating. Why wasn't he scared? He was at the bottom of the sea; why wasn't he scared?

And then came the flash of lightning. A brilliant blue fork of energy that seared his retinas and left the ocean water boiling. In the flash of illumination, for a split second, he saw a face he recognized. Nelson, his brother, looked back at him. But Nelson wasn't a corpse like the others. He was alive, alert and awake. He was looking right at Niall, his mouth moving to make words Niall couldn't make out.

And then Nelson screamed soundlessly, and Niall woke up. He lay in bed for a few minutes, staring at the ceiling. It was so weird; he was sure he hadn't heard Nelson's voice in his dream, but he *had* heard it. These dreams were getting so strange.

He hoped it was just a dream. He'd had other visions like this that had turned out to be true.

The house was silent. He was sure he'd heard Nelson's voice, but that wasn't possible. According to the clock on his bedside table, he must have fallen asleep after school. His parents and Nelson should still be at work, and Nana was usually out for her afternoon walk at this time.

Niall rolled out of bed dressed in only his boxers, nearly stepping on Joey Smallwood. The cat hissed at him. Niall pulled on a Star Wars t-shirt and stumbled to the kitchen to look for food. His mom or Nana would probably get mad at him for ruining his supper, but what was he supposed to do? He was a growing boy.

Niall had barely sat down with a bowl of cereal when a fierce pounding came at the door. Before he could react, the knocking came again, more incessant.

"Niall, open up! I know you're in there."

It was Harper's voice.

Instinctively, he jumped up and rushed to the door. Millions of thoughts race through his head. Why was she here? Did she want to clear the air? Did she want him to apologize? Give him another chance?

He yanked the door open. Harper was standing there in cargo pants and a jean jacket. Her black hair was pinned back hastily and sticking out in numerous directions.

She looked him up and down. "Nice drawers."

Niall, embarrassed, put his hands in front of him. What was he thinking, going to the door with no pants on? You would think all those nightmares about showing up to school naked would have taught him a lesson. Still, he couldn't let this opportunity slip away.

"Harper, I'm sorry about the other night—"

She held up a palm. "Talk to the hand. I don't want to hear it. I don't care who you're seeing or if you're a stoner or a drunk now or what. I'm not here for you or for me."

"What are you talking about?"

Niall saw a horrible fear pass over Harper's face. His stomach clenched. He hadn't seen her like this since the tunnels two years ago. "It's Pius. He's gone. And so is Rebecca."

"What?"

"They disappeared. Pius was watching Rebecca after school yesterday while Aunt Sam ran to the grocery store, and when she got back, they were gone."

Niall's stomach pains moved further south, and his intestines felt like they were tied in knots. Neither Pius nor Harper had been in school today, but he'd barely noticed. He'd been too busy thinking about Stacey and how he'd made a fool of himself in front of Harper's mom... "I'm sure there's a logical explanation..."

"Where the hell would Pius go, Niall? With his baby sister? They've been gone all night."

She was right, of course. Pius was just getting over his fear of the dark and was super-protective of his little sister. He would never take her out of the house unless it was an extreme emergency. And what kind of emergency would have kept him away all night?

"I don't know. What do you want to do?"

"Find them. And as much as I hate to admit it, I might need your help."

Niall nodded. Outside of their awkward conversations the last few days and his puking on her and her mother, Niall and Harper hadn't spoken much in over a year. This was going to be weird. But if Pius was in trouble...

He'd asked Niall to come over yesterday.

"Let's go," said Niall.

He took a step forward, and Harper stopped him. "Put on some pants, butthead."

CHAPTER TWENTY-SEVEN

Basket Case
Thursday, October 27
4:00 pm

Skidmark was sitting across from Craig Muise in a booth at ZigZag Pizza. Craig had his notebook open on the table before him, trying desperately to interview the round, shaggy-haired boy without much success. For his part, Skidmark was shoving a donair in his face, smearing himself, the table, and his backpack beside him with gooey donair sauce. He somehow got some of the sweet garlic sauce on Craig, too.

"C'mon, you must know something about Keith." Craig was on the verge of pulling his hair out. "You guys hang out, right?"

"What do you want from me?" Skidmark licked his fingers. "I thought you were his cousin?"

"We're related, but I barely know him. Cecil Doucette was married to my mom's sister, but most of the family never liked Cec. After Aunt Julia moved away, we never saw him or Keith much."

"I need another Pineapple Crush..."

"Skidmark! Brian! Focus, please. Tell me about Keith."

"We play D&D, Magic and Super Baseball Simulator on the Super NES. Keith always makes teams of giant black dudes. Is that what you mean?"

"No, that's not what I... Keith is a bully and a hard case. Everyone has been beaten up by him or has seen him beat up somebody. Did he ever talk about doing anything to his father?"

Skidmark shrugged. "Like beating him to death with a baseball bat? I mean, haven't we all been mad enough to threaten to kill our parents?"

Craig cringed. "I... guess?"

"I mean, I certainly have, but my parents have been known to lock me in a closet in the basement for days at a time. I have my own toilet bucket and everything. But I doubt Keith can formulate any specific plans about murdering his dad since he's drunk all the time—Keith, not his dad, I don't know anything about the late Mr. Doucette's drinking habits. But Mr. Doucette did rip Keith's earring out in the middle of Main Street the other day, totally humiliating him. If he does that in public, you can imagine what he does at home. I wonder if Keith has his own toilet bucket? I should ask him the next time I see him, probably when he's in jail. Do you know when visiting hours are at jail?"

Craig, who had started taking notes, had since given up and was now staring slack-jawed at Skidmark. He shook his head.

"Oh well, I guess we can go ask. While we're at the police station, we should probably also mention that Keith's dad sent dirtbag redneck assassins to kill him. I don't think it's fair that they're blaming Keith for murder when his dad tried to do it first."

This caught Craig's attention. "Wait, his dad tried to kill him?"

"No, I said his dad hired redneck assassins to kill him. Actually, I don't think they were actually assassins, Keith said he thought one of them was a plumber. Maybe assassination was just a side gig, like how Han Solo rescued Princess Leia for money. Rescuing people wasn't his job. He was a smuggler by trade, he just happened to be in the right place at the right time and was a good enough businessman to know—"

"Skidmark, shut up. Do the cops know about this?"

"I would imagine the cops know about Han Solo. I mean, Star Wars is a classic movie that came out over fifteen years ago..."

"I mean about someone trying to kill Keith! Did anyone else see this?"

"Pius did. The hitmen followed us home from Timmies. At least one of them had a gun."

Craig fell back into his seat, covering his mouth. "There was more than one of them? And they had guns?"

"*One* of them had *a* gun. That we saw. I think it's important to keep your facts straight, otherwise, no one will take you seriously."

"And the next day, Pius disappeared? You don't think this was worth telling the cops about?"

Skidmark shrugged as he stuffed the last bite of donair into his mouth. He swallowed it whole, like a gull, then chased it with a huge gulp of Pepsi. "I think you're majorly overreacting to the situation. Seriously, shit like this happens to us *all the time.*"

"We're going to tell the cops. *Now.*" Craig stood up to leave. When he did, Skidmark caught sight of the woman behind him standing at the counter, and froze.

The donair, which was only halfway down his throat, threatened to come back up again. He tried to swallow it, and it felt like a rock settling into his stomach.

Craig must have noticed his discomfort. "Brian, you okay?"

Skidmark gestured to a tall, buxom woman with jet-black hair standing at the counter. She was wearing what appeared to be a black velvet cape. "That's my wife."

"Your what?"

"I mean, she was supposed to be my wife until her boyfriend died, and she got all depressed, and Mrs. Walsh fell hopelessly in love with me."

"Skidmark, what are you talking about?"

"Shit, she's coming over this way." Brian tried to slip under the table the way he'd seen Niall do countless times, except his middle was much larger than Niall's, and he got stuck halfway.

"Skidmark!" Anna chirped. Her black lips curled into a smile that made Brian's insides shiver. "Fancy running into you here!"

"I'm always here at 4:00 on Wednesday for a large donair and a Pepsi." He struggled to get back to an upright sitting position. "I get my allowance after school on Wednesday, and I have to get my donair before I blow the money on something stupid. Don't touch that!"

Anna had reached to move Skidmark's backpack and sit down, but Skidmark jumped on the bag like a wounded bear protecting her young. "My Magic cards are in there!"

"Right," Anna rolled her eyes under her thick makeup and sat down opposite Skidmark, beside Craig instead. "Who's your friend?"

"This is Craig. He's investigating Keith's dad's murder."

Anna's smile vanished, and she became paler than usual, which was shocking. She was nearly translucent. Craig just grimaced.

Craig looked uncomfortable, but Skidmark could imagine why. If Anna was squeezed into the booth next to him, he would float on sunshine. He cursed himself for jumping on his bag so quickly. But they were his cards, man. He almost had a complete set of Serra Angels.

Craig cleared his throat. "I'm not investigating anything. Cecil was my uncle. I thought I might have a story for the school paper, but this is getting too big for the St. Paul's Examiner."

"I guess so. Keith's dad? That's terrible."

"Not really." Skidmark shrugged. "He's an asshole."

"Anyway," said Craig, "we were just on our way to the police station to tell them some information about Keith, so if you'll excuse us..."

Anna bit her lip, and Skidmark's heart fluttered. Was she flirting with him? "What kind of information?"

"Just some stuff that Craig thinks will get Keith off, but I think he's trying to be Clark Kent without the cape."

Craig had to ask Anna to move twice before she let him out of the booth. She seemed to not want them to go. Maybe she really did have feelings for him that she hadn't realized until she saw him today? Skidmark was conflicted. On the one hand, he should try to help his buddy out. On the other hand... boobs.

Anna sat back down in the booth across from Brian. She looked him directly in the eyes, and Brian found it hard to breathe. "You wanna stay and chat some more?" she asked.

Brian's heart was screaming at his pants. Why didn't Anna tell him how she felt before he started a serious relationship with Mrs. Walsh? Well, serious on his side, anyway. She hadn't expressed her true feelings yet, which was understandable, as she was married and twenty-five years older than him.

Craig called from the door. "Skidmark, come on!"

Crap, now his head was yelling at the rest of his body. He should at least try to help Keith. They'd been through a lot together. If Anna really cared about him, she'd understand.

Skidmark stood up from the booth. Anna looked surprised. "You're going?"

"We can continue this chat later. Where can I find you?"

Anna's black lips turned down, and her eyes became blank and cold. Brian knew he often had trouble reading people's facial expressions, but this one gave him a sense of discomfort and unease he'd never known before. It wasn't sexy at all.

"Don't worry. I'll find *you*."

<u>**CHAPTER TWENTY-EIGHT**</u>

Bounce
Thursday, October 27
4:18 pm

The place across the street from the Jeddores' yellow house was a two-storey with blue vinyl siding. There was always a white pickup truck parked out front. As long as Niall had been coming here, and he had known Pius since the first grade, that truck had never moved.

They had come straight over here without speaking. Despite the situation's awkwardness, Pius was too important to both of them, and Niall would do just about anything for his best friend. Still, he started to feel a bit uncomfortable approaching that weird house on Townsview Street.

"You sure this is a good idea?" Niall asked. Mr. Parsons always creeped Niall out more than Pee-Wee Herman and Mr. Rogers combined. If he had been watching Harper through the window, Niall felt his dislike of the man was well founded.

"Are you sure wearing leather pants was a good idea?"

Niall looked down at the black leather pants he'd pulled on before leaving the house and sighed. The first six times Harper had mentioned it, he'd been embarrassed, but now he was just getting annoyed. "I told you, all my other clothes were in the wash!"

"Where did you even get those?"

Niall did not think stories about hanging out with Stacey and her friends were a good topic of conversation right now. "Don't change the subject. Do you really think we should be questioning random old weirdos?"

"You are not seriously afraid of an old pervert, are you?"

Harper had a point. Next to some of the stuff they'd faced, Mr. Parsons would be a Care Bear.

Harper marched up the cracked concrete steps and pounded on the door. She was always very direct. When no answer came within thirty seconds, she pounded again.

"Maybe he's not home."

"He's always home." She looked into the small window beside the door and nodded. "Yup, I see him creeping behind a chair in the living room."

"He's hiding from you?"

"I did tell him if I caught him peeping on me, I would shoot him in the guts."

"He believed you?"

"I was holding my dad's .22 at the time."

Niall tried to imagine Harper showing up at a neighbour's house with a rifle in her hands. He was not surprised that he could picture it perfectly.

"Mister Parsons!" Harper called through the door. "It's Harper from across the street!"

"Piss off!"

"I'm not here to shoot you. I want to ask you a few questions about what you saw last night."

Harper was so direct and to the point. She would hate to hear it, but she would be a good cop. She reminded Niall of Sergeant Tanguay.

"I didn't see nothing! I already told the Mounties."

Harper tried the knob. "It's locked." She stepped back and nodded to Niall. "Open it."

She had asked Niall to do many things, but this was new. "I don't know how to pick a lock. And if you think I can kick the door in, you must remember my physical prowess through rose-tinted glasses."

Harper rolled her eyes at him. Niall had forgotten how much he missed that. "I didn't bring you along for her stunning fashion sense or sparkling conversation." She removed a safety pin from her jacket. She used it to prick the tip of her finger. A tiny drop of blood pooled on the soft brown flesh. "Use this."

Niall felt cold shivers run through his entire body. "You want me to use magic?" He hadn't used this power in over a year. "Is that enough blood?"

"You don't need to burn the house down. Just open the lock." She held out her finger.

He had told her he never wanted to do this again. Several times since Keenan's death, he tried to look more into magic and spells and started to read a few books, though they were hard to find in a town like Gale Harbour. He always got scared and gave up within a couple of days. He broke up with Harper to ensure they could never use this power and hurt anyone else. Harper accepted his decision, and they'd barely had any contact until the last few days. But now here she was, basically demanding he use it.

"Niall, come on. This is why I asked you here. I need you to do this for Pius."

Niall nodded. Pius and his sister were in trouble. If anything warranted breaking his promise to himself, this was it.

With great trepidation, Niall touched his fingertip to hers. The ice in his veins was replaced with heat—not just because of the unnatural energy that shot through his body but also because of the sheer joy of touching Harper again.

With the blood pounding in his head, Niall concentrated on the lock. He could see every detail with perfect clarity, every scratch in the metal around the thin keyhole. He realized at that moment he had missed the rush of power, though this was strange and different. He had never used his abilities like this before; in the past, he had always lashed out chaotically, desperately, trying to save himself or those around him. Now, using such fine control, he discovered he could not only see the lock, but he could see *inside* the lock. Every tumbler stood out to him, and he was sure that with just a little effort, he could slide them into place...

"Hurry up, Niall," Harper chided, and his concentration slipped. Like a screwdriver sliding off the head of a screw, Niall felt the barely-controlled energy in his mind burst out into the lock, and the mechanism inside the doorknob exploded with a screech. Shards of metal shot out of the handle, scrapping Niall's hand and bouncing off his leather pants.

Harper nodded in approval. "That was pretty impressive," she admitted, opening the door.

Niall didn't bother telling her that it wasn't what he was trying to do. He was happy that the small, controlled use of power didn't leave him feeling as exhausted as usual.

They stepped into the porch and saw just the top of Parsons' bald head as he ducked behind the chair.

"We know you're hiding behind the armchair, dumbass," Harper called out.

"I'm calling the cops! And you owe me for a new door!"

Harper snorted. "Oh please, it was just the doorknob."

"I'm serious, you dirty freaking kids think you can just bust in here and do whatever the hell you want!"

"Like you do, you friggin' creep?"

"I've got a gun! I swear to God, I'm not afraid to use it!"

"Shut up, asswipe!"

Why was Harper aggravating this guy? They broke into *his* house. Niall wanted to leave, but they had to find out what Parsons knew. He just wished the old man would shut up...

Niall felt a twinge of energy leave his body, like when he broke the lock a moment ago. He still had some of the power left in him? Usually, it all went out in a torrent, but he had never used a controlled amount before as he did with the door. How much of Harper's blood power could he hold? And how long could he hold it?

It took Niall a moment to realize the room was quiet. Parsons was silent. Niall's heart rate quickened, and he felt his hands felt cold.

The power. He'd used it on Mr. Parsons.

Had he killed him?

Unaware of the turmoil inside Niall, Harper stepped into the living room. "What did you see at my house last night, Mr. Parsons?"

The answer came slow and slurred as if the man was finding it difficult to speak. The anger and agitation from a moment ago were gone entirely. "I... I already told you... and... and the cops. I saw nothing."

Niall breathed a sigh of relief. So he hadn't killed Parsons, but what had he done? Scrambled his brain in some way? Why did the man sound like a drunk six-year-old?

"I know you're staring at our house all the time. You expected me to believe you didn't see anything?"

A long pause. "I d-don't look at your house..."

"I saw you just a couple of days ago. And last week, and the week before that. You're a dirty peeping Tom, you can't friggin' help yourself. Now you're going to tell me what you saw, or I'm telling the cops that you're a pervert and you'll never be allowed within five hundred feet of a school or playground again."

Another long silence. Was Harper blackmailing this guy? And how long had he been creeping on her? Niall wasn't sure what he would have done if he'd known, but it probably involved setting the man's testicles on fire. He didn't feel so bad about scrambling his brain anymore either.

"So, you w-won't tell the cops?" he asked finally.

"What did you see?"

Parsons sighed. "There w-was a girl over there."

"You're lying. Pius would never have a girl over to the house."

"No, I swear! She was late teens, maybe twenty or so…" His speech was coming faster and clearer now. Fortunately, whatever Niall did to him seemed to be wearing off.

"So too old for you," Harper muttered under her breath.

"She had dark black hair, probably dyed. Dressed all in black, too. Chest out to here."

Parsons was still behind the armchair, so they couldn't see precisely what "out to here" was, but Niall had a pretty good idea. He and Harper stared at each other. Neither said a word, but he was sure they both knew what the other was thinking.

Anna Chaffey? What the hell was she doing in town?

"When did she come by?" Harper demanded.

"I dunno, about 7 o'clock. The Jeddore kid opened the door and let her in. I didn't see them leave, but Samantha got home a little while later and started screaming 'cause the kids were missing."

Niall was disgusted. "And you didn't tell the cops any of this?"

"If he told them, he'd have to explain why he was watching so closely, not to mention the telescope upstairs that's pointed at my bedroom. He's a coward and a pervert."

"I told you everything I know. Now, will you get out of my house?"

"I better not find out there's more to the story you're not telling me, or I'll come back and shoot you in the balls myself."

"Nothing! I know nothing, I swear!"

Harper moved as if to charge at the armchair, stomping her Doc Marten-booted foot and causing a picture frame on the end table to rattle and fall over. Parsons yelped.

"C'mon, Niall," she said, heading for the door.

He followed her out, awkwardly shutting the busted door behind them. "Are we looking for Anna? I wouldn't know where to start…"

"No, we're calling the cops, they need to know—Niall!"

Niall took a step off the front porch and fell into darkness.

He was in deep space. Or underwater, he couldn't be sure. He was surrounded by infinite blackness, but he wasn't afraid. It was the same dream he'd had many times before, but something was different this time.

He was moving. Slowly, inexorably, crawling across—yes, he was definitely crawling—the ocean floor. He couldn't see it but could feel it underneath his... not hands, not exactly—some kind of limbs.

There was a tiny pinprick of light, as if it were a thousand kilometres away, but it was right in front of him—a tiny speck of heat and light into the empty void. Niall felt himself scooping it up with his appendage and stuffing it into something he could only describe as a mouth.

Energy burst inside him. A microscopic spark, not unlike the feeling he'd just gotten from touching Harper's blood. But it wasn't the same. Harper's blood gave him a warm, powerful glow. This energy felt greasy and unpleasant, like a clawed hand grasping his heart.

Red eyes opened—familiar, unmistakable red eyes that were his and not his at the same time. Niall gasped and woke up.

Harper was kneeling over him, haloed by the sun. His knee and head hurt, but the sight of Harper filled his chest with a warm, fluttering strength.

"Niall! Are you okay?"

"What happened?" He tried to get up, and pain shot like stars across his vision. He must have hit his head.

"We were walking out of the house, and you just keeled over."

With great difficulty, Niall brought himself up to a sitting position. "It's alive."

"What?"

"The Primordial One... The Psycho Hose Beast. It's awake. And it's moving."

CHAPTER TWENTY-NINE

Nutshell
Thursday (?)
???

Pius woke up in darkness. The hood was gone off his head, but he still couldn't see. His hands were free, so he felt around and found himself in a small room no bigger than a closet. The walls were rough wood. There was a door, but it was locked from the other side.

He hadn't fought when Anna pulled the knife on him. He froze in terror and went along with everything she said. He asked questions, but she didn't answer any of them. She told him what to do—grab Rebecca, get diapers and formula, move quickly, and be quiet. Rebecca started to fuss when Pius picked her up, but he quickly lulled her back to sleep. She was snoring gently when Anna led them out of the house, where a black van pulled up and two men jumped out and grabbed Pius. Anna took Rebecca carefully and promised she wouldn't be hurt. Pius couldn't say anything else before the men pulled a hood over his head and shoved him into the van.

Pius had a lot of time to think while lying facedown on the van floor. Who were those men? Why was Anna doing this? He should have fought her when she was alone. He might have had a chance, even against her big hunting knife. He could have grabbed a weapon, could have tricked her somehow or locked himself in a bedroom. But he was so shocked and terrified that he couldn't do anything. He just went along like an idiot and handed himself and his sister over to lunatics, and now there was no chance to escape.

During the ride, Pius realized he knew the men who'd grabbed him. It was the guys who had chased Keith that night at Tim Hortons.

Was this related to whatever was going on with Keith and his father? Had Pius gotten himself and Rebecca into some terrible danger just for helping Keith? *Why would they target Rebecca, though?* It didn't make sense.

Then again, what if they had never been following Keith in the first place? What if they had been following him? Pius couldn't imagine any reason why anyone would want to kill or kidnap him. Well, he could imagine quite a few, but they were mostly irrational. The first thought was that it had something to do with burning the school down last year. Or friends of the creepers that were looking for a bomb in Gale Harbour. Or agents working for the United States or the Department of National Defence pissed off about how their schemes to capture the monster were foiled. None of those possibilities made sense to use dirtbag baymen. That Mr. Doucette was after him for being Keith's friend was actually the most likely scenario.

But how was Anna involved in this? What did she have to do with any of those people? Was this part of her revenge for Keenan's death? Keenan's death was an accident, though, and as far as Pius knew, she never blamed Niall for it. Why would she come after him and Rebecca?

Pius' thoughts went in circles as they drove into the night. He must have drifted off to sleep because the next thing he remembered was being dragged out of the van, then his hands tied behind him before being force-marched over rough terrain through trees that scratched and tore at him. At least the heavy cloth bag protected his face. He guessed they travelled about half a kilometre but couldn't be sure. He asked about Rebecca, and Anna said she had the baby and she was safe. Then, one of the men told him to shut up, and Pius felt the barrel of a gun placed against the back of his head. Pius whimpered and spoke no more.

At the end of their journey, he heard a door open and was shoved head-first into open space. With his hands tied behind him, there was no way to catch himself, and Pius landed face-first on the hard wooden floor. He heard Anna admonishing the man as he lost consciousness.

Now he was awake again, his head pounding in time with his heartbeat. There was dry blood on his forehead and a painful gash above his right eye. His hands were free, but he was still trapped. Feeling around, his hands brushed against his glasses, which he put back on his stinging face. At least one of the lenses felt cracked, not that it made a difference in the darkness.

He went over the room three more times before giving up, convinced there was no obvious way out. He returned to the same hopeless cycle of thoughts that brought him no answers before. All he kept coming back to was that he had screwed up, that he should have acted faster, and maybe he and Rebecca wouldn't be in this mess.

The door opened. For a split second, Pius considered charging whoever was there, but then he second-guessed himself and froze. What if it was one of those huge men? What if they had a gun or a knife? He hesitated and did nothing but cower and stare.

Anna stood in the doorway, silhouetted by moonlight. Her figure was unmistakable. She was unarmed.

Of anyone who had opened the door, she might have been the one person he could've gotten past. Pius cursed himself again and nearly started to cry.

"Are you okay?" she asked.

Pius laughed bitterly. "You kidnapped me and my sister, and you're asking if I'm okay?"

Her features were hard to see, but Pius thought she might look concerned. "The brothers were a bit too rough. I'm sorry."

"Where is Rebecca?"

"She's perfectly safe and comfortable. Don't worry. You and your sister will be well cared for. You're too important."

"What are you talking about?"

Anna took a deep breath. "There's no harm in telling you now. If you cooperate, this will all be easier for everyone. The Primordial One—the Psycho Hose Beast—is about to return."

Pius' heart rate quickened. It felt like it was trying to claw its way out of his chest. *That's not possible…*

"The people I'm working with, we've been watching the signs for a long time. We found the creature at the mouth of the Bay, where Niall imprisoned it two years ago. But it's fighting its way out and coming back toward Gale Harbour."

Pius wanted to say that was ridiculous, but he couldn't. It had come after them once. Then killer June bugs fell out of the sky, and another giant monster appeared nine months later. Nothing was impossible in this town.

"Then find Niall and Harper! They're the ones who can stop this, not me."

Anna shook her head. "Niall and Harper are kids. They couldn't stop it before. I don't think they could do it now. But I've studied Theolina Kane's spellbooks."

"I thought your book was destroyed." Pius had burned it himself at the school through sheer negligence and incompetence.

"There were... other copies. Plus, the people I work with have other powers. We can deal with the Primordial One properly this time. We just need your blood."

The blood she was talking about—Pius' blood—went cold. His pounding heart slowed, and everything around him shifted into stark, perfect clarity. It was like time slowed down.

That's why they wanted Pius and Rebecca. Because they thought they had the same magical blood as Harper.

Pius started to open his mouth to say that he and Rebecca didn't have the same blood as Harper, that the blood of Kluskap came from his father, Dick Jeddore, who was the son of William Jeddore. Pius' father, Raymond, was the son of Gerrard Doyle. Gerrard died when Raymond was very young, and his mother then married William Jeddore. Raymond and Pius didn't share the Blood of the Blood, the direct line from Kluskap, the First Hunter.

Pius started to open his mouth to explain this, then stopped himself. He and Rebecca were here because Anna and her cronies thought they had magic blood. They would no longer have value if they found out they didn't. Pius seriously doubted they would just casually let them go if they found out otherwise. Their mistaken belief in them being Blood of the Blood was the only thing keeping them alive.

Pius gritted his teeth and bit his tongue. Finally, he managed to say, "So what is happening now?"

"We wait. But not for long. There's not a lot of time left. Rebecca and you are safe, but I'll try to get you somewhere more comfortable. You're a smart kid, Pius. Surely, you know there's no other way. You're going to help us, right?"

"I guess I don't have a choice, do I?"

Anna looked sad and tired. "No, I guess you don't. But it will make things easier if you help us willingly. The faster we deal with the Primordial One, the fewer people it can hurt."

She turned and went to close the door again, and Pius felt a sudden surge of panic. He didn't want to be locked in there. He was helpless in there, trapped in the darkness like an animal waiting for slaughter. But how could he possibly get out?

"Where are you going?" Pius asked just as Anna was closing the door.

"To get the other piece of the equation. To bring in Nelson."

Pius almost choked. How could she...? But of course. If she thought Pius and Rebecca shared the Blood of the Blood with Harper, then, of course, she would come to the same conclusion that Niall and Nelson shared the same abilities.

Unfortunately for Nelson, Anna didn't know what Pius had figured out last week.

Anna left the small room, and the door closed, the knob glinting silver in the moonlight before it vanished into darkness. Pius took a deep breath. He was alive only by pure chance and wasn't sure how long it would last. He had to act quickly to find Rebecca and get the heck out of there.

Fortunately, thanks to Anna's visit, he had an idea.

<u>**CHAPTER THIRTY**</u>

Hook
Thursday, October 27
5:15 pm

"Well, you've certainly spent a lot of time here lately." Mrs. Murphy led Harper and Niall to a desk at the RCMP detachment, a cheery smile on her round, red face. "You wait here, loves. Constable Bennett will be out in a few minutes to take your statements."

Harper leaned over to Niall. "What's she talking about?"

"I was here with Pius a few days ago. To make a statement about Keith's father abusing him."

"Right. Pius told me about that."

Harper seemed distracted. She was not her usual confident self. She must have been worried about Pius; they both were. Not to mention, there was the imminent return of the Psycho Hose Beast. Niall wished he could hold her hand to comfort her. Their mutual discomfort was not making the situation any better.

Trying to distract them from the crushing dread hanging over their heads like a pick-up truck on a tangled thread of dental floss, Harper blurted out, "So what's going on with you and that Stacey chick?"

Niall's guts contracted into a tight ball in his abdomen. He opened and closed his mouth a few times before remembering how to make words. *This was supposed to be better?* "Nothing. I mean, maybe something? We never really defined it or anything..."

"I'm not surprised. I waited months for you to ask me out. She's probably waiting for the same."

Once they had discovered their feelings for each other—or Harper had acknowledged his existence, anyway—after the incident with the Psycho Hose Beast, it had taken months for Niall to ask Harper on an official date. He had asked other girls out before, but he didn't seem capable when it came to someone he liked. Probably because his track record with the other girls was so miserable.

It was so awkward talking to Harper about Stacey. He liked them both but in different ways. Harper was dark, both in complexion and demeanour. She was not only his first crush but exciting, unobtainable, and *other*. It was hard to describe. They had so much history together. For better or worse, their lives and fates were intertwined.

Stacey was the opposite, as different from Harper as Sega and Nintendo. Stacey was bright and bouncy, both her hair and her personality. Not only was she new and uncomplicated, but there was something normal about her and her friends. Niall was the weird one in that relationship. He had always been surrounded by weirdos and freaks, so he had never imagined being the weird one himself. He kinda liked it.

Niall could contemplate his romantic interests and compare them all day, and doing so was marginally better than thinking about what was lurking out in Bay, but he didn't want to talk to Harper about it. He was more than a little relieved when Constable Murphy led Skidmark and Craig Muise into the office. The oddness of the duo was enough to cut off their current conversation.

"You know these two boys, too, right?" Constable Murphy asked. "Well, I guess Burt is going to be busy taking statements. You can all wait here 'til he gets in."

Craig Muise was tall and skinny, while Skidmark was short and the opposite of skinny. The pair were on opposite ends of the social strata. While Niall wondered what the two of them were doing together, Harper was able to express his feelings very bluntly and to the point.

"What the hell are you two doing here?" she demanded.

"I have no idea," Skidmark grumbled as he and Craig sat in a pair of chairs opposite Niall and Harper. He cocked his head at Niall. "Why are you wearing leather pants?"

Niall ignored him and turned to Craig, who looked like he was about to choke Skidmark with his bare hands. Niall was quite familiar with the expression and had experienced that desire more than once himself. "Skidmark—Brian—has some important news about Keith Doucette that he needs to share with the police."

"About Keith?" Niall asked. "What about Keith?"

"Keith murdered his dad this morning," said Skidmark.

"What?!" Niall and Harper's voices were so perfectly in unison that he wasn't sure she had spoken. He wasn't sure of anything. Keith had killed his father? That wasn't possible.

Craig put up a hand to prevent Skidmark from blurting out anything else. "I guess you didn't know. Sorry that you had to hear it like this. Cecil Doucette was found dead in his home this morning. Keith was arrested under suspicion of murder—I don't know if that part has gotten out to the news yet, but he's probably locked up in this very building. I made Skidmark come down here to tell the police about how he, Keith, and Pius were chased a few nights ago by armed men who possibly worked for Mr. Doucette."

"What?" Niall and Harper were so good at this that you'd swear they practiced.

"Why the hell didn't Pius tell me this?" Harper demanded. Skidmark and Craig shrunk away under her fury.

"You've been busy with your mom," Niall offered. "Did you see him the day before he disappeared?"

Harper bit her lip and said nothing. Niall cringed. He hadn't meant to hurt Harper's feelings, but he suspected a part of her felt guilty for what had happened to Pius. Niall cleared his throat and spoke to break the silence. "That's so messed up. What happened, Skidmark?"

Brian told them the story, but because it was coming from him, it took about ten minutes longer than necessary and included two tangents into the plot of *True Lies*. Niall was pretty sure he'd gotten the gist of it—the story about the rednecks with the guns, not *True Lies*—but taken together with everything else that was going on... "That's just so nuts. So, a day after you are chased by men with guns, Pius goes missing? And then Keith's father turns up dead? This can't be a coincidence."

Gale Harbour was a small town. Weird stuff happened here regularly, and it was always connected somehow.

"And what does Anna Chaffey have to do with this?" Harper asked.

That probably should have been a non sequitur, primarily since they hadn't explained the connection between Anna and Pius' disappearance, but Skidmark answered without missing a beat.

"Oh, we saw Anna at Zig Zag. She's still looking as hot as ever."

"What?"

Seriously, it was like they shared one brain.

Constable Bennett strolled in at this moment, round and sweaty as usual but looking more haggard. His moustache was scraggly, and he hadn't shaved in a few days.

"Hello, kids," he said, managing a yellow-toothed grin. "If you're here to see Keith, I'm sorry, that's not allowed right now. Or are you here to tell me about some new monster in the sewers?"

Bennett winked. Harper and Niall looked at each other and squirmed. How much did he know? They thought only Sergeant Tanguay was supposed to know. Niall hoped they would see her, too, to tell her about his vision.

Bennett chuckled. "Go on with you, I'm just kidding. To tell you the truth though, there's too much seriousness going around right now. I wouldn't mind an alligator in the sewer or maybe a Bigfoot or two."

Craig cleared his throat and spoke first. Niall still wasn't sure why he was here. "Well, sir, I'm sorry we have more seriousness to add to your pile."

And so they told the whole story, going back and forth between Skidmark and Harper, with Niall and Craig interjecting on occasion to keep them on track. They told the Mountie about the men who followed Pius and Keith home. About the neighbour who spotted Anna at Pius' house right before he disappeared. About Craig and Skidmark seeing Anna just hours ago. Niall didn't mention his vision of the Psycho Hose Beast, lest he discredit the rest of their very important story.

Sitting at the desk beside the kids, Bennett scribbled furiously into his notebook as they spoke. He filled several pages. He tapped the spiral binding with his pen when they reached the end, deep in thought.

"That's right odd, now. I was just thinking about Anna Chaffey the other day. I mean, she came up in another investigation. I mean, never mind. You kids don't need to know anything about that." He cleared his throat, his cheeks flushed red. "You have anything to add? I sure hope not. It's going to take me all night to type this up as it is..."

"Well, actually—" Skidmark started to say, but all three other kids raised their hands to stop him.

Niall spoke the quickest, "Brian, does this have anything to do with what we came to tell the Constable?"

Skidmark seemed to mull this over. "No," he said carefully.

"Is Sergeant Tanguay here?" Niall asked him.

The Constable's face fell, and his ruddy cheeks grew pale. He cleared his throat and shuffled the papers on the desk uncomfortably.

"Um, Sergeant Tanguay will be out on leave... until further notice."

Niall's heart sank. "I thought she was back to work?"

"She was, but, uh, she just needs a little more time." He cleared his throat again and tried to shake off his unease. "Anyway, if there's nothing else, you kids run on home, and I'll call you if I have any questions..."

"Hey, Burt!" Constable Murphy called from the other room. "You talking about that Chaffey girl?"

"The one with the knockers, yes," Bennett called back. Niall felt Harper stiffen with indignation.

"Just got a call that someone matching her description was spotted with the O'Neil kid."

All eyes turned to Niall, who somehow felt his face flush and drain simultaneously. It was some sort of negative energy situation. "What?"

"Not you, your brother. Rumour has it they've been canoodling all over town."

CHAPTER THIRTY-ONE

Who Am I (What's My Name)?
Thursday, October 27
Thursday 6:10pm

Brian stood at the counter of Fred's Emporium, seething with anger. On the other side of the glass case, the store's proprietor smirked a sly, shit-eating grin that made Brian want to climb over the cabinet of stolen watches and jewelry to punch the son-of-a-bitch in the face.

Fred's Emporium at the Hansen Mall, not far from the RCMP Detachment, was ostensibly a pawn shop, but realistically, it was just a fence for all the stolen goods in town. The police, the owner, and everyone in town knew this and accepted it. If anyone had a bike, TV, musical instrument or lawn ornament stolen, they reported it to the RCMP, and the cops just walked down the street to the Emporium to pick it up. Nine times out of ten, it was sitting there, and the guy behind the counter handed it over without question. It was a cost of doing business, and he calculated the stolen goods he had to hand over as evidence into his budget. The stolen goods the cops *didn't* find more than made up for it.

The owner of the Emporium was Fred Fudge, a tall, creepy man with long limbs and freakishly long fingers. His pinky nails were trimmed extra long, too, which someone said was used for snorting lines of cocaine, but Brian thought it was to pick guitar strings. Either way, the combined extension from his shoulder to the tip of his fingernail nearly allowed him to touch the floor without bending down.

Fudge's bulging, insect-like eyes stared at Brian with feigned distress, and Brian wanted to slap the taste out of his thick, pink lips.

Brian had stopped at the Hansen Mall, which was an old US-air force building that housed a handful of crappy stores, on his way home from the police station after parting ways with Craig Muise. Craig had seemed extremely relieved and excited to leave Brian standing alone on the side of the street—he probably needed to get home to watch Xena: Warrior Princess or something. So Brian went into the crappy mall alone, walked past the carpet and rug store that always smelled like dog pee, and now stood in the crowded Emporium amidst the racks of old books, magazines, coats, porn, sporting equipment, a shovel that appeared to have blood on it, and various other random junk that Brian couldn't possibly care any less about. He had only one thing on his mind: how Fudge had betrayed him.

Brian jabbed a pudgy finger at a newly reorganized section of the display case. Fudge had removed the old Atari game cartridges and replaced them with several lines of Magic: The Gathering cards in clear plastic sleeves with tiny price tags.

"What the hell is that?" Brian demanded.

"Magic cards," Fudge droned, his voice purring like a cat cleaning its own butthole.

"Last week, you told me you didn't buy and sell Magic cards! Those are some of the same cards I tried to sell you, and you wouldn't buy them."

"I didn't sell them last week. I do now."

"Why?"

Fudge shrugged. "There was an increase in demand."

"I have been asking you for two months to buy and sell cards!"

"You were only one person asking. Now, there are several. That is called an increase in demand."

"Who was it? It was Todd Murphy and his friends, wasn't it? That sonofabitch..."

"It is store policy that I don't divulge the names of any of my customers." Now Fudge purred like the cat had eaten his butthole and most of his back end.

"Except to the cops, right?"

"You are not a cop."

"Yeah, but I know a few." Skidmark sighed and opened his bookbag, pulling out two long, white cardboard boxes full of cards. "Whatever. Can I sell you a Mana Vault and Vesuvan Doppelganger now?"

"No." Fudge gestured to the case. "I already have them."

"Fine. I'll buy yours, then."

Brian left the Hansen Mall fifty dollars poorer and a few slim pieces of cardboard richer. He was not looking forward to the day his parents discovered he was skimming twenties out of his dad's stash. He hid his money in the encyclopedia in the den under the "Money" entry, which was both brilliant and stupid at the same time. The first time Brian did it, he'd felt guilty and worried for weeks that his parents would find out and beat him with a tire iron wrapped in a dish towel. When they didn't, his qualms about stealing from them dropped substantially. He was still afraid of getting beaten to within an inch of life, mind you, but not enough to actually stop what he was doing.

He looked down the street toward the Hansen movie theatre, wishing he had saved a few bucks to see *Timecop*. It was supposed to be pretty dumb, but watching Jean Claude van Damm kick a dude in the face was always good for a laugh. He'd rather see *Stargate*, but the crappy Hansen Theatre was always a month or more behind on their movies. He hated living in Gale Harbour sometimes. Well, pretty much all the time. He would have bugged his parents to take him to Corner Brook to see it, where they usually showed new films, but on the off chance they actually agreed, his dad would likely go to his stash to get money to pay for the movie. Brian didn't feel like a beating right now.

He was so focused on the theatre that he was nearly bowled over by three giggling teenage girls. Brian wasn't bothered by the fact that they likely giggled about him. He knew the girls who laughed at him now would be begging to date him when he was a famous director/movie star/rapper/professional Magic player. Besides, he had Mrs. Walsh, so what did he care about ditzy teenage girls? He would have ignored them altogether, except one of them stopped and actually talked to him.

"Hey, you're Skidmark, right? Niall O'Neil's friend?" She was blond and kinda pretty, Brian supposed, if you liked curvy fourteen-year-old girls. He preferred more mature, curvy girls, like Anna Chaffey, or very mature, skeletally-thin girls, like Eleanor Walsh.

"My name is Brian Hawco," said Brian.

She covered her mouth. "Oh, I'm sorry, Brian! I just heard people call you Skidmark, so I thought..."

"It's okay. Everyone calls me Skidmark, even my dentist. I asked him not to because he always says it in this sarcastic, mocking voice, but he's a tool. A total sadist who gets off on jamming metal implements into kids' mouths, like that guy from *Little Shop of Horrors*, but without the laughing gas and singing. At least if he sang, it would be more entertaining, but my dentist is so boring, and he has no sense of humour. I asked him if he had a leather biker jacket like Steve Martin, and he just looked at me like I was a weirdo."

She swayed, a little bewildered. You know what they said about blondes. "Right, anyway, I'm Stacey. I was wondering if you'd seen Niall today? I called his house, but his mom said he was out and wasn't sure when he'd be back."

Brian raised an eyebrow. "Oh, so you're the new minx that's stealing my friend's heart. I will have you know that he's a sensitive soul, so I hope you're not planning on just using him for his body and then dumping him like the bones of Mary Brown's chicken legs. I once choked on a chicken bone from Mary Brown's. I told my parents to sue the restaurant, but they told me I was being stupid. At least I convinced them to only buy Kentucky Fried Chicken from now on, and I've been working hard to spread a rumour that Mary Brown's chicken is actually deep-fried seagulls."

Stacey looked back at her other friends, who seemed equally confused, which was weird because they weren't blond. "Wow," said the one with the ponytail and glasses. "I had heard about you, but I never imagined..."

"Sorry, toots, no use buttering me up. I'm spoken for. Anyway, Niall isn't home because he's been hanging out with Harper all day."

The third girl, the tall one with frizzy hair and the gap tooth, snorted and growled. "With his ex-girlfriend? What a jerk..."

Stacey's cheeks had turned a little red. "It's fine, Jennifer. He can talk to whoever he wants. We hadn't actually put a label on anything..."

"Oh, they weren't making out or anything," said Brian. "They were at the police station, telling them about how the pervert that lives across the street from Harper saw Anna Chaffey kidnap our friend Pius, but I'm pretty sure that perv didn't know what he's talking about because I know Anna would never do something like that—"

"Wait, what pervert?" asked the one named Jennifer.

"Mr. Parsons, on Townview Avenue."

Jennifer shuddered. "Oh, yeah, he's a real creep. He stares at all the girls that walk by his place, like he's imagining what they look like in their underwear."

Brian did that. *Was he a pervert?* "Anyway, I wanted to tell the cops that it was way more likely that Pius was kidnapped by aliens or government secret agents or Satan worshippers or something because that would be way more likely with our luck, but Niall and Harper were all like, 'No, don't say that, we're not allowed to talk about that,' and I was just like, they're the friggin' cops, they were there for all the crazy stuff. If they can't figure out what's going on, then they're really crappy cops. Or maybe it was a witch; we were all kidnapped by a witch a while back."

The girls looked at each other and then burst out laughing. Were they laughing at him? Or with him? As far as he was aware, he hadn't said anything funny, so it was probably mean-spirited. "This guy is a riot," said the girl with the glasses. "Come on, Skidmark, you totally need to tell us more of your stories."

"Erin, leave the guy alone," said Stacey.

Erin looked insulted. "I'm serious! I bet this guy has plenty of funny stories, and you were just saying you were bored. He probably has all kinds of dirt on Niall and Harper, too."

"Oh, totally," said Skidmark. "Did you know that Harper's mom is a deadbeat drug addict who abandoned her as a baby, so she was raised by her dad, but then her dad was brutally murdered in front of her, so she went to live with her aunt and uncle but her uncle had an affair, and now they're on the verge of splitting up, then Niall broke up with her, and now Harper's mom is back, and Harper is going through like these serious mental issues because she doesn't know if she can trust her mom but she feels like she has no one else here in Gale Harbour, and then her cousin Pius got kidnapped again..."

The girls were silent for a moment. Stacey put her hands over her face. "Oh, my God, I feel so bad for Harper now..."

Erin just burst out laughing again. "Seriously, girls, we have to take this guy with us."

CHAPTER THIRTY-TWO

Interstate Love Song
Thursday, October 27
6:15 pm

"You're looking tired, Anna. Did I keep you up too late last night?"

Nelson met her outside the drugstore in the mall after work. He was wearing a button-down, short-sleeve plaid shirt, having changed out of his ugly pinstriped uniform. Anna was dressed in her usual black lace and leather but was definitely more dishevelled than usual. Her corset wasn't laced properly, her hair was messy, and her makeup was sloppily applied. He could see the purple bags under her eyes.

Anna smiled and squeezed his hand. "I was so excited to meet you that I barely had time to get dressed."

Nelson's stomach made odd little flutters when she took his hand. He was so smitten with this girl—he didn't care what she looked like, but he was worried she wasn't getting enough sleep.

He hadn't gotten much sleep either. He couldn't stop thinking about the other night when he had slept with two other young women. He had never been with any girl before, and then he'd been with three. At the same time! His mind had been reeling ever since.

He'd slept with Anna every night since. Sometimes, she would appear at his window in the middle of the night. Yesterday—his birthday—she had met him on his lunch break, and they'd fooled around in the mall bathroom and then again after work in the backseat of her crappy car. It had been a way better present than the jeans his parents got him, or the packs of Upper Deck hockey cards Niall gave him, but it wasn't really a fair comparison. Anna was insatiable and freaky and did things he had never even fantasized about.

He kissed her, hot on the lips, ignoring the stares of the blue-haired ladies shuffling past them in the lobby. "I'm happy to see you, too. But I'm getting worried about you. Do you sleep at all?"

She pulled away from him and squeezed his hand. He couldn't quite place the strange look she gave him with her stunning grey eyes. Was it sadness? Longing? "Come on," she said. "Let's talk."

She let him out to the parking lot, to her beat-up old green station wagon. Nelson's heart was pounding in his chest. He didn't have a lot of experience with women, but he knew enough to know that "let's talk" was a phrase to strike terror in his heart. As he got into the passenger seat, he wanted to ask what was wrong, but his mouth was too dry to say anything. She started the car and pulled out onto the street.

Anna eventually spoke first, "My church wants me to leave you."

Nelson was confused. He was expecting her to say she was breaking up with him, or that she was pregnant, or that her old boyfriend was coming to kill him. In all honesty, her Church meddling with their relationship was nowhere on his radar.

"Can they do that?" Nelson asked stupidly.

"The Sun Redeemer means everything to me. They took care of me when I was at my lowest, when I was young and into drugs and my life was falling apart. After I ran away from them, after Keenan died and I went to dark places again, they welcomed me back and helped me put my life back together."

Nelson couldn't imagine anyone being so supportive. He'd certainly never experienced anything like that in his own life. "I understand how much they mean to you. They seem like good people."

"They don't want me to have a relationship with an outsider."

Nelson didn't see the issue. "Then I'll join your church."

Anna's face lit up with the brightest smile he'd ever seen. She shrieked like she'd just won the lottery. She pulled the car over, her hands shaking. "Are you serious?"

"Of course I'm serious." Nelson's dad left the Anglican Church to become Catholic when he married his mom. It didn't seem like that big of a thing. "I would do anything to be with you."

"The Sun Redeemer isn't all orgies, you know. We do ministry and other work that's hard sometimes. We expect a lot of our members."

"I don't care. I want to be with you."

"Won't your parents be upset?"

Nelson couldn't help but imagine his parents' shocked faces when he told them he was converting. That might be almost as good as being with Anna. Plus, if he was out of the picture, it would give them more time to fuss over their precious Niall. "I don't care what my parents think."

Anna squealed again and reached across the gear shift to hug and kiss Nelson passionately. He replied in kind, unable to imagine what his family could offer that would be better than this.

She pulled away and yanked the car back into gear. The tires squealed as she spun around in the middle of Main Street, and other drivers slammed on their horns in surprise and annoyance.

"What are you doing?" Nelson yelped.

"I have to go tell everyone the good news!" Anna righted the car in the westbound lane and slammed on the gas.

Shortly, they were on the road to Cape-de-Cape, the same road they had taken a few nights ago to Nelson's eye-opening beach party. He half-thought they might return to the same spot for another round until they passed the turn-off to the secluded beach.

"Where exactly are we going?"

Anna's smile had faded. "I'm taking you to our retreat. I want to tell everyone the good news."

They drove for a few minutes along the long, twisting road. In many places there was nothing between the left side of the asphalt and the Atlantic Ocean except a short guardrail and a steep cliff. Driving out here as a kid always freaked Nelson out. It still made him nervous, especially since Anna seemed to be looking under the weather.

"What's wrong?" he asked her.

She bit her lip a moment, then shook her head. "Are you really sure about this, Nelson? About joining my church?"

"I just told you, yes."

"Because there's really no going back. They don't let you leave. It becomes part of you for life."

"You're making it sound like a cult."

Anna's face was blank. "I ran away once, and they drew me back in. It was the right thing for me. I needed it, and it saved me... but it's not the right thing for everyone."

"Anna, I want—"

"—No, shut up and listen. I care about you. I really care about you. I don't want to see you get hurt or make a mistake that you will regret. I've done a lot of things I regret. I believe they were for the right reasons, but..." She trailed off momentarily. The road began a steep rise. "You have to truly believe what you're doing is right. You have to truly believe that what you're doing is worth all the sacrifices you have to make on the way."

"You're kinda freaking me out, Anna."

She looked at him with her striking grey eyes, and for a split second, all doubt and fear slipped away.

"I need to tell you something, Nelson. The truth."

In that moment of calm, the road reached its zenith, and a large truck came around the corner out of nowhere. Anna screamed and swerved.

Nelson remembered nothing.

Anna was ten years old again.

Her father was screaming at her. Her thighs and palms were bleeding from being beaten with a belt, and her knees were screaming in agony from the broken glass beneath her. When she looked up, her father's eyes glowed an otherworldly blue. His face exploded into a cloud of giant, glowing bugs that flew at her and crawled all over her body. She screamed until her throat was raw.

She fell to the floor. Tired and aching. The lights came on, and her eyes exploded in flashes that blinded her. How long had she been suspended in darkness? She slowly realized that the deafening noises blaring in her ears had fallen silent for the first time in days.

Anna lay naked on the cold floor in a puddle of her own urine, struggling to enjoy a few moments of blissful peace. She wasn't ten but couldn't remember how old she was.

"Anna."

Her father's voice made her tired muscles stiffen, which was agonizing. She had been suspended against the wall for so long...

"Anna, it was wrong for you to run away."

"I'm so hungry..."

"Do not speak back to me!" he roared. Anna couldn't see him standing behind and over her, but she could imagine his face, the red flush to his cheeks and the veins bulging in his forehead.

Anna's body convulsed with sobs she could not control. "I'm sorry, Father."

"Do you know how much time was wasted looking for you? Don't you know how important you are to the Redeemer's plan?"

Anna's throat was so dry it was raw. She thought she could taste blood. "Yes, Father. I'm sorry, Father."

"Are you ready to come back now? To do what you must do to usher in the Redeemer's return?"

"Yes, Father." Anything to make the pain stop.

He touched her hair, and she cringed, but he only patted her head gently. "Brother Vee himself is coming to see you. You are so important, Anna. I don't know why, but you have been born with a great gift. A gift that will save the true believers when the Redeemer returns."

She was so scared—not just of her father but of what she had to do. The Redeemer was returning; she had seen the signs herself but wasn't sure if she could do what they wanted.

She couldn't say that, of course. She would be punished again, or worse.

"We need to get you cleaned up before Brother Vee arrives." He paused for a moment. "But I suppose we still have a bit of time."

He grabbed her forcefully by the wrist and yanked her to her feet. She yelped in pain but was too weak to resist. He slammed her face first into the wall, raised her hands above her head and re-fastened the shackles. She struggled feebly, begged him to stop, and promised she would be a good girl and never run away again, but her father was relentless.

He leaned in close and whispered in her ear. His breath smelled of alcohol and dead things. "I need to ensure you will be on your best behaviour when Brother Vee arrives. You are so important, Anna. We can't risk you doing anything to jeopardize everything we've built."

He left her trembling against the wall, and then the room was plunged into complete and utter blackness. She couldn't see anything, couldn't feel anything but the brick wall against her skin and the steel manacles biting into her wrists. Her hands were so high above her head that her toes barely touched the floor, and her arms and body began to ache already from the tension of holding herself up. Soon, she knew the pain and discomfort would become so great that she would become delirious and start having hallucinations again.

The worst part hadn't started yet. It was a few minutes before the screaming began, the recorded sounds of dying and tortured people who had been sacrificed in the name of the Church. It was a reminder of what would happen if the Redeemer returned and they weren't ready. The screams were so loud, they blocked out all other thoughts and temporarily numbed the pain. It hastened Anna's descent into nightmarish oblivion.

CHAPTER THIRTY-THREE

Cornflake Girl
Thursday, October 27
7:00 pm

Tanguay was sitting on her Chesterfield in a daze when the doorbell rang. The lights were off, the curtains were drawn, and Tanguay had every intention of pretending she wasn't home, except whoever was at the door would not leave her alone.

After the fourth ring, she knew it couldn't be Jehovah's Witnesses or the door-to-door fish salesman, but that still wasn't enough incentive to get her off her backside. She was buzzed on Percocet; she hadn't bathed in days and wasn't sure if she was wearing any clothes. She had to look down at herself to confirm she had on an old Montreal Canadiens sweatshirt, but she still wasn't sure if there was anything on the bottom half.

Finally, a voice called through the door, "Sergeant Tanguay, it's Cheryl Murphy. I just wanted to check on you and see how you're doing. You aren't answering your phone, so if you aren't answering your door either, then I have probable cause to break in to make sure you're not unconscious or dead."

There was a pause while she waited for a response. Finally, she added, "But I hope you answer because I don't really know how to break down a door."

Tanguay struggled to her feet, leaning heavily on her cane for support. It took her a few moments, but she eventually made it to the door and opened it just enough to look out at Cheryl's round, concerned face.

The sunlight hurt Tanguay's eyes, but not as much as the pitying tone in Cheryl's voice hurt her heart.

"Oh, dear. Well, at least you're alive."

Tanguay gave a weak smile. "Yes, I'm alive. You did your good deed for the week, so now if you'd please—"

She tried to close the door, but Cheryl put up her hand to block it. "I brought you some food. I didn't think you'd be feeding yourself properly. You need good, healthy food to heal."

Tanguay wanted to say that fruits and vegetables weren't going to help a shattered pelvis but held her tongue. "Cheryl, I'm not feeling well, and the house is a mess, so..."

"Oh, don't mind that, and I'll just stop in for a minute." Suddenly, Cheryl was in her house, and Tanguay didn't have the strength or the will to stop her. The Constable was carrying a grocery bag full of plastic food containers. "I've got chicken soup, chilli, some tuna casserole—you should probably eat that one first—and potato salad. There was supposed to be lasagna, but Harold and Todd got into it last night and ate half of it. I bawled them out good, I tell you." She put the bag on the counter next to the fridge and started arranging the food containers.

"Thank you, Cheryl. You didn't have to do that."

"Nonsense, you're hurt, and you need some help. It's what friends do."

Friends. Tanguay didn't remember the last time anyone had called her "a friend."

"Let's get some light in here. You're going to start growing mushrooms." Cheryl opened the curtains on the small window over the kitchen sink. The red light of sunset streamed in, revealing a sink stacked with dirty dishes, a garbage can overflowing with waste, and dirty clothes strewn over every visible surface in the kitchen and living room. "On second thought, maybe dark is better."

"I haven't been feeling much up to cleaning."

"I'm just teasing, love. Of course, you haven't. You should sit down and take it easy. I'll put on the kettle. Where are your tea bags? Never mind, I'll find them." Cheryl started going through the cupboards.

While the round woman banged through the kitchen, Tanguay fumbled through the couch cushions, looking for her bottle of pills. She opened the small plastic container, popped two in her mouth and swallowed them with a glass of old water from the end table. She hoped it was water.

"Cupboards are looking pretty bare, my dearie. I'll have to pick you up a few things the next time I'm at the Foodland."

Tanguay didn't answer. She just closed her eyes and sank into the couch, waiting for the pills to kick in.

Cheryl placed a cup of tea on the end table next to her head, and Tanguay awoke with a start. She had no idea if she'd been sleeping for a few minutes or an hour.

"So, how are things going down at the detachment?" Tanguay didn't want to make idle conversation. If she had to talk to someone, at least she could get an update on things.

Cheryl's wide brow wrinkled with concern. "Not good, actually. Pius Jeddore and his baby sister have gone missing."

Tanguay's heart leapt into her throat. She sat up as much as she could manage. "What?"

"There were no signs of foul play; they just up and disappeared the night before last. Peters thought maybe he ran away..."

"No." Pius wouldn't do that. And certainly not with his little sister. "Talk to the other kids. There could be something going on..."

"We're talking to everyone, Sergeant. Niall and the Jeddore girl seem to think that Anna Chaffey has something to do with it."

It took her a few moments to remember why she knew that name. "The girl who was one of the last people to see Shelly Parsons. Her boyfriend was killed last year, the same time I got shot." Why was she involved in everything?

"There's something else. Keith Doucette..." Cheryl's voice trailed off.

The hair on the back of Tanguay's neck prickled. She didn't like the way Cheryl said that. Despite the haze of pain and narcotics, her instincts were on full alert. "What about Keith?"

Cheryl let out a gulp of air like a deflating balloon. "Keith is... Keith was arrested for the murder of Cecil Doucette."

"His father?" *Tabarnak chalice d'hosti.* "No, no, it can't be. I know the kid messed up, but his *father?*"

"Nothing is proven, but it doesn't look good. The murder weapon was Keith's favourite baseball bat. Witnesses saw Keith threaten Cec and trash his office earlier that same day. Not to mention, Pius filed a report a few days ago that Keith's father was abusing him. Keith had a motive, on top of all the evidence."

Tanguay's head was swimming. Keith threatened his father and trashed his office. Cec was abusing him. Pius of all people reported it.

Keith murdered his father.

She knew last year that Keith was in trouble. She saw it with her own eyes and hadn't done anything about it. Now, a man was dead, and Keith's life was as good as done too.

She began to sob. Ugly, gasping sobs. She had never cried like this, not since Lynne died, and certainly had never done it in front of a subordinate. But Tanguay didn't care. Not anymore. None of it mattered anymore.

"I'm sorry, Sarge, I..." Cheryl awkwardly tried to comfort her but didn't seem to know where to put her hands. She never imagined how bad off Tanguay was or how poorly she would react to the news. "I never meant to upset you. I came to ask for your help."

Tanguay choked back the tears and looked up at Cheryl with red, puffy eyes. "*Tu blagues*, right? You're joking? How the hell am I supposed to help anyone?" She gestured vaguely to herself, the mess on the couch, and her life.

"You and those kids have secrets," Cheryl said. "Weird things have been happening in this town, and you and those kids know more than you're letting on. I don't doubt that my Todd would be dead if it wasn't for Niall and the Jeddore girl, and I know you and them killed something far worse than a crazy old lady in the tunnels under the old base. I hoped you might know something or could convince the kids to say what they know to help Pius, or Keith, or that poor little baby girl."

Baby girl. Pius' little sister couldn't have been more than six months old. *Tabarnak.*

Tanguay tried to think, searching her memory for anything that might help. But it was so hard to focus. Her brain was so foggy that she had to grasp and claw for thoughts that drifted by in the haze. Tunnels... Could they have gone into the tunnels? Could there be another monster? Did the Americans leave something else behind in the base?

She shook her head. Tears again began to stream down her face. "I'm sorry, I don't... I can't think of anything... That doesn't mean there isn't something, I just can't think..."

"There is one other thing," Cheryl said, reaching into the bag at her feet and withdrawing a few sheets of folded paper. "Sergeant Peters has been on the ball since he took over for you. He keeps Bennett and Brake in line. He's more by the book than you used to be. He does everything a good Mountie is supposed to do. But I always felt that there was something off about him."

Cheryl handed Tanguay the sheets of paper. "I think this is what was bothering me."

Tanguay took the paper with trembling hands. She read it and couldn't believe it. She had to reread it to make sure she wasn't hallucinating. "Where did you get this?"

"Off his desk. And there have been other things as well." Cheryl told her what they were.

It only took Tanguay a moment to decide. With immense effort, she pulled herself to a standing position. "Cheryl, help me get cleaned up and dressed. We need to go."

CHAPTER THIRTY-FOUR

Sweet Dreams
Thursday, October 27,
7:50 pm

"No way," Erin said between bites of Brian's popcorn. She ate like a snowblower and somehow had butter all over her glasses. "You were held at gunpoint in a bunker under the town by a witch, and you scared off a monster by singing 'Informer.' I call bullshit on, like, all of this."

The three girls and Brian were in the lobby of the Hansen Theatre, waiting for the movie to start. He convinced them to buy him a ticket, a large popcorn and a Pepsi, and in exchange, he would tell them whatever they wanted to know about Niall. They had already been through all the times he'd embarrassed himself in elementary school. How he had a crush on Pius' mom, and how he once stole a Ken Griffey Jr. rookie card from Chad MacDonald, which was not entirely true because it was actually Skidmark who had taken the card, but Niall had somehow gotten the blame for it. Brian just had to keep up the ruse.

They had just gotten to the part about the Psycho Hose Beast. "I know it sounds crazy, and the RCMP told me I wasn't supposed to tell anyone, so I shouldn't be telling you, but I swear it's true. And I'm not 100% sure she was a real witch. I mean, she said she was, and Niall and Harper claimed she could do magic, but I never really saw any myself."

"If the cops told you not to tell anyone about this," began Jennifer, picking popcorn from between her protrusive teeth, "why are you telling us?"

Brian shrugged. "Harper and Keith told the cops that telling me everything was a bad idea, and Sgt. Tanguay didn't want to, but Niall and Pius said it didn't matter what I knew because no one would believe me anyway."

"Keith?" asked Jennifer. "Is he the guy that killed his father?"

"I didn't think that was out in the news yet."

"You just told us a few minutes ago," said Stacey.

That was entirely possible. He remembered telling them the plot of the first few episodes of M.A.N.T.I.S. and his strategies for convincing his parents to get him a 486 computer. There may have been something about Keith murdering his dad in there. "Actually, I don't think Keith really did it. He's an asshole sometimes, but he's our buddy. He plays a really cool red and black deck in Magic, which I guess makes him at least a little evil, but he wouldn't really kill anyone. Keith's cousin Craig, Niall, and Harper seem to think that some kind of Satan worshippers or redneck hitmen did it."

Stacey guffawed. "Satan worshippers or redneck hitmen?"

"Maybe they're both? I mean, the two are not mutually exclusive, are they? The guys who almost kidnapped me last year were both government agents and child molesters. Then again, I guess technically they turned out to be neither."

Erin slapped him on the shoulder, leaving a greasy stain that fit perfectly with the other stains on his shirt. "See? I told you this guy would be a riot. You are nuts, Brian. In a good way. I think."

"The movie's about to start," said Jennifer. "I need to go to the washroom."

"Me too," said Stacey, and soon all three girls disappeared.

Brian stood alone in the corner of the dimly-lit grungy theatre lobby. The carpet, installed when the US Air Force built this place, smelled and looked like it had forty years' worth of popcorn, pop, spit and vomit ground into it. While he wouldn't put his own bag, containing his precious Magic cards, down on such a filthy surface, he noticed one of the girls had left their pink backpack. He wasn't sure which one it belonged to, but whichever it was must be up to date with their Hepatitis vaccine.

With less than five minutes until the movie started, two strange things happened. Well three, if you counted how inconsiderate it was for the girls to make him wait. First, all the lights in the building went out. There were several moans and yelps from inside the theatre. Brian could see the streetlights were out, too, through the tinted windows at the front of the lobby. If they had to cancel the movie, he'd better get his money back. Brian hadn't actually paid for it, but still.

The second odd thing was that the pink bag on the floor started to talk.

Most people would have at least hesitated to consider the morality of searching through someone's bag, but Brian opened it without a second thought. Besides a wallet, a notebook, and a sweater, there was a large, old-fashioned, black walkie-talkie. A cracking, muffled voice was coming from the speaker.

Brian picked it up and turned up the volume knob.

"...phase two complete. Power's out."

A second voice cut in, "Phone lines are still down."

Weird. They didn't sound like utility workers. They sounded almost happy that the power was out.

"So I guess it's all goin' down tonight?"

"Sister Pearl said she wanted to wait, but Brother Vee is sayin' it has to happen tonight. They're getting the tributes ready."

"I feels bad for them, I do. They're just kids."

Brian clicked the talk button on the walkie-talkie. "Who are we talking about?"

There was a pause as the voices probably tried to decide how to deal with this interruption. Brian was merely annoyed by the delay. What did they expect to happen? It was a walkie-talkie, and an old one at that. He highly doubted this channel was secure. Of course, someone was going to hear what they were saying.

One of the voices decided they would try to scare Brian off the line. "Who the hell is this? What's your call sign?"

"Seymour Butts," replied Brian.

"Seymour... get off the friggin' line! This is a private channel!"

"Who were those tributes you were talking about? You said they're just kids. Are you talking about Pius and his sister? Did you find them? Why did you call them tributes? That makes it sound like you're going to sacrifice them... Holy shit, *are* you going to sacrifice them? *Are you the Satan worshippers?!*"

There was radio silence. Brian clicked the call button a few dozen times, making an unpleasant squealing sound each time, but still, no one replied.

He had figured it out. That's why no one could find Pius and Rebecca—they had been kidnapped by Satan worshippers. He had to tell someone! His first thought was Craig Muise for some reason, probably because he never believed Brian when he told him repeatedly that this was the kind of shit that happened to them in Gale Harbour.

Then he figured he should tell the cops... except Stacey's dad was a Mountie, wasn't he? This radio belonged to one of the girls, so one of them must have been a Satan worshipper, too. What if it was Stacey? What if Stacey's dad was one? That would explain why they were so blasé on the radio and not worried about being caught by the cops if the cops were in their blasphemous, red satin pocket (Brian had no idea how Satan worshippers actually dressed).

So he couldn't go to the cops, which sucked because the police station was pretty close. Maybe he should go to the church? Nah, Father Hickey seemed pretty useless unless he was a secret badass with a blessed crossbow and holy water grenades hidden in the basement of St. Paul's. Brian didn't think so, though. He had once been down there for a school function, and it was mostly just folding chairs, an old upright piano, and the weird feeling that you shouldn't swear there because, you know, you were still kinda in church.

That meant the only option was Niall. He had to tell Niall. He would know what to do. The thought made him groan because Niall lived so far from the movie theatre. If the Satan worshippers were correct and the phones were really down, then he couldn't call his parents for a ride.

Brian checked the payphone, just to be sure, because he didn't think Satan worshippers could be trusted to be honest. Finding the line dead, he grumbled and finally left the theatre, just seconds before the girls returned to find him—and the radio—gone.

CHAPTER THIRTY-FIVE

Violet
Thursday, October 27
7:30 pm

Niall walked Harper home after they gave their statement at the police station. The Mounties had ushered them out pretty quickly after the news of Anna came in. Her involvement complicated the growing web of mystery that was pretty much par for the course in Gale Harbour.

They shared theories about what might be going on. Maybe the government—either Canada or the United States—was trying to get revenge for being embarrassed during the fiasco last year and was taking out the kids one by one. Niall and Harper would surely be high-priority targets, so they weren't fond of this theory. Maybe Keith's dad had really hired goons to either frighten or hurt his son, and when Keith confronted him about it—whether by accident or on purpose—the old man ended up dead. There was also the very real possibility that the Psycho Hose Beast was somehow orchestrating the events taking place right now. Maybe not directly, but they didn't understand a fraction of the monster's powers. Subconsciously manipulating people into violence didn't seem like a far-fetched idea.

However, none of these theories explained what Anna Chaffey had to do with any of this. Her involvement didn't make any sense.

They turned onto Townsview Drive and approached the Jeddores' small yellow house. As they grew nearer, they heard sounds from inside—smashing dishes, yelling, and sobbing.

Niall was transported back to this same spot last spring when he approached the house with Pius and Harper to discover Samantha throwing Raymond out for having an affair. She had taken Raymond back after discovering she was pregnant, but Niall had always felt it was a tenuous treaty keeping them together. It sounded like tonight that treaty may have been broken.

Harper must have come to the same conclusion because they both broke into a run toward the house simultaneously. She beat Niall to the front step first, just as she always did, and was in the door, hardly breaking her stride. Niall was right on her heels.

Samantha Jeddore was sitting on the kitchen floor in a beige nightdress, surrounded by shattered plates. Her right hand and arm were covered in blood, and there was a small puddle of red pooling beside her.

Harper was by her side in a second. "Jesus Christ, Aunt Samantha, what happened?"

There was no answer besides choked sobs. Her eyes were unfocused, and she seemed incapable of coherency.

"Niall, the first aid kit is above the fridge!"

He grabbed the white plastic box without hesitation and sat beside Harper. She tore it open and pulled out gauze and bandages, quickly applying them to the nasty-looking gash on Samantha's hand. Samantha herself was a nurse, well-versed in binding wounds of all kinds. Harper picked up her first-aid skills from Girl Guides and her father.

"She must have cut her hand on a broken plate," Harper said, holding pressure on the wound while she inspected the rest of her aunt's arm with her free hand. "Aunt Samantha, where's Uncle Ray?"

She looked at them with terror in her green eyes, but no words would come out. Niall thought she mouthed, *I'm sorry,* but he might have just imagined it.

He had to look away. Seeing an adult like this, the mother of his best friend, who he once had a massive crush on, was too much. He saw Pius in her panicked face, the same fear he'd seen on his friend more than once as they confronted unimaginable terrors. They had been through so much. And now Pius was gone. Niall wanted to burst into tears himself, and he felt his heart tightening inside his chest.

Harper, always the level-headed one, noticed his trepidation and grabbed him by the arm. Her strong fingers digging into his skin seemed to snap him out of it. "Niall, I swear to God, if you go all foolish on me too..."

Niall shook his head and wiped his eyes. "I'm sorry, I'm here. What do you need me to do?"

"She's hysterical. We can't get anything from her in this condition. We need to calm her down."

"How?"

A light came on behind Harper's big brown eyes. "You need to do it. The same way you made Mr. Parsons calm down."

"Excuse me?"

"Use your powers to calm her like you did with Mr. Parsons."

Niall's conviction left him. He had sworn he would never use his powers again, and he'd already done it twice today... "I don't know how I did it. I don't want to hurt her..."

"Parsons was fine. It wore off in just a couple of minutes." Harper sounded too blasé about it, as if she wasn't asking him to melt her aunt's brain with his magic powers. She made it sound as reasonable as stealing an extra cookie from the jar. Samantha was rocking and moaning beside her. "I'm worried if she keeps this up, she's going to hurt herself again."

"I don't want to... What about Keenan?"

Harper was losing her patience. "To hell with Keenan! That was an accident and completely different. You know that! Something is going on here. What if the people who took Pius and Rebecca came back? What if they took Uncle Raymond, too?"

"Harper, that's crazy..."

"Everything is crazy in this town! It might have been OJ Simpson who came in here and stabbed her for all I know, but we won't be able to find out until we calm Aunt Samantha down! Now please, Niall. Just do it."

She could talk him into jumping into a live volcano wearing nothing but Speedos and a snorkel. That's why he had to keep her away. He knew that if he stayed with her, they would keep finding reasons to use their power again.

What she was saying was reasonable. If there was a chance this could be connected to Pius and Rebecca's disappearance, they had to find out. He nodded.

Harper took a pin off her jacket again and pricked her finger. It seemed very unsanitary, with all the other blood and dirt smeared around them, but they had been through worse. He touched her fingertip and felt the familiar rush of energy course through his body.

He held onto it tighter than he ever had before. At Parsons' house, he had used it cautiously, trying to open the lock, but now he was using it on his best friend's mother. He had to be careful and use just the tiniest bit of power necessary. He was terrified of causing permanent damage to her brain.

Niall closed his eyes and imagined Samantha sleeping peacefully. He pictured her as he used to daydream about her—beautiful and serene, her red hair tossed playfully around her head. He could see it so clearly, and he remembered with bitterness that time not long ago when the most exciting thing in his life was having a crush on his friend's mom.

He opened his eyes. "Sleep, Mrs. Jeddore," he said.

Samantha went limp and collapsed.

Niall started to panic, but Harper caught her head and lowered her carefully to the floor. "It's okay, she's just sleeping. Her breathing is already going back to normal, and her heart rate is slowing down."

Niall breathed in relief. "Thank God."

"We need to remember that trick for Skidmark." She gently stroked her aunt's hair. "We can't ask her anything until she wakes up. How long do you think you put her out?"

"I have no idea," Niall said. He looked at the wreckage of the kitchen, trying to find clues to the situation. "I wonder what happened?" He reached out to touch Samanta's arm, and the world turned upside down.

He saw the Jeddore's kitchen, but it wasn't through his eyes. The angles and colours were wrong, and his vision was hazy at the edges. Harper wasn't there anymore, but Mr. Jeddore was. The black eyes in his dark, chiselled face were staring right at Niall.

"Samantha, please calm down. The police are doing everything they can to find Pius and Rebecca."

"*Don't tell me to calm down!*" Niall snapped at him, but it wasn't his voice. It kinda sounded like Samantha, but not exactly, like the opposite of what happened when you heard a recording of your own voice. "Pius was trapped in those tunnels by that crazy old woman. He nearly died. And Rebecca's only a baby..."

"Pius didn't die, he was okay, and I'm sure—"

"He's not okay, Ray! I hear him talking in his sleep! He has nightmares. He won't sleep with the light off. He's more of a basket case than he ever was. He blames himself for everything that happened between us!"

"Don't bring that up right now."

"Why? Why not? He ran away after he came home and found you in bed with that teenager—"

"She wasn't a teenager!"

"How do I know he didn't catch you in bed with someone else, and that's why he ran away again?"

Raymond Jeddore's face was turning red with anger. Niall also felt a strange anger rising in him, but it wasn't his anger. It was in his head with him but somehow compartmentalized, separate from him. "He didn't find me in bed, *you* did, and *you* were the one who threw a fit and made a scene in front of the whole neighbourhood!"

"Oh, don't you dare! Don't throw that back on me. You were the one who had an affair!"

"I did, and I've been trying to make up for it ever since. I swear to you there hasn't been anyone else."

"How can I believe you?"

"Sam, this is not the time—"

"No, it's not the time! I'm worried about my goddamn children. I shouldn't have to be worried about my husband, too!"

"Sam, please calm down—"

"—Stop telling me to calm down!"

Niall grabbed a dinner plate off the counter and hurled it at the wall next to Raymond. He didn't try to hit him, at least he didn't think he did, but he also wouldn't have cared if it had struck him square in the face. Niall was screaming and crying, the rage threatening to burst out from that other place where it had been sealed away until now. Raymond, himself shaking with anger, turned and walked to the door. "I'm going to go look for the kids."

And then Raymond was gone, and the anger exploded inside Niall's head in a blinding flash of red. It frightened him so much that he jerked away, and Niall found himself on the floor, staring at the ceiling.

"Niall!" Harper was calling into his ear. "Say something!"

It took Niall a moment to remember where he was. He was in the Jeddores' kitchen. Samantha was also lying on the floor, snoring softly. Harper was between them, tears on her face, looking scared and confused. "I'm here," Niall responded, and his own voice came out of his mouth again. "I think."

"Dammit, I thought you might have hurt yourself somehow using your power," Harper angrily wiped at her eyes, then punched him in the arm. "Don't make me worry like that again. Butthead."

"I'll try not to." Niall slowly pulled himself into a sitting position.

"Did you have another vision of the Psycho Hose Beast?"

"No, I... I think I saw your aunt's memories. I saw her fighting with Raymond, but I was seeing it from her point of view like I was inside her head. She was scared and angry, worried about Pius and Rebecca, and mad at Raymond. She was throwing dishes, screaming at him, and..." His voice trailed off. He wasn't sure if he should tell Harper the next part.

"And what? Did Uncle Raymond hurt her?"

"No! No, he walked out, and he said he was going to look for the kids."

She sniffled once and nodded. "So what happened to Aunt Samantha?"

"She was hysterical. She was thrashing and throwing things. I had to pull out of the memory, or maybe I was thrown out. I don't know. She must have cut herself in all her flailing around."

Harper nodded. "So what do we do?"

"We should probably get her to the hospital. But we'd better try and get in touch with your uncle."

"Yeah." Harper was quiet a moment, then laughed bitterly. "Niall... you just read someone's mind."

"I am still processing that little nugget of information."

"Is there anything you can't do?"

"Anything *we* can't do," he corrected her. "I can't do any of this without you, remember? We're a team, whether we like it or not."

Harper smiled slightly and punched him in the arm again, much less aggressively this time. Niall was glad. His muscle still ached from the last one.

The phone on the counter above them began to ring, shaking them from their moment. Harper crawled to her feet.

"You're getting that?" Niall asked.

"It might be about Pius or Rebecca." She picked up the phone and said hello. "Nana Josephine?"

Niall jumped to his feet. "What's wrong?"

Harper was intently listening to Niall's grandmother and nodding along. Niall waited to hear the news for an agonizing thirty seconds that seemed like thirty minutes.

"Okay, okay. I'll tell him to come home right away... Hello? Nana Josephine?" Harper clicked the receiver switch a few times, a confused look on her face.

"What's going on?"

Harper hung up the phone. "The line went dead."

"What did she say?"

"Your brother was in a car accident. Out in Cape-de-Cape."

In a flash, Niall saw the rain-drenched road, the glowing red eyes in the dark. He felt the car turning over as it went off the road. "Is he okay?"

She shook her head. "They can't find him."

Niall's legs went weak, and he had to grab the counter to steady himself. What the hell was happening? He had been in a crash, just like they had two years ago. And he disappeared, just like they did. Just when the Psycho Hose Beast was on the verge of returning. Was Nelson alive? Was this connected to Pius and Rebecca?

It was too much. Just too much. This couldn't be a coincidence.

"I have to stay with Aunt Sam," Harper said, though Niall only half heard her. "You need to go home. Your dad's at work, and your mom can't get ahold of him."

Niall nodded and took half a step toward the door. He needed to shake this off and clear his head, or he wouldn't be of any help to his mom or anyone.

What the hell was he going to do?

Before Niall could come up with an answer, all the lights in the house went out.

CHAPTER THIRTY-SIX

Silver
Thursday (?)
???

There was a scene in the new Star Wars novel, *Heir to the Empire,* where Luke Skywalker is locked into a storage closet, much like Pius was stuck in now. In the book, Luke uses the battery from his robotic hand to short out the electronic lock on the door. Pius, unfortunately, didn't have a robotic hand or an electronic lock, but he had the next best thing: a crappy lock he knew how to break through.

When Anna opened the door, Pius caught a glimpse of the doorknob and realized it was the same kind they used on the doors at Doucette Motel. It was the same knobs that Keith had shown them how to break into using a screwdriver. Pius didn't have a screwdriver, but he had something he thought might serve just as well.

Shortly after Anna left, Pius returned to the floor and started feeling around the corner. Earlier, he'd found the head of a loose nail sticking up about half a centimetre from the floorboards. It wasn't much, but it was enough to get his fingernails under and start working it out.

It was an arduous process. At first, he couldn't get it to budge and was worried he wouldn't be able to get it out at all. Then, Pius reminded himself that if he didn't get the nail out, he couldn't get out of the shed, and he and Rebecca were as good as dead.

Pius struggled until his fingertips started to bleed, but the nail was moving. He switched to his left when it got too painful with his right. Soon, his fingers cramped, and tears streamed down his face, but he pushed on. Eventually, he got it up enough to squeeze it between his fingers and wiggle it instead of tearing up his fingernails, and the progress became marginally easier.

He had no idea how much time was passing. It was probably hours, but he couldn't tell what time of day it was in the complete darkness. Finally, after what seemed like forever, the nail came loose from the floor, and Pius collapsed to catch his breath. His hands throbbed with excruciating pain.

He thought about Rebecca and how scared she must be. They had taken formula from the house; he hoped someone was feeding her. He imagined how upset his parents must be. His mother had been a mess after they were trapped in the tunnels two years ago; she would be losing her mind now that he was gone again, as was the baby, no less. He wondered where Niall and Harper were and if they were looking for him. Was anyone looking for him? Probably, if only for Rebecca's sake.

Pius was shaken from his daze when the door opened. The daylight streaming in was blinding, and he shied away from it like he hid from the trailers for that vampire movie with Tom Cruise (it looked terrifying). He did have the presence of mind to slide the nail under him, though.

"What the hell are you doing?" asked a gruff male voice with the accent of a bayman. He couldn't see the man's face, silhouetted as he was by the bright sunlight. "You scratching at the door like a cat? Dumbass."

The man tossed a plate of food on the floor and slammed the door closed. Pius heard the lock click.

He waited a few moments before rising from sitting and crawling over to the plate. The opening door at least put one of Pius' fears to rest. He only heard the one lock close—he was worried there might have been a padlock or bar on the outside that he hadn't noticed last night. At least his efforts weren't totally in vain.

Pius couldn't see the plate of food, but he felt and smelled a slice of stale buttered bread and a handful of Vienna sausages. He wolfed it down, briefly wondering if it might be poisoned. He doubted it. If the crazy stuff Anna said was true, they wanted him alive.

With renewed strength and aching hands, Pius turned his attention to the door. The nail wasn't as long or sturdy as a screwdriver, but it was big enough to wedge into the gap between the door and the frame. He was momentarily stymied by the door stop along the inside of the frame. With a little bit of patience and a lot of effort, Pius was able to use the nail to wedge the strip of trim off the frame enough to get his fingers in and tear it off completely, exposing the door latch underneath.

With his way cleared, it took less than a minute of fumbling for Pius to open the door. He dropped the nail once, and for a few seconds, he was terrified he'd lost it. While he was frantically searching the dark floor, he heard voices outside the door. He sat back, waiting for someone to barge in and drag him off to some kind of sacrificial ceremony, but the voices continued past him. He thought they were arguing about when the NHL lockout might end and when regular hockey could resume.

Pius knew he'd surely have been caught if he had opened the door at that moment. He silently prayed to the God he didn't believe in. Much to his mother's chagrin, he had long ago stopped believing in God since the stories of the Bible and creation made no sense from a logical, scientific point of view. His experiences over the last two years had also caused him to seriously question the hierarchy of the divine.

He found the nail and used it to jimmy the latch open. It was darker outside than he expected as the sun was slipping below the horizon. Had he been in here all day? At least it was easier for his eyes to adjust to the dusky light. Pius found himself in a wooded area, standing outside a long, low wood building with a row of identical doors and no windows. Several other small, utilitarian buildings were nearby, all freshly constructed. Most didn't have the shingles and siding finished yet and were just covered in bare plywood and insulation wrap. The muffled rumble of a motor indicated that one of the buildings must contain a generator, which powered the bare lightbulbs over the doors. A bit farther away was a larger concrete construction that looked much older. Pius guessed it was built by the Americans when they had the base here thirty years ago.

But where was "here?" As far as Pius knew, he could be anywhere on the island. He had to find Rebecca and figure out how to get to safety.

The first place to look was the building behind him. The doors, in a long, even row, were like the ones in Doucette's motel, just with the doorknobs turned around so they were locked from the outside. Were they the only doors you could buy in this town? They must have been on sale or something. Pius counted at least eight doors on this side of the building—how many people were they keeping locked up here?

Fortunately, not as many as they could. The first three doors Pius checked opened into tiny storage-closet-sized rooms just like the one he'd been locked in, but they were all empty. As he approached the next door, he heard voices from around the corner of the jail building. With the choice of hiding in one of the cells or making a break for it, Pius made the split-second decision to run for one of the wooden houses. He didn't want to risk getting trapped in one of the cells again, and the house was only a half-dozen paces away.

With years of practice running away from things, Pius was quicker than he looked. He bolted, then dove behind the wooden steps of the nearest house just as two figures turned the corner by the jail building opposite, less than ten metres away. Both were dressed in the same long, white robes Anna wore. One was wearing a hood that obscured his face, and the other was a balding middle-aged man Pius didn't recognize. They were arguing about who was better, Dave Andreychuk or Vincent Damphousse, so he guessed it was the same voices from earlier.

They were approaching Pius' hiding spot, heading for the house. The wide gaps in the wooden step provided no concealment, so Pius pressed as close as he could to the rocky ground and crawled backwards around the edge of the building. He turned the corner just as the men reached the stairs. They didn't go in but stopped on the steps and continued their chat.

"Buddy, Andreychuk had over fifty goals last season! And a wicked playoff run."

"Man, Damphousse killed it in the playoffs, too. I think this would have been his year."

The other man sighed. "Too bad there won't be playoffs this year."

"Look, don't remind me! There better be hockey on Sirius, that's all I'm saying."

More footsteps and voices approached. "Sister Pearl and Brother Vee are trying another spell in the bunker," said a woman's voice.

"Do they want us there to watch?"

"No."

"Thank Christ. That shit freaks me right the hell out."

Pius wanted to listen to more, but the group was gathered just a few metres from where he was hiding, and he had absolutely no cover where he was crouched by the side of the house. He slowly backed away. The large concrete building was not far from the back of the building he now crept along, and he could see an open rusty door on the treeline side from his vantage point.

He had to search everywhere, and there weren't any better options at the moment. After a quick glance to ensure the coast was clear, Pius dashed to the concrete building and slipped through the door.

The inside was dimly lit and looked not unlike the bunker they'd been trapped in two summers ago. The floors and walls were bare, crumbling concrete. There was garbage scattered about, empty beer bottles where someone had been drinking in this alcove and not bothered to clean it up. And there was only one way out of this small room—a narrow staircase leading down.

He had to find Rebecca. There was no other option.

Trembling, Pius stepped slowly down the stairs. It was cool down here and stank of horrible things he didn't want to think about. He'd been through enough in the last two years to know what dead things smelled like.

The narrow passage opened at the bottom of the stairs into a large room, but it was blocked off by a wall of oil drums and gas cans. The gasoline smell made him suspect it was fuel for the generator above. Why would they store it at the bottom of these steep, narrow stairs? It seemed inconveniently far away from where they needed it. There must have been another way out; sure enough, Pius heard voices from the other side of the drums.

He couldn't make out what they were saying, and he was about to give up and head back up the stairs when he caught a mention of "the child." Were they talking about Rebecca? As much as his soul screamed at him to escape this terrifying hole, Pius knew he had to hear more.

Following the barricade, he found a small gap between the stacked barrels and the wall, leading deeper into the chamber. It was just wide enough for the rail-thin Pius to squeeze through. He pushed his way along until he found a concealed spot where he could hear the voices more clearly and see them through a tiny space between two drums.

"...you have to do it," said a male voice, coming from a tall, cloaked figure.

"Can you just give me some time?" replied a female voice. *Anna's voice.* Pius could just make out the edge of her silhouette and see the side of her face. It was smeared with blood. "I just crawled out of a car wreck. I would appreciate a few hours to pull myself together, you know?"

"That car wreck was your fault! Why did you do that? You risked everything."

"I have a flair for the dramatic, I guess."

The man struck her with a backhand across the face. She nearly fell over but caught herself and returned to a standing position, her head bowed. "I'm sorry. I... had a moment of weakness. I thought... I thought it might be better to be dead than be here when—"

"You are a coward!" The man roared, making Pius jump. He covered his mouth and choked back a startled yelp of surprise. "Just like your parents. Killing yourself will not save you. Simple death is not a release from what we are about to face."

"I know, Brother Vee. Please forgive me."

"We don't have time to wait. You know the timelines we're facing."

"I... I'll do it." The figures adjusted their positioning, and now Pius could see they were standing beside a rough wooden table. Lying atop it was what appeared to be a human corpse. The tall male passed Anna something. "Why are you so certain this will work this time?" Anna asked.

"The scarabs are more active, giving off more energy. I believe it's because the Redeemer is drawing so close." The man opened a large plastic container that looked like the boxes fishermen used to store their catch and reached into it with a pair of metal thongs. He withdrew a giant, twitching beetle.

Pius reached up and bit his own hand to keep from screaming. The space June bugs? The Butt Monkeys, as Harper called them? How did these creeps get one?

The man held the creature over the corpse's pale, bare chest, and Anna held her hand, palm down, over the June bug. She was saying something, but Pius couldn't make out the words. Was she trying to do magic? Did she know you didn't need the words, at least according to Niall? Could she actually do magic like he did?

The man dropped the June bug, and it started to burrow into the corpse's chest like a dog digging into the lawn for a bone. Flesh ripped with a sound like tearing heavy fabric. Ribs cracked and broke. Pius felt like he was going to be sick. He turned his head and started to slip away the way he came, trying to get away from the scene before he began to vomit.

He heard a low groan that seemed to echo through the dark chamber. Anna made a sound between a screech of terror and a squeal of delight.

"It worked!" the man gasped.

"It worked?" The shock in Anna's voice was palpable. "Shit, what about all the other bodies we dumped in the bay?"

Pius risked a look back. Through the space between the metal drums, he saw the corpse slowly lifting itself to a sitting position. Its flesh was still unnaturally pale, and the side of its head was cracked open, revealing bone and brain matter beneath, likely the cause of his death. In the centre of the chest, the Butt Monkey had half-embedded itself in the man's dead flesh, looking like some sort of glossy, messed-up superhero logo.

"Glorious," the man whispered. "The return has begun already. Will this work on a living host?"

"I don't know!" Anna was definitely excited now. "How would I know? We would need a test subject..."

"There are no more prisoners... except the boy and the infant."

"No!" Anna snapped. "You can't!"

"I am well aware, Sister Pearl, you do not need to lecture me. Animating the dead is one thing, but the other rituals require Pius and his sister to be alive and healthy. Not to mention the O'Neil boy. You best not have killed him."

Niall? They captured Niall, too?

"Nelson will be fine. He's banged up, but he's alive. And you know pain and disorientation makes one more... susceptible."

The man, Brother Vee, made a weird chirping sound. "I know it very well," he said. A moment later, he made a sound that might have been a laugh. If it was, it was the most horrifying and gut-curling laugh Pius had ever heard. "We have another test subject arriving any moment. A... poetically appropriate host."

The corpse fell off the table and hit the floor with a thud. Pius jumped and made a tiny, surprised yelp. So did Anna, so he hoped no one heard him.

The walking corpse struggled to its feet, moving like a puppet with tangled strings. It twitched and spasmed grotesquely, and though Pius couldn't be sure, he thought the giant June bug in its chest was also twitching slightly.

And then the corpse raised its head and looked in Pius' direction with glassy, milky white eyes. It was the first time he'd gotten a good look at its face.

It was Keith Doucette's father.

CHAPTER THIRTY-SEVEN

Seether
Thursday October 27
8:28 pm

Niall burst into his house to find his mother and Nana Josephine sitting at the kitchen table. The fluffy orange cat Joey Smallwood rubbed his head on Nana's ankles. The room was lit with only a candle on the tabletop.

Barbara O'Neil jumped to her feet and hugged her son. "Oh, thank God you're safe. Nelson..."

"I know, Mom, I heard." Niall hugged her back. "What happened?"

His mother choked back her tears. "He was in a car that was driven off the road by a truck in Cape-de-Cape. The driver of the truck said they went over the yellow line and then swerved over the embankment, but the police aren't sure. They're still investigating."

Niall felt a slight relief. At least it wasn't a monster. But there was something about how his mom said he was "in a car."

"Who was driving the car?" he asked.

"The police say a couple of people saw him get in a green station wagon with a woman named Anna Chaffey after he left work."

Niall's relief vanished, and he broke out in a cold sweat.

He was in the car with Anna? "The police don't know what happened to them?"

His mother shook her head. "They found the car, but there was no sign of Nelson or Anna."

"He's been running around with that girl for a few weeks now," Nana Josephine chimed in. "I saw the two of them together. I'm sure it was just an accident."

A few weeks? How did he not know his brother had a girlfriend? And that it was Anna Chaffey?

The police knew she was possibly involved in other crimes, but they hadn't told his mother about it yet, which was good. No need to freak her out any more than she already was. Niall was freaking out enough for the both of them. "Mom, if they're gone, then they walked away, right? That means they're okay. Harper, Pius, and I were fine, right?"

He didn't mention that he and his friends were fine when they got into an accident because he had protected them with his magic powers. Niall didn't feel the need to unpack that right now.

"I can't get a hold of your father," she said, wiping her face. "He's at work, and the phone lines are down."

"I'm sure he'll be home soon," Nana reassured her.

Barbara shook her head. "No, if the power's out, then they're going to keep everyone there to make sure the reserve power holds up and then reset the machines when they come back on."

"Then we'll go tell him," said Nana, grabbing the car keys off the rack.

"Mom, I'm in no condition to drive."

"I'll drive. I'm not that senile yet." At sixty-five years old, Nana Josephine was far from senile, especially since they had freed her from the witch's soul that used to share her body. She didn't drive much, but she could replace a car's oil and repair a small engine with ease. She and her late husband had really been into cars.

"We'll all go," Niall added. He wanted to go back to check on Harper, but he couldn't leave his mom in this situation. They had to tell his dad, and then they had to find his brother. Nelson could be a dick sometimes, but he was still his family. Niall just wished he could help everyone.

They opened the door and nearly ran into Stacey, who was just coming up the steps.

"Oh, hi, Niall," she said breathlessly. She looked at the two ladies in the door. "Niall's mom, Niall's grandma, I assume?"

"Mom, Nana, this is Stacey Peters."

She held out a hand. "I'm Niall's... friend." Niall's mom looked at it strangely, but Nana accepted it and shook it firmly. "Look, I was just hoping to talk to Niall for a minute."

Nana brushed past her, ushering her daughter along. "Sorry, we're having a bit of a family emergency."

"I'm sorry, it's really important, and it will only take a minute..."

Niall looked at Stacey carefully. Her blue eyes were filled with fear and panic, as well as eagerness. She really wanted to talk to him—badly.

"Mom, Nana, maybe I should stay here—"

"Nonsense," said Nana cheerfully as she put Niall's mom into the passenger seat of the family's blue Chevrolet Malibu. "We aren't leaving you here alone with your new sweetheart. Get in, Stacey, you can come with us."

Now Stacey looked really uncomfortable. "I don't know if that's a good idea."

"Fine," said Nana as she got into the driver's seat. "Then stay here. Niall, get in the car!"

"What's wrong?" Niall said softly. He took Stacey's hand. He wasn't sure why, but he knew he didn't want her to be upset.

"I don't... I can't... I need to tell you something."

"Then get in the car, come on. We can talk on the way."

Stacey looked on the verge of tears, but she nodded and allowed Niall to lead her to the car, much like Nana had led his mother. What the hell was going on? What was so important that she had to tell him?

Now, Niall was worried about her, Harper, Nelson, Pius, Samantha, and his mom. Why was everyone around him falling apart? Was this his fault somehow? And how was he supposed to help everyone?

The car pulled out of the driveway and turned right down Civil Street. They just started getting a bit of speed when Nana slammed on the brakes, throwing Niall forward in his seatbelt.

A very red-faced and sweaty Skidmark was standing in front of the car. He collapsed on the hood, gasping for breath. Nana rolled down the window to yell at him. "Skidoo, are you okay?"

"I'm... fine..." Skidmark gasped, holding up a hand to beg for a moment. "I just... ran the whole... way here..."

It was the slowest Niall had ever heard Skidmark speak. It would probably be the slowest he would ever speak because the round, sweaty kid looked ready to drop dead any second.

"Well, if you would kindly move out of the way," said Nana, "we're in a bit of a hurry."

"I... just need... to talk to... Niall..."

"Well, our Niall seems popular tonight," joked Nana.

Skidmark finally raised his head, looking past the ladies in the front seat to the kids sitting in the back. His eyes locked on Stacey, sitting beside Niall. His glistening, thick, crimson face turned into a glare of pure anger and hatred.

"You!" he snarled.

A second later, he added, "How the hell did you get here so fast?"

CHAPTER THIRTY-EIGHT

Blind
Thursday October 27
7:48 pm

Tanguay got out of the car and headed for the detachment. She was struck by the memory of making this same walk just last week when she came back to work for the first time in a year and a half. There were several differences.

She didn't drive herself this time. She sat in the passenger seat of Cheryl's car. She couldn't trust herself in her present state.

Last week, she didn't use her cane because she didn't want to appear weak. Now she leaned on it heavily and didn't give a damn.

Then, she was in pain and was using pills to fight it. Now, she was in more pain, and the pills were just to keep her conscious.

Last week, she also hadn't been carrying nearly so many weapons.

She approached the employee entrance of the detachment with more determination than ever, driven by rage and willpower, hoping it was enough to keep her going a little longer.

Tanguay practically kicked the door in, regretting the impact with every bone in her body. She had wanted to catch Peters by surprise if possible, but that might have been too much.

"Where is he?" she demanded into the dimly lit office. "Where is Peters?"

Bennett stood up so quickly from his desk that he spilled his tea. Brake shoved something into his drawer, probably dirty magazines. "What's up, Sarge?" Bennett asked, frantically wiping the tea off the crotch of his pants.

Both men looked thrown—whether it was because she caught them in the middle of something they weren't supposed to be doing or because she was packing an arsenal's worth of weapons, Tanguay didn't know or care.

"Where the hell is Peters?"

"Peters went out," Brake replied, running a hand through his greasy black hair and pulling on his uniform hat. "You feeling okay, Sarge?"

"I told her the guns might be a bit much, but she's a little upset, you understand..." Cheryl muttered behind her.

Tanguay hobbled over to the commanding officer's office and stopped at the door. "Why is my office locked?"

Bennett cleared his throat and pointed at the nameplate. "Sgt. Peters," it read.

The paperwork hadn't been finalized yet, and he'd moved into her office. *That son of a bitch.*

Tanguay put down her cane and, without hesitation, raised the shotgun slung over her shoulder and blasted the knob on her old office door. The gunshot was deafening in the small space. Cheryl screamed, and Brake dove under his desk. He was still jumpy from when he'd gotten shot by that Russian arms dealer a while back.

Bennett choked. "Christ, woman, we have a key!"

"You have a key to Peters' office?"

"We had a key when it was yours, too. How else do you think we could steal the good pens from your cabinet?"

She always wondered why the detachment bought so many of those friggin' pens. It didn't matter now. She opened the door and flicked the light on inside the tiny, clean office. Peters somehow kept it neater than she did. In her experience, psychopaths were always tidy.

"Mind if I ask what's going on?" Bennett asked sheepishly.

"Show them," said Tanguay, not looking up. She began rifling through the desk drawers.

With shaking fingers, Cheryl handed Bennett the paper she had shown Tanguay earlier that day. It was a statement from Cecil Doucette's neighbour, who said that he saw two men visiting the Doucettes' house early the morning of Cecil's death. One of them was carrying something that looked like a baseball bat.

Bennett's face turned white. "None of this is in the official report. Who took this statement?"

"Peters, of course. Where's Keith?"

Bennett slowly lowered the paper. "In holding cell number one."

"I'll get him," Brake called from outside, possibly still under his desk. She heard him scramble away. He returned quickly, though, his usually stoic poker face glowing with dread. "He's gone."

"What do you mean, gone?"

Brake scratched his thin moustache nervously. "The kid, Keith, he's not in the cell. I saw him down there myself about an hour ago."

"Has anyone else been in there?"

"No, I don't..." Bennett's round face lit up with recognition. "About forty minutes ago. Cheryl was out to check on you, and Brake was on a coffee run. I went to the toilet and told Sarge to watch the phones. When I came back, he was gone."

"And so was Keith, I'm guessing," grumbled Tanguay. She gave up on the desk and started going through the filing cabinet.

"Why would he take Keith?" asked Bennett. "And why would he cover up those men at Cec's place?"

Tanguay found what she was looking for. She pulled two file folders from the back of the cabinet and threw them on the desk. Newspaper clippings spilled out of the first one, revealing an odd assortment of headlines.

"UFO's in Clarenville? Mass suicide at the Solar Temple?" Bennett scratched his head. "What do aliens and cults have to do with the Doucettes?"

Brake folded his skinny arms across his narrow chest. "I always knew that Cec Doucette was up to something. He probably knows who shot Kennedy, too."

"It has nothing to do with the Doucettes! It's about Peters." She opened the second folder. It contained a handful of scribbled note pages and a half-filled report. Everyone leaned in and stared at the papers."

"This is about Jake Cutler and Jerome Wheeler, those fishermen who were killed on their boat last week." Cheryl covered her mouth in horror. "This can't be right. I saw the official report; it said it was an accident."

Brake picked up the file and looked at it more closely with his black beady eyes. "Bodies were mutilated... bite marks... a third dead body..." He looked up at Tanguay, his thin face paler than usual. "This can't be right. What the hell is going on?"

Tanguay took a deep breath and sighed. It was time to tell them. She didn't give a shit about anything anymore except finding those kids. "A lot is happening in this town that I haven't told you about..."

So, she started to tell the story of everything that had happened in Gale Harbour over the last two years. And then the lights went out.

Niall did not get a chance to talk to Stacey. He ended up crammed in between her and Skidmark in the backseat while Skidmark berated her the whole time for being a "vile, lying skank trying to ruin Niall's life."

Skidmark had insisted on coming with them. Niall didn't want him to; his mother didn't want him to, but Nana Josephine had a soft spot for Skidmark and told him to hop in. He gladly complied, insisting that his presence was required so that "the evil harlots didn't betray Niall's trust any further."

By the time they had reached the Strip, Niall was fed up with Skidmark's raving, but Nana seemed to think it was quite a joke. "Is this from one of your plays, Brian? I saw you in that one the school put on earlier this year, Rocky Horror Show, was it? You were very good."

"Did you see it the night I fell off the stage and landed on the drummer in the band?"

"No, but you did put your head through the fake wall and knocked down part of the set."

"Oh, you saw the Tuesday show, then. I was pretty good that night."

Mrs. Walsh must have been very thankful for Skidmark saving her life last year because there was no way he should have been on any stage. Even playing Eddie, with only one song and less than five minutes of stage time, he was still a catastrophic disaster every night.

"I thought that might have been a little... *risqué* for a high school show, don't you think?" asked Niall's mom. She had complained about it at the PTA last spring, but her warnings fell on deaf ears. It wasn't until after the show opened that everyone started clutching their pearls. It would seem none of the parents at St. Paul's High School had heard of the Rocky Horror Show before this past June. "I felt sorry for that poor boy who wore the gold speedo through the whole show."

"Oh yeah, that was Aaron Wheeler. Mrs. Walsh kept telling him he looked flabby, and I think it gave him an eating disorder. He looked great for opening night, though."

Stacey leaned into Niall. "Did your school really do the Rocky Horror Show for the school play?" she whispered.

"Unfortunately, yes."

"Who played Dr. Frank N. Furter?

"Mrs. Walsh."

Stacey looked horrified. Niall shook his head. "It's worse than you think. You've never seen Eleanor Walsh in lingerie and fishnets."

"You better not be badmouthing Eleanor!" Skidmark roared.

"No," replied Stacey.

"Good! I don't ever want to hear her beautiful name in your trash hole mouth again!"

"Brian, stop it!" Niall snapped at him.

Stacey seemed to have had enough, too. "What *is* your problem, anyway? Why are you treating me like this? We bought you a movie ticket and popcorn."

"You did?" asked Niall.

"I would never have accepted your filthy handouts if I had known about this!"

Skidmark pulled a walkie-talkie out of his bag. He had insisted on keeping the green bookbag on his lap, which crowded the backseat even more. Stacey stared at the radio blankly. "It's a walkie-talkie."

"I know it's a walkie-talkie. It's yours, right?"

"Um, no?"

"I found it in your backpack at the movie theatre. And guess what I heard on it? Satan worshippers talking about sacrificing Pius and his little sister!"

Stacey's face twisted to a visage of horror and disgust. "What are you talking about?"

"Brian Hawco!" snapped Niall's mom. "Don't you dare say such horrible things."

Niall said nothing. Thanks to his experiences over the last two years, he couldn't completely rule out Skidmark's ramblings.

"Brian…" said Nana. They were approaching the turn-off to the matchstick factory now. "You actually heard people talking about sacrificing the Jeddore children to Satan?"

Skidmark grumbled, "Well, not exactly. But I heard two guys with bay-wop accents going on about Sister-so-and-so and Brother-what's-his-name and tributes and how they were the ones who cut off the phones and electricity!"

Stacey turned on him. "Brian, I barely know you. You certainly don't know me, so I don't know what the hell is wrong with you! How can you accuse me of this nonsense? I've never seen that radio before in my life, and I have no idea what you're talking about! Niall, is he always this insane?"

Niall really wished they hadn't dragged him into this. "I mean, Skidmark's a bit weird at times, but some of it isn't out of the realm of—"

"—Why are the Mounties here?" Niall's mom asked, the breath catching in her throat. They were driving past a high chain-link fence, beyond which was a police cruiser with lights flashing.

Niall was glad for the reprieve. "That's not the factory," Niall corrected her. "That's the power station. They're probably here because of the power outage. The entrance to the matchstick factory is a bit farther down the road."

"See?" Skidmark looked smug. "The cops are in on the power outage, and Stacey's dad is there overseeing it!"

Stacey tried to crawl over Niall to get to Skidmark, and Niall had to hold her back. He felt a brief flash of excitement at having her body pressed so close to his, and he thought for a split second he may have accidentally touched her boob, but then Nana slammed on the brakes, and they were all thrown forward, ending the brief scuffle and Niall's inadvertent attempts at reaching second base.

"We're here," Nana announced.

Before them stood a chain-link gate and a small booth where a lone night watchman sat. He stood up as Nana, Niall's mom, and Skidmark exited the car. Skidmark was trying to escape Stacey, but Stacey didn't chase him out. Instead, she hesitated and put her hand on Niall's. His heart raced again, and his mind flip-flopped with a thousand conflicting thoughts, but he was not expecting the words out of Stacey's mouth.

"Niall… I'm sorry. Part of what Brian said… is true."

And then she was gone, out of the car, and storming off, away from the gate back the way they came. Niall scrambled out after her.

"Stacey!" he called. "Where are you going?"

She looked back but continued walking away. "I'm going to see if that was my dad back there. And Niall, please... don't trust him."

Niall was about to ask who she was talking about, but his mom touched his shoulder, and he nearly leapt out of his Reeboks. "Nana knows the guard. He's going to let us inside to meet your dad. Where's your friend going?"

"She..." *Where was she going?* "She said she saw her dad back at the power station. He's a cop."

"Really? You could do worse than a Mountie's daughter with how much trouble you and your friends get into." His mom smiled, but Niall couldn't tell whether she was kidding. "She's probably upset about what Brian said, and I don't blame her. What is wrong with that boy?"

Skidmark was an idiot, but he was one of the most brutally honest people Niall knew. If he thought he had heard something about Satan worshippers and sacrifices, Niall was inclined to believe him. Of course, Skidmark might have misunderstood what he overheard... "He's just... weird, Mom. Come on, let's go find Dad."

When the guard opened the gate, Nana drove inside and parked in the employee lot. Only one emergency light was on over the guard booth and another near the factory entrance. Otherwise, the parking lot and the large factory building looming over them were dark and oppressive. A few more lights illuminated a ship moored to the loading dock a hundred metres away. St Stephen's Bay was black and still, reflecting only the silver moonlight.

Farther along the coastline, where Gale Harbour was supposed to be, was a complete void of inky darkness. Niall felt his stomach lurch and hoped that it wasn't an omen.

They walked through the door and into blackness. Niall had only been at the factory during daylight hours and did not recognize the dark, shadowy corridors. The group momentarily stood in the employee lounge, unsure which way to go. Two open doors led to two hallways, both dimly lit by distant emergency lights. Fortunately, they weren't waiting long, as another employee in overalls—a short, heavyset man with a grey moustache—appeared and recognized Niall's mom. He said he would return with Johnny in just a moment and hurried off.

"It's so quiet," said Niall's mom. "The last time I was here, you could hear the machines rumbling all the time. Hell, Johnny's going deaf from the noise. It's eerie, being so quiet."

It wasn't the only thing that was eerie. Niall ushered Skidmark away from the adults and confronted him. "Brian, where did you get that walkie-talkie?"

"I told you, it was in Stacey's bag. Or maybe it was in Erin's... or Jennifer's. It was one of the girls' bags, anyway."

That sounded like the Skidmark Niall knew. "And you're *sure* you heard that stuff about sacrifices and Satan worshippers?"

"Yes! I mean, no one called themselves 'Satan worshippers,' I'm sure bad guys don't go around calling themselves 'the bad guys,' except I guess the Nazis called themselves Nazis, but they thought they were the good guys. Of course, how you could be the good guys with a name like 'Nazis,' I have no idea. They had skulls on their hats, for crying out loud!"

"Brian!" Niall snapped. "What did you hear?"

"One of them said Sister Pearl wanted to wait, but Brother Vic, or Vee, maybe it was Ee? said he wanted to do it tonight. And the other guy said he felt bad for the tributes because they were just kids."

Dammit. It didn't necessarily mean it was Pius and Rebecca, but it sounded bad. Maybe they should go back and find Stacey's dad, too. But Stacey said not to trust Brian. Maybe he had misunderstood something. There had to be something else she knew. She was really upset and seemed to want to tell him herself.

Niall's dad burst into the room and rushed to his mother. He wore safety goggles over his glasses, and his sandy hair was cut much shorter than the long golden locks he rocked in his wedding pictures from the seventies. However, when his dad swept into the room and comforted his mother, he looked far more masculine and intimidating than Niall had ever remembered. He was a big guy, over six feet tall with broad shoulders, and in pretty good shape from hockey or whatever it was he did on Wednesday nights. Niall only ever thought of him as his dad, not as a man with a wife and a family to protect.

Niall's mom and Nana quickly explained what had happened—how Nelson had been in a car with a suspicious woman, they'd been in an accident, and now neither could be found. His dad hugged his mom—Niall was reminded again how large his dad actually was—and then he said they would head out immediately.

They didn't have a chance to turn toward the exit before the door opened, and a police officer walked in. It was Sergeant Peters, dressed in full uniform and carrying a flashlight. He, too, was a large man, at least as tall as Niall's dad, and in his bulletproof vest and utility belt, he looked much beefier as well.

"The O'Neils," Sergeant Peters said, smiling. "Just the people I was hoping to find. Stacey told me you would all be here."

"Where is Stacey?" Niall asked dumbly.

"She's in the car."

Niall's dad stepped forward. "Has there been any word about Nelson?"

"Unfortunately, no, not yet, but I would like you all to come to the station with me to answer a few questions..."

Movement in the windows behind Sergeant Peters caught Niall's eye. There were at least two men out there, obscured by shadows. They just appeared to be waiting. But waiting for what?

They didn't look like cops. Niall couldn't make out any details, but one had on a backward baseball cap, and the other's head was bare. It was definitely not like Peters' uniform. Why were they out there? Could they be factory workers on a smoke break? There was no one out there when they came in a few minutes ago. They seemed to have shown up with Stacey's dad.

Stacey's dad. Who was just at the power station with Skidmark's Satan worshippers. Satan worshippers with baymen accents, like the men who had followed Keith and Pius the other day.

"Don't trust him," Stacey had said.

What if she wasn't talking about Skidmark?

Sergeant Peters started to usher his family to the door, but Niall stopped abruptly. "Who's Sister Pearl?"

Niall watched the Mountie's face and saw the surprise and recognition. It lasted only a fraction of a second, and he quickly regained his neutral composure, but Niall saw it.

"I'm sorry?" Peters asked. "I have no idea what you're talking about. Now, please, if you would all come with me—"

"I don't think we will," said Niall defiantly.

"Niall!" His mother gasped. "Don't talk to the Sergeant like that."

"Hey, Niall," said Peters, "I know you're worried about your friends. It's been a stressful week. You're probably not thinking clearly."

"I'm thinking more clearly now than I have in a long time." What he was doing was crazy, but Niall had a feeling in his gut that leaving with this man right now would be a terrible idea. "Who are the men waiting for us outside?"

Now, Peters looked irritated. "Niall, you're being irrational—"

"Are they the same men who chased Pius and Keith home the other night?"

"Could be," said Skidmark, peering out the window. "All baymen look the same to me."

"Who are the tributes?" Niall demanded, feeling more brazen now. "Is it Pius and Rebecca? And what do Nelson and Anna have to do with it?"

Peters grimaced, grinding his teeth. He was pissed. Niall's mother looked horrified, and Peters was probably not used to people standing up to him like this. "Okay, I'm losing my patience. Jimmy, Carl, get in here!"

Peters reached for his gun, but Niall's dad was faster. He crossed the distance between Niall and the Mountie before Niall realized what happened, and his hand was on Peters' wrist before the gun cleared the holster. Johnny O'Neil twisted Peters' arm with practiced fluidity, bending it at an uncomfortable angle and causing him to drop the pistol.

At that exact moment, the door flew open, revealing two very un-police-looking men. One was wearing a backward Blue Jays cap and a flannel jacket; the other wore a hunting vest. The one in the cap took half a step into the room before Skidmark, standing by the window next to the entrance, threw his full weight on the door and slammed it into the thug's face.

"Go!" Niall's dad called to the rest of them. "Down the right hallway!" He twisted Peters' arm some more and flipped him completely over onto his back. The door flew open, and the first guy charged in again. Johnny caught him with a sidekick to the jaw, sending him hurling backwards into the second man behind him.

And then they were running through the dark hallways of the factory. Niall couldn't believe what had just happened. "How did Dad just do that?" He was behind his mother and Nana, ushering them along.

"Your father has a blackbelt in karate!" Niall's mom called back. They came to an intersection in the dark corridor. Without any clear direction, they turned right again.

Niall was flummoxed. "What? How did I not know this?"

"What do you think he does every Wednesday night?"

CHAPTER FORTY

Glycerine
Thursday October 27
9:30 pm

They weren't storing the fuel in the basement of the bunker out of convenience but as a fail-safe. If something went wrong, they could blow up the fuel and the butt monkeys with it.

Pius had reached this conclusion after slipping back up the stairs and finding a safe hideout in the trees outside the bunker. It was ghastly that they were keeping the alien bugs at all, and the fact that they were using them to create some kind of zombie somehow made it even worse.

How had they collected so many of the bugs? It was obvious, Pius quickly realized. The town had been swarmed by butt monkeys on the night of the meteor shower last year. Niall had destroyed many of them, and many more were absorbed into the carapace before it was disintegrated. But there were thousands upon thousands around Gale Harbour that night. Only one or two were found the following day, sparking rumours of some kind of radiated mutant Junebug. As far as Pius knew, neither the RCMP nor the military had made a concerted effort to collect any leftover bugs. Which meant these... cultists or whatever they were must have picked them up. *All of them.*

Who were they? How long had they been in Gale Harbour? Was Anna already with them when she and Keenan rolled through last year? Had her interest in Niall and Theolina been about this plot to animate the dead using the butt monkeys?

No. It wasn't just about the bugs. They had bigger plans, Anna had told him herself. Pius had to find his sister and get out of there. Wherever they were.

He was near the coast; he could smell the seawater, but he had no idea whether that was on the South Shore, somewhere on the Cape-de-Cape peninsula, or north toward Gros Morne. He wished he'd been able to get more clues on the way here.

He would figure out where he was and how to return home later. First, he had to find Rebecca. Since he'd checked the bunker and the cells, only the two houses were left as the likely location...

Pius heard a car approaching in the distance. Fortunately, now that it was dark, he could move around more confidently. Pius hurried back to the bunker's wall and pressed himself against the cool concrete. He tried not to think of what was inside.

He crept around the edge of the building to get a look. While he knew he had been delivered here in a van, he hadn't seen any vehicles come or go since breaking out of his cell. A car and a couple of pickup trucks were parked in a cleared dirt field not far from the bunker, but they were all locked up tight, and so far, he hadn't found any keys. He needed to take stock of any changes in the situation in case a plan or opportunity presented itself.

Having plans and small goals was good. It was the only thing keeping Pius from completely losing his marbles.

A white van appeared through the trees beyond the bunker. It was the same van that had picked him up or was one like it. It pulled up in front of the holding cells, and two men in white robes hopped out. They dragged a third figure out of the van with a bag on their head. Pius was pretty sure it was a young man or teenager. His suspicions were confirmed when they pulled off the bag before tossing him into one of the cells.

"Keith?" Pius asked aloud, dumbfounded. He covered his mouth and flattened himself against the wall so hard he knocked the air out of his lungs. *Stupid, stupid.* He didn't think anyone heard him, but he couldn't risk that. His life, and his sister's, depended on him not getting caught.

After carefully looking in all directions to ensure no hooded zealots were rushing at him, Pius poked his head around the corner just in time to see the two men who had tossed Keith in the storage room disappear into one of the houses. Pius counted to three hundred, then made a wide circle of the compound to return to the holding cells. With no further sight or sound of the hooded people, Pius crept up to Keith's door, unlocked it, and slowly opened it.

A heavy body flung itself on top of Pius, and he inadvertently cried out in shock and pain. Pius was thrown to the ground and winded for the second time in less than ten minutes. He covered his head to protect himself as his assailant hauled back to punch him in the face.

"Pius?" Keith asked stupidly, his fist hanging in the air. "Why are you working with the Satan worshippers?"

"I'm not working with..." Pius started to say, then heard a screen door opening. "Run!" he hissed instead.

Keith, to his credit, didn't hesitate. He leapt to his feet and took off around the side of the jail building toward the tree line. Pius scrambled after him, taking an extra half-second to close Keith's cell door with his foot. If the cultists hadn't already seen them, there was no need to give them a clue that they'd escaped.

Pius tripped about three metres away from the bushes, banging his knee badly. He managed to choke back his cry of pain this time, but he had no idea if the cultists could see him. Before he could react, Keith leapt out of the underbrush, grabbed Pius under the arms, and bodily dragged him into the bushes.

"My leg..." Pius started to moan, but Keith put a hand over his mouth. The bigger boy was staring out through the trees, his blue eyes following something closely, but otherwise, Keith was utterly still and quiet.

"What're you doing, Goulds?" called a voice from the direction of the house.

"Nothing. I thought I heard something." The second voice, a deep man's voice, came from just a few steps away from Pius' head. Pius broke into a cold sweat and willed himself not to shudder. How could the guy have not seen them? Keith must have pulled him to safety in just the nick of time.

Pius heard the crunch of feet on gravel as Brother Goulds walked away, and then a moment later, the screen door of one of the cabins banged closed again. Keith finally removed his hand and smiled down at Pius. "Damn, that was close." He helped Pius to his feet. "What the hell are you doing here?"

"They kidnapped Rebecca and me," Pius explained. "Anna Chaffey is helping them."

Keith's face contorted with recognition and confusion. "The chick with the boobs? I knew she was weird, but I didn't think she was into kidnapping kids."

"They got you too?" Pius asked, realizing they were probably also looking for Niall, Harper, and Skidmark. However, if they were smart, they would probably leave Skidmark alone.

Keith shook his head. "Not exactly. I was in the holding cell down at the police station. That new Sergeant, what's his name, Peters, came in and unlocked the door. I thought they were transferring me or something, but he punched me in the gut and put a bag over my head."

"Why were you in jail?"

"They say I killed my father."

Oh my God. Pius felt sick. Keith's father. The corpse he'd just seen animated by a terrifying magical ritual. Pius' legs went weak, and he sat back on the ground.

Keith crouched down beside him. "It's okay! I didn't do it, I swear! I think those same bastards in the truck framed me. I think they're the same guys chased us from Tim Hortons, too."

Pius nodded but didn't say anything. How was he supposed to tell Keith his father was a possessed monster? The feeble hold Pius had managed to keep on his nerves so far was slipping away. It was too much. This was all too much. How did he possibly think that useless Pius Jeddore was supposed to rescue himself or anyone else?

Keith must have sensed his discomfort and put an uncharacteristic hand on his shoulder. "It's okay, man, it's gonna be okay. We've been in worse spots. We're gonna find your sister and get out of here."

"I don't know where we are," Pius breathed, fighting back tears.

"We're near the Boot," Keith said matter-of-factly. He saw Pius' confusion and explained. "LeBotte, right at the tip of Cape-de-Cape Peninsula. I heard the guys in the van on the way here mention a couple of place names, plus the length of the drive and the shitty road makes me pretty certain. That old bunker, though—" He pointed at the concrete building that housed his zombie father and a thousand alien bugs in the basement. "—is what really did it for me. That's one of the old American monitoring stations. I saw a picture of it in Tricia's office. She's my dad's secretary. Was my dad's secretary."

Fuuuudge. He had to tell him. How was he going to tell him? Pius racked his brain for some way of breaking to Keith that his dead father, the man he'd been accused of murdering, had been reanimated as a zombie. How did you tell a guy that?

"Keith, I—" Pius started to speak, but the words died in his throat. They did not come back to life like Keith's father did.

"What buddy?"

Pius shook his head. "Nothing. I'm just... glad you're here."

"Let's go get your sister from these bastards," Keith said.

CHAPTER FORTY-ONE

Sabotage
Thursday, October 27
10:10 pm

Niall cowered behind a long, quiet conveyor belt with his mother, grandmother and idiot friend. Somewhere in the dark, cavernous room around them, the footsteps of armed men echoed on the concrete floor.

Niall had never been in the matchstick factory before, had never seen where his dad worked. He had never really been interested in it. Hell, he didn't know his dad was a friggin' black belt, so he definitely didn't pay enough attention to conversations around the dinner table. He wished he had. If he'd just taken his dad up on that offer of "take your kid to work day," he might have a general idea of how to get out of this place. But no, he had insisted on going to school instead because it was pizza day at the cafeteria.

They didn't know where his dad was. He could be hurt or captured, and they wouldn't know. Niall's mom was sobbing, Skidmark was clutching his green bookbag and mumbling something about how this was just like an episode of M.A.N.T.I.S., and Nana Josephine was... well, surprisingly calm. That woman was as steady as a rock, more so after the ghost sharing her body was exorcised.

Her pink tracksuit was dirty from crawling around the factory floor, and a few silver strands of hair were out of place, but otherwise, Nana was as calm and put-together as if she were on her way to Church. "Settle down, Barbara," she said, patting her daughter on the arm. Everything is going to be fine."

"How is it going to be fine?" Niall's mom managed between gasps. "There are men with guns chasing us!"

"Niall, check that door to see if it's locked." Nana gestured at a metal door a few metres away behind some other machinery. Niall hadn't noticed it—Nana was as sharp as she was calm. He would have to leave the safety of their hiding spot and cross an open patch of factory floor to reach the door, but Niall agreed it was their best chance. He nodded and crept as quietly as he could, but every soft footfall of his sneakers sounded like a gunshot in his head. He wished Harper was here, she was much better at this sort of thing. Even Pius was pretty quiet when he wanted to be, like a scared mouse creeping behind a wall.

It seemed to take an hour, but Niall finally reached the wall and ducked down near the door. No one cried out or shot at him, so Niall assumed he wasn't spotted. Then, with equal care, he slowly pushed the latch and opened the steel fire door. The other side was equally dark to the factory floor they were now on, except for a single dim emergency light twenty metres away, illuminating a long, empty corridor.

"It's clear," Niall mouthed, hoping Nana could see him well enough in the low lighting. She nodded and then ushered Barbara to hurry across the floor. Niall grabbed his mom's hand and pulled her toward the door. She nearly made it but tripped on a cable and bumped into a heavy plastic container on the machine Niall was hiding behind. It crashed to the ground with a deafening bang.

"Go!" Nana cried out, shoving Skidmark toward the door.

"Hey, they're over there!" someone yelled from the dark room.

Niall shoved his mom through the door just as Skidmark crashed into him. Nana came behind him just as several gunshots rang out. Barbara screamed.

"My Magic cards!" Skidmark shouted.

Niall saw what was happening but was too slow to stop it. Brian's bookbag was still lying next to the conveyor belt. The stupid dumbass dove back across the open aisle, and another gunshot rang out. He grabbed the bag and rolled back to the door just as another bullet smashed into the concrete floor centimetres from his head.

"You idiot!" Niall screamed, shoving Skidmark through the door. Niall dove in behind him and slammed the door closed.

The gunshots stopped. In the other room, Niall could hear muffled voices.

"Stop shooting! You dumb... What if you kill the kid? Brother Vee will have our heads!"

Brother Vee?

"Niall..." Nana Josephine whispered.

Niall turned around and realized that his mother and grandmother hadn't fled down the hall as he expected but were instead just a few steps away. Nana Josephine was slouched against the wall, Barbara kneeling over her.

"It's going to be okay, Mom, you're going to be okay..."

Blood was pooling under Niall's grandmother.

"Go on with you," Nana Josephine said, her voice faltering. "Take Niall, get him out of here."

"Mom, I'm not leaving without you."

"I can't... I'm not walking out of here..."

Niall crawled over and took his grandmother's other hand. His eyes were stinging. "Nana, you don't remember, but we made it through way worse than this in the tunnels under the town. You didn't survive that just to die here..."

Nana looked up at him and smiled. "I do remember, Niall. You gave... an old woman her life back... To let her see her grandson grow... into a fine young man." Nana squeezed Barbara's hand and then turned to smile at her. "You listen to Niall, you hear? Whatever he says... however crazy it sounds... you do it, okay?"

"Mom, what are you talking about?"

"I love you, Barb. Tell your brothers I love them, too... and tell Niall... who Nelson really is..."

Nana went silent, and the hand in Niall's fingers went limp. Niall's mother shook with sobs and threw her arms around the old woman's body. She was gone. She couldn't be gone. Nana was always there. She was the rock that held their family together, stronger than any of them...

And what did she mean about "who Nelson really is?"

"They're coming!" Skidmark yelled, just seconds before the fire door flew open and a shadowy figure appeared. A pistol was pointed directly at Niall's head.

"Come on!" said a rough voice. "All of you out of there. Now!"

"Hey, you just killed Niall's grandmother, you asshole!" Skidmark snapped. The man grabbed him by the shoulder and shoved him through the door to the factory floor. It was the guy in the hunting vest. He gestured at Niall and his mother with the gun. "Both of you too. Move!"

Niall awkwardly pulled his mother to her feet. She was shaking and sobbing.

Please, Mom, hold it together, he begged silently. Between Nelson and now Nana, she was on the verge of completely falling apart. He didn't need her to become a catatonic wreck like Pius did in the tunnels two years ago. There was no one here who could carry her.

Niall led her forward, through the door and toward the man with the gun. As they passed him, Barbara leapt forward and smashed her forehead into the bayman's nose. There was a sickening crunch, and he dropped the gun. He didn't have time to recover before she grabbed the man by the hair and slammed his face into the steel door. He stumbled forward, head down, and Barbara proceeded to slam the door onto the man's temple again and again until he went limp on the floor.

Okay, I don't need to worry about her holding it together. "Mom, did Dad teach your karate?"

"No," she growled and picked up the man's pistol.

"Drop it!" screamed an enraged voice from nearby. Barbara whirled, gun in hand, and Niall followed her gaze to find Sergeant Peters holding his dad with an arm around his neck, a gun to his head. The other bayman in the Blue Jays cap was nearby, his own gun drawn.

A bright red vein was popping in Peters' thick neck, and he was sporting a fresh black eye. "I don't want to hurt you! I only need the kid!"

"You killed my mother!" Barbara growled. She had the gun pointed squarely at Peters, but Niall could see her hands shaking.

"Drop the gun!" Peters demanded again.

"You bastards killed my mother!"

Peters pointed the gun at the floor and pulled the trigger. Niall's father howled in pain.

"You shot him?" Barbara's face was as white as her blood-stained blouse.

"Let's see you do that fancy karate shit now, Bruce Lee," Peters hissed in Niall's dad's ear. Johnny's leg crumpled under him, and Peters' arm around his neck kept him on his feet.

Barbara let the gun fall from her fingers to the floor. Niall tried to tell her to stop, but it was too late. Peters raised his weapon at Barabara.

Niall's father, despite his wound, twisted his body and elbowed Peters in the ribs. The blow didn't do much damage through the

Mountie's protective vest, but it did cause his shot to go wide. Barbara screamed as the bullet ricocheted somewhere in the darkness.

Another gunshot ran through the factory. The thug standing beside Peters fell to the floor.

Niall's father dove clear. Sergeant Peters scanned the darkness, fear creeping into his square-jawed face for the first time. A familiar Quebecois accent called out from the shadows.

"Drop the gun or *jurer devant Dieu*, I will put the next bullet in your skull."

"You aggravating French bitch, you think you can threaten—"

Another gunshot. Peters screamed out in pain and clutched his right arm. His pistol clattered to the floor.

Sergeant Tanguay appeared through the darkness, wearing her bulletproof vest and gun belt over jeans and a Montreal Canadiens jersey. Niall didn't think he'd ever seen her out of uniform. She was limping and sweaty, and her black hair was tangled and matted, but her eyes were deadly clear and focused.

"You're lucky," she growled. "I was aiming for your head."

Niall and his mother rushed to his dad's side. He'd been shot in the foot. There was a lot of blood, but Niall hoped it wasn't too bad. His mom kissed him and then pulled off his belt.

"Mrs. O'Neil!" whistled Skidmark as he slipped into the darkness. "Now is not the time!"

Barbara ignored him and tied the belt around her husband's lower leg to slow the bleeding. Niall was impressed. His mom was actually quite competent under pressure.

Constables Bennett and Brake appeared beside Tanguay.

Peters made a last desperate effort to save his skin. "Constables! Arrest her!"

Bennett and Brake looked at each other. Brake, the tall, skinny one with the creepy moustache, shrugged. "You know what, buddy? I don't think we will."

The portly Bennett nodded. "Yep. She might be an aggravating French bitch, but she's *our* aggravating French bitch."

"Plus," added Brake, "you've gone right off your friggin' rocker."

"Where's the Jeddore kids?" Tanguay demanded. "Where's Nelson O'Neil? Where's Keith Doucette?"

Peters grinned through gritted, pained teeth. "We need them."

"*Need* them?" Her gun never wavered. "For what?"

"For the End Times!" Peters snapped. His face twisted into something horrific. "The Redeemer is returning to Earth! He will burn all the sinners and unbelievers and deliver his chosen unto Sirius! We need the blood of the first hunter and the descendant of the witches of Kelly's Island to protect us and show our devotion."

Niall's heart stopped. It was worse than he thought.

Bennett looked at Brake. "He really is off his rocker, ain't he?"

Skidmark, who had run off during the scuffle, called out of the darkness, "If you're his chosen ones, why do you need protection?"

Peters' mania shifted slightly, revealing a hint of fear and confusion. "The Redeemer will want revenge on the unworthy. We need to protect ourselves until we can prove our faith."

"Sounds like a terrible version of Christ to me," muttered Tanguay. "Now, where are the kids?"

Peters snarled, "You would be pissed off, too, if you'd been trapped under the ocean."

Oh, no.

Bennett chuckled. "I don't remember much from Sunday school, but Jesus Christ is not rising up from under the ocean."

"They don't have oceans in Palestine," agreed Skidmark.

"We saw him! We saw the Redeemer beneath the waves, and he accepted our offerings of the scarabs and the unbelievers."

"Scarabs?" Niall asked, already knowing the answer. "Do you mean creatures that look like giant June bugs?"

Peters staggered a little, whether from loss of blood or lunacy, it was hard to say. "Yes. We feed them to the unbelievers and then give them to the Redeemer beneath the waves."

Niall whirled on Tanguay. "They're feeding the butt monkeys to the Psycho Hose Beast! They're trying to bring it back!"

Niall's mother and father said, "What" simultaneously, just like Niall and Harper did. It would be kind of cute if the situation wasn't so terrifying.

Tanguay nodded. "And the Jeddore kids and your brother... They want them to do some kind of magic like you do with Harper?"

Again, his parents were yelling questions, but he didn't have time for answers.

"They will provide the power that Brother Vee and Sister Pearl need to protect us."

Skidmark called out again from the darkness. This time, his voice seemed to be coming from somewhere in the catwalks above the factory floor. "Are you going to tell him, or can I tell him?"

"Brian, now is not the time…"

"Oh, come on, he's totally mental. If we tell him, it will make his head explode."

"Brian…"

"Please? Let me tell him. Please?"

Niall sighed. "Fine."

Skidmark yelled, "Neener, neener, neener," and made fart noises at the disgraced, bleeding cop. "Pius' dad and Harper's dad had different fathers. Pius isn't 'blood of the Blood,' you moron. He can't do magic."

Peters' face went pale. "But but Sister Pearl said…"

"Who the hell is Sister Pearl?" Tanguay asked.

Please don't be Anna, please don't be Anna. "It's Anna Chaffey, isn't it?"

Peters didn't respond, but his look told Niall the answer he didn't want to hear.

"Where are Pius, Keith, and Nelson?" Niall asked.

"It doesn't matter. The Redeemer is already awake." Peters curled up on the floor. "The Redeemer is going to consume everything. You can't save them. You can't save anyone."

"Shoot him in the other arm," suggested Brake.

Tanguay shook her head. "Look at him. He's gone. We're not going to get anything from him." Peters was rocking and sobbing on the floor.

"They're at my church's campgrounds," said a new voice. All eyes turned to see a blonde girl standing at the door to the factory floor. "At LeBotte, at the tip of the Cape-de-Cape Peninsula."

"Stacey?" Niall's heart couldn't take any more shocks tonight.

"I know the place," said Bennett. "It's those weird Pentecostals' camp."

"We're not Pentecostal," Stacey said. "We're from the Church of Christ the Sun Redeemer. It's an offshoot of the Solar Temple."

Why did Niall know that name?

"The cultists that killed themselves in Quebec?" Tanguay asked.

Stacey nodded. "Niall, I'm sorry. I was trying to tell you earlier. My dad wanted me to spy on you to learn about you and your friends. He was planning to kidnap you, but I refused to tell him anything. He's been so weird since he joined that Church… I'm so sorry! I didn't want to be part of this!"

"Stacey, shut up." Peters' head raised from his position on the floor.

"They got Anna to do it to your brother instead, Niall. She's so brainwashed that she'll do anything for the Church. She helped them take him, I'm sure of it."

"Shut up, you little bitch!" Peters came up off the floor faster than a snake. He wrapped his good hand around Stacey's throat with murder in his eyes.

Niall was closest to them. He grabbed the Sergeant and tried to pull him off, but the man was shockingly strong. Niall grabbed his blond hair and yanked his head back, causing him to yelp and loosen his grip for a split second, just enough for Stacey to catch a breath. Peters flung Niall aside.

Peters shifted, getting behind Stacey and wrapping his beefy arm around his daughter's throat. "Put down your guns, or I swear I will break her neck!"

"Dad…" Stacey wheezed.

Tanguay didn't drop her gun, but she didn't pull the trigger, either.

"Shoot him!" Brake barked.

Tanguay, obviously worried about hitting Stacey, lowered her weapon. Peters seemed less concerned about hurting his daughter. He squeezed her neck harder as he backed away from Tanguay until he hit the metal steps up to the catwalk. He began to walk backwards up the stairs, dragging Stacey after him.

"They're going to get away!" Niall's mom cried out.

"Sergeant, just say the word!" Brake bellowed. "I can take the shot."

Tanguay, who had been frozen and unresponsive for a moment, shook her head. "No! You might hit the girl. Peters, there's nowhere for you to go. Let her go, she's your daughter, for Christ's sake."

"Me killing her now would be a mercy, instead of leaving her to suffer at the hands of the Redeemer." His voice was manic, squealing at a high pitch.

"Dad, please," Stacey begged through sobs.

The next few seconds were chaos, but Niall saw every detail as if in slow motion. The lights came back on, with a roar of beeping and grinding as machines throughout the factory came back to life. Stacey used the moment of distraction to wiggle free from her father's grasp. Peters reached for her again, but a heavy green bookbag came out of nowhere and smacked him in the face. Both Peters and the bag fell over the side of the catwalk into the whirling blades of the industrial woodchipper below.

"Dad!" Stacey screamed.

"My Magic cards!" howled Skidmark.

Gore mixed with bits of coloured cardboard sprayed out of the machine, raining down upon a horrified Stacey, staining her blond hair red. She stared down into the machine, paralyzed with shock and unimaginable horror.

"*Tabarnak*," Tanguay breathed, leaning heavily on a support column. She glanced at Brake. "Go get her."

Niall wanted to throw up. He knew he should go to Stacey, but he couldn't remember how his feet worked.

A firm hand wrapped around Niall's shoulders and pulled his gaze away. It was his mother, and she hugged him close. "Don't look, Niall," she whispered into his ear.

Skidmark rushed down the stairs to the woodchipper, his face nearly as manic as Peters' had been a moment before. He picked up the remains of his shredded backpack from the floor and screamed an animalistic cry at the ceiling. The portly constable Bennett put a hand on his shoulder. "It's okay, son, you did the right thing. It was self-defence, and you saved the girl—"

"My cards!" Tears were streaming down Skidmark's face. "I didn't know they were standing over a woodchipper!"

Niall wanted to cry, give up, and hide in his mother's arms until all of this was over. He hadn't realized how much he missed her or how hard the last few days—hell, the last few years—had been. He was just a kid; none of this should be his responsibility.

He wanted his parents to fix everything so he could just go home and hide in his room, but he knew that wasn't an option.

His mother was squeezing him tightly. "Niall... what the hell is going on?"

Niall sighed. "A lot. I'm going to explain it to you, but I need you to tell me a few things, too."

Ask her who Nelson really is...

There would be time for mourning later. Niall choked back the sobs that were threatening to climb up his throat and looked over to Tanguay. She looked deathly pale, and tears were streaming down her cheeks, but when she noticed Niall looking at her, she shook her head and seemed to pull herself together.

"Sergeant... we need to get Harper."

CHAPTER FORTY-TWO

Kiss From a Rose
Thursday October 27
10:00 pm

Ivy Glenn had grown up on the Cape-de-Cape Peninsula. Born Ivy White in Limeville, she married Bob Glenn from Keating and they built a house together in Bugger Arm on a low hill beside a brook that emptied into the bay. The house had only washed away once in the big flood of '83, which was two times fewer than their neighbours' house down the road.

Hardships like storms, poverty, and houses washing out to sea were accepted and everyday aspects of life among older generations in Newfoundland. If you hadn't nearly died of some disease that would be readily curable in a town with a better hospital or didn't have a sibling or at least a cousin who had drowned, then you could hardly call yourself a true Newfoundlander. Ivy herself had survived a near-fatal childhood bout of measles and had both a brother *and* an uncle killed at sea. She was as hard-core a Newfie as you were likely to find outside of a song by Simani.

Ivy and Bob were now retired and living a quiet life in Bugger Arm with their black Labrador Retriever, Blackie. Bob had named the faithful animal and was not known for his imagination. Ivy and Bob's children, Jeff and Delilah, had long moved away and had their own families. Jeff was a firefighter up in Ottawa, and Delilah worked for a bank in Halifax. When Jeff was born, Bob had wanted to name him "Pinky," which Ivy had been forced to vigorously veto.

When the lights went out, Ivy suggested they take Blackie for his evening walk, and if the power wasn't back on by the time they returned home, they would turn in for bed. In truth, the walk was more for Bob's benefit than the dog's. The doctor had been on Ivy's husband to get more exercise and lose some weight, as the sedentary lifestyle of a retired man did not agree with his cholesterol and blood pressure. Ivy wasn't particularly distraught by the thought of Bob's death—she was far more concerned he would survive a heart attack or stroke, and she would end up nursing him for the rest of his tortured life. At least until she got fed up with him and smothered him with a pillow. Ivy sighed. She would never be able to go through with it. Bob damn well wasn't worth going to prison for.

The beach behind their house was beautiful that evening. The waves were rolling a few metres away, a slow, relentless crashing sound that had haunted Ivy's life since childhood. She had trouble sleeping while away from home because she couldn't hear the ocean. She found it too quiet. Across the bay, lights twinkled along the coast in the town of St. Stephen's. They obviously still had power. Ivy was momentarily jealous that they could watch that new E.R. show.

The dog ran off ahead as usual, splashing in the waves and running back and forth across the beach like a crazy beast. It was a sin Blackie didn't get walked more, instead of just left on a chain to crap in the yard most of the day. Ivy hounded Bob to walk the poor creature, but he was too busy sitting on his arse and watching talk shows.

"Delilah call today?" Bob asked absently, tossing a rock into the water. The crashing waves were so loud they didn't hear a splash.

Bob knew damn well she had, he had complained that Ivy was on the phone for an hour. She tightened her blue windbreaker around her neck against the cold wind. "Yes, she's good. The twins have the flu, though. Sally had a fever of thirty-nine-point-five last night."

"She never dresses those kids warm enough," Bob grumbled. He was dressed in two sweaters and a thick grey winter coat. He was sweating under it all, but he believed that the slightest draft could cause pneumonia, and there was no use trying to talk him out of it. He wore a jacket and wool socks in the middle of August.

"Oh, go on, she dresses them fine. Probably picked something up at school, is all."

"Damn kids eating each other's snot and licking each other's faces. Filthy buggers."

Ivy sighed. The man was obsessed with germs and illness. "They're ten years old, Bob. I don't think they're out there sticking their fingers up each other's noses."

Ahead, Blackie started to growl and bark wildly. "Ah, Christ, he probably found a dead animal again," Bob grumbled and trotted toward the sound. Last year Blackie had found a dead seal on the beach and had rolled on it. It was disgusting, but it was the happiest Ivy had ever seen the animal. Bob had thrown up three times and washed Blackie until the poor dog barely had any fur left.

Ivy chased her husband. It wasn't hard to keep up as Bob's jog was more for show than speed, and she crashed into him when he stopped abruptly.

"What is it? What's wrong?"

Bob was white as a sheet. His hand raised, trembling, and pointed to where the dog was barking. It was a dark shape lying on the rocky shore, with details impossible to make out in the dim light.

It was definitely human-shaped.

"Is that a person?" Ivy asked. Her heart was beating so hard she could hear it over the waves, but she felt icy cold.

Bob didn't respond. He was completely frozen.

"Get away from that, Blackie!" Ivy called out, but the dog didn't stop. *Odd.* He was usually very well-behaved. He came when they caught him in the seal-corpse jamboree. Cautiously she stepped forward and grabbed the dog by his collar, pulling Blackie away. She looked closer at the shape at the same time—it was definitely a person, face down and shirtless. She couldn't tell if it was male or female; its body was bloated and purple, and half its head was gone.

Ivy let go of the dog and turned away to vomit. She may have buried several relatives, but she had never seen a body, let alone find one like this. The poor soul must have drowned; it looked like it had been floating in the bay for days. But what had happened to its head? They would have to call the police. She hoped the phone lines were working again.

Blackie continued to bark louder than before. He sounded downright hysterical, which was hardly surprising. The dog must recognize it as a person, too.

"Dammit, Bob, get the dog!" Ivy snapped, wiping her mouth. She couldn't turn back to the corpse, but from the corner of her eye, she saw Bob snap out of his stupor and step forward.

The dog howled a horrible, terrified yelp. Ivy had never heard it make a sound like that. She whirled around to see the body had reached up and grabbed Blackie by the neck. Ivy felt a scream emerge from her own throat. *How could it be alive?*

The bloated figure on the ground wrenched Blackie's neck so forcefully that Ivy heard it snap like a dry branch. The dog went silent. Bob lunged forward to grab his pet, but it was too late. The figure tossed the dog aside and came up off the rocks with horrifying speed. It snatched Bob's coat with strong hands and pulled itself in close. Its face was a gruesome mess—its skull was cracked open, one eye and most of its nose was gone. Its lower jaw was hanging loose, and strips of torn black flesh and muscle barely held on.

However, the top teeth were sharp, and the creature pulled Bob in and sank those teeth into his throat. Bob screamed briefly before his voice was lost to choked gurgling. Hot blood, black in the moonlight, spurted across the beach and the dead dog.

Ivy screamed again, unwillingly. She was not in control of her body and mind. She was not seeing Bob, her husband of forty years, being torn apart by an unearthly monster. Her focus was only on the corpse monster and the insectoid, throbbing alien thing in its chest. It looked like a giant bug that was half-burrowed into the monster's body. It was pulsing, creating a mocking impression that the corpse was breathing. And it was *glowing*.

The monster turned its fractured, blood-spattered face toward Ivy's scream. It dropped Bob's body. She turned to run but knew she had no chance. She only got three steps before she tripped on the rocky beach and fell hard to her knees.

The monster was on her in seconds.

CHAPTER FORTY-THREE

Hallelujah
Friday, October 28
Midnight

Tanguay sat at the Jeddores' dining room table. She hated sitting down at a time like this; she wanted to be up and moving, but her body ached so much that she needed the rest. She was in agony, running on adrenaline, and she couldn't take any more pills. She needed what little clarity she had left.

And Niall and Harper needed to tell their story.

Though the power was back on, the phone lines were still a mess. Tanguay had sent Brake and Bennett to get a message to other RCMP detachments on the island, but all the roads into Gale Harbour had been blocked with logs and rubble. They'd blown up the bridge on the North side of town. Peters' church had really covered their bases. The Constables were working to get the roads cleared for when reinforcements did arrive, and Tanguay was here to make sure these kids got to the end of their story, whatever that may be.

Harper and Niall were seated beside her. Across from them sat Niall's mother, Barbara, and Harper's uncle Raymond. His wife, Samantha Jeddore, was lying down in her bed beside herself with grief and fear. The kids had already told her what they'd found earlier that evening, and the broken glass and blood in the kitchen corroborated their story. This poor family was a mess, and it was about to get more complicated.

Harper and Niall told Barbara and Raymond everything. They told them that Theolina Kane wasn't just a crazy old woman but a witch trying to seal away a monster older than time that had escaped its tomb beneath the Atlantic Ocean. They told them that the monster had possessed the body of Theolina's dead sister and that the ghost of said sister had possessed Barbara's mother. The monster, in the animated corpse of the dead witch, had killed Harper's father—Raymond's brother—and a half-dozen other people before Niall and Harper, using blood magic, had banished it back under the Atlantic.

Tanguay thought the adults' heads would explode, yet they hadn't gotten to the part about the giant alien bugs.

When the kids finished, Raymond's lean, dark face was flushed with anger. He'd lost weight since the last time that Tanguay had seen him. "What the hell is this nonsense? This is one of your dungeon games, isn't it? Sergeant, please tell me this is all horseshit."

Tanguay shook her head. "Mr. Jeddore, I'm sorry, *mais c'est vrai*. It's all true."

"And you're telling me that some cultists have kidnapped my son and daughter?"

"Yes. They think they can use your children's blood in a ritual to control the monster."

"But they can't," added Harper. "It won't work. They need my blood. I don't think they know Pius and I have different grandfathers."

Raymond ran his fingers through his thinning hair. "Even if I believe you, what happens if they find out the kids aren't who they think they are? How do we know they're still alive?"

"We don't." Tanguay sighed. It was harsh but true. "Which is why we have to hurry. We would already be gone, but Niall said he needed to talk to his mother first."

All eyes fell on Barbara O'Neil. Unlike Raymond, she'd been very quiet throughout the whole story. She sat with her hands folded in her lap. Her pale blond hair was sticking off in all directions, her make-up was smeared, and her white blouse was stained with her mother's blood. The fire Niall had seen when she'd fought back at the factory was gone.

"What do you want to know?" She didn't look up, her voice hoarse.

Niall slid his chair over and put his hand on his mother's. He was growing into a caring young man and had come a long way from the weird, awkward boy she'd met two years ago. All the kids had. They were still weird of course—why was Niall wearing leather pants, anyway?—but they were good kids. Tanguay just wanted them to live and grow into good adults.

"Mom, before Nana..." He couldn't bring himself to say "died." "...she said to ask you who Nelson really was. What did she mean by that?"

Barbara was quiet. She wouldn't look at her son.

"I figured out that he's probably not Dad's son," Niall said matter-of-factly. Raymond shifted uncomfortably in his chair. "I mean, Pius figured it out. It didn't line up with the dates Dad was gone on his bowling tournaments."

Those kids were too smart for their own good. Barbara didn't deny it, either. She didn't say anything for another long moment but finally nodded. "He's not your father's, no. I thought he wasn't mine for the longest time."

"What do you mean?"

Barbara wiped tears from her eyes. "When I was away at school, I went to a wedding in Clarenville. Your father and I weren't together at the time. We had broken up over something stupid.

"My car broke down on the side of the highway. It was the middle of the night, and I walked until I found a payphone. While I was dialling the number, there was a flash of light, and I think I blacked out. When I came to, there was a cop there. He offered to give me and my son a ride."

Son? What son?

Barbara saw the confused looks around the table and sighed. "After I blacked out, when I woke up, there was a three-year-old boy beside me. I had never seen him before, I had no idea where he came from, but he called me 'Mommy.' I was so freaked out, I didn't know what to do, so the cop brought him and me back to my hotel."

Tanguay felt a cold shiver down her spine. It made her body ache. Raymond was incredulous, but Niall and Harper didn't bat an eye.

"Where did he come from?" Niall asked.

Barbara O'Neil shrugged. "I don't know. I looked around for weeks but couldn't find any missing child reports. He kept insisting I was his mother. I know I should have told the police, but I didn't. I was terrified.

"Then Johnny showed up. It was him I had called without thinking the night Nelson appeared. He was worried about me. He saw the boy, and he was so shocked. I still didn't know what to do... so I told him Nelson was his. That I was pregnant when I left, which is why I ran away. My parents wanted me to get rid of it, but I couldn't go through with it."

Tears were streaming down Barbara's face. Raymond shook his head. "He believed you?"

"He said he did. But I could never know for sure. He always treated Nelson like his own, and I was grateful for that. My mother never believed it. She was too smart for that."

The mention of Josephine caused Barabra to choke up again. Niall reached across the table to take his mother's hand. "Nelson's birthday, October 26. Was that the night you found him?"

She nodded. "But it wasn't 1975, it was—"

"—1978." Both Niall and Tanguay said it at the same time.

"How did you know?"

"The night of the UFO sighting in Clarenville," said Niall. "I saw a newspaper clipping on Sergeant Peters' desk."

Tanguay nodded. "I saw the same article."

Raymond's face was aghast with horror. "Are you saying Nelson is some kind of... alien?"

Barbara shrugged. "I don't know. I don't know where he came from, but he's my son, and I love him."

Raymond shook his head. "Barabra, I know you think of him as a son, but..."

"I don't think, I know. I had a blood test done. He's my son."

The room was quiet. A thousand thoughts flooded through Tanguay's clouded mind. So Nelson was an alien, but he wasn't? He was Barbara's son somehow, though he appeared as a three-year-old boy? *Tabarnak*, this stuff didn't make sense at the best of times, and now she was hopped up on Percocet.

"Niall," said Harper, breaking the silence. "I don't know if it will help us deal with the Psycho Hose Beast, but I think we should figure out what's really going on with Nelson. We need all the info—and help—we can get."

"I think I know where you're going with this, Harper, and I don't know..."

"It's in her head, Niall. She was there. If she was abducted by aliens, there may still be memories in there of what happened. You did it with Aunt Samantha; you can do it with your mom, too."

"Do what with Samantha?" Raymond asked. "What the hell are you talking about?"

"Whatever you need to do, Niall," Barbara said softly. "Please show me the truth about Nelson."

CHAPTER FORTY-FOUR

Undone (The Sweater Song)
Friday, October 28
12:20 am

Nelson woke up in a bed that wasn't his, in a room he didn't recognize. The walls were mostly bare, save for a picture of Jesus by the door and a crucifix above the bed.

There was a woman he didn't know sitting on a chair beside him. She was about his mother's age, with black hair and wearing too much make-up. She wore a long white robe, the hood hanging back over her shoulders.

When Nelson tried to ask her where he was, she jumped to her feet and fled the room. Well, that was rude and really unhelpful. He wanted to call out after her, but his throat was dry and sore. He was in so much pain. What happened to him? He vaguely remembered being in a car with Anna before she swerved to avoid a truck and ran them off the road. There was something about him agreeing to join her church and her trying to talk him out of it. You'd swear she was in a cult or something.

His head was pounding. He touched bandages on his forehead, then winced at the slight pressure. There must be a pretty bad gash under there. He tried to get up from the bed but couldn't. His right leg wouldn't move. Gingerly, he pulled back the thin white blanket that covered him to reveal his leg was swollen and bloody, wrapped in bandages and a crude splint. His foot was turned at a weird angle, and his kneecap was not where it was supposed to be.

He nearly threw up. This was worse than when he'd got hit from behind in Pee-Wee hockey. Sure, he'd got a concussion then, too, but with it, only a broken nose and a lost tooth when his face hit the ice. This was so much worse. He looked like the moose his buddy Steve Budger had hit with his truck...

Why the hell was he in this weirdo church lady's room? Why wasn't he in the hospital?

He tried to call for help again, but it came out a garbled moan. Nelson coughed, which brought a stabbing pain to his chest. He thought he tasted blood. Great. This was just great.

His eyes fell on the picture of Jesus staring down at him. He hadn't looked closely at it before, but this was different from the one in his grandmother's bedroom. Usually, Jesus looked serene and occasionally smiled, but this Jesus was scowling at him menacingly. His hand was raised not in an open sign of peace but in a fist. Like he was threatening to punch anyone who dared look at his picture.

This Jesus had wings. And not feathery, fluffy angel wings, but black, bat-like wings, like on the cover of a Meatloaf album. And there were tentacles coming from... somewhere. Nelson couldn't tell if they were coming from Jesus himself or some monster behind him, but all in all, he decided he didn't like this picture very much. It probably wasn't Jesus at all. Maybe it was Jesus' crappy cousin that no one wanted to talk about.

The door flew open, and Anna burst into the room. She was wearing the same weird white robe as the other woman. She had a black eye and dried blood across her hairline. She smiled in a mixture of relief and concern.

"Nelson, thank goodness you're awake! I was so worried."

"What happened?"

Anna sat on the edge of the bed. "We were in a car accident."

"You drove us off the road."

She shook her head. "What? I had to swerve. Don't you remember what happened?"

Nelson was quiet. He was sure he remembered Anna yanking the wheel *toward* the embankment, but his memory was foggy. He did have a concussion the size of a watermelon. Did concussions come in sizes? Whatever, it felt like he'd got kicked in the face by a boot stapled to a garbage truck. "It's all really fuzzy. Where are we?"

"We're at my church's camp."

Nelson very pointedly did not look at the picture of "Jesus." "Yeah, I saw the... religious stuff. Why aren't we at a hospital? My leg looks like it's been through a trash compactor."

"We'll get you medical attention soon, but... you're in danger. We need to keep you safe, and this is the best place to do it for now."

"What are you talking about?"

"Don't you remember what happened right before we crashed?"

Nelson wanted to say, "You drove us off a cliff," but he held his tongue in an uncharacteristic moment of restraint. "I don't. I just remember you were driving, and we were heading to your church's camp..."

"We swerved to avoid a woman who was standing in the road. A very bad woman. We went through the barricade over the embankment, and both of us got banged up really bad. Another car came along, and the woman got scared off, but fortunately, I knew them from my church. They gave us a ride here. Don't you remember?"

Nelson vaguely remembered something about a scary woman driving a car off the road. It was all so hazy, though. He thought there was a truck, but maybe his brains were scrambled. "I don't remember anything..." Nelson settled back into the uncomfortable mattress. "Who was this woman? Who's out to get me?"

She put her hand on his. "Nelson, your brother has been involved in some bad stuff the last couple of years."

"Niall is just a kid."

"Just a kid who's disappeared several times, was witness to numerous murders, was at the site of several explosions, got in the way of military and police investigations. He's made enemies."

Crap. He'd heard bits and pieces of what Niall was up to, but he had no idea the extent of it. Did their parents know? Their parents...

"Are my mom and dad in danger?"

"Don't worry, Sergeant Peters is taking care of them right now."

"Who's Sergeant Peters?"

"He's the RCMP Sergeant here in town. He's a good guy. He's a member of my church, too. He's trying to protect Gale Harbour from the bad stuff your brother and his friends stirred up."

Nelson was now having visions of shady government agents or murderous mobsters. Nelson thought Niall and his friends had just been kidnapped by a crazy old lady. "What the hell did my brother do?"

Anna's answer was pre-empted by a knock at the door. She looked annoyed, but before she could stand up, the door opened, and a bald man's head poked in. "Sister, the kid's gone."

Anna leapt to her feet and shoved the man out the door. She and the bald man talked animatedly, but Nelson could only pick up snippets of their conversation.

"...both kids..."

"How?"

"...dunno where..."

"Find them! Get everyone out there looking for them!"

Anna yelled that last part, then stepped back into the room and slammed the door. She took a deep breath and composed herself.

"I'm sorry about that."

"What kids? What's going on?"

She sat back down on the bed. "A couple of kids from our congregation wandered off. The person who was supposed to be watching them isn't very bright and doesn't seem to realize how dangerous it is for children to be out right now by themselves."

Nelson was getting annoyed at her evasiveness. He raised his voice as much as his sore throat and head would allow. "Why is it so dangerous? Anna, what is going on?"

Anna took his hand again. She looked at him and smiled. A genuine smile, like she was happy to be there with him. Like she was glad he was alive. But the smile faded, and concerned lines crossed her perfect pale forehead. "Nelson, I'm going to tell you things now that will be difficult to believe, but please hear me out. Gale Harbour, and maybe the whole world, is in danger and it's all your brother's fault..."

Dale and Nancy Chaffey knelt on the floor the same way they had forced their daughter countless times before. At least they weren't kneeling on uncooked rice, gravel or broken glass.

"What happened?" the voice asked behind them.

The couple was in a nice house in a small town in Quebec. The sun was setting, casting long shadows across the dimly lit living room. Neither of them dared look back.

"The Mounties were waiting for us," Dale mumbled. His thick face was red and glistening with sweat. "Somehow, they knew the deal was going to go down."

Something struck Dale across the back of the head, and he fell forward. Nancy tried to catch him, but Dale was much larger than her, and his skull smacked the hardwood floor with a crack.

"They knew because you left a trail so obvious that an idiot could follow it!" the voice bellowed like the roar of an angry dragon. "What the hell were you thinking? You might as well have posted an ad in the newspaper classifieds asking to buy assault rifles!"

"We've never had to buy guns before!" Nancy wailed, trying to sop the blood from her husband's face.

"No," the voice growled. "Di Mambro shouldn't have given you the job. Your failure will lead the authorities directly to him and the Temple. Worse, we don't have the weapons we need for the coming ordeals."

Joseph Di Mambro was one of the church's highest-ranking bishops and their face to the world. Unfortunately, as far as Brother Vee was concerned, he was nearly as stupid as Dale and Nancy Chaffey.

Dale finally looked back at Brother Vee, his face a crimson mask. "Is it true? Is the Redeemer truly returning?"

Vee gazed down at this pathetic, miserable creature and bit back his rage. "Yes. Unfortunately for you, you will not live to see it."

The High Priest of the Church of Christ the Sun Redeemer withdrew a semi-automatic handgun from inside his robe and placed it on the floor between the Chaffeys. "You must be punished for your failures. If the Redeemer is truly forgiving, perhaps you will be transported to Sirius early."

Dale and Nancy looked at the gun in horror. Neither of them moved.

"Take it," ordered Brother Vee. "Send your wife to Sirius, and then join her."

Dale reached for the weapon with trembling fingers. He had known for years that he would someday give his life for his church. The Golden Way, the Solar Temple, the Church of the Redeemer, whatever it called itself, Dale believed in it with all his heart and would do whatever his God or church asked of it.

With trembling fingers, Dale took the gun and placed the muzzle against his wife's head, just above the scar their daughter gave her years ago. That was the last time the bitch fled and slashed her mother in the face on her way out the door. Nancy's face was twisted in a mask of terror. Tears streamed from her eyes, but she said nothing. Dale's own vision was blurred with tears and blood. The gun felt like it weighed a hundred kilograms.

His finger touched the trigger, but he couldn't squeeze it. Nancy had been by his side through all the hardships and struggles and through all the tests of faith God had put him through.

Dale's hand fell. "I... I can't."

Another hand snatched the pistol from Dale's fingers. The muzzle was placed against his temple.

Dale looked up into remorseless, cold, grey eyes. "It finally worked, you know," said the woman holding the weapon. "All your years of torture and abuse, and all it took was for me to lose the one person I really loved."

Dale started to open his mouth to speak but didn't get any words out. The gun fired, the shot echoing like an explosion in the small living room. Nancy screamed, and a second shot quickly sent her to her eternal reward as well.

"Sister Pearl..." Brother Vee said, looking at the woman who had just ended the life of both her parents. There wasn't sympathy in his voice, not quite, but there was the slightest hint of pity. "I could have done that."

"It needed to be done," she said coldly. She had dreamed of this day her entire life. She scarcely believed it would ever happen, but now that it had...She thought she would feel relief. Or maybe remorse. Something.

Instead, Anna Chaffey felt absolutely empty.

CHAPTER FORTY-FIVE

The Mirror
Friday, October 28
1:00 am

Niall helped his mother sit down on Harper's bed, with Harper on her other side. It was one of the weirder positions he'd been in as of late.

He hadn't been in Harper's room in over a year. She had updated her posters of Kurt Cobain and The Smashing Pumpkins, and added posters of Tori Amos, Courtney Love and Pearl Jam. There was also more girly stuff, like make-up and hairspray on the dresser, and... was that a bra on the back of the chair?

Niall tried to keep his mind on the task at hand. Lives were literally at stake. He could fantasize about Harper's undergarments later.

"Niall, I don't know what's happening." His mom was a mess. Her blouse was spattered with blood and dirt, and her straw-coloured hair looked like it could use some of Harper's hairspray. Her face was trembling. She'd been on the verge of tears since they'd left the matchstick factory, often slipping into pained wallowing.

"I'm going to use the powers we told you about to see what happened the night you found Nelson." He had no idea if it would actually work. He read Pius' mother's mind accidentally, and it was only her most recent surface memory. How was he supposed to find memories she'd suppressed for nearly twenty years?

"Can you read her?" Harper asked. "Like you did with Aunt Samantha?"

Niall looked at his mother. He didn't want to do this to her. It was so invasive, so intimate. The things he'd seen in Samantha's head were private. He couldn't imagine knowing those same things about his mother.

Barbara must have sensed his trepidation. "Do it."

Niall nodded. "Lay down and try to relax. When I do this, you'll probably pass out, and I don't want you to hurt yourself."

Barbara let Niall and Harper lay her down on the bed. "Will this hurt?" she asked Niall.

"I don't think so," Niall lied. Truthfully, he had no idea. "I've only done this once before and kinda slipped into it. I may have to dig through your memories to find what we need. I'm really not sure how this is going to work."

"You can do this," Harper said firmly. She squeezed Niall's hand. "And you are going to be fine, Mrs. O'Neil. We're going to find Nelson, and Pius, and Rebecca, and everyone is going to be fine."

She looked directly at Niall when she said the last part. Her brown eyes were focused, but he thought they looked wet and glossy. Was she telling him that everything was going to be okay? Was she telling his mom? Or herself?

If Harper was starting to crack, they were in real trouble.

Harper pricked her finger and touched Niall's hand. He felt her strength flow into him like an electric shock. His senses became sharper. He could see every hair and line on his mother's face. He could hear her heart beating and smell the blood in her veins. Weird. The power seemed to be growing more... potent? Maybe it was because he'd been using it so much lately.

Niall laid his hands on his mother's head. He concentrated and reached out with the tiniest speck of power he could, imagining that he was brushing her forehead with a feather. She gasped, and he pulled back.

"Niall, what are you doing?" his mother asked, her panicked blue eyes looking up at him. He had no idea what she was feeling, but it was probably unpleasant.

"Sleep, Mom," he said, touching her again, using the same trick he'd used on Samantha. Her eyes closed immediately, and her breathing levelled off. Her face looked serene, the calmest he'd seen it all day.

"It will probably be better if she's not awake for this," Niall said to Harper, and he dove back in.

The light touch he'd used before wasn't enough. He found he had to gently pry into her mind, like pushing his finger into Play-Doh. He told himself it wasn't actually her brain he was shoving his dirty digits into, but it certainly felt like it. He saw the scene at the kitchen table just a few minutes before but from his mother's point of view. Niall watched himself, telling him/her about the Psycho Hose Beast and Theolina Kane. He could feel his mother's fear, but he noted there wasn't a trace of doubt in her. She believed everything he was saying.

He needed to go farther back. He was at the matchstick factory, and he saw Nana Josphine die. He saw Sergeant Peters shoot his dad. He heard his mother scream in his own head, and the shock, the fear and the sadness were overwhelming. Niall found himself forced out of her mind and fell back on Harper's bed.

Niall was shaking. "How is she still going? She's been through so much today..."

He also thought of Stacey and what she had witnessed that night. He could not imagine what she was going through right now.

Harper put her hands on his shoulder. "Come on, Niall, you can do this. You have to do this. For Nelson and for her."

Niall went back in. He pushed farther back. He saw an argument she had with Niall a few months ago, then saw his father comforting her when Niall and the others were lost two years ago. Her emotions then were nearly as strong as they'd been today, but they didn't hurt Niall so much this time. He realized that, even in his mother's memories, seeing the world through her eyes, he could still feel Harper's hand on his shoulder. It was like she was there with him.

"I am here," she whispered. "I'm with you."

That should have freaked Niall out. He hoped she had never read his mind before because there was definitely a thought or two about her that he should probably keep to himself. Instead of embarrassment, Harper's presence brought Niall peace and strength. He pushed onward.

He saw himself as a young boy, crying because he'd dropped his ice cream cone. He felt Harper smile. Moving on.

A brief flash of his father's face. Grunting noises. Niall quickly rushed past that one, hoping he hadn't just witnessed his own conception.

He saw his parents' wedding day. His dad looked so young and handsome, dressed in a white suit with a big pink carnation on his lapel.

With his shoulder-length hair, thick moustache, and tinted glasses, he looked like a hippy. Niall had never seen him look so happy.

Nelson was there. He was three or four years old, dressed in a white suit, just like his dad. It never clicked with Niall that Nelson had been at his parents' wedding. He didn't remember ever seeing a picture with Nelson there.

And then Niall found it. A dark road. His mother's terror. A phone booth, a cop pulling up, and then Nelson, a tiny, healthy little boy with round cheeks and bushy brown hair. Niall went a little farther back and found himself at another wedding with people he didn't recognize. He realized they were his mother's friends from college.

Something was missing. He waded back and forth, like sifting through sand on the beach, trying to find the memory between breaking down on the side of the road and the police officer finding her and Nelson. Why was nothing there?

No, there was something there. Flashes of light. Just blinding light. And behind it...

"Deeper," Harper whispered. "It's behind the light."

Niall needed to push harder into his mother's mind. Now, it didn't just feel like poking Play-Doh but scooping pieces out. Little blobs of coloured, squashed clay, falling discarded to the floor. It felt dirty and obscene. He prayed he wasn't doing permanent damage to his mother's brain. But there was something there; he knew it and could almost see it.

And then, without warning or fanfare, he was in.

The light was still blinding, but Niall and Barbara could just make out the edges of a room in the periphery of their vision. The curved walls were made of dark metal. Blue and green lights blinked on and off somewhere, and a low, constant hum seemed to make the entire world vibrate.

They were not alone in the room.

Niall/Barbara couldn't see their faces. Vague, shadowy figures moved around in the bright light, devoid of any details. But they could hear voices.

At first, they were just droning and buzzing, composed of no recognizable human words. But slowly, Niall and Barbara realized that the voices weren't in their *ears* but in their *heads*. And the longer they concentrated on it, Niall and Barbara realized they could understand it...

"...certain the prisoner arrived on this planet?"

"Affirmative. Over four billion cycles ago."

"Where is it?"

"Currently trapped beneath the ocean by the natives of this planet."

Niall/Barbara realized they were lying on a table and unable to move. There were no restraints. It was just like their body wouldn't respond.

"How?"

"Others have visited this world. The apes are compatible with multiple life forms. Some of their offspring must have developed abilities to confine the prisoner."

"It will escape."

"Affirmative."

"We cannot linger. But if it escapes, it will wreak havoc among the native flora and fauna. The prisoner is our responsibility, we cannot allow that."

"We will leave them a failsafe, a last resort. It will trigger if the prisoner attempts to assimilate it."

A vaguely humanoid shadow leaned into Niall/Barbara's field of vision. He tried desperately to make out any details but only saw a dark blob.

"The female?"

"Affirmative. Begin retrieval of genetic material. Set the synthesis pod to maximum growth speed."

"What if their physiology is not compatible with the weapon?"

"Leave a backup inside the female. Let it conceive and grow naturally."

"It will not be as potent."

"It will be more likely to be compatible. It is only a backup."

"The solar winds are changing. There is little time. Shall we proceed?"

"Affirmative. Let it be done, then."

"The female is awake."

"Re-induce unconsciousness. It would be cruel if she were alert for the procedure."

A hot, white light exploded across Niall's vision. He was flung out of the memory, out of his mother's head, and physically thrown across the bed into the wall. He tore Harper's Courtney Love poster and fell to the floor.

CHAPTER FORTY-SIX

"There's a lot more of those freaks in dresses running around," Keith muttered from their hiding spot in the trees. They had moved several times in the last hour, scouting the perimeter of the compound twice over and investigating every door and window they could reach. In one of the rooms of the storage shed where Pius and Keith were held, they found a pile of tools and hardware. Keith grabbed a crowbar, which was much shorter than his trusty Easton but would serve as a weapon in a pinch. He also tucked a utility knife into his pocket. Pius ended up with a regular claw hammer and a screwdriver.

"They know we're out," Pius grumbled, watching the third cult member in the last five minutes trip over the hem of their robe as they ran across the yard in the compound's centre. *Why did they wear the dumb things?* "We're taking too much time."

"Well, until we figure out how to get your sister out of that house, we don't have many options."

They had found the house where Rebecca was being held. Pius had seen her himself when Keith boosted him to look through the window. She seemed fine, asleep in a crib, dressed warmly and cared for. Unfortunately, there was a guard in the room with her, two more by the outside door, and who knows how many more inside. They would not be able to just walk in and grab her. They would have to get as many guards away from the house as possible.

"Distraction, we need a distraction," Pius said, thinking aloud.

"Usually, in the movies, they blow something up." Always helpful, Keith made a "boom" gesture with his hands and mouthed the sound at the same time. "Too bad we don't have something to explode."

"Actually," Pius sat bolt upright. "The lower level of the bunker is full of fuel tanks. We can set them on fire."

"The bunker that's full of butt monkeys?"

"My plan has the added bonus of taking the bugs with it, yes."

"And us, too. How are you planning on lighting it?"

Pius was already thinking about this too. "There were wires and batteries with the tools we found in the storage shed. I could probably rig up a remote detonator." It was pretty simple, actually. He was *pretty* sure that an electric spark would ignite a puddle of gasoline.

"Look at you go, MacGyver!" Keith slapped him on the back, nearly knocking Pius over. He righted himself and adjusted his glasses. "Alright, let's move. Stay close, stay low, and for the love of God, try to be quieter this time, okay?"

Keith was referring to the moment half an hour ago when Pius saw a chipmunk skitter through the undergrowth, which caused him to yelp, trip, and crash loudly into a dogberry bush. The boys beat a quick retreat and shockingly had not been caught, but Pius knew that if they relied solely on his athletic ability, it was only a matter of time.

"Why don't you get the stuff, and I'll wait here?" Pius suggested.

"I don't know what you need. Now, come on! It'll be just like my fighter, Snoop Doggius, taking care of your wussy wizard Rat-gas."

"His name is *Radagast*," Pius corrected him, annoyed that Keith never bothered to learn the other characters' names. "He's the brown wizard from the Lord of the Rings?"

"He's a shit-wizard?"

Pius sputtered and grumbled, unable to form a suitable response. Finally, he managed to spit out, "At least he's not named after a misogynistic dope head!"

Keith winked and smiled. He turned back to their task at hand. "Just keep your head down."

Pius continued to grumble under his breath as they moved from bush to bush, shadow to shadow. Light streamed from several spotlights around the campground, but there was darkness between the pools of illumination. Just stay in the shadows and try not to get spooked by chipmunks.

They made it back to the storage shed without incident. Keith kept watch while Pius rummaged through the tools. There were lots of basic stuff—hammers, boxes of nails, screwdrivers, a couple of handsaws—the cultists were obviously handy, but it begged the question: Did they do their repairs and construction while wearing those robes? It seemed terribly dangerous and impractical. Surely, they must just be wearing them for a special occasion tonight. There's no way they shingled a roof wearing ankle-length robes, right?

Pius quickly found what he needed; he'd noticed them earlier when searching the shed: a pack of 9-volt batteries and a large coil of wire. He also grabbed some pliers and a roll of electrical tape, just in case.

"You got what you need?" Keith asked over his shoulder, causing Pius to startle and nearly jump out of his skin.

"Yes!" he hissed, listening to his heartbeat in his ears. "You just keep an eye out, okay?"

"It's all good. We're clear—*ughf*!"

Someone grabbed Keith and yanked him from view. Pius jumped to his feet and looked around the door to see a large woman in a white robe, her arm wrapped around Keith's neck. She squeezed her wrist with her other hand, trying to choke the life out of Keith.

"Tric—Tricia?" Keith gasped. He dropped his crowbar and feebly grabbed at the woman's meaty forearm.

"They call me Sister Mary around here, Keith," said the woman. She barely looked at Pius, obviously thinking him to be no threat. "I'm sorry about your dad. I'm glad you came in and busted up the office, though. It made a real nice alibi for me and Brother Limeville when we beat him to death with your baseball bat."

Pius was frozen in fear. *She killed Keith's dad?*

Keith was turning purple, but somehow, he squeaked out, "Why?"

"He didn't accept Christ the Redeemer. We were trying to get him to join us, but he refused. Unfortunately, he already knew too much. Getting you involved was a happy little accident."

Keith stopped fighting, and his eyes rolled back into his head. Sister Mary smiled, half turned and opened her mouth to call for help—

Pius didn't think. He might not have committed the shocking act he was about to perform if he had. Pius leapt forward, his hammer in hand, and smashed the cultist in the side of the head with everything he had. He didn't weigh much, but the adrenaline strengthened his thin arms. Pius felt the woman's skull crack under the head of the hammer.

He heard it, too, a sickening crunch as the steel tool sank a couple of centimetres into the woman's temple.

The cultist let go of Keith and collapsed to the ground. Pius dropped his hammer.

It took Keith a few moments to come around. "Come on, we gotta go!" Keith hissed when he finally caught his breath. He picked up his crowbar and yanked Pius' arm. Numbly, Pius bent down and picked up his discarded batteries and wire. His gaze never left the crumpled white form on the ground before him. The woman wasn't breathing. Blood was pooling around her head.

Pius didn't argue as Keith led him away from the scene. "Shit, I'm sorry," Keith whispered to him. "She came out of nowhere, I should have seen her coming." After a moment, when Pius didn't respond, he continued. "Look, it's not your fault. She would've killed you. She was trying to kill me. Thank you."

Pius nodded, his mind still blank. His arms and legs weighed a thousand kilograms.

"When they find her, they'll know we're still nearby." Keith pushed Pius down behind some trees as a man and a woman in robes passed them a few metres away. When the coast was clear, he continued. "We need to set up your distraction. *Now.*"

Right. The fuel. He had a mission. He couldn't fall apart now; too much was depending on them. With supreme effort, Pius followed Keith around the outer perimeter of the compound once again until they were in line with the side door of the bunker that Pius had used earlier.

"The coast is clear," Keith said, scanning every direction. He was being extra careful now. "They're spread out looking for us. Hopefully, they're not expecting us to sneak back inside."

Pius nodded dimly, and Keith grabbed his hand to lead him across the open field. Pius noted that Keith's palm was warm and sweaty, which was unusual for him. He was probably just scared. Pius himself was terrified, but he somehow managed to compartmentalize those feelings like a first-rate narcissist. Or Skidmark. He would have to remember how to do that. He was never very good at dealing with strong emotions.

They slinked down the dark concrete stairs into the storage area behind the fuel tanks. "What is that smell?" Keith asked as they slunk down behind the gas drums and containers. He looked through the gap between the containers and pulled away. "Holy—The space bugs? Where the hell did those come from?"

Pius, still numb, started to work on his plan. He found a jerry can that was mostly empty and slid one end of the wire inside. He tied it onto the container's handle, keeping the exposed wire ends above the surface of the fuel. He needed the spark to ignite the vapours, but he wasn't sure if it would work if submerged in liquid gasoline. Pius also made sure to wrap the other ends of the wire in electrical tape so as not to accidentally set it off by picking up a static charge.

"There are people over there," Keith whispered, but Pius wasn't paying attention. He was already working his way back up the stairs, letting out the wire behind him. He didn't think that the gas cans would explode like in the movies, but he had no idea how fast the flames would go up and wanted to be as far away as possible when they did.

"They look like... zombies?" Keith was saying, a mixture of panic and excitement causing his voice to rise an octave higher than usual. "Holy frig, these Satan-worshipper guys are making zombies?!"

Pius told himself to focus on the task of laying out the wire. He paused momentarily to knot it around some rebar sticking out of the wall to ensure it didn't accidentally get pulled loose. *Don't think about the lady you just killed, don't think about the zombies...*

"Dad?"

Crap.

Pius hadn't told him. Why hadn't he told him? He was so focused on just surviving.

There were gunshots outside. Screams and cries for help. What the hell was going on? Pius grabbed the wire and ran up the stairs. At the top, he peered out into the dark compound to find numerous people in white robes running toward the tree line. Many of them were carrying guns. "They're coming from the beach!" someone called out.

Who was coming? The cops? The army? Pius didn't care. Whoever it was would help them.

Maybe they didn't need Pius' distraction after all. But it wouldn't hurt to ensure the alien bugs in the basement couldn't hurt anyone else. He called back down the stairs. "Keith! We have to go!"

There was crashing and banging in the room down below. Pius heard the crunch of bones and the tearing of flesh, sounding like when his dad butchered a moose in the shed. He heard the guttural screams of something unnatural, and for a moment, he was afraid the zombie Mr. Doucette had got its hands on Keith. But then Keith staggered up the stairs out of the darkness, spattered with gore. His crowbar was slick with blood.

"Sorry. I had to take care of something."
Pius said nothing.

CHAPTER FORTY-SEVEN

Shine
Friday, October 28
1:25 am

Nelson looked out the window, watching the chaos in the gloomy darkness. People in white—Anna's church friends, if she was telling the truth—were shooting other people. But they weren't people, not anymore. They didn't move, act or speak like people. They were monsters, corpses raised from the dead to kill and eat the flesh of the living.

It was *Night of the Living Dead* out there, and it was all Niall's fault.

Nelson's grip on the windowsill slipped, and he nearly fell over. He let Anna help him back onto the bed, and he felt immense relief as the pressure was removed from his injured leg. Standing at the window was agony, but he had to see it himself. He wouldn't have believed it otherwise.

"So a witch taught my brother and his girlfriend how to do magic," Nelson said, breathing slowly through the pain. "And they used it to wake up some kind of demon sleeping under the ocean. Now it's coming toward Gale Harbour, and its presence is bringing the dead back as zombies."

"That's the gist of it, yeah." Anna nodded, sitting on the edge of the bed, her hand on Nelson's arm. "I don't think they meant to awaken the monster, but they're playing with powers they don't understand and can't control."

"And you think that somehow I can control it?"

"The elders in my church think that what's happening right now is the Second Coming prophesied in the Book of Revelations. They think that whatever woke up beneath the Atlantic is coming to destroy all the unbelievers and then deliver the worthy to Heaven. They think you have the same powers as your brother, which you can use to protect us and show the Redeemer that we are worthy."

Yeah, he heard all of this a few minutes ago, but it didn't sound any less crazy the second time. It sounded like the crap from one of Niall's dungeon games, and he would have called Anna mental to her face, except that he saw the zombies out there with his own eyes...

"What do you believe?"

Anna was quiet for a moment. Her gaze was far away, and her grey eyes were watering. She sniffed and wiped her cheeks, and when she finally started to talk, her voice was less confident than before. Her words sounded less rehearsed. "I don't think what's out there is coming to save anyone. My parents were obsessed with the end of the world, and from the time I was a baby, they told me it was coming in my lifetime. They tried to beat the fear of God into me, but all their screaming and abuse only made me fear them.

"This thing that's coming wasn't sent by a benevolent god. It's a monster older than time that doesn't care any more about humans than we care about ants. It's going to destroy everything in its path. I don't think we can stop it. I just want us to protect as many people as we can."

"Why didn't you ask Niall for help? If he summoned it, he's probably better qualified to get rid of it."

"Because he killed my boyfriend!" Anna snapped. "I'm sorry. Niall is a kid. He's careless and selfish, and he doesn't have the maturity and sense to do this. Last year, when half of Gale Harbour nearly burned down? Your brother and his friends caused it. Niall caused it, irresponsibly using his powers, and he killed my boyfriend in the process."

"I'm sorry. I'm sure he didn't mean to..."

"He didn't mean to because he's reckless! He didn't care who died. He never even spoke to me afterward, never apologized for what happened."

That didn't sound like Niall. His little brother was usually a snivelling little goody-goody. But then, it seemed he didn't know Niall very well.

"We need your help, Nelson, please. *I* need your help. I don't want anyone else to get hurt like Keenan."

Nelson didn't know how he was supposed to help anyone, lying here half-dead with a busted leg. Besides mowing the lawn or taking out the garbage, no one ever asked him for help. Not for anything important. His parents never expected anything from him. They were surprised he actually finished high school. Niall was the one they doted on, the one who was supposed to be smart and successful. As long as Nelson didn't kill anyone or get anyone pregnant, that was enough.

And now this beautiful woman was asking him to help save the world.

"What do you need me to do?"

CHAPTER FORTY-EIGHT

Vasoline
Friday, October 28
2:30 am

Sergeant Tanguay drove through the flimsy gate at the compound's entrance without slowing down. Someone screamed. Niall wasn't sure if it was Harper or him.

The police car screeched to a stop beside a long, low building with numerous doors. "No guards at the gate," the Mountie said vaguely, slamming the car into park.

"I think they're busy." Harper pointed across a hard-packed dirt field, where two people in white robes were wrestling with a topless woman. The figures were illuminated by the car's headlights so that they could see that the half-naked woman was biting one of the robed people on the neck. The woman was pale and scarred, marked by numerous gaping holes and wounds across her body. Her victim's white robes were drenched in a rapidly growing red stain.

The other robed figure stepped back and levelled a long gun at the grotesque woman's head. There was a bang and an explosion of gore. Both the woman and the person she was chewing on slumped to the ground.

Tanguay stepped out of the car. Niall noticed she held the door with white knuckles to pull herself up.

"Brother Gambo," the surviving robed figure called, rushing toward the Mountie. "Thank God you're here! "Wait, you're not Peters—"

The robed man started to raise his gun, but despite her reduced state, Tanguay was still faster. She drew her sidearm and put two bullets in his chest. He flopped to the ground in a swirl of white cloth and blood.

She opened the back door of her patrol car to let Niall and Harper out. "What happened here?" Harper asked, gawking at the field. Now that he got a good look, he could see another dozen bodies strewn about the ground. Some were dressed in white robes, and more were stripped half-bare with pallid flesh.

"Niall, make sure none of them are Pius or anyone else we know." Tanguay gestured to him while training her gun on buildings around the clearing.

Niall's stomach knotted. "Seriously?"

"Harper will cover you."

Niall glanced over and realized Harper had already picked up the rifle from the guy Tanguay shot. She checked the chamber and magazine, then went back to the corpse to look for spare bullets.

Harper was nothing if not resourceful, and Tanguay was already approaching the nearest building with her gun at the ready. Niall could do much worse than these two badass women having his back.

Holding his breath, Niall moved from body to body, prodding them with the toe of his sneaker. The white-robed cultists had all been killed in horrific ways, with chunks of flesh torn from their faces or necks. A couple of them looked like they were chewed on, and he knew it wasn't by animals.

The other bodies were somehow worse. Their flesh was desiccated and peeling or purple and bloated. All of them were rotten and blackened. The stuff that was oozing from their wounds was not blood but some kind of thick black fluid that reeked of decay and seawater.

Some of the zombie bodies were still moving. They twitched feebly trying to pull themselves up though their legs, arms and sometimes heads had been blown away by close-range gunshots. There was something else, too...

"I think I'm going to be sick," Niall said aloud. "Something's crawling around inside their chests."

"Like a rat?" Tanguay asked, raising her shotgun and aiming it at the nearest corpse.

"No, I feel... I think it's—don't shoot!"

The warning came a split second too late. Tanguay fired, the chest of the corpse a few metres from Niall exploded, and a pillar of blue flame shot up into the sky. The force of the blast knocked Niall backward onto his ass and singed his hair and eyebrows.

"*Merde*, I'm sorry, Niall." Tanguay hovered over him. "Are you okay?"

"Butt monkeys," Harper whispered, kneeling on his other side. "There are butt monkeys inside the corpses."

"Those beetle things?" Tanguay asked. "Why is someone putting them inside dead bodies?"

"It's animating them like zombies," said a familiar voice from nearby.

Tanguay whirled but fortunately did not fire as Pius and Keith slowly approached them out of the gloom.

Harper dropped her gun and ran to Pius, throwing her arms around him. "I'm so glad you're safe. Are you okay?"

"I'm alive," he responded, smiling weakly. He looked terrible, covered in dirt and blood, but he was most definitely alive.

"Hey, so am I," added Keith, who somehow looked in worse shape than Pius.

Harper punched him in the arm. "Believe it or not, I'm glad you're alive too."

"That's the nicest thing you've ever said to me. Niall, buddy, why are you wearing leather pants?"

"That's not important right now." Niall got to his feet and, discovering no serious injuries, approached Pius and hugged him too. "Why are they bringing the dead back to life? How are they doing it?"

"Anna is doing it. She's doing some kind of magic. I'm not sure how, but she's using magic just like you do."

Harper shook her head. "Not just like Niall. She doesn't have my blood."

Niall had a hunch about this. He'd felt something happening, some force that was growing like an unseen pressure on the back of his mind, getting stronger as they approached LeBotte and the cultists' camp. "I don't think she's doing it alone. It's the Primordial One. It's getting closer, and it's stirring up the bugs."

Keith groaned. "Well, that's really bad then because there's a shitload of them in that bunker over there."

"What?" Niall and Harper asked, once again nailing their simultaneous bit.

"It's true," Pius confirmed. "There's hundreds of them down there, maybe thousands. Anna and some other guy they call 'Brother

Vee' are trying to do a ritual to summon the Psycho Hose Beast. I don't know if they're trying to control it or what, but I don't think they actually know what we're doing."

"We know, Pius," Harper said. "Niall's bimbo girlfriend's dad told us about it before he fell into a woodchipper."

Niall started to protest, but Pius spoke over him, "I set up a firebomb in the basement of the bunker to destroy the bugs, but—"

"But what, Pius?"

Pius looked pale. Keith stepped in to finish. "They just took Rebecca and Nelson into the bunker. There were too many of them for us to stop them. They're doing their ritual thing right now."

CHAPTER FORTY-NINE

The River
Friday, October 28
2:30 am

Nelson realized he may have gotten in over his head when they led him into a dark underground chamber lit by flickering candles, surrounded by robed figures and cages full of skittering, squealing, fist-sized bugs. He wondered briefly if he'd stumbled into one of Niall's stupid games.

"What the hell have I done?" he whispered.

Nelson was leaning heavily on Anna. He had no choice. His right leg wouldn't work, and he couldn't put any weight on it. Anna gave him pills for the pain, but all it did was make his head fuzzy. The candles seemed to float and swirl at the edges of his vision.

Anna took his hand and squeezed it firmly. "It's okay," she assured him. "I know this all seems crazy, and some of it is just for the effect, but it's all under control. Just focus on me, okay?"

"Are those giant... June bugs?" Nelson asked in horror.

"No, they're aliens, technically. They just look like June bugs. Don't look at the bugs, okay? Just look at me."

That was easier said than done. Anna looked calm and smiling, but the anxiety rising in Nelson's throat needed more than a pretty face to settle it. They seated him in a chair in the centre of a circle of the robed figures. Anna stood beside him, and from the circle emerged two people, their faces hidden by their hoods. One was a tall man, and the other, Nelson believed, was the woman in his room when he woke up.

She was holding a baby.

Nelson's mind whirled. What were they doing with a baby? No one mentioned a baby. Anna placed a battered red notebook on a pedestal in front of her. She flipped through the pages while keeping one hand on Nelson. The other woman tried to place the baby in Nelson's arms.

"What? No! I don't want to hold the baby!"

"You have to," Anna said softly. "It's okay. You don't have to do anything. Just sit there and hold her."

With great apprehension, Nelson took the child into his arms. She was all dressed in white and was fussing and crying a little; Nelson tried weakly to gently rock and shush her. The bugs continued to skitter and hiss in the cages around them, just outside the circle of candles.

He felt something warm and sticky on the baby's back. He pulled his hand away, blood smeared on his fingers.

"The baby's hurt!" Nelson screeched. "Someone help me!"

"She's fine," Anna said calmly. "It's just a scratch. She'll be fine."

"I don't like this!" Nelson tried to get up. "Someone, please come check on the kid. I don't know how to tell if she's okay!"

"She's fine!" Anna screamed in his face. Nelson was so shocked that he flopped back down into the hard wooden chair. His leg screamed in agony. Anna took a deep breath and focused her attention back on her book. "I'm sorry, Nelson, but I need to concentrate. The Primordial One will be here any moment, and we must be ready."

The circle of robed figures was still, but Nelson noticed the tall male standing ominously over him. He heard gunshots outside, and a few figures near the stairs shuffled and glanced around, but no one said a word. The bugs continued to scratch and hiss in their cages.

Anna was speaking quietly, and Nelson couldn't make out the words. It didn't sound English. She was squeezing his shoulder so tightly it hurt, her fingernails digging deeper and deeper into his flesh every time she repeated the strange set of phrases. It sounded like gibberish to Nelson, but Anna kept saying them louder and louder as if yelling them at the top of her lungs would make them coherent.

Fear began to slip into Anna's voice, and the tall man twitched.

"What's wrong?" he demanded. His voice was familiar.

"I don't know!" Anna screeched. "It's not working!"

"You have a legion of the harbinger beetles. You have the blood of the Blood. What are you doing wrong?"

"I'm not doing anything wrong!" Her voice was growing panicked. More gunshots burst outside the bunker.

The man's voice was impatient and angry, but he also had a hint of fear. "Is it the boy? Are you not making a connection with him?"

"No, I can feel his power the same way I could with Niall. It's not that, it's..." Her voice trailed off. Her eyes fell on the baby in Nelson's lap.

"We don't have any more time! The Primordial One is on our doorstep!"

"It's the baby!" Anna gasped. "It has to be!"

"You said she was blood of the Blood," growled the man.

"She should be... She's Harper's cousin. But maybe she doesn't have the same father, maybe... we need to get Pius in here."

"He escaped!"

"What the hell is going on?" Nelson demanded. "You said I was going to help you save the world, but this seems all wrong..."

"It is all wrong!" the man roared. "The Primordial One is about to rise! The Redeemer that has been prophesied for thousands of years to cleanse the world of all sinners and heathens! We were supposed to be ready for Him. We were supposed to be prepared with a sacrifice to appease Him, to show Him that we were worthy, that we would be His greatest servants in the new world..."

Nelson recognized that voice from somewhere... "Sacrifice? Anna didn't tell me anything about a sacrifice."

"Anna was too gentle with you." The tall man leaned in, placing his hands on the armrests to either side of Nelson as if he were imprisoning him. Nelson couldn't see his face clearly but could smell his rank breath. It stank of rot and booze. "Anna thought she could convince you of our need and greater purpose..."

"I just needed more time," she said weakly.

"But she is a coward like her parents. She nearly killed you and ruined everything we planned for."

"Just a little more time..."

"There is no time!" The tall man reared back, pulling a long, silver knife from beneath his robes. His hood fell back to reveal a shiny bald head and a beak-like nose. "The Primordial One will stop at nothing to destroy us all, don't you understand? It doesn't care about us feeble mortals. It doesn't want followers or believe in rituals. It's an otherworldly monster we can never hope to understand, let alone control."

The robed figures in the circle were getting very uncomfortable now. They shifted and swayed, and muttering broke out among them.

Nelson barely paid any attention to them. His focus was on the beady-eyed man standing over him with a knife.

"Mr. Bourgeois?" Nelson asked dumbly. The principal of St. Paul's High School? The Jesus-loving bible-thumper?

"We knew it was coming, but we couldn't stop it. Our one chance was to create a spell to protect us. Maybe if we made it happy, it would go easy on us. At the very least, we could protect our circle from the destruction that was coming. We could survive the devastation of this sacrilegious world to build a new one, a better one, where we could live under God's love and light."

Okay, now *that* sounded like Mr. Bourgeois.

"But now it's all ruined. Ruined! My trust in this woman and these other idiots has doomed us all." Bourgeois looked down at Nelson and the crying baby in his lap. "But maybe there's enough magic to protect just one of us. The power is in the blood. The blood will protect me."

Bourgeois raised the knife to strike. Nelson never found out whether he was aiming for him or the baby. A gunshot rang out inside the bunker, a deafening bang that caused Nelson to jump and the baby to start screaming in his lap.

A red circle appeared in the centre of Bourgeois' forehead. He dropped the knife and went slack, then slumped lifeless to the floor.

"Do it again."

The vulture-like gaze of William Bourgeois' dead eyes bore twin holes into Anna Chaffey. The tall bald man ground his teeth. "You will continue doing it until you get it to work."

Anna stood in the centre of a circle of candles. Upon a table before her lay several arcane texts, a vivisected scarab, and the naked corpse of a man she didn't know. The young woman's hands and arms dripped with the alien creature's fluorescent green blood, and she had used the ichor to draw glowing symbols on the dead man's face and chest. Anna stared at her faintly luminescent fingers, which trembled from fear and exhaustion.

"I can't... I can feel the power in the creature's blood, but it's not answering me. I don't know if I can do this."

Bourgeois was seated on a wooden chair outside the circle. His gaze hadn't moved from Anna in hours. "You made it work with the dog." He was referring to the large black stray she enchanted, which was now locked up elsewhere in the compound. The magic drove the poor animal mad, and now it paced and clawed at its cage without rest. It had not slept or eaten in days.

"The dog was still alive when we found it. These people have all been dead for too long."

"Then we'll start doing the ritual on living subjects."

Anna knew he was going to suggest that. The idea of killing someone as an experiment didn't particularly bother her; she would do anything to make this work, but she still held reservations. "I'm still not sure if it will work. More life force is required to do this to a human. I don't think the scarabs have enough power."

Anna had dreamed of being able to do this, of casting real magic, for as long as she could remember. She was so excited when she found Theolina's journals and to be so close to the real thing. Then, when she had met Niall, she was jealous of him but also inspired. He was living proof that magic was real and that maybe she would have a chance to do it herself.

Only later did Anna discover what her parents had been doing to her.

Bourgeois steepled his long, thin fingers under his chin, his bony elbows resting on his knees. "We need the blood of Kluskap."

Anna took a deep breath. He was right, of course. Bourgeois was always right. From her research, she discovered that about one in a hundred thousand people possessed the potential to do magic. Different cultures held different beliefs and rituals around it—some believed that only virgins could cast spells, which was bullshit— but the truth was that only a limited number of humans were born with the ability. A rare few, like Theolina Benoit, were particularly adept at it and could perform simple spells even without sacrificial blood. Niall O'Neil seemed an anomaly; he could cast magic of immense power with little effort, but only if he was in contact with the blood. Anna's own abilities, she discovered, were middling. She was special, but not that special.

"Harper's not going to help us," she said.

"Don't worry about Harper, there is another way."

Anna's throat clenched. He meant Pius and his little sister, a baby less than a year old. He would sacrifice them to ease the Redeemer's passage into the world. They would die anyway if Anna did nothing; if they gave their blood, she might be able to get the real ritual to work, the one she'd been secretly planning for so long.

Bourgeois must have sensed her unease. He tilted his head slightly. "What is on your mind, Sister Pearl?"

She was so close. She could try the ritual to banish the monster if she could get the Blood. Anna was trying to seal it away permanently, not summon it. She had been lying to the Church the whole time. If Brother Vee figured out the truth, she was dead, but she didn't fear for her own life. She feared for the entire planet if the Church got their way.

It was tearing her apart. The lying, the killing, and the end of the world hanging over their heads was all too much. Anna felt the darkness creeping into her mind like prickly weeds. "Brother Vee... William..." A tear rolled down her face. "I'm afraid. I saw what happened last year, and the kids told me about their encounters with the Primordial One. I'm not sure if I'm strong enough to do this..."

William Bourgeois—Brother Vee—suddenly changed in demeanour. The harsh coldness of his features vanished, revealing a softer side his students never experienced. He stood up, approached Anna, and put a hand on top of the young woman's.

"Anna. We must be brave. The Lord will test us to prove our faith, to weed out the liars and the heathens. We must endure these trials and come out stronger. We must be ready for the new world Our Lord will bring us. Do not let Keenan's sacrifice be in vain."

Keenan. His death had been the catalyst that unlocked her dream.

For decades, the Church of Christ the Sun Redeemer knew that trauma could unlock magical abilities in those born with the potential. They groomed children from a young age in hopes that the abuse and torture would unlock the power that could help usher in the new world.

Anna's parents spent her entire life torturing her body and mind in the name of their Church, but none of the physical and emotional trauma they inflicted unlocked her meagre magical abilities. The thing that finally triggered her was the death of the only person who had ever really loved her.

Sister Pearl nodded and wiped her tears. She had seen this other side of Brother Vee only once or twice before, and she wasn't sure if it was the real him, long buried under the layers of brutality required by leadership, or if it was just another mask he wore to deceive his followers.

It didn't matter. If Bourgeois figured out she was lying, she was dead. If she failed to perform the ritual properly, they were all dead. There was only a slim chance this could turn out well for them.

Anna had to keep the others believing she was trying to summon the Primordial one. She told Bourgeois she had doubts it would ever work, but he waved them off.

"There are other possibilities. It is a long shot, but Peters has an idea of how to use your dog to bring Niall closer to us. If that doesn't work, there's also his brother." Bourgeois' empathy faded, replaced with the cold, focused obsession of madness. His dark eyes glistened in the dim light. "Yes, I think you should start working on the brother immediately."

CHAPTER FIFTY

Zombie
Friday, October 28
3:00 am

"You have a choice," Tanguay called into the cavernous bunker. "Either leave now, or I will start shooting every last one of you bastards until I'm out of bullets and up to my knees in white-hooded idiots."

She meant it, too. She had a dozen magazines tucked into her pockets and inside her bullet-proof vest and was more than happy to use every single one. She had nothing to lose and hated every one of these scum-sucking freaks with fiery passion.

What the hell was wrong with these people? Tanguay had never been much of a religious person, but following this nonsense, believing that this creature was some kind of messenger from God and sacrificing babies to appease it? These people were more monstrous than the walking dead outside.

A handful of the cultists broke and fled. A few more fell to their knees, praying. The rest shuffled uncomfortably, trying to decide which was more painful: being shot in the face or an eternity of torturous damnation. Tanguay scanned the crowd quickly, her finger on the trigger of her Smith & Wesson. If any of them so much as scratched their ass, they were dead.

"There are bugs here," Harper called out, walking past the cages of skittering, undulating creatures.

"I told you, there are thousands of them," Pius said, pushing past the cultists and marching to Nelson. He picked up Rebecca from the shocked boy's arms and held her close. "There are more of those zombie things somewhere here, too."

"Over there, in the corner." Keith pointed to a dark area of the bunker. "There's a bunch of them in a cage."

"What the hell happened to you?" Niall asked his brother, leaning over him.

"I was in a car accident," he said numbly. "What happened to you? Anna told me you summoned some kind of demon to destroy the world?"

Niall and Harper turned on Anna. She crumpled, throwing up her hands in supplication.

"I'm sorry. We needed Nelson's help." Tears welled in her black-painted eyes. "I thought we could stop it. I thought we could at least slow it down..."

"You were trying to summon the Hose Beast!" Harper snapped. "Peters told us it was the stupid cult's plan all along!"

"No! Please believe me!" Anna was sobbing now. "I was trying to stop it. They knew I could do some simple magic spells, so they wanted me to release it from where Niall banished it. Peters and Bourgeois wanted to summon the Primordial One. They thought it was foretold in their scriptures. I thought I could stop it. I was trying to work out a ritual that could permanently banish it."

Harper didn't point her rifle at the young woman, but she kept it at the ready. "Why did you go along with them at all?"

"You don't understand. My parents were obsessed with this Church. They followed Joseph di Mambro and then Bourgeois. They drilled into my head my whole life that I was worthless, and my only purpose was to help the Redeemer return. They tortured me my whole life, trying to unlock magic powers in me like Niall has. That was their only purpose; they gave their whole lives to the temple, and then the Bourgeois had them killed. Bourgeois would have killed me too if I didn't help them."

Tanguay felt sorry for the young woman. She'd seen people brainwashed like this, tortured and abused. Anna nearly got out of it, but the death of her boyfriend drew her into a spiral that sealed her fate.

"But you did wake it up," Niall said, standing by his brother. "Feeding it the bugs. They powered the carapace, and now the Primordial One has reclaimed it, and it's animated the dead bodies you stuffed the bugs in!"

Anna's pale face was twisted in hysteria and horror. "I didn't know! I didn't think the bugs were working! It was meant to buy time until I figured out the real spell and could get Nelson and Pius' blood to banish the Primordial One for good. But the only spell I ever got to work was the stupid dog we sent after Stacey."

"That was you?" Niall asked, horrified.

Anna nodded. "Her dad wanted to recruit you. It wasn't a coincidence that the dog attacked her right in front of your house. It was a long-term plan to try and bring you into the fold. They knew you wouldn't come along willingly, so they would use Stacey to lure you, just like I lured Nelson."

Nelson made weird, shocked, choking sounds. Tanguay was disgusted. All of these fools were sick.

"I knew there was something wrong with Stacey," grumbled Harper.

"She wasn't in on it," Anna said. "And when she found out what we were doing, she tried to refuse. Peters beat her, but she wouldn't give in."

"You said you have a way to banish the Primordial One?" Niall asked. "How?"

Anna held up the battered red notebook. "It's in Theolina's notes."

"But I destroyed..." Pius stammered. "I saw that book destroyed. In the filing cabinet at the school. Didn't I?"

Anna shrugged. "It must have been another notebook. Bourgeois never put this one in his filing cabinet. He knew what it was and realized how valuable it was. Once it fell into his hands, that's what set all of this into motion."

Niall froze. "We did that... We let him take the book..."

"Niall..." Harper began, but he cut her off.

"It's our fault. We caused all of this."

Anna laughed bitterly. "No, Niall. I did. It's *my* notebook, remember? My parents would have found me and the book, eventually. It's too bad Pius didn't destroy it. That might have actually ended all of this before it began."

There was a commotion in the dark corner of the bunker. During Anna's explanation, Tanguay had watched a few more cultists slip away quietly, but now several more broke into a frantic run up the stairs.

"The zombies!" Keith called, running out of the dark. "One of the Satan worshippers snuck out and opened the cage!"

Tabarnak. Tanguay should have been watching them more closely.

"Out!" she called, gesturing toward the stairs. "Everybody out!"

A cultist screamed and fell, grabbed by unseen, undead hands from out of the darkness. Then, a second one disappeared. Something crashed into one of the other cages, spilling a wave of giant bugs across the floor.

Niall and Anna grabbed Nelson and headed for the door. The other kids cleared a path, shoving the cultists aside as everyone rushed for the exit. Tanguay took up the rear, keeping one eye on the fleeing white robes while glancing back at whatever was coming up from the basement. The last thing she saw was the corpse of William Bourgeois as it was swarmed by the giant June bugs. They gnawed on his face, trying to burrow into his dead mouth.

Once she got outside, she slammed the bunker door closed. She didn't wait to see if all the cultists got out. The kids were clear; that's all that mattered. The surviving white robes were scattering in all directions.

"The beach," Niall said. He looked pale, his sandy hair plastered to his head with sweat. "The Primordial One is almost at the beach. It's being drawn to the bugs. It's feeding on them, making it stronger."

Tanguay took a moment to note their similarities, seeing Niall and his brother side by side for the first time. Niall's hair was a lot lighter, but they had very similar faces and the same blue-green eyes. Whatever the aliens put in them, their looks must have come from their mother's side.

"Wait a minute!" Pius handed Rebecca off to Keith, then ran around the side of the bunker. Cursing under her breath, Tanguay followed him. She couldn't cover all the kids if they didn't stay together.

"We need to deal with the butt monkeys," Pius explained, heading to a small side door. "I just need to give the bomb I set up earlier a spark, and it should send the whole bunker up."

The kid was resourceful; Tanguay had to give him that. He was also a lot more focused and confident than she remembered. The last time she'd seen Pius, he was still a little boy, scared of his own shadow. Had he grown up in the last year? Or was it protecting his sister that gave him that extra boost of courage?

Pius pulled a 9-volt battery out of his pocket and carefully fished a wire from the corner of the door. He unwrapped black tape from the bare ends and began touching them to the battery leads. Nothing happened.

"Is it working?" Tanguay asked.

"Give it a minute. It's not going to go boom. Gasoline doesn't explode, but it does ignite and burn fast. We should see the flames in a second."

Niall and the others appeared around the corner behind them. "The way to the beach is blocked with dozens of those ghouls." He turned to Anna. "How many of those things did you make?"

Anna was paler than usual. "Two? Three hundred?"

"*Calisse hosti*, where the hell did you find three hundred dead bodies?"

"A lot of them were cult members from Quebec. The rest were people who had disappeared around the island in the last year. You'd be amazed how many people can vanish and never be missed."

Robbie Brown and Shelly Parsons. Those fishermen from Port Hansen. Who knew how many more? They had started getting more brazen as the deadline loomed.

Maybe if Tanguay hadn't been suffering so badly from her injuries, she would have pieced it together sooner. Maybe if she hadn't been injured at all, none of this would have happened.

"It's not working!" Pius screamed, frantically touching the wires to the battery over and over.

"Maybe you didn't connect something properly," said Harper.

"I know how to set this up!" Pius snapped. "It's a simple circuit! There shouldn't be a problem unless something got disconnected—"

"I tripped over the wire," Keith said abruptly. He was holding Rebecca in his arms, rocking back and forth from foot to foot. His face was white as a sheet. "When we came out earlier, I tripped over it. I'm sorry, I didn't know I ripped it out!"

"We've got to go," Niall said. "I can feel it. It's almost here."

"We can't leave the bugs!" Harper snapped. "If we don't stop the Hose Beast, and it gets to them, it will only get more powerful!"

"Or it could turn more people into zombies," Anna added helpfully.

"I'll do it." Pius sighed. "I'll set off the firebomb. The rest of you go."

"No!" Harper cried. "We're not leaving you."

Pius shook his head. "Harper, you and Niall need to stop Primordial One, maybe with Nelson's help. Anna needs to help Nelson walk, and Sergeant Tanguay needs to protect you guys."

"What about me?" Keith said. "I'm the one who screwed up your bomb. I'm the one who should—"

"I need you to take care of Rebecca. You're bigger, stronger and faster than me. She has a much better chance of getting out of here with you than with me."

"But I'm just a big screw-up, I'm the one who—"

"I know," Pius said calmly. He approached Keith and put his arms around Rebecca, giving her a fierce hug. He kissed her on top of her tiny crying head. Pius stepped back and looked Keith dead in the eyes. "I know I can trust you to protect her. You won't make a mistake again."

Keith nodded savagely. He wiped his eyes with the back of his sleeve. "I will protect her with my life, man."

Harper threw her arms around Pius. "You be careful!" He struggled to get free of her.

"I'll be fine, I'll catch up with you in a few minutes, okay?"

Tanguay knew he was lying. She knew they were probably never going to see him again. But she didn't want to say that, and she couldn't drag out the goodbyes any longer. Tanguay had to make sure Harper and Niall got to the monster in one piece. That was their only hope. If Pius could also destroy the bugs, they might end this madness once and for all.

She hoped no one could see her tears in the dim light. "You are the bravest kid I know," she said, then turned and led the others away.

Pius went back into the bunker and slammed the door behind him.

CHAPTER FIFTY-ONE

99 Ways to Die
Friday, October 28
3:20 am

They followed a path through the trees toward the beach. Several times, the waterlogged ghouls blocked their way. Tanguay and Harper dealt with them quickly and efficiently, but there were always more to replace them.

"Three hundred people?" the Sergeant muttered under her breath. "I'd have you all locked up for life if most of you weren't dead already."

Sergeant Tanguay was looking nearly as rough as Nelson. She was limping badly, and she grimaced with almost every step. Her angular face glistened with sweat. She looked thinner, frailer than Niall remembered, too. He knew the wounds she suffered last year were severe, and they were taking their toll on the once mighty, tireless Mountie.

They found a few dead cultists on the path. Keith retrieved a pistol from one of them, and Harper grabbed a shotgun, which she slung over her shoulder. She offered a gun to Niall, too, but he turned it down. His hands were full, holding Nelson up. He didn't know how to use it anyway and would probably end up shooting himself in the face.

He was still trying to figure out what to do with Nelson. First, Niall was still trying to get over the fact that his brother was a freakin' alien. He hadn't even begun to process that he was also part alien. Second, he had no idea how to use Nelson to combat the Psycho Hose Beast. Third, Nelson was being scarily quiet. In his entire life, Niall had never known his older sibling to go so long without insulting or teasing him in some way.

"You okay?" Niall asked, cringing as Tanguay and Harper brought down another ghoul with multiple shots to the head and chest. This one was a teenage girl, not much older than Niall. One of her arms was torn off at the elbow, and half of her head was caved in. She exploded in a ball of searing blue flame.

Nelson couldn't seem to peel his gaze from the smouldering pile of ash and bone at their feet. "I still don't believe any of this…"

"It kinda becomes normal after a while." Niall smiled weakly. "Kinda boring, really."

"Really?"

"No. Not even remotely."

"Anna," Harper called out, reloading her rifle. "How do we stop the Psycho Hose Beast?"

She shifted most of Nelson's weight onto Niall, causing him to nearly topple over, and pulled out the red notebook from within her robes. "There's a ritual here, with weird words and symbols and stuff, but from what I understand, Niall has never needed that part."

"It's true," he grunted, speaking mainly to Nelson. "Lesson number one—with this kind of magic, the *intention* matters, not the words or gestures."

"So, basically the opposite of dating, then?" Nelson replied weakly.

Anna continued, "I think this is the important part: Theolina said the reason she and her sister couldn't defeat the Primordial One permanently, the same reason the First Hunter couldn't do it ten thousand years ago, was because the monster wasn't complete. It couldn't be banished without having all of it."

"What the hell does that mean?" asked Keith, rocking Rebecca and trying to coo her into silence. "Like Canadian Tire won't take back a barbeque without the gas regulator?"

"Kinda?" Anna shrugged. "She didn't know what was missing, exactly. There are several mentions of a shell, though, and the Primordial One being like a snail without its home."

Niall looked at Harper, and she stared back at him. "The carapace," he said.

"The what?" Nelson asked.

"Carapace. It's an exoskeleton we fought last year. The alien bugs have been coming to Earth looking for it for thousands of years, but it has been buried somewhere forever. The Americans found it thirty years ago and hid it on the base. It got out last year."

"And now the Primordial One has it."

"That's a good thing, right?" asked Nelson. "That means you can defeat it, right?"

Niall shrugged. "It means it's going to be even more powerful, I know that."

Nelson nodded. He looked so weak and defeated. "What do you need me to do?"

"We need to push it away. That's how I got rid of it the first time. I just couldn't push it far enough. You can."

"Why am I stronger? Because I'm older?"

"Something like that." Niall hadn't told him the whole truth. It was too complicated to explain, and Nelson didn't have enough time to come to grips with it now.

"So how do I do it?"

Another ghoul was approaching them, an older man wearing a ragged coat. He was limping badly due to a missing right foot, but he dragged the stump of his ankle along without complaint. His face, like most of the others, was mangled and crushed. Niall raised his hand at the ghoul. "Picture it going away. Far away. The farther away, the better. When I got rid of the Psycho Hose Beast last time, I pictured the ocean. If you can, think about sending it to the moon instead. Or Pluto. Then you just kinda *push* it with your mind."

Nelson looked at him the way he did when Niall broke his Vanilla Ice cassette. That is to say, thoroughly unimpressed. "That's it?"

"Well, no. You also need her."

Niall gestured to Harper, who was already on her way over, removing a safety pin from her jacket. She pricked her finger and offered her hand to Nelson. He took it carefully as if picking up a lobster, expecting it to pinch him.

When their hands touched, Nelson's eyes lit up. "I feel... a weird kind of tingling?"

"Yes!" Niall exclaimed. "That's it! That's the power! Now, do it. Push the monster away!"

The ghoul shambled progressively closer. It was just a few paces away, reaching out for them with black, crooked fingers. Tanguay and Keith stood by, watching nervously.

Nelson closed his eyes. He let go of Niall and let Harper take him by the arm instead; with his other hand, he reached out toward the ghoul. Niall could see the strain in Nelson's face, and his fingers grasped weakly and uselessly toward the rotting corpse. What was going on? It came so easily to Niall.

"Nelson," Harper said, the fear rising in her voice. "Hey, dipwad, hurry up and banish the thing, okay?"

"It's not working!" He said through gritted teeth. "How long is this supposed to take?"

Not this long. The ghoul was within grabbing distance. Niall pushed his way between Nelson and Harper, took Harper's hand, and pushed the ghoul, willing it to go away with nothing more than a thought. He felt the power flow from Harper into him and then into the ghoul.

The monster vanished in a heartbeat. It was not disintegrated, not teleported, but thrown, as if with incredible force, through the air and into the sky so that it vanished in the blackness. It left two furrows in the ground where its feet briefly dragged before becoming airborne.

"That was sick!" Keith called, bobbing up and down with the baby.

"That was a good one," Harper added.

It was. Better than Niall expected, actually. He meant to push the ghoul back so Tanguay could get a clear shot at it. He hadn't wanted to use too much power; they needed to conserve their strength for the Primordial One. And yet...

"It's here..." Anna said softly. Somehow, they all heard her. Over the crash of the waves, over the groaning of the remaining ghouls, over the ringing in their ears from the gunshots, they all heard her whispers.

Niall already knew. He felt the monster seconds before Anna announced it. An invisible beam connected the bugs in the bunker to whatever was under the water. Niall couldn't explain how he sensed the connection was there; he just knew.

"Get Rebecca out of here," Niall called to Keith.

A hundred metres away, beyond the edge of the rocky shoreline, a blue glow appeared beneath the surface of the waves. The waters churned and boiled, then crashed and crested like massive waves rolling across the shallows. Something began to rise from the dark waters.

It's too late, Niall realized. It was here, and they had no way to stop it.

The carapace looked bigger than Niall remembered. Maybe it was bigger, swollen with the power of the bugs and the cult's sacrifices of God knows how many souls. Huge, glossy black, a humanoid beetle over three meters tall, with long arms ending in scythe-like claws. The last time, it was a mindless, hollow engine of destruction, acting on self-preservation instinct. Looking for its soul, the life force to fully power it. Now, the monster had found its power, and Niall could feel it inside the jet-black shell.

It could feel Niall too.

Mortal... you will die a thousand deaths of immeasurable suffering...

The voice was inside his head, rattling around his skull like a steel ball bearing bouncing around a fishbowl. It caused him agony, like insects were trying to burrow out of his head. Niall stumbled to his knees.

He closed his eyes, but he could still see, not through his eyes, but through the eyes of the Primordial One. He saw the beach in front of him, below him, and saw the tiny, frail bodies of himself, Harper, Nelson, Tanguay, and Anna. Strange. They all glowed, like when the Predator used his heat vision to track Arnold Schwarzenegger in the jungle. Tanguay's glow was the dimmest, just a trickle of life force. Anna was brighter, and Harper and Niall were significantly more intense. But Nelson's light was nearly blinding and weirdly *appetizing.*

Whatever they were, whatever power the humans had, it paled in comparison to the limitless power that thrummed inside the monster. Before, whenever Niall saw through the Primordial One's eyes, he sensed the alien mind and the desire to kill and destroy, but it was different now. Now, the monster's senses reached to the ends of the universe, with power and abilities that Niall's mortal brain could not comprehend. He could feel the heat from the hearts of stars, smell the gases of distant nebulae, and hear the waves breaking on the shores of another world a million light-years distant. All of it was focused through the beast, through a beam of crackling white light he could clearly see now. It lanced through the dark sky and vanished beyond the trees toward the cult's compound. The Primordial One needed those bugs to unlock the total limit of its power.

Glancing down, Niall saw Anna approach, sobbing, waving her arms as if to get the monster's attention. She was begging for it to let them go, to not harm them. She was apologizing, throwing herself at its mercy. Niall was uncomfortably reminded of a penitent giving confession to a priest.

And then the Primordial One flicked a clawed finger, using no more effort than one would use to wave away a fly. A beam of blue-white energy flashed across Anna's body, from her toes to the top of her head. It lanced into the sky, booming with a crack of thunder.

In the fraction of a second the light lasted—both microseconds and millennia in the monster's eyes—Niall could clearly see every detail of her expression. He saw every freckle on her pale, soft flesh, saw the tiny dry cracks in her lips. He witnessed the life fade from her grey eyes.

An instant later, her body exploded into bits of roasted meat and bone, splattering across the beach. Niall felt her last anguished screams of guilt and pain, and then he felt no more.

CHAPTER FIFTY-TWO

Hurt
Friday, October 28
3:20 am

Pius tripped, returning down the concrete stairs, and stumbled head over heels into the darkness.

Through the haze of pain and disorientation, he wished he'd brought a flashlight.

He came to a stop at the bottom of the stairs in a twisted pile of his own limbs. His head throbbed. His left arm was bent underneath him at an awkward angle, and he feared moving it. Great, just great. All he had to do was light some gas on fire, and instead, he was going to end up dead in a dark basement.

He heard the shuffle of feet and the groan of undead lungs, and Pius suddenly wasn't so eager to give up.

He jumped to his feet and howled in pain, then nearly fell over again. His arm was in agony; his shoulder was likely dislocated. His head pounded, and when he reached up, he felt hot, sticky blood all across his forehead. He wanted to fall down and cry, but he heard the groans grow louder, and the shuffling of feet became more agitated.

He felt around, his hands falling on the drums and tanks that stored the gasoline he was planning to light on fire. He hoped there wasn't enough space between them for the ghouls to reach him.

As his eyes adjusted to the blackness, he realized the basement was not completely dark. There was a soft glow coming from the butt monkeys that were scurrying about on the other side of the chamber. It looked like a thick black carpet that was slithering across the floor, and the sight of it would have sent shivers down Pius' spine if it wasn't already so busy processing the agonizing pain in his head and arm.

The glow illuminated numerous ghouls that were bent over the bodies of the cultists who hadn't made it out. They were ripping their victims apart with their bare hands and teeth. The cracking and tearing sounds were nauseating.

Don't throw up, don't throw up. Pius didn't think his battered body could handle it.

Pius reached into the pocket of his jeans to find the 9-volt battery was no longer there. He wasn't sure whether to swear or cry. After everything, he had dropped the battery? That's how it was going to end?

It couldn't end this way. He would not give up now. The old Pius would have rolled over like a puppy and begged for mercy, but that Pius was long gone. He was not the kid who burned the high school down by accident. He was going to burn this damn place down on purpose.

Biting back sobs, he tried to think of another plan. He could go back and look for another battery, matches, or something to light the gas with, but that would take time, and he wasn't sure where to look. The monsters down here were growing restless and could escape at any moment. Plus, if the Primordial One was feeding on the bugs and growing stronger, he couldn't risk it reaching this very large and tasty snack...

He looked around the dimly lit basement instead. There wasn't much except the gas drums, the butt monkeys, the corpses, and the ghouls. He could just make out the circle drawn on the floor, where the cultists planned to perform their ritual with Nelson and Rebecca. The circle. It had been surrounded by candles.

Yes. Pius saw them now in the dim light. None were still lit; the tapers kicked and scattered across the floor in all directions. He'd thought about it, at the time, how monumentally stupid it was for the cultists to have open flames in a room full of gasoline. But they were trying to summon an eldritch outer space god, so their judgement was hardly sound.

If they had candles, that meant they needed something to light them. There had to be matches or a lighter here somewhere.

It was worth a shot. He didn't have many other options.

Pius tested several large barrels between him and the main chamber, finding one partly empty and light enough to tip with his limited and diminished strength. Gritting his teeth, he threw all his weight behind his good shoulder and crashed into the barrel. It rocked but didn't fall over. He heard the groans and shuffle change pitch again. Taking a few steps back, Pius made a short run and threw himself against the barrel. It rocked and tipped farther but still didn't fall. The bang of the steel drum slamming back onto the concrete floor alerted every monster in the room, and the groans and scraping increased in volume dramatically. They were coming his way.

Finally, backing up the stairs, Pius ran and threw himself off his feet, landing full force with everything he had. The barrel tipped and fell, and he went along with it. He felt the crunch as the drum fell onto one of the dead bodies, crushing limbs and bones beneath. Pius hit the ground and rolled onto his bad arm, causing him to howl in pain.

He couldn't stop, couldn't black out. Through hazy vision, he could make out the shapes of the ghouls closing around him. He could see the dull glow of the butt monkeys swarming across the floor. He could smell the gasoline leaking from the container, pooling across the room.

Driven by instinct and willpower alone, Pius struggled to his feet. He made his way toward the chair where Nelson had been seated. There was a small table beside it where Anna had kept some of her supplies. He figured it was his best chance of finding something.

A ghoul lunged at him in the dark, and Pius barely sidestepped out of the way. Its fingers grazed his cheek as it stumbled by. Pius limped toward the chair, and he thought he saw, yes! There was a box of matches on the side table! It was only a few steps away. All he had to do was—

Pius' feet went out from under him, and the floor came up to meet his face. He realized, too late, that he'd tripped over the mangled body of one of the cultists. The table was just out of reach. He could see the matches right there. But his head hurt so bad that he could barely tell which way was up anymore.

Teeth sank into his leg, and Pius screamed in pain. The haze and numbness gone, he looked down in perfect clarity to watch the desiccated face of a young man chewing on his calf. Pius tried uselessly to shake the ghoul off, but its claw-like hand gripped his ankle like a vise.

The gas was pooling around them. Pius reached for the matches, but they were just beyond his fingers. He feebly kicked at the ghoul with his other leg, but he didn't have the strength or leverage to get a solid blow. An icy chill spread through his body, and Pius knew he would black out at any moment. He tried to ignore the pain, to separate his mind from the searing fire in his leg, and tried everything he could to reach the stupid matches.

He clawed feebly at the robes of the cultist beside him, trying to get enough purchase to pull himself just a little farther. It was no use. He didn't have the strength, and what little remained quickly faded. He would soon become like the cold, stiff body lying next to him, and Pius' pathetic attempt to find another human form to touch in his final moments just reminded him how sad and useless he was.

His fingers brushed a small box in the corpse's pocket. Cigarettes.

With the last of his strength and the remaining shreds of his consciousness, Pius slid the small cardboard box out. He couldn't feel his leg anymore but could hear the monster chewing. Everything was so cold, so numb.

The fingers of Pius' right hand shook the box. Three cigarettes and a small plastic lighter fell out to splash in the gasoline. Blackness was engulfing him. He couldn't feel his fingers anymore but watched as they fumbled with the lighter, flicking the igniter. Click. No spark. Click. No spark.

His eyelids were so heavy, but he dared not close them. He knew he would never open them again.

He clicked it one last time, and the lighter slipped from his numb fingertips.

Pius closed his eyes.

CHAPTER FIFTY-THREE

Lightning Crashes
Friday, October 28
3:25 am

Tanguay watched the girl Anna vaporize in the blink of an eye, and a heavy blackness settled on her heart. She always knew she probably wouldn't survive this night, but for the first time, she truly realized that none of them were getting out of this alive.

The enemy they were facing was not remotely human, mortal, or even of this world. It was a being of unfathomable power that they could never begin to understand, let alone fight. They had already failed.

Tanguay knew she should have died on the airfield tarmac eighteen months ago. She'd fought on and made it this far, hoping she could keep these kids safe a little longer.

It had all been for nothing.

And then the bunker in the compound exploded, sending a pillar of blue flame a kilometre into the dark sky.

The Primordial One made a sound that was not of the Earth. It was a high-frequency screech, like the cross between microphone feedback and the roar of an impossibly large tiger. The sound alone nearly knocked Tanguay off her feet, but somehow, she kept her footing, and through the haze and the ringing in her ears, she watched the black glossy creature take a step back and stumble.

Did the death of hundreds of those space bugs scare the monster? Or did it actually hurt it?

There were still ghouls on the beach, shuffling out of the waves and slowly moving toward the three surviving kids. Keith had fled moments ago with the baby; Tanguay could only hope and pray they made it to safety—if there was anywhere safe left in the world.

Marie-Ann knew she couldn't fight the monster. She had to trust the kids to do that. But she could buy them time and keep the zombies away from them as long as she could.

"Harper! Niall! I'll keep those damn things away from you! Do whatever you have to!"

Tanguay began to fire. She used the shotgun first, blasting the things in the chest and sending them backward. Some of them tumbled over. One of them exploded in a blue fireball.

She reloaded the shotgun once, but the process was too slow. There were too many, and they were too close to the kids. Harper and Niall seemed to be yelling and pleading with Nelson, but she didn't know what they were saying. After emptying it a second time, Tanguay tossed the shotgun aside and switched to her sidearm.

She could shoot and reload faster with her Smith & Wesson, but she had to aim more carefully. Tanguay took out the glowing lights of the bugs when she could; if she couldn't see them, she would aim for kneecaps to slow the monsters down. Headshots barely fazed the bastards.

Soon, the blast of gunfire and eldritch screams of the monster blurred together and were replaced by an incessant, high-pitched droning in Tanguay's ears. Flashes of lightning exploded across the sky, searing her vision, too, so she could soon barely sense anything around her. She felt the jump of the gun in her hands and saw the shadows of the ghouls moving around her and the kids.

And the pain, the incredible pain that wracked her body.

The handful of pills she'd taken early that day were worn off, and the adrenaline could carry her no farther. Her limbs felt like lead. Her spine sent shots of lancing, fiery pain to her brain with every retort of the handgun. She needed to keep fighting. If she stopped, the kids would die, and that was all that mattered anymore.

She reached into her belt and found herself out of magazines just as a shadowy ghoul approached Harper on the left. Unarmed, Tanguay threw herself at the blurry figure, knocking it away from the girl and landing hard on top of it. Tanguay screamed as she felt something pop in her lower back. She pulled her spare revolver from her leg holster, acting only on instinct and muscle memory because her mind couldn't form a coherent thought. It was the .38 her father had given her as a gift when she graduated from the academy, the only thing he'd ever given her besides genetic material.

Tanguay fired three shots into the ghoul's head and three more into its chest. With the last of her strength, she rolled off of it just as the corpse exploded in blue flame. The heat was unbearable. She felt the flesh on her face crack and split, but in her left arm and leg, she felt nothing. Nothing at all. The pain would come a few moments later when her severed nerves realized that the limbs were gone.

She couldn't see out of her left eye, and her right eye was nothing but a white haze. She still couldn't hear anything.

Marie Ann Tanguay saw the shape of a girl appear before her. Not a girl, a young woman, almost. It must have been Harper. Tanguay tried to speak, to ask her if they had won, but no words would come out.

The girl knelt down, her features coming into focus. It wasn't Harper. The girl was about the same age and height but was fair-haired, with the same sharp features as Tanguay herself and the same blue eyes that Tanguay knew so well.

"Lynne," Tanguay sighed. She wasn't sure if the words came out, but the girl must have heard them. She nodded.

"*Bonjour, maman*," she said.

Tanguay felt hot tears on her cheeks. She realized it was the only thing she could feel at all anymore. "I'm sorry. I'm sorry I couldn't save you."

Lynne smiled. "It wasn't your fault, *maman*. I was sick. The doctors did everything they could. You did nothing wrong, and nothing you could have done would have changed anything."

"You're so big. I love you."

"I love you, too."

Lynne took her mother's hand. Tanguay smiled.

CHAPTER FIFTY-FOUR

The Man Who Sold the World
Friday, October 28
3:25 am

When Niall O'Neil was five years old and his brother Nelson was about ten, Niall fell off his bike while learning to ride. The accident happened in the driveway in front of their house when their parents were not around. His mom was likely at work, and his dad was probably asleep after a night shift. Nelson, as usual, had been pressed into watching his little brother while the adults weren't around, and he was none too keen about it. Honestly, their parents didn't expect much from them—as long as both boys were still alive when the adults got home, that was all they could hope for.

If Niall remembered it correctly, Nelson had been genuinely trying to help him ride, though he would have rather been anywhere else, and Niall was not being very easy to get along with. He had whined and kicked and tried to ignore Nelson's advice. Finally, when Nelson's head was turned momentarily, Niall jumped on his little blue bicycle and pedalled it as hard as he could, right into their dad's car. Niall went headfirst into the paved driveway.

Niall's face was bleeding, his palms were scraped, and there was a substantial scratch on the front fender of the new Chevy. Nelson tried to comfort his brother, but Niall had cried, kicked and screamed, and nearly bit his big brother's hand while he tried to look at the cut on his face.

When their mother arrived home a few minutes later, Nelson tried to explain what had happened and how he never wanted to watch Niall anyway, but his words fell on deaf ears. She screamed at Nelson as she fawned over Niall, calling him careless and stupid and ranting about what would have happened if Niall had been more seriously hurt. The noise woke their father, who stomped outside, saw the damage to the new car, then smacked Nelson hard upside the head.

Nelson never again tried to teach his brother to ride a bike or anything else after that. There was always tension between them, and Niall eventually realized that their parents gave him, their youngest, preferential treatment. Did they really love Niall more? Or did they keep Nelson at arm's length because they knew there was something... unusual about him?

Why Niall took this moment, with death staring them in the face, to dredge up this particular memory, he had no idea. It probably had something to do with Niall doing everything he could to keep Nelson alive.

He blacked out for a moment after Anna died—he assumed it was a defence mechanism of his brain to protect itself from the alien mind of the Primordial One. It took Niall only a few seconds to regain his senses, and when he came to, he was shocked to find himself and the others still alive. By rights, the monster could have killed them a thousand times over in that brief span. *So, why were they still alive?*

And then he felt it—the gaping hole where a huge chunk of the Primordial One's power had been abruptly torn away. He glanced over his shoulder and saw the pillar of blue flame still flickering in the sky near the site of the cult's compound.

Pius had done it. He destroyed the scarabs, which hurt the Hose Beast in the process. Severing the connection to its power source staggered it as surely as it had Niall when he broke his own connection.

The monster was still stunned. Sergeant Tanguay and Harper were fighting off the ghouls, which the explosion did not seem to have affected. Nelson was kneeling on the beach rocks, sobbing and shaking his head.

"I don't know what to do!"

"You have to kill it!" Harper screamed at him, then shot a ghoul point-blank in the face with her rifle so its head exploded. She kicked it over, and it flopped around uselessly. "Use the Force, cast a spell, do whatever you need to do, okay?"

"I don't know how!"

"Holy shitcrackers, Niall did it with hardly an effort."

"I'm not as smart as Niall!" Nelson screamed. "He's the special one! He's always been the special one. Mom and Dad's favourite! I'm the screw-up who got tricked into joining a cult!"

There was no time for Nelson's self-pity. They needed to make their move while the monster was incapacitated. Harper was right. Niall had always been able to use the power with little effort. It came to him easily, too easily, sometimes. That's how he had killed Keenan. His comfort and control of his abilities continued to increase, yet he still grossly misjudged the power he used to fling that ghoul away earlier...

Or had he? Something about that didn't feel right. He usually could feel precisely the power that flowed out of him, no matter how big or small the expenditure. For something as big as throwing that ghoul halfway to Toronto, Niall should have been drained and exhausted. Often, he passed out. But he hadn't felt a thing. Almost as if he hadn't used his power at all...

"Nelson!" Niall called out. "It's not your fault!"

"Niall!" Now out of bullets, Harper swung her rifle like a club at the remaining ghouls. "Nice of you to join us!"

Niall crawled to his feet to stand between Harper and his brother. "Nelson, you can't use your power because, well, you *can't.* The aliens in Mom's memories said something about their incompatible genetic material. I don't think you can make the right connection with Harper to use the magic."

"What are you talking about?" Nelson asked.

"When I pushed that ghoul away earlier, I didn't use my power—"

"—you used Nelson's," Harper finished for him. "I knew it felt different."

Niall nodded. "Because I was touching both of you at the same time. I was like a conduit between you. I think that's what we have to do to destroy the Primordial One."

The giant, black-shelled creature began to stir. "We don't have much time."

"Nelson, take my hand. Harper, other side."

The Primordial One turned its attention to the three kids standing on the shore.

The three held hands in a circle, and Niall felt the energy flow through him. It was different than usual. It felt like a cold snowball in his hands when it was just Harper. Now, it felt like a freezing waterfall bathing over his entire body.

He felt the power flow from Nelson into him, and he tried to channel it into the Hose Beast. Niall thought about the farthest corner of the universe he could imagine, a supernova he and Pius had read about, millions of light years away.

But it wasn't working. The power wasn't going into the monster but back into his brother. They were creating a massive feedback loop, increasing the energy exponentially. Niall was trapped in it, and like his hand grasping a live electrical wire, he couldn't let it go.

"Niall!" Harper screamed, and Niall realized too late that the massive, claw-like appendage of the hose beast was slashing toward them. There was nothing he could do. He couldn't move, couldn't use his power, couldn't do anything except close his eyes and wait to die...

There was a flash of blinding light, and the hose beast emitted a high-pitched squeal, an ear-splitting frequency Niall felt in his bones. The monster's claw bounced off an invisible field around the trio, and it staggered back as if stunned.

Nelson was glowing, a green, unearthly aura pulsing from somewhere inside him. He looked terrified, his blue eyes blank and empty. "I don't know what's happening..."

Niall couldn't explain it succinctly, but whether instinctively or by accident, Nelson had shielded them from the monster. The power flowing from Nelson was *massive*. It was too much. Niall heard his brother groan and felt him shudder. Nelson fell to his knees.

"You have to release the power!" Niall cried. "It's going to kill you. You have to be the one to banish the Hose Beast!"

"Do it! Don't let that thing come back again!" Harper was trying to sound encouraging, but Niall could see the fear in her face, too. He wasn't sure how much she could sense what was happening.

The Hose Beast unleashed a beam of blue-white flame, which also reflected harmlessly off Nelson's shield.

What are you doing?

Niall didn't hear the voice so much as he felt it. It appeared directly in his mind.

How are you doing this?

The Hose Beast spoke to him, trying to get inside his head again. It couldn't defeat them physically, but if it wormed itself into his mind, if it got inside their shields...

Nelson's clothes burst into flames. He was screaming in agony. He was either going to drop dead or explode at any moment. Niall needed him to release the power and focus it on the Hose Beast, but how? How could he defend them at the same time?

"Let it in," Harper whispered to him.

"What?"

"It's a vessel, right? The carapace? It can travel between worlds, between universes. It's connected with you. If it's inside your head, you're inside it, too."

What was she talking about? Nelson was going to die any second. They were all going to die. "I don't..."

"Turn it on." Her voice was firm. Commanding. Certain.

She *could* see inside his head, Niall realized. At least some of it. And she was right.

Niall relaxed, and he felt the alien presence seep inside his brain. It was oily and disgusting. The inside of his skull felt like sandpaper, and his stomach clenched in knots. If he lived with this for long, it would drive him insane or turn him into a pillar of smouldering ash—probably both.

But he only needed a few seconds. Images flashed through his mind. Distance stars and moons, endless blackness, all-consuming black holes.

He picked a beach with a red sky and a black sea, a billion light years away. The world orbited a star that had just gone supernova, destroying a civilization that had spanned thousands of years. All that remained were the fractured ruins of a race that would have been forgotten if anyone had known about them in the first place.

Niall picked this spot, and with the tiniest effort, the slightest flick of his mind against the quasi-organic controls inside the monster, a shimmering glow of blue energy haloed the Primordial One. The carapace could travel between worlds, and he just opened the gate.

He immediately cut off the connection. Niall found himself back on Earth, on a beach on the Cape-de-Cape Peninsula near Gale Harbour. And the Hose Beast had one of its black claws wrapped around his brother's waist.

Niall let go of Harper and grabbed Nelson with both hands. Harper grabbed his other arm. Nelson continued to glow, and Niall could feel an impossible heat inside his brother. It was so hot that Niall's hands were burning. Nelson's skin was sizzling and cracking.

"I can't..." Nelson gasped. "It's too much..."

"How do we stop it?" Harper groaned, bracing her feet as the monster was pulled into the glow, and it, in turn, tried to pull Nelson with this.

"I don't know how," Niall said, his eyes hot with tears. "I don't know how to stop it. You need to let go of it, Nelson!" It had been too much to ask Nelson to do. He didn't know he possessed this power until a few hours ago; how could he possibly know how to control it? They heard bones cracking as the Primordial One's grip tightened on Nelson's lower body.

Nelson bellowed in pain, then shook his head feebly. "You let go."

Niall was shocked. "No! I'm not letting you go!"

"It's okay. It's over... Tell Mom and Dad, I love them..."

"No!"

"It's okay. I finally... finally found my purpose..."

Harper was struggling to keep a grip on Nelson's arm. Niall could smell her flesh burning. "We can't hold him!"

Niall's own arms were in agony, his hands numb from the pain of the searing heat. He could barely see Nelson's features; the glow inside his flesh was growing so bright. "Nelson... thank you... I love you."

He wasn't sure, but he thought Nelson smiled. "Those pants make you look like a tool."

And then Nelson was gone. Niall couldn't be sure if he consciously let go or if his hands gave out. His brother was flying away from him, drawn with the glossy black beast into a glowing orb of light hovering above the waves. Through the orb, Niall was sure he saw the same beach with the red sky he'd seen through the Primordial One's mind's eye.

A split second before the portal closed, he saw the crack of blue-white lightning, tracing from his brother up into the red sky. Nelson vanished in a ball of blinding light as bright as the supernova that hung in the heavens above the black sea.

Niall collapsed, and Harper caught him before he hit the ground.

CHAPTER FIFTY-FIVE

God
Friday, October 28
3:35 am

Heat. Unbelievable, searing heat.

Pius had gone to Hell. That was the only explanation. Oddly, Hell smelled like gasoline.

He heard Rebecca crying.

Pius could believe that he would be sent to eternal damnation for murdering a woman with a hammer and maybe for burning down the school. But why would Rebecca be there?

"Wake up, buddy."

It was Keith's voice. Keith was in Hell, too? That was harsh. He may have been a jerk, but he had mostly cleaned up his act, and it wasn't like he had killed anyone—

"Pius, wake up!"

He opened his eyes. The sky above him was full of black smoke, and the heat came from a towering inferno of flame about a hundred metres away.

His entire body was in agony.

Keith was kneeling over him, trying to rock a hysterical Rebecca with one arm while he gently shook Pius with the other hand. Pius tried to turn his head and immediately winced as indescribable pain lanced through him. He noted he was soaking wet, still drenched in gasoline.

"Thank Christ, you're awake." Keith sighed. "Don't try to move, buddy, okay? Just stay with me and keep talking. Your breathing got really shallow for a minute, and I want to make sure you didn't pass out again."

Dead, Pius thought. *I should be dead. I dropped the lighter; the monsters were on top of me. Why am I still alive?*

"You came back for me," Pius said weakly.

"Of course I did." Keith moved Rebecca to the other arm and adjusted his position while he continued to rock her. "The others were about to fight the Hose Beast on the beach. You were taking too long in the bunker, so I came looking for you. Good thing I did; you were about to become zombie chow for those bastards. Speaking of which, don't look down at your leg. They got it pretty good."

Pius couldn't look down if he wanted to. He could move the fingers on both hands and the toes of his right foot, so he didn't think he was paralyzed, but everything hurt so bad he wished he couldn't feel anything.

"You set off the gas."

Keith nodded. Pius could see the palpable relief on his friend's face out of the corner of his eye. "Yeah, I found the lighter right by your hand. I figured you must have dropped it before you blacked out. Thank cripes, it still worked. And good thing you don't weigh very much because it was a bitch to drag you out with a screaming baby in a bag on my back."

He saved them. Keith saved them when Pius failed. Again.

"What about Niall and Harper?"

"There was a big bang down by the beach a minute ago, and everything went quiet. I think they finally got the bitch."

Tears began to roll down Pius' cheeks. Keith quickly put a hand back on Pius' shoulder. "I'm sure they're fine," he said quickly.

"I know they are." Pius closed his eyes and tried to take a deep breath. Even that hurt. "They always make it out. I told you to get Rebecca to safety."

Pius couldn't see, but he guessed Keith was embarrassed from his voice. "I know, man, but I just couldn't leave you. I'm sorry, but I couldn't."

"It's okay. You still saved her. And me. You did a hell of a lot better than I did."

"What are you talking about?"

The tears were coming hot and fast now, but Pius could do nothing to stop them. His voice was trembling. "I couldn't save anybody. I screwed up again, and you had to rescue me."

"Shut up, Pius."

"I'm useless! The first time the Psycho Hose Beast came after us, I spent the whole weekend peeing myself, curled up in a ball in the corner. Last year, I burned down the high school and nearly killed Keenan and myself in the process. What the Hell am I good for? I couldn't even light a giant stupid puddle of gasoline on fire. I'm a coward and a loser. You should have left me in the bunker…"

Pius' eyes were closed, but he could feel Keith shuffling uncomfortably beside him.

"For a smart guy, Pius, you're being a dumbass," Keith growled. "If you didn't already look like someone ran over you with a lawnmower, I would punch you in the head. You're a friggin' hero, you little shit!"

"Keith…"

"No, you listen to me. I know you went to the cops to tell them about my dad, and I know you didn't do it to be a goody-goody. You did it because you were worried about me. Even after all the times I bullied you and treated you like crap, you were looking out for me. You even came down to help my sorry ass when Skidmark found me pissed out of my mind behind that dumpster."

"I was just—"

"I said shut up! It's not just me. When Niall and Harper acted like idiots and wouldn't talk to each other, you went out of your way not to hurt anyone's feelings. You made that stupid binder to make sure you didn't upset anyone when they were the damn morons who should have been looking out for your feelings and how their stupid row was making you feel."

Pius didn't know anyone knew about the binder. He could feel the tears continue to run down his face, but he couldn't bring himself to open his eyes and look at Keith.

"And what about Rebecca? You did everything you could to take care of her. You tried to be a good son and brother to help your family. You even quit all your stupid clubs and math camps to help your mom, and even your marks are dropping. The Pius I knew from a few years ago cared more about school than anything, but you were willing to give it up for the people you cared about."

Pius felt something on his shoulder, but it didn't feel like Keith's hand. He finally forced his eyes open and discovered Rebecca lying beside him, her tiny head pressed against his chest. She had finally quieted down. With supreme effort and no small amount of pain, Pius put his arm around her.

Keith was still talking. "You got yourself out of that cell tonight. And when you did, you didn't run away. You went back looking for Rebecca. You refused to give up until you found her. You saved my life tonight, too, more than once. And your plan would have blown up those bugs a while ago if I hadn't screwed up and wrecked your trap. After all that, you should have taken your sister and gotten the Hell out of here. No one would have blamed you. Instead, you went back down into that bunker with every intention of giving your life to save all of us and stop that stupid monster once and for all.

"Pius Jeddore. You are the bravest string of spaghetti I have ever met, and we're all lucky to have you in our lives. You're a goddamn hero, you nerd."

Keith took Pius' hand and held it while the sounds of sirens approached in the distance.

Lost Together
December 31st, 1994
Gale Harbour Airport
10:45 am

Niall arrived at the airport to say goodbye to Harper.

He didn't see her much after he woke up in an ambulance near the cult's compound. She held his hand—awkwardly because they were both bandaged from the burns—and rode with him to the hospital, explaining to him that the police, having finally broken through the barricades, reached the beach just moments after Nelson and the Psycho Hose Beast disappeared.

Harper confirmed that Sergeant Tanguay was dead, killed by the bug zombies while trying to keep them away from the kids. Keith and Pius had survived and gotten clear of the bunker with Rebecca when they blew up the butt monkeys.

Thank God Pius made it. After Nana, Sergeant Tanguay and Nelson, Niall didn't think he could lose anyone else.

When they reached the hospital, Harper kissed Niall on the forehead and slipped away. The next few days were a whirlwind of activity around town as authorities attempted to identify the dead, cleared away debris, and generally tried to make sense of it all. The people of Gale Harbour walked around in a daze, not yet capable of understanding what had happened. Niall missed almost all of this, stuck in a hospital bed. Besides a few burns, he had no physical wounds; he was just completely drained of energy. Great expenditures of his and Harper's power always weakened him, but it had never been like this.

The feedback loop with Nelson completely scraped out his insides, and now he was nothing but a hollow shell.

Niall didn't cry or move for the first three days and hardly spoke or ate. Then, they moved Pius out of intensive care and into a room with him. That's when Harper started coming around too. He, Harper and Pius held each other on Pius' bed while they sobbed for hours.

After that, once he let it out and burned away all of the lingering pain in his bones, Niall finally started to come around a little.

His parents were with him all the time. His father's leg was in a cast, but he was healing well. His mother put on a brave face, but she looked a wreck—she never combed her hair, and her eyes were always sunken and bloodshot. Niall heard her, often, crying in the hall outside his hospital room. Barbara O'Neil had lost her mother and her eldest son within hours of each other. Niall didn't know how long it would take her to come back from that if ever she could.

Pius' parents were also there every day, so the hospital room was always crowded. Niall was thankful; he didn't want to be alone.

Keith, Skidmark, Stacey, Craig Muise and several other kids from the school came to visit him. Keith was working his damnedest to be positive, telling jokes and making fun of Skidmark, trying to get Niall to laugh. He had lost his father, too, so Niall couldn't understand how he was so upbeat. Unlike the rest of them, the tragedy of the last few days seemed to have released Keith, turning him into a different person. He had come so far from the selfish bully that used to terrorize Niall and Pius.

Skidmark was always Skidmark. He seemed unfazed by it all. He told Niall about the TV shows he was missing and brought him comic books, but he refused to talk about Magic cards. He swore he would never touch them again and ordered Niall and the others never to talk about it. It was, of course, one of the things for which Keith made fun of him.

Stacey was an odd one. Their relationship had changed. She only came in once and hugged him tentatively when she did, but Niall's limp body didn't react to it. They made polite conversation and smiled a bit, but it didn't feel the same. Maybe it was because her father tried to kill him. Maybe it was because Niall burned out all his care, affection, and everything else when he fought the Hose Beast. She had certainly lost her carefree, bubbly personality after her father revealed himself to be a homicidal lunatic that got turned into so much cherry-coloured slurry and splattered all over her face. There was probably no coming back from that.

Harper came to visit him and Pius every day. She didn't say much the first couple of times, but after they moved Pius in, and they finally accepted the relief that it was really over, everyone started to brighten up. The three of them talked for hours about stuff they'd done together, and she told him and Pius what was happening around town. Even Harper's Mom came to visit him to thank him for saving Harper. He said that Harper had saved him more times than he had her, and she said that maybe he'd catch up with her someday. She turned out to be a pretty nice lady when she wasn't glaring at him loathingly. Unfortunately, she also let slip that Harper was coming to live with her after Christmas.

So that's how Niall ended up at the Gale Harbour airport, standing at the security gate with Pius and Harper on a snowy New Year's Eve. His parents stood aside, talking to the Jeddores and Harper's mom, while the kids stood by the gate, struggling to find a way to say goodbye.

"So make sure you get a computer as soon as possible, okay?" Pius was leaning heavily on crutches, but his physiotherapy was going well, and the doctors said he should get most of his leg function back. Fortunately, he was never exactly a top-notch athlete to begin with. "Then we can chat through email and message boards and—"

Harper cut him off, "—My mom is not getting a computer anytime soon, buttmunch. I will call you, okay? On a telephone like a normal person?"

Pius deflated, but only momentarily. "Well, you call as soon as you get in, okay? And call us again at midnight."

"Newfoundland time or Ontario time?"

"Both."

Harper threw her arms around Pius and hugged him fiercely. He winced a little but didn't complain. "You're gonna be fine, dipwad. But I will miss you."

Niall turned his head, and when he looked back, he saw they had separated and were wiping their eyes. Pius awkwardly shuffled away. "I will give you two a moment."

And so, Niall and Harper were left alone for the last time, and despite having two months to prepare, Niall had no idea what to say.

"So. I never thought this was actually going to happen." It wasn't much, but it was all he could come up with.

Harper, her hands in the pockets of her puffy winter coat, seemed to be looking everywhere but at Niall. "I need to go. This place has too many messed-up memories. And there's nothing holding me anymore."

"There's Pius. And there's me."

She smiled but still didn't quite meet his gaze. "I need to get to know my mom."

"I know. I wouldn't expect you to stay here for me. But I will come to you. As soon as I graduate high school."

Harper snorted. "Sure you will. As soon as I'm gone, you will be after every girl at St. Paul's."

"No." Niall shocked himself with how certain he sounded. "I was wrong. There's no one else for me. We're supposed to be together, Harper."

"We're fourteen years old. No one stays together with their first crush."

"We didn't stay together. We broke up once. Now that we have that out of the way, we're golden."

Harper opened and closed her mouth several times, then bit her lip. Finally, her gaze fell fully on him. Her brown eyes were shiny, but she never blinked. Her lips turned up in an awkward smile. "You're wearing eyeliner."

Niall had been trying new things. "Just a little. Do you like it?"

She shrugged. "I guess you were serious about keeping other girls away from you."

That sounded more like the Harper he remembered. She took a couple of steps closer to him.

"You are an idiot."

That was Harper, alright. He didn't care. He missed her insults. "I will write you every day."

"Yeah, right." She seemed to forget how to look at him again but pointedly refused to wipe the tears from her eyes. Niall felt his own eyes starting to sting.

"Every week, then." He wondered how much stamps cost. "And I will come find you as soon as I can."

Harper took a step back, now vigorously trying to blink back tears. "Whatever. See you around, dork-pie. Take care of Pius."

"I love you," said Niall.

She stopped, frozen for a moment. She stared at him again, sniffled a little, but said nothing. Finally, she smiled, turned and walked away toward the security gate.

Niall didn't care. He'd been waiting forever to say that and knew there might never be another chance.

A moment later, Harper burst out of the gate and stomped toward him in her Doc Martens. She grabbed his face with both hands and kissed him. After a moment that seemed to last forever and nowhere near long enough, she came up for breath. "You're such an idiot."

A disembodied voice announced the final boarding for the flight to Toronto. Harper's mom pulled her away; she smiled at him one last time and then was gone.

<u>**ABOUT THE AUTHOR**</u>

C.D. Gallant-King is a writer, tabletop gamer, pro-wrestling aficionado, father and husband. He was born and raised in a town that looks suspiciously like Gale Harbour, and currently resides in Ottawa, Ontario, Canada. Find out more at www.cdgallantking.ca

The Gale Harbour Series
Psycho Hose Beast From Outer Space
Revenge of the Space-Surfing Butt Monkeys
Dirtbag Satan Worshippers From Down by the Bay

Also by C.D. Gallant-King
Ten Thousand Days
Hell Comes to Hogtown